BLOOD AND STEEL

BY THE SWORD - BOOK ONE

Palmer Blackstock

By The Sword: Blood and Steel

MORE BY PALMER BLACKSTOCK

BY THE SWORD

Blood and Steel

Rise and Fall (Coming 2020)

Life and Death (Coming 2020)

THE FULL DECK

(Coming 2020)

For all of the readers, authors, and friends I have met along the way. This would not be possible without your support. Thank you.

CHAPTER ONE

Live by the sword, die by the sword. That was the way I lived for so long.

It was an old adage—ancient even, depending on the version being told, but it was a useful one for someone like me.

I was first told it by my father during the final years of his life. It came only a few short months after I started training, in fact. A few short months of becoming fascinated by the art of sword-fighting and spending every waking minute trying to master it.

My father was proud of me for my effort. He always gave me the largest smile when I explained this stance or that, detailing my dreams of becoming the greatest swordsman of them all. Of becoming a Knight of Credon and protecting our kingdom more effectively than any before me. He entertained my teenage ramblings without complaint. And since he'd been a swordsman himself during his formative years, he made sure to pass off that ancient wisdom before it became too late.

It was the last gift he ever gave me.

If only I'd known how true it was.

That mantra repeated in my head now as I stared across my path. Standing out there in my field, only a few dozen paces away from me, the reaper stared right back. Wind billowed through its tattered black cloak. It made no effort to conceal the bleached bone underneath. All it did was balance its scythe in skeletal fingers as though taunting me to come and fight.

I wondered why it didn't simply attack me for my ignorance, why it didn't finish the job after I had ignored all of the signs. A tense pain in my chest and a sudden shortness of breath were the only warnings I'd gotten during my morning walk. But before the reaper had appeared, I'd shrugged them both off. I'd been stupid and short-sighted enough to allow my time to come.

Yet the reaper just stood there, watching me.

With my sword held at the ready, I considered if it was scared. Whether or not it was doubting the frozen moment in time when its scythe would harvest my soul. Perhaps it hadn't expected me to resist, I ventured. After all, landing a strike on a swordsman of my calibre wasn't easy for anyone.

The rational part of me didn't think that was it, though. It didn't fit with the concept of the end-bringer at all. The beast of decay was part of nature as we were told; it was integral to the cycle of the world. And while I'd never entirely agreed with that interpretation, especially not after my father had been ripped away from his life, it still shouldn't have had any issue with a measly swordsman.

Then again, the word measly hadn't described me for decades.

I stepped forward, my foot crunching on the path I walked almost every morning. *My* path, I reminded myself. The tranquil sanctuary that I'd cultivated for years. I was supposed to be safe when I walked it, and I had been until *it* had shown up.

A sneer formed on my face as I continued to approach. Its tattered cloak still drifted on the wind. Its scythe still balanced in silence. But as I neared, it looked up. It stared at me, nearly striking fear into my heart.

The reaper stopped and raised its scythe. It angled the ever-sharpened metal in my direction. For a moment, I could've sworn I saw a smile on its face. But I wasn't sure, as it was already charging my way.

My body surged into action. The reaper disappeared from its spot and struck through the air like lightning to force me down with its scythe. Yet as the frozen moment passed with the shriek of clashing metal, I was left standing. The resistance was still fresh in my bones.

I'd parried it, I realized, on instinct and fear alone. As I glared back at its still form once more, picking apart details of the bone, I saw the surprise. I knew what it meant. The beast had never been parried before.

A grin grew across my lips as I readied my blade again. Its surprise would keep the scythe at bay for the moment, but I still had to be ready. I would never let my guard down.

As I'd expected, the surprise faded in short time and it was on me again. I watched it charge with inhuman speed, almost gliding over the ground. I only dodged with a stumble as its scythe cut right through where I'd been.

That attack had been faster than before, I noted. It had hit closer. I had to be

2

ready.

I furrowed my brows and felt ice-cold fire flood my veins. It signaled the onset of battle, and I took the change in stride. Feeling the burn of sunlight on my skin, I stared back at the beast with everything I had and only barely ducked its next attempt at my life. The blade came through right where my head had been.

The scythe, however, never reached my former location. Instead, it turned at the last second. But even with the turn of steel, I was ready. It was one of the oldest tricks in the book.

I parried the hit without a second thought.

Surprise returned to its hooded, bleach-white face. The beast stared down at its unstained scythe, and I had to stifle a chuckle. It didn't matter how fast it was. I would never let my guard down.

I leapt backward, my feet already positioning themselves for the next attack. The beast growled, its tone dark enough to strike terror in any ordinary mind. But I was no ordinary mind—even at my age, I was as sharp.

I narrowed my eyes, brought my sword out to the defense, and ignored the call to blunder. Its skeletal form charged me again—just as I'd predicted. My lips curled slightly as I turned in the nick of time and whipped the hilt of my blade around my wrist.

The clang that rang out was one to split mountains.

Both of our weapons fell, but I was more than ready for it. I swept mine up in an instant and was already twisting away. A smile blossomed across my lips. I would never let my guard down.

Then, spinning back with my blade in hand, I shoved steel deep into the hooded cloak. My ears twitched at the screech of metal tearing through bone.

As soon as I heard it, I retracted my arm. My feet pushed me backward, and I swung my blade out to guard. Looking over the serene path turned battlefield, I saw too many familiar things. The ornate stone lining in the dirt. The shaded patch of trees. My humble homestead barely visible over the hills.

It had no right to be here, I told myself. It had no right to take me here. This was my *home*, world's dammit. And I would never let my guard down.

Images flashed through my mind—parries, deflects, attacks. I was ready. The power in my muscles was already responding to clean commands. But as it turned out, none of it was needed.

The beast stood, paralyzed.

Carrying the same surprise it had shown seconds before, the reaper stared at the grass. Its ash-black robe wavered in the breeze and its skeletal form hunched as though responding to a weight. Watching it, I relaxed my shoulders a hair. The situation was painted clear as day on its face. It had never been hit before either.

Ragged black cloth lifted back off its head to expose pale white bone to the sunlight above. Its dark eyes were riddled with confusion when it turned to me. It stared, and I almost looked, almost sealed my glorious fate. But at the last moment, I recognized the trick.

Darkness crawled out of its eyes. I snapped mine shut before it could take me, my father's proud face flashing in my mind. Another one of his warnings played back through my head.

Never look into the face of death.

The embodiment of decay rushed at me anew—I felt it in the air. Heard it. *Smelled* it. Its speed was even greater than before and I only barely shook off the strike. Even with my eyes closed, with my most important sense stripped away, I would never let my guard down.

I snapped my eyes open while sprinting away, readied for the attacks that were sure to hit my unarmed side. I waited, my ears perked and my eyes sharp. The strikes never came.

After a dozen strides, I turned back to the beast, expecting to see the same dry surprise as before. I didn't. Instead, I saw the beast's cracked, white skull with the hood completely off.

Bitterness fell on my tongue. It coated my mouth with disgust. I felt power radiating from in front of me; I felt it washing off the bone. Simply looking into its face forced my blood to run cold. Where I'd expected to see the same complete and utter shock, I saw confirmation of what I hadn't wanted to be true. An expression more terrifying than any other.

A smile.

The crooked, skeletal grin was perfect and horrid at the same time. It spawned a sense of worry deep within me that I rejected as unnatural. I was a warrior, a swordsman, a *knight*—I didn't have time for worry. And yet, as I felt my gaze stay frozen, the dread only deepened.

The beast didn't rush at me. It didn't move to attack. It didn't even reach for its scythe. For some reason, it seemed done with the fight.

"Impressive display," it said, words reaching my ears on the wind. Its voice came like the concept of decay itself, forcing me to shudder as it ate at my mind. I hadn't seen its bony mouth move an inch.

"Thank you," I replied through gritted teeth, unconsciously getting myself into stance.

The beast noticed and raised a dismissive hand. "There is no need for that. I have no intention of keeping this up."

"Then what do we do now?" I asked, keeping my gaze as harsh as nails. My fingers curled around my blade's loyal grip. I knew it was playing with me—I knew the reaper's words were a trick, but I would never let my guard down.

The beast chuckled dryly. "You are unique."

I glared at the thing, barely avoiding its eyes. It was toying with me and I knew it. Why couldn't I take advantage? Why couldn't I just strike now? No, I thought, dismissing the questions. It was smarter than that. It knew I wouldn't let my guard down, and it wouldn't let its guard down either.

"And?" was the only word I mustered in response.

"It would be a shame to let someone like you fall to the house of the dead."

My gaze lifted, brows furrowing on my face. "What are you getting at?"

"I could give you another chance," it said, the tone of its voice spawning hatred deep in my chest. The beast's smile all but dropped as the force in its words made one thing abundantly clear.

It was serious.

My mind raced, remembering my younger form longing for more time by the sword. Would it really give me another chance?

"Yes," it said, the dark words dragging hope out of my soul.

"What's the catch?" I asked.

Its grin returned, more devilish than before. A chill ran down my spine. "You will have a different body. But you will retain your mind. Life would be more a curse if I were to take that from you."

I considered the offer against my better judgment. The same instincts that were guiding my stance screamed at me to stop. But as I stared at the beast, sunlight dancing on cracked bone, I could find no fault in its intentions.

"What do I have to do?"

Its grin grew wider. "One touch—and a new life is yours."

Overcome by a dark, sudden, inexorable urge, I agreed. As though manipulated by some outside force, the desperation in my mind preyed on my memories and won out over all doubt. The reaper appeared next to me like a shot of ashen lightning.

Its finger approached my shoulder, cooling the air around it as it went. My grip tightened and my mind screamed, but it was already too late. The bleach-white bone touched my skin and my body filled with ice.

My mind burned. My bones froze. And I experienced the most agonizing second of the rest of my life before everything went black.

———

A jolt of motion startled me up from my slumber. I twisted, feeling only the most distant of pain. Everything was numb. A cold, unfamiliar haze was draped over my mind. I stared into the black, faintly wishing for the ability to feel again. Unfortunately, my wish was granted in short time.

My body snapped up. A frigid wind crashed against my face, sending shivers down my spine and a howl through my ears. In a second, everything came back and my mind spun through the images. New mixed with old and familiar with foreign as my mind swirled, but I couldn't make sense of any of it. I clenched my jaw and waited for it to stop. And yet, as soon as it did, one thought was left, one that forced my lips into a smile.

The beast hadn't lied.

When I opened my eyes, I hoped to see my land. I hoped to see my fields, the rows of crops that I was no longer even required to tend. I hoped to see my wife, the beautiful face that just barely escaped me. But the eyes that only vaguely felt like my own were met with a completely different sight.

All around me, spinning in the wind as if just to mock me for my choices, was a dark forest that I couldn't recognize. Feeling the horrid cold cut deeper, my smile faded.

I forced myself up, noting soreness in my bones. My muscles were hollow. My arms were shorter. My legs were... different. Everything about me felt *frail*, as if on the verge of collapse. And as I sat up on whatever rock my body had been strewn across, I felt sharp pain cut a deep pit through my stomach.

My brain started to spin again, the foreign thoughts, worries, and memories all coming back at once. As the waves passed, they were replaced with regret that was only my own. I shivered, the truth cementing in my mind.

This wasn't what I'd wanted. It wasn't what I'd wanted at all. I closed my eyes—if they even were my eyes—and shook my head, trying to force it all away. My efforts were useless as the world set in and one horrible thought echoed out in my head.

I'd let my guard down.

CHAPTER TWO

The cold wind nearly shredded me.

My thin body wavered in the sharp breeze like paper, and I wanted to close my eyes through all of it. I wanted the nightmare to be over. But it wasn't that simple. I had to find shelter, a town, anything. My second chance was ruined if I died again. In this body, even with all my knowledge, I wouldn't stand a chance against the beast for a second time.

The wind smacked my face as if taunting me with more pain. I pressed right through it. My eyes scanned the trees, catching only brief glimpses of movement between the dark, gnarled forms.

My body, once a formidable force in the land, was now weak and frail. The weakness of it stung to my core with each step on the path. My right hand twitched uselessly, grasping for a sword that wasn't there. I cringed again, forcing myself to focus on thoughts instead of the cold. The events of it all swirled through my head.

How could I have been so stupid? Why had I agreed? Had the beast manipulated my mind? The entire encounter now seemed fuzzy, like a distant memory that still hurt too much. What had I been thinking? The prospect had seemed so good at the time.

Pushing back the thoughts, I walked on with clenched fists and keen eyes at the ready. If I was to die, to be tricked into a second death, I wouldn't allow it. The beast wouldn't get the better of me. It had tricked me without lying, and that burned like a wound in my side. I'd been weak. I'd let my guard down.

I would not succumb to the mere will of death; I was better than that. My whole life I'd trained with the sword. I'd become the best in the land. None had been able to challenge my might. Some had said I was blessed by the World Soul itself. I was stronger than the best of the knights, faster than any ranger in the woods, and more powerful than the most coveted of mages. I'd worked my whole life—planning, training, and building myself up. Even in my old age, I was the best of the best.

And I'd fallen for a trick.

As my stick legs carried me down the winding path, I ignored it their screams for relief. I shook my head instead, watching stray locks of brown hair fall in front of my gaze. My eyes widened as I pushed them away. That hair wasn't my own—it was just another reminder of my mistake.

But before my rage could cloud judgement again, something else caught my eye. Something much less natural than the shades of green waving in the shadows, but something that filled me with hope.

A light.

Beyond the next bend in the path, I recognized the perfect orange glow of firelight. It was a signal of deliverance. Salvation was near.

I picked up my pace, slicing through the air as best I could. My feet pounded on dirt, thankfully not missing a step while I clenched my fist and pushed on. My body swiveled awkwardly at the turn.

The sight of the flame warmed my eyes.

It looked so sweet, so delicate, so innocent. It was a beacon of safety that split the night like the halo of an angel coming down to save me from my suffering.

My eyes focused on it and watched in detail. Each fiery tendril and each crackling spark as it put up resistance against the wind. It was being produced by a torch, I noticed, on the front of a building. I couldn't make out what the building was, but that fact didn't matter. The possibility of safety held me up.

I pushed my legs to run, slicing through the cold with abandon. If I could get inside, I would be safe. That fact echoed loud and clear. Legs screamed and muscles burned, bringing back a painful feeling that I hadn't truly felt in years. My body needed rest—*I* needed rest, and it was so close.

As the building rushed toward me, I finally recognized what it was. An old tavern with a red sign on it, the paint cracked and worn. It wasn't large, and it definitely didn't look busy, but I didn't care. It would be warm and it would have food.

The tavern's form filled my vision as I neared, my muscles on the verge of giving out. I clenched my fist tight, stabbing my palm with cold pain and forcing out a breath.

Eventually, I made it. Stumbling up the porch and straining myself just to stay stable, I pushed in the door. My legs buckled under me and I dropped to the floor. I hit the wood with a painful thud that warmed my heart simply because of the fact that it had sounded on wood. Skidding on the carpet, I sprawled myself out and took advantage of the newfound comfort. I'd made it.

A grin grew on my new face as I realized what I'd done. I'd bested the reaper. In one way, at least. When it had tried to reap my soul, I'd warded off its attacks. And when it had tried to trick me, I'd still come out alive.

"Excuse me?" a voice asked, firm and bewildered. It split through the soft crackling of fire and dragged me up from my thoughts.

What? I wanted to ask as I lifted my gaze. My mouth opened a sliver, but no sound came out. Even the small patch of breath that slipped from my lips hurt, causing me not to bother again.

The creaking of wood rang out through the room in complete clarity as a large form walked over to me. A bushy beard draped over a soft face filled my vision.

The large barkeep, with sweat on his brow and what looked like food stains on his shirt, looked down at my embarrassment of a body. As soon as he noticed my daze and my starvation though, all anger faded from his face. The large, gruff man picked me up off his rug, guiding me with strong hands, and sat me down on a barstool. I didn't resist; I couldn't have if I'd wanted to. Despite walking only for less than an hour, all of my energy was gone.

My eyelids grew heavy as I rested on the bar. All of the tension slowly bled from my bones, taunting me with sleep. But the tavernkeep wasn't having any of it. He lifted my head up, forcing me to look into his blue eyes, and placed a bowl of soup in front of me. I looked at him in confusion, disoriented by tiredness. He only nodded back, his beard bobbing as he pointed to the bowl.

Recognition flashed in my head, the simple concept finally making sense. My face flushing, I nodded a quick thanks. The smell of the bowl filled my nose. A hearty stew, from what I could tell—thick broth filled with what I instantly recognized as beef and other random vegetables. My mind flashed back to the feasts of pure elegance that I'd eaten in my king's court. The perfectly prepared dishes that had been lined up one after another. Bread, stew, pastries. What was sitting in front of me now couldn't hold a candle to that, but it was definitely good enough.

I hadn't realized how hungry I'd been until I started eating, my mouth working faster than my mind. Apparently, my stomach had been empty because before I knew it, the stew was gone. The warm elixir satisfied my stomach, swirling with flavors that were but shadows on my tongue.

The wooden spoon clattered softly in the bowl, confirming that I'd finished my meal. I looked up. The now-smiling barkeep stared at me with warm eyes. For the entire time, he'd let me eat in peace. But as soon as I was done, he took the empty bowl and finally asked another question.

"Are you okay?" he asked, the gruff voice reminding me of my father. I winced at the memory, finding the image of him further out of reach than it should've been. I shook my head, chalking it all up to exhaustion before returning to the question. For much of my life, I would've answered easily. As my stomach rumbled, despite being filled with an entire bowl of stew, I found it difficult to find words.

I shook my head lightly, not having the courage to speak. The barkeep nodded. He grasped the empty bowl, walked into a back room, and came back within seconds holding another steaming bowl of the brew. He raised it to me. My eyes tracked it greedily. As soon as he placed the bowl down, I was on it like a starved wolf hunting its prey.

Again, I picked up the spoon and shoveled food straight into my mouth. I gulped it down readily, filling my stomach anew. The feeling was blissful as I sat there, realizing how nice it was to simply sit and *eat*. Though this time, the barkeep had more to say.

"So what's your story?" he asked, the smile on his lips obvious before I'd even raised my eyes. I stared at his face, so full of life and care. And before I knew it, my lips had curled into a dry smile. How was I supposed to answer that question? Even after living a life of fantastical journeys and achievement, my story seemed a little far-fetched for the likes of a humble barkeep.

I offered a shrug as I found my voice. "It's a long story," I said, hoping that he would take it and leave me alone. That didn't happen. He persisted.

The barkeep smiled, looking me straight in the face. "I've got time."

CHAPTER THREE

I really did go on for much longer than I needed to.

The stories just poured out of me, detail by detail. Over the next few bowls of stew, the tavernkeep heard the tale of my entire life.

I told him of my interests, the wondrous curiosity that had pervaded my youth. I told him of my home, the one I'd still owned when my time had come, the one that had taught me everything I knew. I told him about my quests, the ones that I'd taken as odd-jobs just to make enough money to afford a sword. I told him of my training, about how the Knights of Credon had taken notice of me. I'd never forgotten that day; it was burned into my memory.

I still remembered the reactions when I'd bested one of their combatants. I remembered their pure, awe-stricken faces clearly, even if their names were… strangely out of reach. They hadn't wanted to accept that a teenage boy could dance better with a sword than well-trained knights, but I'd damn sure made them. The memory danced in my head as the story poured out. In all of my life, I'd seen few things sweeter than the look of principled admiration on my king's face as he'd knighted me for the first time.

I could tell the barkeep didn't believe me as I went on about my experiences as a knight, as I almost bragged about my accomplishments. But really, it didn't matter. I couldn't have stopped myself if I'd wanted, and he didn't stop to question me at any point. He didn't even flinch when I told him about my fight with the reaper itself. He just kept nodding along, listening intently to the young and crazy homeless man that had stumbled into his tavern.

"So Death gave you a second chance?" he asked, the question forcing a smile onto my face.

"Yeah," I replied. I knew that he thought I was crazy, and I couldn't blame him. I was weak, hungry, and draped in clothes more comparable to rags. My story really didn't make much sense. And yet, none of that mattered to him; he'd listened anyway.

The barkeep smiled and humored me for a while longer. "So what is the mighty Agil going to do now?" He rolled his hand, raising it up into the air in an overly dramatic fashion. Normally I would've scowled, the sarcasm acting as a threat to my reputation. But his tone was so light that I barely even noticed.

"I don't know," I said with a chuckle before the pang of uncertainty stabbed me in the gut. My shoulders slumped as it all set in at once. I really *didn't* know what I was going to do.

On the dark forest trail, I'd been so single-minded. I'd just wanted to get out alive. But now, in a warm tavern with a full stomach—in a place where my life wasn't at risk... I was at a loss. My home was gone, ripped away by the mindless reaper. My body was gone, stripped from me by the bringer of end. My *life* was gone, now too far out of my reach because of my own stupid actions. What did I even *have* to do?

"I suppose you're going to want to take revenge on Death huh?" the barkeep said, chuckling. I blinked at him, shaking my head slightly and furrowing my brow.

Take revenge on Death? Could I even do that? The prospect was daunting, seemingly impossible, and I didn't even know if it was what I wanted. Though, then again... what *did* I want?

The answer to my question came in an instant, emerging as an island of certainty among a sea of increasing chaos. It was the same thing I'd wanted ever since I'd been a boy. It was what drove me to wield a blade, to master it and its every art.

I wanted to be the best.

For my entire life, I'd worked hard, spending every ounce of my time working toward what I saw as my perfect life. And yet, even after achieving what I thought came as close as I could get, I'd still been beaten by the beast. I'd still been beaten by the reaper, the end of all things. The fact still stung. I *wasn't* the best.

A fire ignited inside me, stoked by a force foreign to me. It was the fire of passion, the fire that pushed me on to take the impossible and make it bow before my sword. I wanted to be the *best*. The beast had tricked me—it had kicked me off the pedestal I'd spent my whole life building up. All with a simple trick. But it had also given me a second chance—a second chance that would be its greatest undoing. A second chance to be the best.

I didn't even notice the grin growing on my face; I was too lost in thought. I knew the barkeep saw it as he snapped at me, the sound lifting me out of my stupor. The bearded, sympathetic man looked at me with concern. My grin lowered. I ran my hand—if I could even call it that yet—through my new, youthful brown hair.

"Yeah," I said, remembering his question. My voice was but a shadow of the true passion I felt. "I suppose I do want to take revenge."

The barkeep smiled back and nodded. Even if I was just a crazy person to him, just a bum off the street, he still understood. Studying me again, his eyes exploring with indescribable interest, he took the empty bowl from the bar. He turned around in a huff, filling my vision with the pale blue shirt draped over his shoulders before disappearing entirely off into the back room.

With his leave, I was left in a room threatened by silence. All I could hear was the faint crackling of the fire behind me. I relished in the sound. I felt its warmth, letting it melt the worries from my mind. My eyes drooped, the worry giving way to an exhaustion that I'd been ignoring. The white-hot fire of passion I'd felt moments before dwindled, fading from my mind. I dropped my chin on the bar and thought of sleep, almost giving in to it right there.

The tavernkeep barged back into the room, a loud creak accompanying his entrance. I snapped up, shaken by the sudden noise.

"Do you have a room I can stay in?" I blurted out, my voice filled with desperate sincerity. In my tired state, it was the only thing I had.

He nodded shortly, walking out from behind the wooden bar and up the tavern's small set of stairs. I let out a small breath, pulling up whatever dregs of strength I could still find. And I followed after him.

He brought me up old wooden stairs that creaked with every step and into a small hallway. The hall cut deep into the inn, revealing a plethora of rooms housed within. My smile grew wider as I stared at the doors, the prospect of sleep closer than ever before. The barkeep huffed, stopped at the second door, and took out a key from his pocket. The metal jingle rang out in my ears—a pleasant sound that made my foreign heart flutter—and he unlocked the door. Wood swung inward with a creak to reveal an old, cramped space. At once, a musty, unused smell attacked my nose, but I didn't care. The barkeep's gesture for me to enter was all I needed.

I nodded a quick thanks and let my feet push me through the door, the squeaking of the floor under me acting as my introduction to space. I pressed in further, immediately finding the only thing that mattered. I completely ignored the scratchy rug and the wooden dresser and the blight-ridden desk. None of it mattered.

My body collapsed in an instant as I came up to the bed. Arms flailed wildly as I grasped the sheets. The not-so-smooth cloth felt like heaven on my skin. I flopped my head on the pillow, feeling the softness coddle my body. My eyes slipped shut, releasing all the tension I'd still been holding in. And before I'd even noticed, my body drifted off to sleep.

———

The sun shined down on my face, dousing me in lush, yellow-orange light. Brushing a hand through my hair, I watched the thin blond locks fall through my fingers. I felt warmth on my face, the perfect, intricate kind of warmth that I knew I'd only ever feel here.

Glancing around, I watched the slow spring wind follow our simple dirt trail out to the fields. The grass, the wheat, the corn. It all wavered steadily in the slight breeze. I took a deep breath, smelling the fresh, natural air around me.

"Agil!" a voice called from behind me. It rang sweet in my ears, reminding me of a place somehow even more intimate than my home. It was a voice I would've followed through the widest plain, the densest forest, the most desolate desert. I would've followed it through *hell*, using only the mere sound of it to push me on. No matter where I went or what I had to do to get there, if I followed that voice, my destination would always be worth it.

Turning around, I watched the door to our home slide shut as my wife came out onto the path. The sight alone distracted me from everything. Her brown hair was done in braids—probably the work of a palace girl—and it was decorated sparsely with flowers. I smiled at her, offering the same long smile that tried to replicate just how she made me feel.

"Lynn," I said. My wife's name felt like honey on my tongue. "Are you out here to appreciate the scene as I am?" She smiled at me, the wind blowing a strand of brown hair in front of her face. She fixed it quickly, but I didn't miss the red entering at her cheeks.

Beyond her, our homestead loomed in the background. I couldn't have denied its grandeur if I'd tried. But all things considered, it was modest. With all of my accomplishments—being the greatest swordsman in the land had its perks, after all—I could've had my pick of luxury.

None of that had mattered to me when I'd picked our house, and it didn't matter to me now. The simple, sweeping design of our wooden home was merely a background to the much more beautiful sight walking over to me.

"You're off for your morning walk?" Lynn asked. I nodded with a chuckle. She knew me too well.

"Of course. My duties have slowed down enough that if I didn't do these every morning, I'd just be sitting inside all day."

"Is that such a bad thing?" she asked, the slightest laugh in her voice. I stepped toward her, tilting my head.

"I would love nothing more than to lay with you in bed as the sun made its cycles, day after day." My words made her blush, the rosy color complimenting her hazel eyes. "But I still have status here. I can't let myself waste away with the king able to call me at any time of the day."

Lynn draped her arm over my shoulder. "You could retire."

I laughed. "I'm still a high-knight, m'lady. Could you imagine what would happen if the king lost someone like me?"

She laughed at my confidence. I only smiled more. From anyone else, I would've taken offense; I would've looked them in the eye and reminded them of just who I was. But with her, it was different.

"The world might end," she said, rolling her eyes playfully. "Everything around us would *die* if that happened." Her voice distorted for a second, going to a much lower tone than before as she rolled over the word die. A sharp pang hit at the bottom of my stomach, filling me with a dread that made me double-take.

"What?"

"I'm just saying that it could be catastrophic for the kingdom." Lynn's voice returned to normal. "What is the king to do without Agil the *Great*, at his beck and call?" The burning of my ears was enough to melt all dread away, the little epithet she'd added to my name making me almost too flustered to think.

"You build me up too much," I started. "Give yourself more credit my dear."

"Of course," she teased. "You can build yourself up enough all on your own." She smirked at me. Or, she made her best effort. No matter how hard she tried, she could never really be smug, only offer a sort of tilted smile. Her teasing had the same effect either way.

"And I'll build you up as well." I pulled her closer to me. "We both save lives, you know."

Lynn blushed, her eyes immediately starting to glare with embarrassment. "You know that's not fair!"

"I disagree," I said. "Apothecaries save lives all the time."

Lynn's smile tilted again. A wild intent danced in her eyes, one just barely tinged at the back with something I didn't recognize. "That's not what I meant. You end lives just as much as you save them, you know."

I opened my mouth, a retort ready at my lips. I wanted to defend my honor, to tell her how much I truly didn't like killing and how I only did it for the common good. She'd heard it all before. And before a sound even escaped my lips, words were cut off by her lips pressed against mine.

My eyes widened. Lynn's kiss was soft and quick, but it was exactly what I'd needed. The surprised look on my face was nothing compared to the absolute peace that followed. On her lips I tasted fruit—somehow—just like always… but there was also something else.

As soon as our lips parted, an unfamiliar taste settled on my tongue. Something bitter and gross, as if I'd tasted decay itself. I scraped my tongue on the top of my mouth and winced. Then, swallowing hard in hope of washing it away, I only got bile rising in my throat. I swallowed again, forcing the bile down. A pang of painful dread stung my stomach as I settled. I almost spat the taste out of my mouth.

"Lynn? What the—" I started, my question furious. I was stopped by her face. With the way she stared at me, her innocent hazel eyes peering into my soul, I couldn't have snapped. The horrible bitter taste faded from my tongue, leaving only the faint, sweet taste that I'd always known.

"What?" she asked. Her eyebrows angled upward and her hand gripped my shoulder.

"N-Nothing, dear," was all I could muster. Nothing else would have made any sense. After all, what was I supposed to say? Was I supposed to continue with my question, asking why her kiss, which usually tasted sweeter than a plum, made my mouth want to die? No, I couldn't do that.

"Oh," Lynn replied, not fully convinced. I smiled at her. She smiled back. "So when are you thinking of heading off?"

I scanned back over to the fields as wind brushed my tunic. The fields of crops, still growing before harvest, and the rolling hills that came after. Even the city, its large monumental walls some of the most impressive I'd ever seen, was far in the distance. I could've stared at the scene for ages.

"In a bit," I said absently. My right hand fell over the sword on my waist, its presence calming every single thought in my mind. "Right now, I'd rather watch the world. Just you and me."

She smiled. I didn't see it, but I knew that she did. From the corner of my eye, I could see her stepping forward and pressing herself beside me. "Of course."

And so that was what we did. The two of us stood there, feeling the warmth of the sun and the brisk cold of the wind as we stared out at the impossibly quaint scene in front of us. A weight settled on my shoulder. The strands of brown hair spreading out in the corner of my eye told me exactly what it was.

My lips curled up. "I love you, Lynn."

A sharp breath followed by a giggle was all the response I got as Lynn picked her head up and stared at me. I didn't look back, waiting for the three magical words to come out of her mouth. I'd heard them before, of course. On the day of our twelfth date. On the beautiful day of our wedding. On the night my mother had died. I'd heard those three words from her more times than I could count, but it didn't matter. They were still worth it each and every time.

I focused on her at the edge of my vision. I saw the tilted smile, the long gaze, the slight blush on her cheek. But I didn't turn her way. Not until I heard the words.

After a few more seconds of silence that I knew she couldn't bear, I saw strawberry color growing in her cheeks. She threw up her hands, pulling closer to me.

"Fine," she spat with no malice in her voice. "Agil, I love y—"

My vision flashed black and everything around me went cold. For a moment, I heard the familiar shrieking sound of metal scraping on bone, and I tried to turn toward it. My body went numb, responding blankly to the spinning world that I only saw once it was far, far too late.

Suddenly, my sight came back and the numbness receded. I felt my hand clutched tightly on the blade by my side. The light blinded my eyes, keeping the truth of the new cold world from me for another second. And when I finally saw that truth, I damn-near almost fell to my knees.

Lynn's body was wilted, matching the now-decaying flowers in her hair. My eyes widened and my breathing accelerated, thoughts spinning in my head. Scanning over her body, I saw the singular, impossible bloodstain that ripped all the way down her dress. My legs started to shake, threatening to buckle. My eyes froze on her face, the beautiful, lively face of my wife laid in all too permanent peace while the light drained from her eyes.

"Lynn?" I found myself asking into the air. My hand trembled; a fear stronger than I'd ever felt before struck itself straight to my core. "Lynn?"

My words fell on dead ears, something I found nearly impossible to accept. The air around me grew colder, freezing itself on my skin as new fire pumped through my veins. My mind raced. My muscles tensed. But no matter what, I couldn't move. All I could do was stare at the death of the woman I loved as the countryside around me froze in her wake.

"*Lynn!*" a voice screamed. I barely recognized it as my own.

A chill raced down my spine, one colder than the air around me. I felt a presence behind me, staring greedily at my back. Somehow, I found it in myself to turn.

"She will not respond to your cries," the beast said, my vision filling with its tattered black cloak contrasting heavily on its bleach-white bone. The air only froze further, but I found the warmth to draw my blade.

"Give her *back*," I ordered. It only chuckled at me. I averted my gaze, only barely avoiding the darkness in its eyes as I held my blade.

A second of silence passed. That was all the time I allowed.

A flurry of movement took my muscles by storm as I pushed through the frozen air. My blade came down with more power than should've been possible and my feet were already moving away. All of my thoughts screeched to a halt in my mind, one singular feeling consolidating as the one and only truth.

Revenge.

The horribly familiar shriek of metal and the tremors spreading out through my arm told me my strike had connected. But not with its bone. I rushed away, my feet beating on the dirt as I navigated a terrain I'd trained on thousands of times. My brow furrowed. My grip tightened. I turned around and—

Pain.

Unbelievable, inconceivable pain took my body. Everything went numb for a second, leaving only aftershocks bouncing in my skull, but feeling soon came back. And as I felt the horrible metal scythe ripping through my back, I wished that oblivion had stayed.

I stared it in the face, my now-lazy eyes searching over the bony surface for any explanation. I found none. Only the lifeless, terrifying gaze of death itself.

"Not good enough," was the last thing I heard before all thoughts died. The pain became too great and my vision faded into black.

———

I woke with a start, cold sweat dripping down my back. I coughed, breathing hard as I sat up in the lumpy bed. My hand shook. For a moment, I wondered what I must've done to myself. Then, as a shadow of pain raced down my spine, it all came back. I grimaced, closing my eyes as the images played back. My heartbeat grew until the sound filled my ears.

Snapping my eyes open, I tried to force my body to be still. A ray of sunlight entered my vision, barely catching my eye as I looked over the room. The scraggly sheets, the lumpy bed, the unorganized desk that I knew wasn't mine. My breathing slowed as I remembered what had really happened—where I really *was*. The truth of it all stuck out and lifted a million-pound weight off my shoulders.

Adream.

The thought repeated, making itself as clear as possible to my addled mind while I stayed sprawled under the sheets. Slowly, my muscles relaxed and my heartbeat slowed back down. The worries of my dream faded into the back of my mind, leaving only the worries of my true situation to fill the void. But I'd known those already. They were ones that could actually be addressed.

And as I felt the ache in my back from lying far too long in the lumpy bed, I decided to address them. I had to get up.

After a couple more seconds, I pushed the covers off and got out of the bed. As soon as my feet touched the floor, I felt unstable. The world wobbled around me, tilting and shaking every few moments while I tried to regain my balance. Feeling the lack of muscle, I knew that I wasn't used to my new legs.

Eventually finding my stance, I stumbled out into the hallway and made my way down the stairs. The crackling fire was still going, or it had been restarted—but either way, it felt good. I blinked groggy eyes, flicking them across the peacefully still room. From what I could tell, nobody was around.

The tables were empty. The bar was barren. The tavern looked like a wasteland. So, not knowing what else to do, I plopped myself down on one of the stools and waited. The barkeep had to be around here somewhere.

Then, as if on cue, the burly, bearded man barged out of a wooden door behind the bar holding a plate of food. He noticed me and moved in an instant, placing the plate on the counter before my face.

"Good morning, sir Agil," he said. I smiled at the light sarcasm. "I do hope you slept well. I prepared a breakfast for you and some supplies you'll need before you head into town."

Town? My eyes widened briefly. Did he want me to leave already? I was still getting adjusted to my own body, and I didn't even know where town *was*.

The cheery man saw my expression and assured me. "Don't fret. I'm not kicking you out. I just thought that you'd want to get going as quickly as possible. Sarin is just up the road anyhow." He smiled once again, nodding to the food on the bar.

His smile was infectious. I almost wanted to stay in the tavern forever. But that wouldn't do. The barkeep was right, after all. I didn't really want to stay. I had more important things to do and some things to seriously figure out. Things that I knew I wouldn't be able to accomplish if I stayed in a lonely inn forever.

I showed the barkeep a weak nod. He left again, pushing open the creaky door on his way into the back room. I looked down at my food—a couple of pieces of bread and some warm, nondescript meat. It wasn't the royal food that I'd grown accustomed to in my later years, but I was hungry enough.

I picked up one of the pieces of bread, and I started eating.

By the time the barkeep had come back, I'd eaten more than half of the plate while my stomach roared in agreement. Apparently the meal I'd had the previous night hadn't been enough to satisfy my body's desperate needs. And the more I ate, the hungrier I seemed to get. As I chewed on with greed, finishing yet another piece of the wonderful sliced bread the barkeep had placed right on the bar, the man dumped supplies out on the counter. I took the time to glance up, the strange assortment of goods stopping me in my tracks A plain brown pair of slacks, a slightly-too-big white tunic, a leather bag. And, I noticed with a curl of my lip, there was a small curved dagger too.

"Something wrong with the knife?" the barkeep asked, noticing my hesitation. I swallowed the food still in my mouth and squinted.

"No," I offered. "It's just not my… weapon of choice."

The man raised an eyebrow. "Then what would you rather have?"

A smile sprouted on my face, the image rising up in my mind. I looked up at the large man and grinned wildly before he could even react. "Do you have a spare sword?"

CHAPTER FOUR

I walked.

A groan slipped between my lips, instantly masked by the brisk wind. My once-tight grip loosened on the small and ineffective shortsword sheathed by my side. The groan only rang louder as I felt the growing burn in my feet while I marched. Shaking my head uselessly to rid myself of fatigue, I was met, once again, with a frustrating truth.

My body couldn't keep up.

Even while walking the supposedly short distance to the nearest town, I was already slowing down. My muscles, even though they belonged to a young man, now grew tired easily and wound down with each passing second. There was nothing I could do. The experience didn't make sense. My mind, conditioned to control and react to the body I'd once called my own, was stuck. Each time I tried to go faster—to break into a run or even a slightly faster jog, I was met with resistance. Either my breathing was too heavy, or my muscles began to ache, or my legs were too short—it was a different problem every time. But no matter what I tried, my mind just spun in confusion, failing to understand the feeble vessel it had been paired with.

After the first half-hour of walking, my legs started to falter and my frustration became unbearable. It made sense to me that I should've been able to push on—that I should've been able to make the trip without stopping, but the curse of exhaustion begged to differ. I huffed, puffing my chest out for a moment to emulate my previously attainable stature, but it did no good. The air just burned the insides of my lungs and my body just screamed at me to stop. So, reluctantly accepting the truth that fatigue was pounding into my brain, I set out to look for rest.

I slowed my walk to a crawl and pushed frustration away before sitting down on a small rock. My head pounded for a second, sending me yet another warning about just how tired I was. I nodded to no one, taking the hint and letting myself slump into rest.

Seconds bled on, one into the next as I sat on that rock. My heartbeat slowed and my breathing lightened up after a time. But my muscles still ached, and I had no intention of angering them again. The passion and resolve I'd built up back in the tavern was all but useless while just sitting on a rock. I felt… bored.

As exhaustion gave way to lethargy, my gaze wandered from the ground. Before I knew it, I was scanning the world around me. And only shortly after that, my eyes widened in wonder. The world around me was… stunning. Maybe it was the euphoria of rest, or maybe it was just my fresh eyes, but the landscape looked more beautiful than most of the things I'd seen in the entirety of my past life.

Right in front of me, only a few paces away, was the stone-lined dirt path that I'd been walking all morning. If I squinted my eyes, I could still see where the path met up with that tavern and the forest in the distance. Beyond the dirt path, though, was a wide and flat plain that seemed to extend for thousands of paces. It was filled with tall grasses, sparse trees, and crop fields from farms scattered around. Almost exactly like a sight I would've seen in the rural parts of my home kingdom.

But… no, it wasn't. It almost looked like that, but it was clearly different as well. The plains were wider and less hilly than any of the ones I would've found in Credon and the farmhouses were more scattered—less tied together by organization. The tall grasses of the fields were unkept and badly managed, as if they'd been able to just grow wild for eons. And there were large, sharp jutting rocks that stuck out of the ground at random, forming some incomprehensible pattern among the green.

It looked serene, like the scene of a painting my father would've bought, but something about it was wrong. The plains felt… chaotic. Tumultuous just past the point of untenability. There was no rhyme or reason to the grasses or to the farms built on top of them. It was as if it had been designed just past the cusp of beauty, but just past the cusp of insanity as well.

As my gaze lifted higher, moving over the messy growth, I saw something else on the horizon. Just past where the last slivers of grass fled out into the distance, mountains grew right from the void. From where I sat on my rock, I could only see the top half of the range, solid snow-tipped peaks extending high into the sky. And they… they looked beautiful as *well*, jutting through clouds like ancient guards keeping watch over the chaos below.

Wind ruffled my hair, sending strands of unfamiliar brown down into my eyes. I blinked away the scene, squinting at myself in confusion before I realized yet again. My hand pushed the brunette locks back up onto my head without so much as a grumble. I felt strain in my hand, the exhaustion in my bones having spread there, too. My eyes drooped as the tiredness crept right back up.

I was awake, and that was nothing if not a good thing, but one night's rest didn't cure months of mistreatment. My new body was still frail—despite its young appearance—and it still ached like I'd been lifting boulders for days. Feeling the heaviness in my eyes, I could've gone to sleep right there. I shook my head instead and snapped my eyes wide.

I had to stay vigilant, I reminded myself. There was no time for me to sleep. The town—Sarin, the barkeep had called it—was waiting. I had to get there for answers. When I got there, I'd see the town's local lord, and I'd be back on my way to Credon in no time at all.

I straightened my back and tried to stay focused.

But something was… off. Sitting on the rock and trying to keep myself alert, I felt something strange inside my mind. *Deep* inside my mind. No matter how awake I felt or how much rest I'd gotten, it still slept. Some part of me, far in the back of my consciousness, stayed dormant, refusing to come see the light like a well-fed creature walled in for the winter.

My eyes narrowed, trying to stare at the inside of my brain. I'd noticed it before, I realized as sleep-hazed memories rose up. After I'd woken up in the tavern. Only a few long hours ago. I'd felt that part of me still sleeping. Back then, I'd chalked it up to nothing more than residual fatigue or the unfamiliarity of my own body. But now, forcing myself to be awake, I couldn't feel that same way. I couldn't—

A bird screeched behind me, tearing the quiet air into pieces and my mind back to the present. I whipped my head around, clutching the hilt of my sword. The world spun in a blur around me as I twisted, but once I got there, what I saw was quite marvelous.

A hitch caught in my throat as my sharp new eyes were met with another sight too foreign to really understand. A ways away from me, a large bird sat on the top of a jutting rock. Its feathers were a bright, dazzling green that sparkled in the sunlight and radiated an almost regal kind of power. The feathers played down its body, mixing and mingling into an impressive pattern of different shades that mesmerized my eyes.

Its claws were sharp and golden. Its head was held high in a sweeping, defined shape. And its eyes were the same color of pure gold, staring right at me.

I jerked my head back for a second, surprised by the glare of the bird. Its golden eyes looked intimidating, stirring something within me that I couldn't quite define. My hand twitched over the shortsword sheathed by my side. But for some reason, I didn't take it out.

The bird tilted its head at me, causing my hands to relax even more. Its royal feathers ruffled in the wind. I stared and… got lost in its eyes, the air freezing around my enchanted soul. My lips parted slowly to—

A loud screech split the air, sending time back to its normal speed. I blinked again, finding the bird nowhere and feeling dizzied by what had just happened. My head whirled, searching the empty sky above for any sign of the creature. But my keen eyes searched uselessly, catching only sights of blue.

It was gone.

Eyelids flitted at the sky, my breath quickening by the second. It was *gone*. My head tilted to the side, the series of events that had just taken place spinning through my mind. One second it was there, but the next second it was just… not.

Another version of me might've sat there in confusion, pondering the bird's disappearance for hours to no avail. But now, with energy as still a sparse resource in my body, I didn't. It wasn't worth the work. It wasn't worth the *time*. So I didn't. I just tore my gaze away, forced what determination I could back onto my face, and looked back at the plains.

Eventually, I turned my attention to the path. Looking down the dirt road, I saw only sparse wooden buildings scattered far on either side. But the barkeep had said Sarin was close, I reminded myself. And he'd seemed trustworthy, hadn't he?

I wasn't all that sure, especially with everything that had happened in the past day, but he'd given me a place to stay and some food to eat without so much as a peep about compensation. I gave the man the benefit of the doubt. Sitting around thinking about a bird was not going to get me anywhere, I recognized quickly with a shake of my head. I had to push on. I had to get to town.

So, stretching my youthfully frail legs, I pushed the barkeep's sword fully back into its scabbard and walked on.

———

My legs had felt much better when I'd set off the second time. Another half-hour and a few hundred paces later, I was in the exact same spot. My muscles burned. My body wasn't able to take the paltry exertion. And on top of that, I was hungry again. I gritted my teeth, feeling the increasingly sharp pain in my left foot as I walked on. I didn't want to rest. I *wanted* to keep walking all the way to town like I should've been able to do. But the exhaustion was back, and the pain was only getting worse. So, biting back a sigh, I did what I had to do and sat down in the grass.

A few hundred paces back, with the sun a little lower in the sky, there'd been a convenient rock on the side of the road. Now that rock was much too far away, and I didn't have any better option. I sat right there in the dirt like an indignant child. A sigh fell from my lips as my muscles cheered in relief, and I nodded to myself lazily, letting my still-active eyes once again wander the scene.

Laid out in front of me was the same sparse plain, the same random farm-houses, the same jutting rocks, the same mountain range. But, as I realized with a breath of cool air into my lungs, I hadn't yet looked behind. Blinking, I twisted my body while my scabbard dragged through the dirt.

Behind me, after only a few hundred paces of plain, was a forest. The forest was made up of low, winding trees formed into an intricate pattern of leaves that reminded me a little too clearly of the bird I'd seen a while back. The gentle, organic pattern was sparse and chaotic, yet more controlled than the plains. It was covered in dozens of slightly different shades of green, all making up a sweeping canopy that both beckoned explorers and intimately hid what stayed inside.

My stomach rumbled, a dull pain stabbing me from the bottom of my gut. I clenched my jaw, just sitting there and feeling the breeze until the horrible quivering of my insides had stopped. Feeling the pain start to lighten up, I parted my lips and whispered a soft curse into the wind.

A dark forest flashed in my mind, one with gnarled, impossibly taunting trees. A phantom sensation brushed up against my skin, one that stung me to the core with such a frigid lack of grace that I shivered right there in the grass. I felt my eyes widen, my heart thundering as I relived the moments I'd only just gotten past. But *no*, I told myself. I shook my head and let the warmth of the sunlight pull me back to the world.

Staring at the forest, I wondered if it was the same one I'd emerged less than a day before. I couldn't be sure. And no matter how much I wanted to look back the way I'd come, I was interrupted each time. When I looked in that direction, a film of unease built up in my gut. It made me snarl and was the kind of feeling foreign enough that I would've suspected tampering if not for the fact that nobody else was around.

I shook my head again, letting the ragged dread settle below as I turned away from the forest. The twisted brown trunks and patterned green canopy fell away in a blur. Sitting there in silence, I noted something. The thing inside me had stirred. As if being startled from its slumber, the dormant layer somewhere deep in the back of my mind shook. I tilted my head, feeling the movement as intimately as I could. But the change was so minor that I couldn't tell if it was real.

I was probably imagining things because of exhaustion, I told myself. I still seriously had to get used to my new body, and without all of the luxuries I was normally—

Movement. In the corner of my eye. My thoughts ground to a halt. I noticed them instantly. Two forms, probably male, walking down the path from ahead. One of them was wearing light armor with metal reinforcements on the shoulders and wrists. The other was also wearing light armor, but his wasn't meant to protect. The dark, fitting half-robe was tinged with purple and had winding symbols inscribed on it. I recognized his kind of wear in an instant.

A mage.

My eyes narrowed as I kept track of the pair walking towards me. My grip tightened on my blade slowly, acclimating still-unknown fingers to the style of my hold. My body slumped further down in the grass, going just far enough that I would've been hidden from view, but not far enough to keep the two men out of my vision. I had to stop a grin from overtaking my face. I'd just been thinking about the limitations of my new body, and it was nice to see that with the same mind, my instincts were still very much intact.

I glared daggers at the men, studying their every move. They seemed suspicious. Dangerous. Maybe I was being overly cautious, or maybe it was a side effect of the fire seeping into my blood, but I couldn't trust the way they walked. The way they moved in sharp jolts and reacted to each other a little too suddenly and carefully to just be friends. It looked like they were hunting.

And I did not want to be their prey.

They continued to approach me, meandering down the path in fake nonchalance. Their grips were still tight, and their eyes were still sharp. But they hadn't noticed me yet, which only really felt like half reassurance. They didn't stop. They just kept wandering along with equal parts confidence and cautiousness, growing closer every second. A trickle of sweat rolled down my back; I stayed motionless.

Then they stopped. One of them, the one in mage robes, halted his movements while standing only a few paces away from me. The man held his arm out, making his more heavily armored companion stop as well, and drew his gaze in my direction.

From his angle, he still shouldn't have been able to see me through the grass. But he had, somehow, and I could feel the battle ready to start. I tightened my grip further, twisting pale fingers around the leather hilt of the blade. I wanted to curse into the air—to berate myself for being too obvious, but I didn't move. I couldn't move.

"What are you looking at?" the armored man asked, pushing the arm in front of him out of the way.

His friend gave a long, pointed glare that looked like it could've broken steel. "There's something here," he said, his voice more like a hiss than anything else.

The one in armor straightened at the mage's warning. His hands gripped what looked to be a longsword on his waist.

"How do you know?" the readying warrior asked.

"I can feel the energy of… something." The mage didn't seem too sure. "It's a mage, I think."

The sword-user rolled his eyes, but he kept his stance. "You think there's something hiding in the grass over there?" His hand gestured to me through the grass, seeming to cut through air and right into my soul. My breath hitched for a moment, but I didn't move.

The mage nodded, his eyes slits.

His friend unsheathed a blade. "Okay, so if they're there, then they're *listening* to us."

The mage nodded again, which was seemingly all his eager friend needed. The warrior readied his sword and took a couple steps forward, coming directly into my view.

I unsheathed my blade silently, nearly scoffing at the low-quality shortsword that the damned barkeep had given me. I flicked my gaze back, clenching my jaw and forcing power into my legs. I readied myself, waiting by the wind before I dashed out and took a swipe at the man's calf.

What I had meant to be an elegant slash and retreat, a maneuver that was taught in elementary practice, ended up being nothing more than a clumsy blunt strike that forced my unkind body to scramble away. My blade slashed through the man's light armor, piercing his skin only a sliver. I dashed off, air flushing around me as I pulled my blade with unceremonious grace.

I was clumsy. My body was different. I didn't have the strength I used to have. I didn't have the *training* I used to have. None of the pointed reflexes or refined muscle memory I'd built up over years. I was *weak*. Uncoordinated. And I was exhausted on top of all my other shortcomings. Staring back at the swords-man with anger flaring up in his eyes, I forced an all too dry swallow. This did not bode well for me.

The now-bleeding man shot his eyes toward me, seething with rage. By the time I'd adjusted my grip, he was already on me, swinging his two-handed blade down with all the force he could muster. My eyes widened in a second, the command to dodge echoing out in my mind *seconds* before I moved.

I barely got away. My awkward hand lazily brought up the old shortsword to deflect his blade, causing him only to cut my left shoulder as I twisted away. I winced in pain that my body wasn't acclimated to and backpedaled with my strength as I stared at the still-raging man.

He turned to me, holding his longsword with one hand, and grinned. "Now we're even."

His lips tweaked upward, twitching in a confident rage. But I didn't wait for him to finish fueling his arrogance. I rushed to interrupt, my instincts screaming this stance or that at my blundering body. I tried to focus, to pull the movements of the attacks out of my mind while he had his guard down.

However, by the time I neared him, my feet were still beating on the dirt ground with a hurried lack of elegance that stung my own pride. I was the one to get interrupted.

Something hot tickled my legs and I reflexively jumped back. Pain radiated onto my skin, flicking off and on through my newly singed pants. My eyes scanned the ground for the source of the heat, and when I found it, my jaw nearly dropped.

Sitting there in the dirt, burning all on its own was a flaring, menacing purple flame. It was fueled by nothing and seemed to burn off only what it could find in the air.

I heard a chuckle from my side, and I knew in an instant. The mage. He was able to conjure such fire with nothing but his own will.

My heart raced. I stepped further away, blinking rapidly and trying to get my thoughts to calm. Only one question stuck out with any kind of weight.

Why was such a powerful mage walking down such a desolate path?

I stood there, gaping while I pondered the question in an ice-cold haze before I was rudely ripped from my thoughts by a screaming man. I twisted on my heel, bringing my sword up as quickly as I could. My eyes flitted intensely. I tried to block the strike already coming down on my form and dodged to the side.

The sword-bearer's blade split the air, missing its target with impressive precision. But my eyes narrowed as I realized something. Only an inexperienced fighter would announce his attack with sound.

I scanned the area around, noting the position of everything I could as more maneuvers floated through my head. But when I went to move, I stumbled awkwardly and evenly, my legs almost laughing at their own incompetence. My mouth hung open as I staggered, my heart wrenching for the fall.

After a moment of instinct-driven thought and painfully strict movements, I found my balance. For a second, I smiled, relishing in the fact that I hadn't buried my nose in the dirt. But, unlike I very much wanted to think, my opponent wasn't dumb; he took the opportunity to charge. I turned on my heel, feeling the incredible strain in my ankles as the larger man rammed right into me. His shoulder collided with mine, sending my feet off the ground and my body through the air before I could even get out a wince of pain. I fell *hard*, my borrowed blade clattering uselessly into the grass beside me.

As quickly as I could, I went to grab for my weapon, but I didn't move very far. Before even getting a chance to save myself, I was stopped. The horribly sweet sound of a sword whipping through the air kept me in place. The arrogant swordsman had his sword raised above me. I could feel it in the air. I knew the position all too well; I'd put enough people in it myself. If I moved, I died.

"What a pathetic excuse for a fighter," he muttered above me. The comment hurt far more than the bleeding gash in my shoulder. "Can I kill him?"

"No," the mage said, his serious tone coming right back. "He's useful… I think." His uncertainty returned with the same kind of speed.

The swordsman growled, keeping the sword steady above me. "Whatever. But you're helping me carry him back." I heard the soft mumbling of complaint as the mage took steps toward my prone form.

I let out a soft breath right into the dirt as relief washed off my shoulders. I might not have been in the best situation, but my rematch with the beast was still yet to come. Behind me, I felt the air shift and the soft metallic sound of a sword raising again. I tensed up, my hands already starting to push against the ground.

He raised his arm high then brought it down, striking the handle of his blade on the back of my head. My insides tumbled terribly, whirling in a dizzying way that I knew wasn't right. But my concern didn't last long as all resistance drained away.

Before another thought could cross my mind, everything had already faded to black.

CHAPTER FIVE

My head pounded. My body felt numb. Everything seemed to slow down around me, twisting and turning like the blur of battle in shifting vision.

I was lying on a metal floor, I realized after my tactile sense returned. The cold surface barely registered through my pulsing haze. I forced open my heavy eyes and dragged them around the still-spinning room. It was a cell, or some sort of cage from the look of it. I couldn't really tell through the fog. But with the thick metal bars and the low, nearly claustrophobic ceiling, I thought it was a good guess.

Memories rose up in my head. My eyelids fluttered uselessly, trying to focus. I saw images of a fight—a long, gleaming sword slicing the air into pieces. I saw a purple flame burning on nothing. I saw blackness. Shaking my head clear, it made some sense. The images were familiar—I knew that much from the incessant recognition pounding in my head, but they were also just too far out of reach to truly grasp.

Pain washed over me again. I tilted my head back, resting it against the cold metal wall. I forced my eyes closed and focused on the pain—on pushing it away. My breathing slowed; the spinning in my head calmed. The fog started to part, letting me see straight into the darkness behind it. But by then, it was already too late, and I was drifting away, whether I liked it or not.

Lost in a swirling blackness, I just sat there for a time. I didn't know how long, but it didn't really matter. I could've been sitting there for minutes or for days. It was all the same to my aching limbs. My body sat there helpless, relishing in what little relief it could find up until I heard a loud metal clang split the room as though a door had just slammed shut. I jerked my head up and snapped my eyes open, feeling a rush of blood to my brain.

My vision was still blurry as I twisted in dismay, but the fog cleared quickly. With another pulse of pain, a wave of nausea rushed up, accompanied by strict, unbridled annoyance that I knew I hadn't created. Squinting for a second, I tried to look inward, but with another pulse I was lost again.

"Huh," a voice grunted, making me lift my head. "Looks like they finally found me a cellmate." The voice was low and grumpy, but also somehow amused. It sounded distinctly feminine in a way purely noticeable by the twinge of sound in my ears. And as I blinked away the fog, my thoughts were only further confirmed.

Standing there with her arms folded in front of the now-closed metal door of the cell, was a woman. She was tall, probably at least half a head taller than my current body, and she had short but flowing chestnut hair. She stared at me with narrow eyes, looking me up and down. I could see the glower hiding on her face and the pointed suspicion in her eyes as if she couldn't believe I existed at all. After a few seconds, she flashed me a sly grin.

"You look like shit."

I angled my eyes at the woman, barely able to glare before just resting my head back. I wanted to respond, but I was overcome. The fatigue plagued my bones with an annoying, superfluous intensity, twitching and wailing all over my muscles as if to drag out every signal of pain my body could produce.

A breath fell from my lips, letting my sore muscles relax. My head was throbbing, and as my body soon reminded me, I had a cut in my shoulder. I winced, trying to control the next intake of air that stung my lungs. But still, I caught a hitch in my throat, stopping me dead for a moment before I slumped further back and focused harder on the air.

I had to steady my breathing.

As with all other instances of complete and utter defeat, I knew what to do. If I could clear my mind, everything would be a lot easier to deal with. I had to keep my breath steady and my body relaxed.

In… and out.

"You're just gonna ignore me then?"

The woman's tired voice interrupted my thoughts, causing me to take a sharp breath. The warm, dry air of the cell cracked against my lungs as I pushed it out. Swallowing harshly and rubbing my desert of a throat, I prayed to the world that I wouldn't start coughing. I snapped open my eyes to glare, but she just she sat down with a huff.

I took that as a good sign and let my eyes droop again. After a while, I was taking in coordinated breaths and I could focus on my body. The painful numbness was starting to fade. All I had to do was breathe.

In… and out.

The heavy curtains of my eyelids forced the scene around me into black. Before I knew it, my body had gone limp. And I drifted away into the long, lovely abyss.

———

"What is this—"

"Where am—"

"I thought I died—"

I picked up on a muffled sound. Someone talking. They kept cutting off. The sound felt light, like a bird's song on the breeze. But I couldn't feel it on my ears. In fact, I couldn't feel my ears—I couldn't feel anything at all. Not my eyes, my mouth, my hands, or any other part of my body. I just drifted about in seeming nothingness, existing almost like a bare soul in a void.

"Please…"

The voice didn't cut off, this time only trailing off into an incomprehensible softness.

"Please…"

Something flashed the black. A white spark of light. My vision came rushing back.

"Please…"

The soft words repeated again, still not getting further than the one word.

"Please…"

Another flash of light. A small, white spark whipped through the darkness like a shooting star before it was gone. No words at all followed the light this time.

Another spark. The white light streaked through black, glowing for longer than before. The spark hit… something in the dark; its light vanished. I blinked, hoping with a foreign sense of desperation that the little light would come back.

Then it flared again. My eyes lit up with glee and my mind filled with joy.

There, right in front of my eyes and revealing its innocent beauty, was a small white flame waving in a nonexistent wind. My eyes widened, taking in as much of the little light as they possibly could. It danced and drifted, wavering in the nothingness it had sprung from.

Then it burned out.

A sharp bolt of pain struck right in the center of my mind, and an unfamiliar sense of longing grew within me. The last remnants of light faded quietly into the dark before leaving me drifting. Suddenly, impossibly alone.

———

I woke up unbearably slow; the seconds felt like decades as I lifted my head. My eyelids dragged open and I winced, stung by the sudden influx of light.

I saw the same cell, the same metal bars, and the same woman from before. She was sitting against the wall now, her plated boots scraping it with every tiny movement. And she was staring at something outside of the cell with intent flashing on her irises. Squinting harder, the lines at the corners of her eyes sharpened enough to cut through steel. She hadn't even noticed that I'd woken up.

I stopped looking at her by closing my eyes and steadying my breaths. The fog of sleep cleared, letting me take stock of my situation. And as soon as I did, I snapped my eyes right back open, blinking in complete and utter disbelief. As I felt my body, moving and flexing each individual muscle, I found myself feeling better than before. Most of the pain was gone, with only a white-hot warmth left in its wake.

My head wasn't pounding.

My shoulder didn't sting.

My mind wasn't foggy.

Everything inside of me just felt… better. My muscles flexed with ease, twitching with more power than I'd felt in this body before. The ghost of a smile broke against my tired expression. Given time, I would've even been able to fight again. I smiled. Then my stomach rumbled, responding to my thoughts.

"Awake again?" the woman asked, her voice lilting to my ears. I pried my eyes wide to look at her.

Sitting there, she had her knees up and her metal boots planted firmly on the floor. Her arms were draped over her knees—draped over the dark blue cloth that covered her body—and she wasn't looking at me. She was still staring to the left, at whatever was so interesting outside of the cell.

"Yeah," I mumbled, my voice scrappy and hoarse.

She nodded, an edge entering her expression with a curl of her lips. "So I can ask you questions now?"

I grunted, pushing myself up into a more comfortable position. My glare softened, becoming more of a squint, and I shook my head. "Sure, I guess."

My voice was unconvincing as it echoed off the metal walls of the cell, but I really couldn't help it. I didn't know where I was. I didn't know who *she* was. And I was still pulling myself out a the painful, foggy abyss. Letting her ask a few questions was the least of my concerns.

She grinned. Her eyes didn't move. "So why are you here?"

I tilted my gaze upward, my lips parting in confusion. "I… I'm not sure."

"Me neither," she scoffed, her grin tilting. "But what I meant was, why do they want you?"

I furrowed my brow. "Excuse me?"

"Let me rephrase," she said, a sharpness entering at the corner of her voice. "Why are you useful to them?" Her gaze hardened but still avoided mine, and she rolled her wrist as if that had cleared everything up.

It hadn't.

"What?"

Her grin drooped. She leaned further forward, pushing her boots against the metal and sending the soft, tinny scraping noises echoing off the walls. "What are your powers? What is your soul most attuned to?" I shook my head. She stifled a grumble building in her throat. "Why did they take you here instead of killing you?"

"I don't know what you're asking," I said, raising my voice. A thundering storm formed from the remnants of my fog and my nostrils flared out. I wasn't used to people being so disrespectful to me. "What are you even looking at?"

The sly grin that had wormed its way onto her face in tandem with my annoyance left as quickly as it had come. She pointed outside of the cell. Her eyebrows dropped and her lips pressed together, but she held her tongue. I only stared at her for a few seconds longer before dragging my gaze across to look through the rusty bars. I blinked when my eyes met the sight.

I swallowed, noting the lump in my throat. A vague scraping sound echoed on the edge of my skull.

There, in the cell next to ours and draped in black robes, was a young girl. My stomach rolled as I realized she couldn't have been older than eighteen. Her pale body was sprawled on the ground and her black hair was disheveled, covering a large part of the metal floor. Adorning her fitting black robe were sets of thin, silver strips that twitched and ripped like scars. I swallowed again, still not getting the dry cotton down. Then, as my eyes dropped lower, staring at her impossibly pale complexion, a bitter taste fell on my tongue. Growing directly out of her skin were shaped black scales, like she had been cursed, infected with some sort of parasitic monster.

But that wasn't even the strangest part.

A shiver raced down my spine as I lifted my gaze up. There, draped over her back and extruding directly from her spine were grey, bony wings that sent shots of both wonder and terror straight to my soul.

I shuddered again and pulled my head backward to avert my eyes. The soft, idle scraping grew louder in my ears, pulling at fearful memories I'd long since pushed down.

My world went black, and for a moment, I didn't know why. Then, as I grew aware of my body again, I twisted my neck and pried my eyelids open. The sunlight glinting off the metal ground calmed me, even while stabbing me in the eye. At least it wasn't her.

"Who is…" I started, trying to suppress another shudder. The words slipped away through my teeth.

My cellmate shivered, taking a deep breath that was way more ragged than it should've been. She adjusted her position, sending a soft scrape of metal bouncing through the cell.

"I don't know," she said bluntly. "She's been here for longer than I have and I've never even seen her awake."

I nodded, the blank cloth of the girl's robes flashing in the corner of my eye. I wanted to look, drawn in by a renewed sense of morbid curiosity. But with the vile cracking sound fading from my mind, I knew better than to test it.

"I don't recommend looking at her for long," the woman said. She shook her head. "It'll mess with your mind."

I shook my head too, removing the images from my eyes. My cellmate was right and I knew it.

"So, why are you useful?" she asked again. The past minute of strangely interesting terror was all but ripped from reality by the onset of confusion. I widened my eyes and curled my lips at her, gawking at the question that still didn't make any sense.

Why was I useful? What kind of question was that? For a moment, I thought of my prowess with the blade. But looking down at my thin and inept body, I tossed the thought away rather quickly. It wasn't true anymore. So, through annoyance that was still bubbling under the surface, I just replied the same was as before.

"I don't know what you're asking."

She rolled her eyes at me. "Okay, I'll start from scratch then." She flexed her fingers and gestured to the world around us outside of the cell. The single small wooden building and collection of tents confirmed what she would say next. "This camp is a farm for mages. They send mercenaries and scouters out to find anyone who even has a little prowess with magic and bring them here." She gestured to the cell we were sitting in. "They keep us here until we're useful."

My eyes widened, the information being both vile and incompatible with my mind. Mages were rare, and the ones that could even be considered useful enough to capture would be guarded and capable of defending themselves. The camp... couldn't have been lucrative. It shouldn't have been.

I narrowed my eyes at her, immediately suspicious. I squared my shoulders and pressed myself against the wall even harder as if trying to block off her lies from my ears. What she was saying didn't make any sense.

"So," she continued, not even noticing my movement. "All that I'm asking is why they brought *you* here. What are your powers?"

It clicked, the question fitting like a puzzle piece suddenly forced into place.

She thought I was a mage.

I'd never been good at magic. For my entire life, I'd been completely inept. Even after becoming a high-knight and gaining the opportunity to study with the best mages in the land, I still hadn't been able to do it. The process didn't make sense—being able to move energy at will sounded illogical to me.

It wasn't the greatest loss, though. Most people couldn't perform magic and my physical prowess was greater than the boost some puny flames could've given me. Well, it *used* to be, at least.

My eyebrows dropped. I shoved my head to the side on the metal wall, hearing a dull clang ring out through the cell. A bitter taste fell on my tongue, but I was quick to wash it away, forcing a deep breath through my nose as I responded to her question.

"I… don't have any," I said. "I'm not a mage."

The woman squinted at me, raising an eyebrow in the process. She opened her mouth before snapping it shut only a moment later, her lips contorting in confusion. "If you're here, you have to be a mage."

I let out a long breath, tilting my head forward and repeating exactly what I'd said before. "I'm not a mage."

She blinked and raised her hand. For a moment, she just looked at me, her mouth open. But she didn't say anything. Instead, she squinted ever-harder, rolling her wrist through the air as if in an attempt to turn the gears in her head. After a while, it became clear that it hadn't worked.

A confused grunt rose up in her throat. "That makes no sense."

I shrugged, seeing no further need to repeat myself. *She* just continued her stare for a few more seconds before throwing her hands up, crossing her arms, and sitting back against the wall.

"Whatever," she mumbled, still glancing toward me. "I'll learn what your power is when they test you anyway."

I blinked, my eyebrows already raising to the sky. "Test me?" I asked, trying to keep my tone steady. "What do you mean by that?"

She chuckled, a smirk rushing right back to mask the confusion she'd displayed moments before. "With every new mage they capture, they test them to see what power their souls are attuned to. It's to see whether or not a prisoner is truly useful." Her shoulders were steadily raising again, and the confident edge from before was marching its way back. "If they are, they're sent back to their cell to be called on for future use. If they aren't… then they're killed on the spot."

My eyelids flitted. Thoughts spun in my head, asking questions that I didn't have the answers to. They fed a growing sensation—a sensation I really hadn't felt in years. A sensation that pressed against the inside of my skull.

I swallowed, washing nothing from my suddenly dry mouth. I tried to calm my thoughts, to steady my breathing, but I couldn't. Each time, a new question— a new possibility to consider would spring up.

They'd taken me here. They'd said I was a mage. The scene of my most recent defeat played out in my head. I'd heard the words the mage had used. He'd called me useful, and even that simple fact alone was enough to send shivers down my spine.

I thought about running, but my legs groaned at that. Even if whatever rest I'd gotten had healed me, I still wasn't in the best shape. And I didn't have my sword. No, I thought. I couldn't run. Running would just get me caught and killed.

But I would be killed anyway, the rising sensation whispered into my ears. I shuddered, pressing myself firmly back against the wall.

I had to think of something. I had to get out. I'd only had this body for a day, and I already hated it. The beast had cursed me, cursed me to live a new life that wasn't mine. For that, it was going to *pay*. But as my eyes flicked around and I realized more and more that I wasn't in a situation that had an easy way out, I cursed under my breath.

My cellmate chuckled. "You really aren't a mage, are you?"

I stared at her, shaking my head slowly. "No."

"You're screwed then," she said. "They're almost here."

My brows knitted at that, throwing lines on my forehead. I opened my mouth, another question ready at my lips, but that question never made it out. Familiar noises registered at the edge of my hearing.

Footsteps.

Distinct, heavy, boot-made steps ripped through the air. I heard the crunch of grass, the shifting of dirt. They were coming.

"By the way," my cellmate started, narrowing her eyes, "you're not from Sarin, are you?"

I widened my eyes, the name registering. "No, I was just on my way—"

The jingle of metal. I stopped, my lips freezing as I dragged my gaze to the door. As I stared out at the bulky man dressed in light armor opening the door. He wore a shallow grin and kept his eyes on me while the hand *not* opening the door settled on the daggers strapped to his waist.

"Well," the woman started again. "I'm Kye, anyway."

She laughed after that, but I didn't pay her any mind. As the long-forgotten sensation of fear—real fear—pricked my skin, the man wrenched the keys in the door and opened it up.

As soon as he stepped inside, he pointed directly at me.

CHAPTER SIX

"Get the fuck up."

The man barked at me. I obeyed without hesitation, fearing another hit. My eye twitched, but I averted my gaze and turned back to the small pile of kindling I was supposed to be lighting. I did *not* want to come out of this more damaged than necessary.

"Try again," the brute of a man said from behind me.

I breathed in, closed my eyes, and tried again.

The man was trying to get me to conjure a flame. Because apparently, a flame was the easiest thing to make as a mage; it was the simplest way for the soul to shape energy. As even a basic user of magic, I was supposed to be able to do it. What the man didn't want to hear was that I *wasn't* a mage and no matter how many times he yelled at me, it wasn't going to happen.

With his sharp gaze cutting into my back, though, and even sharper knives strapped to his waist, I tried anyway. Collecting my thoughts, clearing my mind, and feeling every bit of energy I could, I tried again to force heat out through my hand.

Nothing happened. Just like before. There was no flame, no light, no magic. Not even a noticeable change in temperature.

I sighed, biting back a curse as I knew what would come next. Accepting my failure for the third time in a row, I turned to the man and looked him directly in the eyes. My eyes narrowed a sliver, unwavering under the pressure of his stature. His brows raised in anticipation. Hope sparked in his light brown eyes, but I squashed that in a heartbeat. I shook my head.

The man hardened his gaze and stepped forward. For a moment, nothing happened, with only the man's accelerating breaths filling the suddenly still air. Then his fist flew out, and I was knocked to my knees.

Spit flew out of my mouth, my jaw stiffened unnaturally, and my own teeth slashed at the inside of my cheek. Breathing heavily and spitting droplets of blood out onto the ground, I grunted. I couldn't help it. It *hurt*.

The man growled. "Stop playing with me! Drel said you were useful, dammit. He felt it on you. So just *do it* before I have to kill you."

I had to swallow a scoff, wincing at the way the man's raspy voice invaded my ears. His words hung in the air. I paid them no mind. Instead, I spat into the dirt and turned my head, looking at the pile of splinters I was meant to light.

I wasn't going to be able to do it. I knew I wasn't. The realization made me sick. Yet, I knew that if I *didn't* do it, I was going to die.

So I quelled my anger as best I could and stood back up. My frustration simmered, bubbling just beneath the surface. I had to stop it from getting the better of me. But as I closed my eyes, focusing back on the pile of splinters, I felt nothing. No heat. No energy. No magic. It felt like bashing my brain against the inside of my skull—I just wasn't able to do it.

A growl slipped through my teeth and I turned, not seeing any other real option. The man glared at me with both hands clenched into tight fists. I wasn't intimidated. I didn't show any fear. If I showed my fear to him, it would only be even worse.

Instead, I looked him right in the eyes, making sure he met my gaze, and shook my head.

The man trembled with anger, veins bulging out of his forehead. "You won't do it, rat? Well you can't say I didn't warn you."

His low, grating tone reached my ears at the same time as his fist. It plowed into the side of my head, sending jolts of blunt, white-hot pain streaming through my skin and throwing my body to the side like a rag doll. I yelled, clattering to the ground like an charred piece of firewood.

When I picked myself back up, I was coughing, spitting even more blood into the dirt as I pulled my teeth apart. I winced in pain, afternoon sunlight burning on the side of my face. Patting my skin, I tried to brush away the light, and only ended up getting blood on my fingers instead.

I closed my eyes tight, trying to steady my breathing. I coughed hard, again, and trembled as I tried to get myself under control. Feeling a burning rage seep into my veins, I slammed my eyes open and twisted back toward the man of wrath. He was already standing above me, fists raised and twitching confidence in his eyes. But he didn't strike. Instead, he just took a ragged breath like he was remembering something.

"Try again."

I jerked my head back, blinking. But I didn't argue. I shoved down the rage burning in my chest and uncurled my fists. Sparing only one glance at the man, I tried again.

Taking a deep breath and realizing that this was probably my last chance, I gave it another shot. My mind went clear. I felt my entire body. I felt the energy within it, swirling as it fed through my bones and through the back of my mind. I grasped onto that energy. I gripped it tight.

And I moved it.

Or I attempted to, at least. When I opened my eyes and focused on the pile of wood though, nothing happened. All I got was another wave of frustration and more banging on my skull. Wind brushed over my skin, twirling through my fingers with impossible grace. And at that exact moment, that grace froze me as the breeze barreled through, taking my last shred of hope along with it. My hands shook in morbid anticipation as I turned to stare at the man a final time.

I winced internally, keeping the expression away from my face. I shook my head, and he was on me in a second.

The first punch made me stumble backward. As I stabilized myself, adjusting on shorter legs, I glanced back at the man only to see him already moving. I was more ready for the second strike. I brought my arm up to defend, hoping to hinder the blow. But with my new, weak limbs, it still hurt like hell and it still knocked me back.

He rushed anew, fists raised and not letting up. I barely dodged out of the way, but he was faster than me anyway. He turned on his heel, barely losing any speed, and slammed into me with all of his weight.

I fell to the ground, breath vanishing from my lungs. Pain itched at my insides and I tried to wail, to scream in agony as air rushed back into my throat. The man crouched beside me, grinning, and hit me again. This punch only halfway landed on my raised arm. I grimaced, my face contorting into a horrible display of pain that I hadn't shown in years. Ashamed, I covered myself, but another punch never came.

After a few long moments, I lowered my hands. Just enough to see the man again. And when I saw him, the vile rage still burning in his eyes, his grin split wider. My hands tried to shield my face, but he had something different in mind. All heavy breathing stopped as his hands wrapped around my neck.

My eyes bugged out. I scratched the man, desperately trying to save my windpipe. Anger, fear, surprise, and pain all mixed together, swirling in my mind. I gasped, feeling nothing touch my lungs. My desperation grew, and as it grew, my drive grew with it. But as moments bled together, my fingers weakened. There seemed no way to get out.

The banging on the inside of my skull returned, harder this time, and I frantically kicked out. Weak legs pushed against an immovable object, but the pain didn't stop.

My brain screamed, my mind burned, and everything slowed. My eyes drooped and pain got clouded over by fog. Blood ran cold in my veins, thickening with each passing second. And yet, somewhere along the line, I must've become able to breathe.

"Get *off!*" my voice screamed. The piercing sound broke through the pain and left me seething in power and confusion. My voice... wasn't entirely mine. I hadn't ordered the words. But they'd come out nonetheless.

In the back of my mind, a sleeping force stirred, and I felt energy filling my body. Slowly, as time sped back to its normal space, power trickled out through my veins and into my muscles, twitching in wait. My eyesight sharpened, my hearing deepened, and the slow-motion faded.

Not fully in control, my fingers grabbed at the hands around my neck and pried them off. In the corners of my vision, a white haze danced as I attacked, but I couldn't pay it much attention. My hands moved rapidly, flailing in strangely coordinated movements as I tracked the man's face.

Everything became hot as I punched him, over and over. The white haze in my vision deepened and my hands erupted into white flames. Something about the pale fire was familiar to me, but I couldn't place it through the crazed attack.

My fists rammed into the man's armor, creating a burn mark each time. He grunted and staggered, scrambling backward. His eyes filled with burning terror as he stared. I just growled and slammed right back into him. A flurry of blows followed, seeming to crack the air around me as I knocked the man to the ground. Then, standing above him and seething, I stopped.

Slowly, unsteadily, and with a whole lot of effort, I came down from my craze.

My eyes widened. I could do little more than gasp. As the white haze dampened, the blockade broke and questions flooded my mind. The power, the fighting, the flames—I didn't understand any of it.

Shaking my head, I darted my eyes to the man. Charcoal-black singe marks covered his body and he was shifting unconsciously as if trying to squirm away from the torment. Blood ran out of his nose, but even that was burned. Reality hit me like a falling temple, the truth of the situation sending bile up in my throat.

I swallowed it down while the white haze receded, leaving me cold and bare. Energy flowed out of me just as readily as it had flowed in and evaporated into the air. And after a while, it was just me. Standing, staring, and trembling over a much larger man in the middle of the camp.

I could've freaked out—I wanted to—but I knew better than that. After being a fighter for my entire life, my instincts were honed sharper than that. I forced my thoughts into order and pushed back against the raging sea in my head as I realized what I had to do next. The thought came to me slowly, scraping its way to prominence.

I had to get out.

My impulse-driven body leaped into action and shots of ice-cold steel flooded my veins. I gritted my teeth and tore my gaze from the man, the objects of necessity revealing themselves one by one. I had to get out of this camp. I had to get to town. I had to get *help*.

Running through the options still spinning in my head, I grasped onto a plan of action. Then, swallowing harder, I crouched down next to the unconscious man and produced the keys from his pocket.

For a moment as I stood back up, I gawked. The blood. The bruises. The burns. A shiver raced down my spine. I didn't understand any of what I'd done, but I tore away enough to compose myself. Clutching the keys, I turned on my heel and sprinted back the way I'd come. I sprinted all the way back to the cell.

The worn and uncomfortable shoes the barkeep had given me beat furiously on the dirt as I worked my way back. Weaving around the trail we'd used to get there, I retraced my steps and pushed on. The small metal cell lined together with about a half-dozen others on the plain came into view in short time. I hoped and prayed that nobody in the camp would see me.

By the time I came up to the cell, my muscles were screaming and I was far beyond out of breath. I ignored the desperation. I didn't need it now. I would have time to be exhausted after I got out of this world's forsaken camp.

Running up on shaky legs, I jammed the key into the lock and threw open the door to wake the woman inside.

She jumped, her metal boots scraping against the floor. "What?" was all she was able to ask before she noticed my glare.

"We need to get out of here," I said, breathy and cold.

The woman—Kye, she'd told me—rubbed her eyes. "What happened? How did you—"

I didn't let her finish. I couldn't let her finish. We didn't have time for it. I needed to leave, and I needed her help to do it.

"It doesn't matter right now," I said. "We need to *leave.*"

She opened her mouth but nodded instead. After a few moments of sitting with pursed lips, she pushed herself off the ground and looked me right in the eyes. "Okay," she sighed. "What's the plan?"

I stopped, freezing in place. Her words echoed off my skull, nearly sending everything spinning again. The plan? I didn't know. I didn't *have* a plan. I just needed to get out.

Words came slowly but surely. "Do you know where Sarin is from here?" I asked.

She scoffed. "Of course. But how are we supposed to get out of *here?*"

"I…" I started, but nothing more came out. A hurried breath fell from my lips with a painful realization. I truly didn't know.

The tall woman eyed me, tapping her foot. I could feel the weight of her gaze, the intent behind it. But as I thought, wracking my brain for any semblance of a plan, I was at a loss.

Finally, she sighed. "Okay. We're going to have to wing it then."

I blinked. But she didn't wait up, pushing past me and into the grass. I turned on my heel, glaring at her. "*Wing it*? We can't just—"

"You haven't said anything about a better idea," she shot back before I could continue. "Now, I don't know how you got away from being tested, but that doesn't matter now. I'm in full agreement that we need to get *out*." She squinted out at the camp around us. "This place isn't guarded all over… I'm sure we can sneak off." The ghost of a smirk floated at her lips, but she was right. I didn't have a better idea.

So, ignoring the pointed comments she'd made, I nodded. And when she nodded back, her smile breaking through, I pursed my lips.

"How do you suggest we 'wing it' then?"

Her expression wavered for a moment. She whirled around, her eyes almost swirling with energy as she scanned the land around us. "Nobody is around for a little ways," she said as if it was natural to know. I furrowed my brow. She continued on. "If we keep close to the cells, we should be okay."

I nodded slowly, unsure. But I was forced to agree. "So we're just going to sneak off and hope they don't notice?"

Kye shook her head, flashing a toothy smile my way. "Follow my lead."

I opened my mouth to complain, but she was already moving. Stepping back to the cell, she took the metal door and slammed it shut. The sharp metal clang shook the world around me. I froze in place. She was gone in a flash, hurrying down the line of cells.

Far slower than I would've enjoyed, I unfroze and followed right after her. "What the hell was that?" I hissed as I struggled to catch up.

She didn't look back at me, only squinting in a direction beyond the line of metal cages. "Sarin is that way," she said, tilting her head. "And if we don't get spotted, we should be able to get to the main path from here."

My pace slowed as lines appeared on my forehead. I stared at the woman draped in unfamiliar blue cloth, doubt rising up. She'd just ignored my question completely. Pretended it didn't exist. And the things she was doing didn't inspire me with much hope.

But as shouts sounded off in the distance, I sped right back up. My muscles screamed. I ignored them as I once more matched her pace. By the time I was only a few paces away again, we were almost at the end of the line. After glancing back, her eyes danced on me for only a moment before she swept around the corner.

A soft wail, long and hollow, lilted to my ears from the cell to my side. I gritted my teeth and stiffened my neck. I wanted to look, but it wouldn't have been any use. I was having enough trouble saving myself.

When I ducked around the last corner as well, my breath accelerating with each step, Kye's form caught my eye. She glared frozen daggers at me, energy dancing in her eyes, and held a finger to her lips.

"They're coming," she said.

I swallowed, my mouth suddenly dry, and pressed myself against the metal wall. Standing there in wait, I strained my ears. But I couldn't hear anything. The shouting was gone. My lips parted to speak, but a heavy breath consumed my words. I almost burst out coughing, only barely holding back the sound as light air tickled my lungs.

Hearing my soft coughs, Kye glared at me again. I stifled the last of the sounds still slipping from my lips. Then, glancing over at her, I saw her angling her head as if tracking a sound in the distance. I furrowed my brow and perked my ears again, hearing nothing.

Then, slowly but surely, the sound revealed itself to me.

Footsteps.

Again, in the distance, I heard the distinct sound of boots on dirt. I froze. Someone *was* coming. Kye was right somehow, though I still didn't know how the hell she could've known before me.

I turned to her and opened my mouth. She shook her head and went back to listening. She didn't want me to talk. She was waiting for something, something that I apparently couldn't hear.

"What?" a voice called from a familiar distance, shaky and full of shock. Immediately, I understood.

Whoever was walking toward us had found our cell. *Empty*. After a couple more seconds of silence, the distant voice started yelling and Kye looked to me again. Her lips curled up and she only nodded once before surging off the wall and running straight into the field.

With a smile of my own, I followed right behind.

It was actually quite genius. Whoever had heard our cell door slamming shut had come to investigate. And when they'd gotten there, they'd seen only an empty cell and had started yelling. Their booming voice and the commotion around us drowned out the sounds of our escape. As our feet pounded on dry ground, nobody could detect us over the clamor raised in the camp.

I didn't know if Kye had planned it or if she just got lucky, but either way, it worked. And either way, I was impressed.

So we ran, her much faster than me, out of the low, sparse field and up into greener plains. Grass crunched beneath my feet as I ran for my life. I pushed away fatigue as well as I could and eventually, the lined dirt path came into view behind increasingly tall grass. Kye then ducked behind a large rock formation jutting out of the ground.

I did the exact same thing seconds later as I finally caught up.

My legs slowed. Air rushed into my lungs. And it was that exact moment that my body chose to remind me of its weak, miserable existence. Leaning against the jutting rock, I slid to the ground.

Above me, I heard the woman let out a breathy laugh. When I looked up at her though, she had me fixed with a deadly stare. "*Now*," she said. "You have some serious explaining to do."

CHAPTER SEVEN

All in all, she had much more to explain than I did, but I'd gone first.

Kye shifted her weight, glaring at me with an intensity I wished I could've gotten used to. "So you *are* a mage?" she asked, tilting her head at my cringing face. "But I thought you—"

My hands waved through the air as if trying to disperse her misconceptions physically. "No. I'm *not* a mage," I said, nearly breathless. Oppressive afternoon sun beat down on my face, making my ever-frustrating body sweat through the collar. The exhaustion setting into my bones along with Kye's ever-present stare only made all of it worse.

The tall woman's lips curled, her eyes sharpening. "You said your hands were engulfed in flames. That sounds like magic to me."

Wincing again under the weight of her scrutiny, I nodded. Then I immediately shook my head. "It does sound like magic, but I'm not a mage. There were flames, but they weren't *my* flames."

My walking partner nodded slowly, her expression unreadable. "And how does that work?"

I gritted my teeth, trying to quell the frustration building inside. "I don't know—I wish I did. But it wasn't me."

She clicked her tongue softly, turning her narrowed eyes away and down the lined dirt path. Angling her head from side to side, she just stared out at the horizon, eventually dragging my gaze along with her.

In front of us, the dirt path extended for hundreds of paces, cutting through the plains just as it always had. It looked, from where we walked in idle arbitration, that there wasn't a town anywhere near. But slowly and steadily, the farms around us were growing less sparse; they were becoming less chaotic. Some semblance of actual, organized civilization was returning to the land.

Turning back to me with one of her eyebrows half raised, Kye finally responded. "So. It wasn't your magic. Does that mean someone else did the magic... for you? Some other soul bent energy from a far range just to help *you*?"

My face scrunched up. I found my head shaking again. Though, when I opened my mouth to retort, nothing came out. I just… didn't know how to describe it. When I'd been choking, I'd thought I was going to die. I'd thought I was at the end of the line—that the beast was waiting mere minutes away. But something had stopped that out of pure rage and desire to survive. Something had saved me.

"It only happened when I was about to die," I said, trying to keep the bitter bite from my tone. "When he'd tested me—asked me only to make a simple flame, I hadn't been able to do it." I watched Kye nod skeptically. The disbelief in her eyes didn't waver. "Before it happened, there was some sort of *banging* in my head, as if my skull was a cage and something desperately wanted to get out."

Finally, something changed in Kye's eyes. The light brown quivered for a second, responding to a shift in her thoughts. "That *is* the most unusual way I've ever heard of a mage realizing their potential."

"But I'm not a mage," I said, nearly spitting the words through my teeth.

"Right. So something *inside* of you is a mage."

I blinked, half-nodding before jerking my head backward. "What? That doesn't even make any sense."

She just shrugged, chuckling dryly to herself. "Does it make less sense than sudden magical abilities happening for you this late in your life?"

I nearly scoffed. "This late in my—" Then I stopped, my eyes widening as I realized my new, youthful self. Looking down at my body, I knew I was young. I couldn't have been older than the practiced woman in front of me. But I didn't actually know how old. I didn't even know my own world's damned age. "How early is a mage *supposed* to realize their powers?"

Kye's little chuckle turned into an all-out laugh at my statement. "Way earlier than this," she said. "Although, I'm not so sure. Maybe you're just a bit slow."

My eyebrows dropped and I glared. The disrespect burned my skin. I'd earned better than this, I told myself. But she didn't even notice. As the seconds wore on, her laughter only picked up.

"That doesn't matter though," I said with as little emotion in my voice as I could manage. "All I know is that it wasn't me."

Then with a realization coming to me steadily, I checked the back of my mind.

Whatever was there, it was sleeping again. An irritated noise crawled out of my throat. Sarin couldn't come fast enough.

Kye stared at me skeptically after calming herself. "How did you get captured anyway?"

I blinked, the question hitting harder than it should've. Recent memories rushed back. So much had happened in the past two days. I'd been *reborn* only a day ago, and now I was escaping from a prison camp and questioning my own magic? It didn't make much sense. None of it really made much sense.

Remembering her question, I said, "I was on my way to town and they ambushed me." I did not want to go into detail about what had happened before that. My story still confused even me, and I doubted that her understanding would've reached the same heights as the warm barkeep.

She raised an eyebrow. I didn't miss the way her fingers curled into a careful fist. "Where were you coming from?"

I shrugged and gave the shortest answer. "From some old tavern back down the road."

Kye's face lit up in an instant. Then she remembered the suspicion she held and chose her words carefully. "The rustic one?" I hesitated before nodding. "The one with the cheerful and caring owner?" I nodded again. A genuine smile ghosted at her lips. "You came from Sal's place?" She nudged me on the shoulder playfully, causing my weak muscles to scream. I would've rolled my eyes if I hadn't been forced to grimace in pain.

Regaining my composure, I shrugged. "I didn't know that was its name."

She nodded knowingly, looking forward and clicking her tongue. "Then you probably didn't stay for very long."

"I only stayed one night," I said. From the corner of my eye, I could see Kye glancing over every few seconds. My fingers curled. and I forced myself to take a breath.

Kye made a knowing sound and turned to me. "If you could be staying at Sal's right now, why are you walking to Sarin? You are not in *any* condition to be walking this far." I didn't miss the amusement that floated on her lips, but I also couldn't ignore that she was right.

Her words churned through my head as I shook away the disrespect yet again. Hesitating, I considered how much to reveal. "I need to get to Credon as quickly as possible."

She squinted at me. The questions in her eyes didn't disappear. "Credon? The town is called *Sarin*."

I nearly stopped in my tracks, my brow furrowing. For a moment, I just blinked in disbelief. "I know what the town is called. I am *trying* to get to Credon. I thought Sarin would be a good place to start."

Kye's fists tightened. "Where is Credon? I don't think I've ever heard of it."

My brows knitted together. Again, the woman's words didn't make any sense. Credon was the capital. It was the richest city on the continent. It was my *home*. How could she not know of it? "It's near the coast, on the centerline of the kingdom by the same name. Do you really not know where it is?"

Kye raised an eyebrow at me, smirked, then scoffed. "I can't just know every little place on this continent by heart, you know."

I was already shaking my head. "Little? It's the capital. You must've heard of it."

"The capital of what?" she asked, narrowing her eyes. Once more, I could feel the burn of her antagonism against my skin. Meeting her gaze with my own, I pride for my kingdom swelled up.

"The capital of Credon," I said shortly. "The greatest kingdom on the continent."

She snickered. I shot her a glare, but that only seemed to amuse her even more. The stubborn suspicion broke away in a storm of chuckles. "Which continent?" she asked. "There hasn't been a kingdom here for hundreds of years. Did you get lost in someone's accounts of the past before you got yourself captured and locked in a cell?"

I blinked, tilting my head. The words she'd used stuck out like sore thumbs. They flooded my mind, spinning and spinning until I could make enough sense of each of them. Unfortunately for me, that time wasn't very close at hand. I shook my head, setting aside the confusion and returning to her question.

"Tecta," I said slowly. "There are at least a dozen kingdoms in Tecta."

She jerked her head back, still chuckling. Then she blinked, the sounds escaping her lips morphing into light breaths. Finally, the slight glimmer of recognition lit up in her eyes. "Tecta? You mean the continent to the north?"

Continent to the north? What was she talking about? There was nothing north of Tecta. It was surrounded on that side by the eternal sea.

Doubt rose up but I forced it down, summoning what information I'd learned from my lessons as a child. For some reason, they felt slippery and hard to grasp, but I got enough. Slowly, steadily, I pieced it all together. And all at once, the conclusion came down on me like a collapsed church.

There was nothing to the north of Tecta. But there was a continent to the south. I swallowed, turning back to my walking partner. "Where are we, again?"

She stared at me, bewildered. I widened my eyes and nodded, trying to push past the wall of dread building up between me and all of my goals. "We're in the middle of the road right now."

I shook my head. "No. Which *continent* are we on?"

She snorted but played along. "We're in Ruia."

I cringed, the world shattering around me. In an instant, my mind was sent whirling and everything I'd known since the night I'd been reborn was called into question. Looking back at the woman in the blue cloth uniform, I tried to find a joke. I tried to find some semblance of a lie.

There wasn't any. She was telling the truth.

The beast—the vile, mindless reaper had given me a second chance at life. It had thought I would fail, setting me up for a return visit from the very start. And on top of all of that, it had put me in *Ruia*. The corrupted continent. The outlands of the world. A lawless wasteland from everything that I knew, one filled with barbarians.

"Shit," I mumbled.

"What the hell is up with you?" Kye asked, an edge entering her voice. My hand dropped down to my side, but there was no sword there. I was unarmed. Completely and utterly defenseless.

"I must be confused," I spat through my teeth.

She eyed me still, obviously not impressed by my response. I clenched my jaw and hung my head, just continuing to walk on. Kye kept pace with me though and glared with increasing curiosity the whole way. "What's your name?"

I blinked, her calm tone catching me off guard. "Agil," I said. "My name is Agil." I didn't look up, but I could see her rolling the name over in her mind. The momentary silence felt nice. Especially now that I had far too much to think about.

"Why were you at Sal's in the first place?" Kye asked. She didn't seem to care for the fact that I didn't want to talk.

Remembering my feeble body, I complied. "I needed a place to sleep. As you can see, I don't have all that much to my name."

She exhaled sharply through her nose. "I can see that rather well. What happened to you anyway?"

I scrunched my nose, distaste rising on my tongue. And it seemed I wasn't the only one bothered by the question as I felt movement in the back of my mind. Whatever was back there shuddered, shying away from even the idea of a response.

"I'd rather not talk about it," I said instead, complying with the wishes of everything in my brain.

Kye made an unsure sound in her throat but nodded. "Alright. I won't push it. You did break me out of that cell." I nodded. It was good that she remembered something like that. "And… you're interesting enough. It wouldn't do well to have you dead."

The smirk that accompanied the last of her words stung, but I let it go. Silence crept in afterward. That was good, I decided. Thoughts were still spinning in my head, barely catching a foothold anywhere. I didn't *like* it—in fact, I hated it with a passion. But as I clenched my fist and felt pain in my fingers, I knew it was a useless resistance. This was my life now, whether I liked it or not.

From what I knew, Ruia was a continent of disorder. It was the spawn of discord, of all chaotic magic in the world. Almost all of the folktales I'd been told as a child had been set in Ruia. Maybe it was just a convenient spot, I thought now as I glanced around. But still, remembering the purple flame that the bandit had summoned out of thin air, I couldn't shrug it off so easily. No matter what I came up with, it didn't sit right. Nothing sat right. I felt like I was out of the loop —kept in the dark because of some trick on my mind.

I needed answers.

"Is capturing mages common practice here?" I started. I tried to keep all indignation from my tone. Some still crept through.

And Kye heard it too, putting poison into her own voice. "Common practice? Not exactly. But groups of bandits like the one we had the misfortune of interacting with are more common than I'd like."

"Why?" I asked, fighting my pride to the side.

"Usually to use stray mages for work or sell them as slaves to anyone depraved enough to buy."

I swallowed a bitter taste. "That's allowed to happen?"

"Allowed to happen..." Kye got a small chuckle out of that. "Not sure what you remember, but there's not much 'allowing' here. It's allowed to happen because people are able to do it. And with a group as large as the one we got tangled with, there isn't some magical police force ready to put them in line. People are trying to survive, and getting themselves killed doesn't really further that goal."

I blinked, furrowing my brow. In Credon, vigilante organizations got dealt with in quick time. *I* dealt with them in quick time. Maybe it made sense with everything I knew about Ruia already, but it was still hard to accept. My fist clenched at just the thought of the poor people getting stomped on and slaughtered, forced to meet the same beast I'd met. Here, it seemed, they barely had a chance.

"How did you get captured?" I asked.

Kye's confidence rushed back onto her face and an eyebrow shot up. "I didn't."

Her arrogance was grating. I had to keep myself from rolling my eyes. "Excuse me? I saw you in that cell."

"Sure," she said. "But I didn't get captured. Captured implies that it wasn't all planned."

"So you *wanted* to get captured?"

"I *did* get captured. On purpose. Those bastards have been a thorn in our side for a while, but we heard that they'd taken citizens from Sarin. And if there's one thing that is alive and well in Ruia, its revenge. I was tasked with exacting just that."

I chuckled—I actually chuckled at that. For the first time since I'd died, amusement flooded into my voice. "It doesn't seem that you were very success-ful."

Kye shot me a glare. "I didn't see or hear of any of the rumored prisoners while in there anyway. You weren't very useful in that department, that's for sure. And I got out while leaving a few more bandits dead. I see that as that a success."

"What's the point of going alone anyway if you're just going to get captured?" As a knight, I barely ever went on missions alone. My fellow knights and I were the backbone of the kingdom's order.

"It's not like we have an unlimited reserve of rangers." She cracked her knuckles. "Especially not ones as competent as I am. Plus, I'm fully capable of handling myself. I wasn't worried about staying there for very long."

A comment rose to my lips, one that took a jab at her, but I bit it back. Getting too comfortable so quickly wasn't something I was keen on doing. And neither was making any unneeded enemies.

Instead, I asked a different question. "Rangers?"

Kye shot be a sidelong glance. "The Rangers of Sarin. We're as close as it gets to something organized outside of a simple town government."

I squinted. The idea of a ranger was familiar—we'd had them back in Credon. But, as I was having to face over and over, things were different now. Further questions rose to my lips, but I swallowed them. Stashed them away for some other time.

"It really is a lawless wasteland outside a town, then?"

Kye grinned. When she looked at me again, her gaze was no longer sharp. The careful caution from before was gone. Or, at least it was slightly hidden away. Her hands still didn't spend much time out of a clenched fist. "Yeah. That's how it goes." She watched as I bit my lip and worked through more of my thoughts. "You don't seem to have a lot of experience around this place. A lot to learn, I reckon." She chuckled. "I sense a rude awakening in your future."

She looked down at me—she was half a head taller, after all—and smiled. I sneered back, pushing away all thoughts reminiscent of my past life. I didn't like being talked down to; I didn't like being treated like some blundering child. But again, I held my tongue.

"I'm not used to it, is all," I said. "I haven't spent much time in the wastes of —" I stopped myself, reconsidering. "It's a long story."

Kye eyed me with one eyebrow raised. Her doubt crept back, but she didn't push just like she'd said. "Well. You'll have to tell me about it some day." Then she turned and started to walk more quickly. I furrowed my brows and followed her lead. For a moment, I could've sworn I saw the face of the world. Lying in front of us, only about a hundred paces down the path, was a town. Small wooden buildings and an unpaved cobblestone road, but a town all the same.

It was salvation. That was all that mattered.

CHAPTER EIGHT

It may have been small, but Sarin was livelier than most other towns I'd seen. As Kye sped through the streets and I tried to keep up with her, it almost felt like sensory overload. People rushed all around us, talking, laughing, or shopping to their heart's content. They all moved in a slow, relaxed hurry as if some force of nature was making sure every interaction happened at exactly the correct pace.

On the sides of the rough road, dozens of stalls were selling dozens of different goods. From produce and bread to pastries and jewelry, there didn't seem to be a shortage of things to pick from. My nose twitched at the heavenly smells and, despite the knots still tied in my stomach, I couldn't help it when my mouth started to water.

Although, as I weaved through the crowds of people on my tear to keep up with Kye, I didn't feel in pristine shape. On the unpaved street, the pain in my feet only sharpened, and half of my expressions turned into some variation of a wince. The road wasn't as nice as any I'd seen in Credon, and as I looked around, the houses weren't either. Yet still, as I passed an older woman breaking a pastry in half to give to two children, I couldn't help but cheer up. The thriving community made me feel warm. It made me feel at home. For a moment, I almost forgot where I really was.

Kye, on the other hand, didn't pay much attention to Sarin at all. She maneuvered through the streets with ease and didn't so much as raise an eyebrow at anything we came across. I knew that she must've known the place already, but she was moving even faster than that. There was pointed intent in each of her steps, as though she was making her way through a maze while already knowing the correct route.

"Where are we going?" I asked when the commotion from the crowds had died down enough. Kye slowed her pace as if remembering I was even there.

"We're going…" She hesitated for only a second. "We're going to where I live."

I twisted, avoiding a grumbling man pushing past me on the street. "And where exactly is that?"

She glanced back at me with an eyebrow cocked up. "The Ranger's Lodge. I have to report back."

I furrowed my brow. "A lodge? You don't live in a house?"

Kye bit back a chuckle. "All rangers live in the lodge. It gives us the best access to the forest while providing a place for all of us to eat, sleep, and train." I nodded slowly. It was their equivalent of a Knight's Quarters, then. "It's not that hard of a concept to grasp."

My lips contorted into a sneer. "I understand the *concept*."

"Good," she shot back, her tone sharp. "Don't mess anything up while we're there."

I swallowed my protests and nodded. At least I knew how to follow orders still. And with my new, frail body looking over a town I'd never even been in before, I decided against testing her any further.

As we ambled on, the buildings around us began to change. The cobblestone road expanded into a larger town square, and the stalls became larger in turn. The quaint buildings went along the same way, basic wooden houses turning into larger shops and structures with sweeping roofs and intricate designs. At the end of the square, a large, raised wooden building loomed over the rest of the town with such intense importance that it reminded me of a palace I would've found in my old city.

"We're not going in there," Kye said, seemingly reading my thoughts. My parted lips pressed shut as she turned and dragged me in her wake.

The street we moved onto was narrower than the main one, and it was much less lively. At its onset, it cut between two of the larger buildings in the square and led along a downward slope.

Despite myself, my lips curled into a smile as I watched the town fly by. Even with the basic architecture, I couldn't help but be impressed by the cozy road and the houses that lined its sides. At the bottom of the hill, the uneven cobblestone petered off, leading into a clearing right next to a forest. A forest that, as I noted with widening eyes, housed a decorated wooden building that seemed intentionally separated from the rest of town.

"*This* is where I live," Kye said, her words ripping me back to the present. She gestured forward as we made our way into the clearing.

"This is the lodge?" I asked, making no effort to hide how affected I was. Compared to everything else I'd seen, the smooth stone foundation and polished wooden frame looked positively regal to my eyes. In fact, to say that the lodge was huge would've been… exactly correct. The structure wasn't tall, but it was wide and made use of all the space it could get by extending a good ways out into the trees.

In the corner of my eye, I saw Kye's lips curl. "Don't act so surprised." She pushed past me and made her way up to the lodge's front entrance. A dark wooden door inlaid with a golden crescent-shaped arrow swung open to let the chestnut-haired woman inside.

I blinked, remembering myself, and rushed forward as well. Then, after the heavy door slammed shut behind me too, my eyes widened yet again. If the outside of the building had been ornate and regal, the inside didn't fit very well. Instead of a setting for legends, the interior felt cozy. Homey. Oddly comfortable.

Soft footsteps rang out on the sturdy wooden floor as I made my way out of the entrance hallway and into a large room that expanded out. On one wall of the room, the same golden symbol of a curved arrow stared down at me. And on the other wall, multiple racks of gear beckoned me forward with their variety. Bows and arrows, swords and daggers, cloaks and gloves—there was everything I could've wanted. My hand twitched in the air, suddenly desperate at the absence of my sword.

From the look of it, the space was a training room. And it was one the swordsman in me desperately wanted to try out.

"You live here?" I asked, turning toward where Kye stood at the edge of a black mat in the center of the room.

She stopped, turning on her heel. "Yeah. Not *here* exactly, but our quarters are just back there." She gestured behind her to where the training room ended, meeting up with a long horizontal hall that had doors littering its far side.

I nodded. "All of the rangers live here?"

Kye folded her arms. "This place is bigger than you'd expect."

My head bobbed up and down, eyes drifting across the room. After a few moments, they settled on the golden sigil emblazoned on the wall.

"What is your purpose here?" I asked. "The Rangers, I mean." From the corner of my eye, I saw Kye squint at me. She straightened up, doubt showing in her eyes the same way it had on our way into town. I turned, squaring her gaze with mine.

My home kingdom had employed its own version of the Rangers, who were really just a special force of scouters that provided information and backup to the royal guard. But, as I had to keep reminding myself over and over, I wasn't in Credon anymore. Things were different, and I wanted to know in exactly what ways.

"We have a contract with Sarin," she said carefully. I could tell she was cherry-picking her words. "We agree to provide them with information and protection, as well as keeping the... dangers of the forest at bay in exchange for hospitality and the gear we need to hunt."

I furrowed my brow, part of her explanation jutting out like a rock. "Dangers of the forest? What do you mean by that?"

The ranger in front of me stiffened. "I mean exactly that. The forest is full dangerous creatures. We deal with them."

My eyes widened, but I fought to keep the shock contained. Dangerous creatures. Her words repeated in my head. The same mythical stories from my youth—ones that my father had told me about Ruia—rose up like steam.

"Dangerous creatures as in... magical ones?" I asked, keeping myself composed. I tried to play it off like I'd already known what she meant.

"Yes," she muttered through her teeth. It didn't seem that she wanted to give the answer she did. "We deal with whatever hybrids or magical concoctions the world decides to throw at us. We hunt them. That's our job."

I nodded, connecting everything she was saying with the ideas of rangers from my home. They were similar, I realized. Very similar. But in Credon, we didn't have magical beasts to put down. A shiver raced down my spine as I remembered all of the *things* I'd learned about as a child.

"Hybrids?" I asked. "Like hulking wolves or flying rats?" My fingers curled as I remembered the scary stories that had been tossed around in Credon's town square during the night. "Or, say, vampires?"

Kye's face contorted and she held up her hand. *"Kanir*, first of all. And yes… things like that."

"Kanir?" I asked. I wasn't sure if I even really wanted to know.

Kye scowled. "You're already familiar with the concept of vampirism. You have to be. Kanir are what humans infected with vampirism are called."

I rubbed my neck, scowling. But under Kye's scruntinous gaze, I nodded. I *was* familiar with the concept of vampirism, after all. A human who experiment- ed with their magic—someone who'd been cursed by the world with the urge to consume the energy of other living beings—was a popular figure in horror stories. I just didn't want to believe they were real.

"You hunt those things?" I asked, trying not to sound like an ignorant child.

"In some cases," Kye started. "We usually only deal with cases that aren't serious, but with kanir… their minds deteriorate quickly. We hunt them because we have to, and even then, they're about as powerful as we can go." She shifted her weight, eyes narrowing. "We stop short of creatures like wisps and obviously dragons." With that, Kye shot me a resolute glance and turned away, signaling the end of our conversation.

Shaking away the mention of wisps and dragons, I stepped forward. After all, I still had more that I wanted to know. "People really use magic that way?"

Kye stopped and let out an annoyed chuckle. "What do you expect? The only rules for magic are those set by the world. We can't change that."

"I know," I said, pushing off her condescension again. "But if someone doesn't experiment with magic, they can't become a vamp—*kanir*, right?"

"Look," Kye started as she whipped back around. "I don't know how you were taught where you're from, but it doesn't work like that. People experiment with their magic because they want *power*. Everyone does."

I stopped, leaning back on my heel. Her words echoed in my ears, striking a familiar chord among my memories. Before I knew it, my father's words were playing back in my head.

Everyone wants power. Don't ever forget that.

Another one of his warnings. Another one of his pieces of advice that had made me the man I'd become. I'd vowed never to forget any of them, and even now I still wouldn't. His words stuck out like lightning among the fog; I knew they were true. Even in Credon, people craved power. Crazed nobles, obsessed scholars, cruel merchants. There was no reason for it to be different here.

"Right," I said in a voice that barely sounded like my own. "I guess you're right."

Kye huffed. Then, seeing the dark expression on my face, her eyes narrowed as if trying to pull a reason out without having to ask. After a few moments, though, she opened her mouth.

"Oh, look who's back," came a sarcastic voice that kicked me from my thoughts. Kye's lips snapped shut. Looking up, I saw a young, sandy-haired man in the same dark blue clothing as Kye standing on the far side of the room.

"What do you want, Jason?" Kye asked.

The smirking man threw his hands up. "Hey. I wasn't trying to intrude. I'm just glad you came back alive."

The previously confident woman grumbled as if the presence of the man named Jason sapped her of all will to be arrogant. "None of the people rumored to be captured were there."

Jason's eyebrows dropped a sliver, but his smug smile stayed strong. "So you failed?"

"No," Kye shot back. "I didn't come back with any because there weren't any to come back with."

Finally, the blonde man's arrogance wavered. He gestured to me. "Then who's this?"

Kye turned to me slowly. "He's... the one who got me out of my cell. He was on his way to Sarin as well, and it didn't feel right to just drop him in the first street."

"Sure, sure," Jason said slowly.

My fingers curled. I had to fight myself not to scoff. "I'm Agil."

"Well, *Agil*," he said. I scrunched my nose at his emphasis. "Thanks for getting Kye out of her jam." His smug grin rushed right back and I nearly rolled my eyes.

"Shut up, Jason," Kye said, glaring daggers in his direction.

"Just glad that you're back," he said as he pushed off the doorway and started walking across the room. "Oh, and Lorah wanted to see you when you got back."

Kye straightened and her eyes widened. Sharing a glance with Jason, she nodded gratefully. I tilted my head and opened my mouth, about to ask who Lorah was, but the words died on my lips when the man slapped me on the shoulder. His eyes bored into me for a moment, glinting dangerously before he nodded and walked all the way out the door.

I swallowed the distaste in my mouth. "Who was *that*?"

Kye chuckled. "*That*, was Jason. Our resident, self-proclaimed swords-master." My ears perked up at that. "And as you can probably tell, our resident asshole as well."

"It doesn't take a genius to see," I said, rolling my shoulder.

Kye nodded shortly, eyeing me. "Anyway, Lorah must be able to sense me already so I should go see her."

I blinked. "Sense you?"

Kye raised an eyebrow. "She's sensitive to magical energy. I'm sure she knows that I'm here already."

I stopped, realizing something. "You're a mage?"

"Of course I am," came her off-handed response as though it was the most natural thing in the world. Remembering where I was—which *continent* I was on, I shook my head. Right. Things were different.

"What kind of magic do you specialize in?" I asked, continuing to push my luck.

She didn't even look back at me. "I enhance my own abilities." A cold note of finality entered her voice and I snapped my lips shut, swallowing my pride and taking the hint. I didn't want to pry too much. She'd been nice enough not to is for my life, after all.

Yet, as soon as I decided not to ask any more questions, my body rebelled. It took the moment of silence as an opportunity to remind me of my condition. The pain in my bones, the exhaustion and fatigue—it all rushed back at once.

Hesitantly, I opened my mouth again. "Do you have any empty rooms?"

Nearly out of my vision, I saw Kye stop. A soft, gritted sigh lilted to my ears. I could already feel her irritation.

"Yeah," she eventually said. "Down the hall. The… very last room is vacant.

It should already be unlocked."

Tension slipped off my shoulders. "Got it."

"Don't mess anything up."

I held my head up and nodded, seeing no need for a response. Even if she was a little arrogant, even if she had been condescending, and even if she'd been full of disrespect despite me breaking her out of a cell, I didn't have to be the same way. Plus, as the idea of sleep floated in my head, I didn't care. My limbs felt like anchors dragging me to the ground, and I wanted nothing more than for them to pull me down into the abyss.

Sparing a silent and grateful glance to the woman still swiftly walking away, I turned around and made my way down the hall.

———

"Agil?" came a familiar voice, breaking through the dull commotion. All around me, rangers were finishing up their breakfasts and preparing for something I knew nothing about.

I turned in an instant, my mind craving an explanation. I'd already been up since the crack of dawn, but no matter where I tried to go or who I tried to ask, I hadn't gotten even a hair of information. I was a ghost, floating in a sea of pre-established connections and dynamics. The sight of Kye, then, was more than a relief.

"Kye," I said, weaving my way around a tall, black-haired ranger and a group that seemed to follow him around. "What's going—"

"I didn't think you'd still be here," she said without even looking at me. A grey-haired ranger beside her handed over a bundle of arrows. Then he glared at me. The older man tilted his head and raised his eyebrow almost imperceptibly as if to tell me that he'd keep an eye out.

"Where else am I supposed to go?" I asked.

"Thanks Myris," Kye responded but not to me. When the grey-haired ranger stopped watching me like he thought he was a hawk, Kye turned her attention back. "Sorry, what?"

I took a deep breath, flexing my feeble fingers in the air. "Where else am I supposed to go? It's not like I'm very familiar with this town." A dull jolt of pain hit my sore shoulder as yet another ranger who was at least a head taller than me rushed toward the weapon rack. "What's going on here anyway?"

"Everyone got new assignments yesterday," she said. Her lips curled up into a grin. "Most of us are preparing for a hunt."

Glancing around, I did see almost all of the rangers gathering supplies or changing out weapons for whatever worked best for them. "I didn't realize there were so many of you," I said off-handedly. There couldn't have been much more than a dozen in the room, but it easily felt like hundreds.

"You've got a lot to learn if you're gonna stay in Sarin then," Kye said as she organized arrows into a quiver strapped to her waist. "Look, I assumed you would sleep here for the night and be on your way. I mean, I'm thankful that you broke me out of that cell, but it's not like I have a plan for the rest of your life."

I gritted my teeth, frustration bubbling just under the surface of my mind. I knew she was right. I shouldn't have expected her to accommodate me for very long. But I was on a whole new *continent*, dammit. I'd been tricked by the reaper itself and cursed to a life in what amounted to little more than a lawless waste-land. I was a knight. The least I could get was a place to stay while I figured things out.

Shaking my head, I tried to block out the racket bouncing in my ears. "Is there at least something I can *do*?"

Kye's grin faltered, turning more awkward by the second. Around us, the rest of the rangers started to finish up their preparations. Most of them were already making their way to the door. The chestnut-haired woman scrunched her face, warring with something in her head before she sighed. Her hands fell to her belt and she unfastened a small brown pouch of something I could only assume to be coin.

"You can make a grocery run, I guess." She held out the pouch and tilted her head at me. Her foot tapped on the wood as she waited for me to accept.

Blinking, I took the pouch in my own hands. "That I can do."

"Go into town and buy food. Nothing fancy. And buy blue cloth for uniforms. That coin should be enough for whatever you need."

Feeling the weight of the money now in my hands, I smiled. "Thank you."

"Don't mess anything up," Kye said, a cold edge entering her tone. I straightened up, feeling the burn of her gaze on my skin. "If you don't come back with all the coin you have left, you won't be smiling again for a very long time."

For the first time in a long while, I felt intimidated. With my weak, sore muscles reminding me of their useless existence, I knew that her threat wasn't in vain.

"Kye, are you coming?" came another familiar voice from the door. The smirk on Jason's face told me everything I needed to know.

Kye whipped around, stringing the bow across her back. "Yeah. We all ready to go?"

Jason nodded, his fingers drumming on the hilt of his. "Just waiting on you."

"I get it. I get it," was all Kye gave in response as she tore across the now-empty room. Jason disappeared from sight, and with one last frozen glare my way, my former cellmate was gone as well.

The door slammed shut and I was the only one left. Instead of the commotion I'd been dealing with all morning and the knots that had tied in my mind, I was left alone in silence.

Suddenly, the weight of the little pouch of silvery coins in my hand felt more real. It made me remember something. The task I'd been given. For the first time since my cursed rebirth, I wasn't fighting for my life. I was standing in a comfortable room, in an actual *town*, and I had something to do. Mundane and boring, but something to do nonetheless.

Inside me, burning deep within my soul, I still wanted to be the best. I still wanted to make the beast pay for what it had done. But feeling the stiff soreness in my legs and the lack of a weight on my waist, I knew *that* wasn't happening anytime soon. So I just held the pouch tight and made my way to the door.

And with everything that had happened, that would have to be enough.

CHAPTER NINE

I was on my ass again.

Jason stood above me triumphant. His lips split slowly into a smirk so arrogant I could've sworn it was demonic. But before I could glare at him—before I could even think about saying anything else, he extended his arm.

The gesture calmed my temper and I nodded, accepting his outstretched hand. He pulled me up with more strength than I expected, causing me to stumble on shaky legs. I had to bite back a curse as it took me far too long to even balance myself.

"Want to go again?" he asked, making sure that same smug grin was there for each and every word. I narrowed my eyes, my lips tweaking upward at his question. At this point, it might as well have been rhetorical. Jason *knew* I wanted to go again; he was just taunting me. Remembering where I was—remembering that it was a privilege for me to be using their training room at all, I gave an answer anyway.

"Of course. You don't think I'm done already, do you?"

Jason chuckled. "I'd like to think not, but from the way you fight I can't be so sure." He tilted his head at me and twirled the wooden training sword in his hand. I almost wanted to laugh, but I stopped myself. Because he was right. We'd sparred thrice already, and I'd lost pitifully each time, even despite the fact that he hadn't used any of his magic.

Ever since arriving in the Ranger's lodge, all I'd done were menial tasks. It was all I'd been *able* to do in order to keep my place to stay. No matter how much I disliked it, running to get groceries, cleaning, and sorting weapons were all better alternatives to living out on the street. To them I was some nobody that just happened to get lucky enough to break one of their own out of prison, but I still wanted more.

And for my new, painfully incapable body, sparring with Jason was exactly that. For the first time in a while, it was an actual uphill battle. It was a *challenge*. The kind of thing that made my blood boil in the best way.

Seeing the way I flexed my fingers on the training blade and readied my stance, Jason must've assumed I was ready to go. Instead of dragging it out, he readied himself as well and stared me right in the eyes. "Same rules as last time?"

I nodded, dropping the grin off my face. Truly, I knew the techniques. I knew how my body was supposed to move. The maneuvers, the attacks, the dodges—they were all clear in my mind. I could even anticipate most of his strikes.

But in the previous duels, I hadn't been able to execute. That had been the common theme. No matter how much I knew, I wasn't able to stop his attacks amid my unrefined movements.

Jason's smug smile dropped off with each passing second. I took the moment to consider him as well. He was a more talented swordsman than I'd first thought; I had to give him that. I'd *assumed* he was average at best, attributing most of his talent to the sheer force of his strikes. But he wasn't. He could easily execute at least intermediate fighting patterns, he knew how to block, and his strikes came with an unexpected level of finesse.

All things considered, I still would've wiped the floor with him in my previous body, but I was a little bit impressed. A grin crept onto my face as I heard blood starting to pound in my ears.

"You want the countdown again?" Kye asked from across the room.

"Yeah, that'd be great," Jason aid. "Make it as fair as possible."

My eyebrows dropped. I could hear the bait in his comment, but I pushed it away. I had to focus if I wanted even the tiniest chance of winning.

"Alright," Kye said. She nodded in the corner of my vision, her arms folded as she leaned against the wall. "Three... Two... One..."

Jason rushed at me like he'd done before. It wasn't the greatest of strategies, especially with the telegraphed way he was executing it. But against an inexperienced opponent like the one he thought he was facing, it was dangerously effective.

Seconds before he reached me, I ducked off to the side. His eyes widened a hair, but he twisted to bring his sword down on me. Summoning all the speed I could, however, my blade was already colliding with his leg. I forced myself backward before his counterstrike could land.

"One," I said, my voice a flurry of breaths.

Instead of a normal duel until yield, we were doing matches to five hits. Everything depended on the dexterity of our strikes—whether or not we could actually *hit* our opponent instead of how much damage we could do. As the first number fled desperately from my lips, I would've taken a moment to be thankful, but I didn't even have time to think.

Jason's sneer was all I saw as he dashed. Slightly ahead of my movements, I noted. Probably trying to catch me off guard. Before he got to me though, I stopped in place. Banking all trust on my legs to keep me balanced, I aimed my sword as his shoulder. But somehow, he expected me to do that and swiped his blade sideways before he arrived. My sword wrenched away and I stumbled, already gritting my teeth.

The next maneuver flashed in my head as clear as day. Following it, I would've ducked under his reach and struck his leg while pushing out of range. But for the first time in forever, my sword slipped. My smaller, weaker fingers couldn't grasp it like I'd expected and it glided into the air. The blunt wooden blade landed silently on the ground, leaving me defenseless to his barrage of hits.

"One, two, and three," Jason said as I cursed under my breath. I only barely dodged the fourth hit with a stumble backward in the direction of my fallen blade.

Swallowing my anger, I snatched it up in a flash. And before I knew it, I was sprinting as fast as I could. The failed maneuver was a rusted rod in the cogs of my mind. I needed distance. I needed time enough to think.

Time, however, was not particularly on my side.

Jason darted. I narrowed my eyes on him. My fingers relaxed on the hilt of my training blade. Something was different in his form and I knew it. I caught it in the distinct glint in his eye, the same glint I'd seen my whole life—the shine of a swordsman who was sure of victory.

Deep breaths circled in my lungs. I readied my sword and nodded, prepared to go along with his deceptive play.

He lunged at me, feigning a rightward attack and then shifting the strike left with all of his remaining strength. I'd been ready for it, though, and I hadn't raised my blade to the right. With a toothy grin breaking through on my face, our swords collided in a dull blunt strike that wasn't to his advantage at all. There was no time to think. My instincts carried me forward as I dashed, tearing right through his open side. By the time I was out of range, I'd counted three solid jabs through his broken guard.

"Two, three, and four," I breathed as soon as I was a good distance away. Feeling muscles shriek in my leg, I slowed.

For a moment frozen in time, Jason's eyes flashed in pure surprise. In a different situation, I would've laughed. It was an expression I hadn't seen on the smug man yet; it didn't even seem to fit his face. But I didn't get to appreciate it for long as he found his bearings.

In my breathless and unthinking state, I expected him to come all the way to me. Once again, I underestimated the swordsman and his skills.

Instead, Jason stopped short. His feet moved almost in a graceful little dance and circled over to my unarmed side. He jabbed at me rapidly, but I was able to blunder away. With shock building on my face, I nearly fell to the ground.

The sandy-haired blur in my vision slowed, coming to a full stop only paces away. He smiled at me with confidence. Another trick up his sleeve. It was obvious to any trained eye. But despite myself, I just couldn't see what it really was.

The realization came too late as the arrogant swordsman faked a dash. I saw right through it, of course. Then he started to swing his sword. I flung mine out to counter, yet I recognized it too late. As soon as my blade only connected with thin air, I was defenseless.

In a move that I didn't know he could've executed, Jason rolled onto the floor. A perfect, coordinated movement was all it took. He'd struck me in the leg by the time I even recognized what was going on.

Cursing myself, I repositioned. Swinging my leg back and my sword down, I tried to catch him. He was already gone. A scan over the ground told me he was running away. Still crouched low, I noted too. Still moving faster than I'd thought he could.

I shook my head. Then surged forward without a second thought. I didn't *have* a second thought. It was my chance to get on the offense and I wasn't letting it go to waste. Dashing at Jason from behind, I caught him shortly after he'd stood up.

"Fou—" he started, biting off the word. At my overhead strike. Jason was forced to do something he'd forced me to do many times in the past: block without the power to back it up. He was barely able to keep the tip of my blade from his face.

He leapt backward, keeping the wooden sword close on guard. He was ready for another strike. It was to be expected from anybody who got overzealous in a fight.

Mine, however, was one that was never to come.

Instead of playing into some expected and basic attack, I saw an opportunity in his stumble. I dashed to the side and came up under his unarmed side—where he had no hope of deflecting.

Feeling victory at hand, my arms moved on their own. I could taste it. It was close. My blade sliced through the air at exactly the angle I wanted, aimed at his hip. And a smile tugged at my lips as premature celebration filled my head. I had it.

Or… maybe not.

Feeling a harsh tremor of contact rip through my hand, my brows knitted like a quilt. Based on my instinctual calculations, I should've hit his hip before he was even able to react. Yet, as happened far too often these days, I was wrong. In my new body, my arm just wasn't quick enough. Jason's blade came down and he shuffled away in the nick of time.

In a moment that was all too fleeting, his navy-covered hip swung away from me and the next thing I knew, my blade was lying on the ground.

The sad wooden sword hit the black mat with an odd silence that kicked my pride while it was down. In that moment and the next dozen that came after it, I was completely defenseless.

Jason's foot came down too, holding my sword in place. I knew I'd lost before he even muttered his next word. Slowly and steadily, if only to raise my annoyance ever-higher, Jason brought his blade up and brushed it against my shoulder. My lips pressed into a thin line as I looked up at his cocky gaze.

"And five," he said with a warm tinge. I just tore my shoulder away and rolled my eyes.

Then I shoved Jason's metal-booted foot away and picked up my blade. The absolute scowl on my face would've been enough to make fresh trees rot. At the time, I didn't know whether it was more directed at Jason or myself.

"Impressive display," a voice said from behind. My eyes split wide in an instant. It sounded cold in my ears, freezing at oncoming memories that sparked a shiver down my spine. I'd heard those words before. I hated them with a passion. Panic filling my bones, I twisted on my heel, not at all ready to confront my fate yet again. "You both have quite well-refined technique."

A white, tailor-made suit gleamed in my vision. It quelled my fears. A soft sigh fell from my lips, and I nodded a little too thankfully when I realized that it wasn't the beast.

Instead, the source of the deep, confident voice was another thing that I didn't quite expect. It hadn't come from the type of person that I normally expected in the lodge. The man standing in the narrow entryway was not a warrior or a hunter. He was a handsome young man. He wasn't wearing armor, much to the contrast of the guards flanking his sides. And his bright face was filled with an overly genuine kind of interest.

"The fake-out," he continued. "Where he ended up faking *you* out. Oh, that was fantastic! And that last moment as well." The man rolled his wrist. "I was on the edge of my figurative seat."

I squinted at the man, his deep yet chipper voice streaming onto my eardrums. It was practiced and unburdened, like a perfect sweet spring breeze. The sound of it radiated a sort of regal power, and it reminded me of people I'd become acquainted with in my past life. Even a bit of myself, if I was to be honest.

Breathing a little more heavily than I'm sure he would've admitted, Jason shook his head. "What are you doing here, Arathorn?" The signature leer on his face was gone, replaced with an expression lined in respect.

I bit back a grumble about why he hadn't used that expression with me.

The charming man of authority flashed both of us a toothy smile. "I'm only here to speak with Lorah, but I couldn't resist such a duel. I had to stop and watch it." The sweet breeze of his words blew over me once more. It felt nice. So nice, in fact, that I almost missed the way his attention landed on me.

The man was staring, even while responding to Jason. His eyes *stayed* on me as if frozen in place. They studied me carefully, something odd glinting in his irises. Breaking out of his charming gaze, I tried to sift it out. Tried to see what was hiding in his eyes.

Whatever it was, it left a bitter taste on my tongue, but it was shielded well. I couldn't see very deep, and with his cheerful and pleasant demeanor, I couldn't even tell if it was real or not.

I shifted in place, stepping forward toward the man. "Who are you?"

He laughed, tilting his head in my direction. "My name is Arathorn Gairen. I'm the currently sitting Lord of Sarin." His title came down like an anvil on my shoulders, making me straighten up. "And who would you be, promising young warrior?"

For a second, I just furrowed my brow. Confusion rose within me and I shook my head, my own internal reasoning saying that he couldn't have been referring to me. I wasn't young. And I wasn't a *promising* warrior. I was a warrior that had already been promised. After another second of silence and a glance down at myself, I cringed.

"Agil," I said, trying not to stutter. "My name is Agil." Seconds of pure silence ticked by after my response. Arathorn didn't seem to mind.

"Well. Nice to meet you *Agil*," he said. Despite his strange stare, his tone was exactly the same as before, cheerful and confident.

"Lorah's in her office," came Kye's uninterested voice from the other side of the room. "She might've sensed you already, but I'd knock before you walk in."

Arathorn's expression tightened but he smiled at Kye. "Thank you," was the last thing he said before nodding to both of his escorts and tearing through the room, full of poise. My eyes followed, squinting more and more the longer they stared at the man.

As soon as he was gone, a breath slipped between my lips. A breath I hadn't even known I'd been holding in. "What's up with that guy?"

Kye turned to me, pushing off the wall as she made her way over. "Was there something different about him?"

I shook my head lightly. Doubting the lord of the town I would be living in for the foreseeable future wasn't on the top of my list of wants, but I couldn't ignore it. "I don't know. Something was off, as if he was hiding something."

Jason scoffed. "He's always hiding something, but he's the lord. He has to. If he weren't as amicable as he is, I might be suspicious of him too. He's so charismatic that some people get caught off guard by it." I nodded slowly. It made some sense, but it didn't satisfy me. Something still nagged me—a newly forming theory still in its stages of infancy kicking at my skull in an effort to develop faster.

"I wouldn't bother with it too much," Kye said, eyeing me carefully. The antagonism in her gaze was back and I had to fight to shrug it off. As much as Jason's arrogance grated on me, at least he wasn't holding shriveled pieces of doubt for just about everything I did.

"By the way," the swordsman cut in with one eyebrow raised. "You do have some technique that isn't half bad. Where'd you learn that kind of stuff?"

My eyebrows dropped at the half-assed, unexpected compliment. In my past life, I would've gotten glowing praise from someone of his ilk. My new and clumsier fighting, however, barely deserved what he gave me.

I twisted my neck, trying to pick my words. Explaining my entire life story was off the table, but I didn't particularly want to lie. "It's something I taught myself back home."

Jason nodded, curling his lip. He wasn't satisfied. "Were there any great… warriors or instructors back at your home? It's hard to believe you are *only* self-taught."

I suppressed the grin tugging at my lips and clenched my jaw to restrain myself. "No… not particularly. At least not that I had much interaction with. I've just always been fascinated with swordplay."

The man who'd just bested me scrunched his face. He nodded once more, trying to put a smile back onto his face. His smirk, however, felt uncharacteristically vacant. "I have a certain love for swordplay as well." My fingers twitched. "But if you've never trained with someone seasoned, that would explain your pitiful form." Seeing the way I stiffened and gritted my teeth, his grin returned to full force.

I brushed off the backhanded statement and tried to push the conversation forward instead. "I've always wanted to be a swords-master." I had to stop myself from cringing. "Though I've never had to fight anyone who could use magic."

Jason laughed. "Yeah. If I'd used magic, that would've been over much quicker."

I let out a breath through my teeth. "I bet it would've. What *can* you do, anyway?" If I was going to have to listen to him stroke his ego, I wanted some information out of it.

Jason's smugness returned to a humorous degree. "I'm rather good at manipulating energy in relation to objects. Even the air at times. I can heat things up, make them heavier, all depending on how much I expend. Obviously, it's easier to make something hotter than heavier, though."

I furrowed my brow. "Why's that?"

Jason stopped twirling the training sword. He looked over at me with arched eyebrows as if he felt bad for my ignorance. "Heat is a more basic state of energy... it's easier to manipulate." My head bobbed, trying to burn the information into my mind. Jason glanced back at Kye, who only offered a shrug in return. He continued. "Increasing something's weight is more complex. It requires more finesse and strains the soul more. I have to put in more effort."

Jason looked at me in silence for a second, a perplexed expression on his face as though he'd just been handed an arithmetic test.

"Interesting," I said, feigning some sense of childish wonder. "I would stand no chance against that." My own discipline and previous training berated me, lashing out at my words. I ignored both calls and just tried my best to keep a smile.

I tried so hard, in fact, that I didn't even notice when another ranger entered the room. Her presence completely ghosted my senses up until the point that Kye spoke up.

"Hey Tan, are you heading out?" she asked. I *didn't* miss the fact that her tone was far lighter and friendlier than any she'd used with me. I looked up, flicking my eyes over to the new woman standing by the wall. Picking arrows from one of the quivers on the rack—one of the quivers *I* had put in place, I reminded myself—was a tall, brunette woman wearing the same blue clothes that all the rest of the rangers wore.

The woman looked in our direction, smiling at Kye. As her eyes glossed over Jason, a glint of familiar annoyance popped up. But her gaze froze completely as soon as she locked eyes with me.

"Yeah," she said, responding to Kye's question. Her eyes narrowed as if the recognition of my face was taking longer than expected. "You're new here, aren't you?"

I nodded, the fact that *someone* around here had bothered to remember my face bolstering me more than I wanted to admit. "Agil," I said. "My name's Agil."

"You're the one Kye brought in," she said carefully. Her fingers thumbed through arrows almost all on their own. "The one that's been taking the bottom-feeder assignments for us."

All the pride that had built up before fell down like a crumbling wall. My eyebrows dropped and I grumbled under my breath, only confirming what the woman knew to be true. "Yeah," I said despite myself. "That's me."

The tall, brunette woman stifled a chuckle. "You're already dueling with Jason, then?"

My frustrated expression contorted. "How did you figure?"

"Well, it's not like his expression leaves anything to the imagination. And I figured he *hadn't* just dueled with Kye, because he only looks that pompous whenever he actually wins."

Beside me, Jason scoffed. "And what's that supposed to mean?"

"Nothing at all," the woman said. It was as if her backhanded insult had slapped the arrogance right off of Jason's face and transferred it onto hers.

Kye snickered. "So, Tan, what are you heading out for?"

The woman apparently named Tan ripped her gaze away from the definition of conceit to look at Kye. "There's a contest today."

"Yeah, I knew *that*, but they left for it more than an hour ago."

"Oh?" Tan asked, raising an eyebrow and stopping her fingers. "I thought they were holding two rounds today because the forest has been particularly active." She finished picking the arrows she wanted and placed them in her own quiver.

Kye grumbled, the smile on her face betraying the friendly nature of it all.

"Why did nobody feel the need to tell me about that? I'm coming with."

"The more the merrier," Tan said with a warm grin. "I want to see who places second this time."

"Oh," Kye shot back before questions could even form in my head. "That's some confidence. What, are you pairing up with Myris again this time?" Tan's grin widened, but she couldn't hide the slight blush in her cheeks. "Of course you are."

"Fine, I'll come," said a voice from beside me. Jason stepped forward with a grin.

Both of the other two rangers shared a glance before glaring back at the swordsman. Kye was the first to let out a laugh as she twisted to face him. "I don't think there was any doubt that you were coming."

Jason's wicked grin deepened and he let off some boastful response. I didn't listen, drowning him out while I tried to collect my thoughts. I curled my fingers around the training sword still within my grip. Whatever the rangers in front of me were talking about, it didn't seem to include me. In the mere minute since Tan had entered the room, I'd gone from a part of the conversation to little more than a fly on the wall. And after they left for whatever contest kept being thrown around, I already knew things wouldn't change. I'd be left alone and bored, cooped up in a lodge while the only people I actually *knew* on this corrupted continent were off galavanting in the woods.

No, I told myself as I collected my breaths. Sparring with Jason was nice; it gave an actual challenge and some purpose beyond being a glorified butler. But it would only take me so far. I'd sparred with him multiple times, and I was still in the same feeble body as before. I needed more than stray fights. I needed training. I needed *experience*.

And so, with resolve building back up in my head, I took a step forward. As soon as a lull in the conversation sprung up, I grabbed the chance with an iron grip. The eyes of each of them bored into me, threatening to poke holes in my soul as I tried to find the words I wanted. There was no going back now, I told myself and tried to force up a grin.

"So, what exactly does this contest entail?"

CHAPTER TEN

The pumping of blood in my ears and the rustling of leaves behind me were the only things I heard as I dashed through the trees. With my brows furrowed into a line and sweat dripping down my back, I was moving as fast as I could. I was moving as fast as my frail, uncoordinated body could push me. And it was still catching up.

This hunt had not been a good idea for me.

Shaking away the unneeded thought, I pushed my foot into the ground again. The worn-in boot that the barkeep had given me all those days ago dug into the dirt at the worst possible angle. I stumbled. My arms shot out and my eyes shot wide. But with all of my might, I managed to keep upright just enough to continue sprinting.

The symphony of my desperation filled the air. It sounded in tandem with my roaring blood. The leaping bounds of the creature on my tail were just an uncomfortable addition. Each sound, each sight, each jolt of movement felt like it lasted a thousand years.

Thoughts raced in my head as I tried to figure out what to do. Ways to fight the creature, ways to evade it, ways to *live*. All I had was my mind and my sword since my companion had left me somewhere down the line. Usually, that was enough for me. But right now, I was coming up short. I couldn't think the way I normally did. I couldn't fight back like normal. Death was too much to risk.

I just had to stay ahead of it, I told myself. I just had to stay ahead.

A sharp rustle sounded behind me along with the creature's low growl. I turned, twisting on my heel and surging through the trees to my side. Thorns of a bush tore into my leg, but I wrenched out in quick time. I ducked and weaved through the next few trees, scrambling to cover as much ground as possible.

If the bounding creature caught me now, the reaper would take me with swift ease. I couldn't let that happen; I continued to push on. Cold fire seeped into my veins and resolve solidified in my head. With each new step, my bones ached more and more. I was slowing down and I knew it, but that didn't mean I had to give in. As the hulking creature tore out of thorns, I still had hope. Hope that in however much time I had, something would change. That something would save me. Some miracle would—

A rustle to my left. All thoughts screeched to a halt.

I perked my ears up and twisted my neck. Beside me, a form was barreling through the trees. That was all I needed to know. Whatever or whoever it was, it was aiming for the creature instead of me.

And fortunately for me, my pace was quick enough because within the next few seconds, the form clad in blue cloth lunged out of the trees. A strangled snarl slipped into the air. I flicked my eyes back, glancing at the ranger who'd saved me. The flash of chestnut hair and the toothy, cheerful smirk told me everything I needed to know. All at once, tension slipped right out of my muscles and I turned around to face Kye.

Or, that's what I'd intended to do. Instead, my thundering feet struggled to slow, twisting on the ground and causing me to stumble into the dirt. Air pressed out of my lungs and a jolt of pain shot through my chest as I skidded on grass, my sword slipping from grip.

I cursed under my breath, berating my body once again. No matter how many times I tried, it didn't listen to my calls. It was too slow. It was unconditioned. It was unresponsive. Those facts grated on my mind.

"Mine!" a voice exclaimed, far too excited for the circumstances. I blinked past heavy breaths as Kye retracted her knife from the back of the whimpering wolf. The hulking thing growled once more, wrenching its head over to bite her, but she evaded with ease and dragged the blade through its neck.

Blood poured out and the creature shrieked as soon as it made contact with her knife. The bounding wolf that which had looked so intimidating before teetered on shaky paws before crumpling to the ground, life pouring from its wounds.

I gasped, blinking in disbelief at the woman who'd reluctantly chosen to partner up with me. When she flicked her gaze over to meet mine, the prideful look on her face only deepened. She ripped her knife from the wolf's neck and wiped off the blood, all the while squinting at me.

"You're not very useful," she said with the same humorless edge she'd used back at the lodge. After I'd asked about the competition, neither her nor the other rangers in the room had particularly wanted to tell me. Eventually, Tan had let out that it was a competitive hunt that most of the rangers participated in. It was a game to them. A thing of status that, at the time, had really piqued my interest.

As I stood up now, aches already setting into my bones, I wasn't so it was worth it.

"Insightful," I said as I wiped dirt off my pants.

Kye snickered, but didn't take her eyes off me. "When I'd agreed to let you come along, I'd at least thought you would be more of a help than a hindrance."

I rolled my eyes. "Maybe I would have if you hadn't wandered off without telling me."

"This is a hunt," she said, crouching down to inspect the now-dying animal. "It isn't my fault that you can't handle yourself."

I glared at her, my gaze harsh as nails. She wasn't bothered in the slightest. Instead, she looked down at the hulking wolf-like beast. Reluctantly, I followed her gaze.

The large and muscular monster that had been chasing me through the woods, for all intents and purposes, was a wolf. It was enormous and had fur patches of mismatched shades of grey, but it was a wolf. My problem with it related more to the charred marks it had been leaving behind with its fiery claws and the terrifying black protrusion sticking out of its left eye.

A shiver raced down my spine.

It was the kind of creature talked about only in old folklore or exaggerated horror stories back in Credon. It wasn't the kind of nightmare that was *real*. But, as I reminded myself again with a heavy breath, things were different now. Here, the ghastly creature *was* real, and apparently it had been killed with the simple use of a dagger.

"It's not like I'm out hunting deer or something," I said, not even trying to hide the bitterness in my tone. After a few more seconds, I had to tear my gaze away. "That thing looks like it would feed on my world's damned dreams."

Kye chuckled. "These are the kinds of creatures we hunt here." I didn't miss the way her lips tweaked up. "Probably something you should get used to if you're going to stick around."

I closed my eyes and forced myself to take a deep breath. Instead of sending a quip back, I opted for a question instead. "How did you kill it so quickly anyway?"

Kye raised an eyebrow. "My dagger is tipped with blue silver."

I blinked, my fingers curling. A squint of confusion threatened my face, but I kept it at bay. I didn't want to give her the satisfaction of that. "And blue silver is…"

The ranger in front of me didn't even look up. "A metal. It's poisonous to most mammals, and fast acting too."

My eyes narrowed, but I nodded at that. "Right," I said, adding the new information to the pile in my head.

In my past life, I hadn't been much of a hunter. I'd been able to do it, of course. Even quite well, if a mission called for it. But we hadn't had magical beasts with fiery claws. I'd trained against other *people* because they were the largest threat. I'd only ever hunted for food. I had to be stronger than a boar or a deer and that was it. I had *not* been forced to deal with hulking beasts of corruption that could cauterize any wound they inflicted.

In front of me, Kye cut off the wolf's paw. She held it up to the light and inspected it, a small spark flying off her finger to make sure the wound didn't bleed.

"What's that for?" I asked, not even commenting on the display of magic. Before, I would've gawked at the ability to produce a spark that easily. But at this point, I'd heard Jason bragging about his abilities enough to know it was standard.

Kye shot me a sidelong glance. "It's a trophy." She placed it in the small bag on her waist.

My eyebrows dropped. Right. The competition. For each of the targets we killed, we were supposed to bring a trophy back to the lodge. Apparently, there was some point system determined by mages who inspected the trophies of each team.

A flash of chestnut hair ripped me out of my thoughts. Kye narrowed her eyes, glaring at the murky black spike coming out of the wolf's eye. All along it, thin silver streaks sent fear to my core.

I shuddered. "What even *is* that?"

Kye raised her head, but she didn't respond instantly. She leaned toward the disgusting thing instead. "I don't exactly know."

Well, I thought to myself with a snort, that was a first.

But rather than being scared of the thing or leaving it where it was, Kye had another idea. She poked it with her dagger. It shuddered, and I did as well. Kye kept picking at it, eventually tearing open the creature's eye socket with her knife in an effort to pull it out.

A few seconds, a few slices, and one grunt later, she was holding the spike. It stopped shaking as soon as she ripped it from its parasitic lodging.

I felt a tickle in my throat, bile inching its way up. I swallowed it down quickly and clutched my sword as comfort. "*That* is terrifying."

The confident ranger raised her eyebrows. She looked over at me and twirled the spike in her hand. "I won't disagree with that. It almost reminds me of terror flesh." The mention of yet another thing I didn't understand almost sparked a question. Kye barreled on before I could let it out. "Either way, it has to be worth a lot. Whatever it is."

"Great," I said as I sheathed my blade. At once, the aches in my body caught up with me and I had to grit my teeth through fatigue. "When is this hunt going to end anyway?"

I still wanted to train my body. I still wanted to become stronger, faster, and more experienced. Especially considering how little I knew about my new environment. But at some point, I'd reached my limit. The complaints of my weak muscles had become too much and my training had bled into overexertion. No matter how much I hated it, I had to accept that.

Kye furrowed her brows, looking into the sky as if to judge the sun's position. "It should be almost over, actually, which makes your incompetence a little more forgivable." She gestured to the wolf now lying in the dirt. "With this thing, I might even beat Jason this time."

I still remembered Jason beating me in four straight duels before the hunt had started. If I were her, I knew I would've been as excited as she was to wipe the smug smile off his face.

Yet, as I envisioned the moment, I didn't feel as excited as I'd hoped. Because

I wasn't excited. I *was* tired, and not particularly in the mood to hear any more of Kye's cocky comments. So instead of staying, I just let a breath slip through my lips and walked off.

Pushing through the same brush that Kye had unexpectedly arrived through, I followed her very obvious footprints in an attempt to find my way back. Through the gnarled trees and twisting paths, I knew I wouldn't make it back without her help. But that didn't worry me much.

"Ready for the end of the hunt so soon?" she asked sarcastically as she caught up.

I nodded. "I'm *ready* to get out of these woods."

"Oh really? But you've just gotten to know them, with all your aimless running and all."

My eyebrows dropped, the insult scraping against my discipline. "It's not like the place is particularly welcoming."

"I guess for a beginner like you"—I clutched the hilt of my blade—"dealing with a pyre wolf may not have been ideal." Her smirk bared its shining teeth in the corner of my eye. "Especially if you don't have blue silver in your arsenal."

I nodded dryly. "Right. Or if you're not a mage."

Kye scoffed. "If you're capable, you don't need magic. Most of the time it's just an extra convenience."

I allowed myself an exhale of amusement at that and let her words stew in my head. As seconds slipped by, my brows furrowed together. Jason's explanation of magic rose up again, and something nagged at my brain.

"If…" I started. One of Kye's eyebrows shot up. "If heat is the easiest thing to create with magic, how are you able to enhance your body at will?"

Kye stared at me for a second as my question hung in the air. Her feet masterfully avoided all obstacles on the forest floor while we walked. "It's not as simple as that," she eventually said. "The soul is like a muscle—like something you can train. And the more you use it for a purpose, the easier that purpose becomes. I've always enhanced my actions, so that's what I mainly do."

Recognition flickered in my head like a white flame as I processed her words. My brows knitted together and I nodded, something about her explanation ringing true against the lessons in magic I'd been taught in my youth. Lessons that I'd quickly thrown out, in fact, because I'd never been able to use what they'd taught me.

A chuckle rose in my throat. "So, what—"

I tripped.

A brief moment of panic was all I got before I found myself face-first in the dirt. A slight burn scraped my skin as the rock tore on my shin. Above me, Kye snickered.

"World's dammit," I muttered as I picked myself up. Standing up, I brushed the dirt from my face and already-ragged clothing before Kye started laughing beside me. As soon as she did, I gritted my teeth and shot her a glare to shut up. All that did was make her laugh even louder.

I could barely hear my own grumbles over her bellowing amusement as we pushed on through the trees.

CHAPTER ELEVEN

"How big is this damn forest?"

The question forced itself out of my mouth after about the twentieth minute of walking. Beside me, Kye laughed, but I didn't even stop to glare at her. She wouldn't have looked up anyway. She was still counting all the trophies she'd collected in her bag.

"I think you're just impatient," she said. I didn't need to turn around to see her face. Truthfully, she was right. But that didn't help me much. My chest still burned. My feet still hurt, and I was still going over the encounter we'd had back in the middle of the forest. Still berating myself for succumbing to the fear and not being able to keep up.

However, I could see Kye's point; groaning further wasn't doing me any good. Instead, I twirled the short sword the rangers had given me through my fingers. I focused on the strain in each individual muscle. It was a simple technique to improve dexterity and build muscle memory, but it was also the technique I'd used when I was first studying the blade. Back when I was a *teenager*, I reminded myself. A gravelly sigh fell from my lips.

"We're almost there anyway," Kye said. When I looked over, her eyes were narrowed on the trophy in her hand. The murky black spike.

I shook a shiver from my spine and focused on her words. Furrowing my brow, I flicked my eyes across the scene, seeing only the same twisting trees and unkempt brush that we'd been hunting in the whole time. There was no way we were almost there.

I'd never been much of a hunter in my day, but I'd been in forests enough to know we were still deep in its heart. From the looks of the trees intermittently spliced by rays of sunlight around us, we were hundreds of paces from the nearest tree line at the least. There was no way we were almost there.

As it turned out, Kye was right.

After walking for only another minute, we were met with the clearing. Looking ahead, I could even see the lodge. My vision was flooded with at least a dozen rangers, a few tables, and the sight of Sarin in the distance.

While gawking, I'd apparently slowed down because Kye ended walking out in front of me. She whipped her head around with doubt flickering in her eyes. As soon as she caught the surprised expression on my face, she only let out another laugh.

"You should get to know these woods better," she said, tilting her head. "But don't ever doubt me on it. I know this place like the back of my hand."

Finding no aggravation to counter her accusatory glare, I nodded. After all, it was pretty clear that she did. I had no idea *how* she'd known where we were going, but it would've been a lie to say I wasn't impressed. And as we walked into the autumn sun, it would've been a lie to say I wasn't thankful as well.

As soon as we entered the clearing, I didn't have much time to enjoy it. Kye sped up and I had to match her pace. Barely even looking about, we weaved through the crowd of people who'd gone on the hunt.

All around us, a myriad of rangers sprawled out in the most casual formation I'd seen them in yet. They weren't organized and confirming orders with each other; they were standing around and talking as if on their way to a tavern. Out of the lot, I recognized almost every face, but it frustrated me to realize I couldn't place all of their names.

I recognized Myris, the older, grey-haired ranger who was even more suspicious of me than Kye was. He was standing near the middle of the clearing with his arm around Tan, who was laughing at whatever the ranger in front of them had said. But it bothered me that I didn't know who the ranger in front of them *was*. As a knight, I'd made it my mission to bond with every other knight in my king's court. I'd known their names by heart. And now, not only could I barely recall those names, I couldn't place half of the rangers I'd been living with for over a week. What I once held close was being blown from my fingers by an ethereal wind I was helpless to resist.

Unconsciously, I scowled and slowed my pace. A few dozen paces away, a particular sight caught my eye. Arathorn—the town's lord who I'd met only hours before—was talking with a few rangers at the front of the lodge. I even recognized the slim, brown-haired ranger who was laughing his ass off. Narrowing my eyes, I watched the handsome lord in expensive garments trade jokes with the rangers who had just returned from a hunt.

Yet, unlike too many lords that I'd known in my time, he didn't look bored. His smile was small and genuine, and the sparkle of charm in his eyes didn't falter for even a moment during the exchange. After what looked like just a conversation to catch up, Arathorn gestured back to his guards. With an amicable wave, he was gone, walking back up the hill toward Sarin to attend to the town's official business.

Even watching him go, I couldn't help the smile on my lips. Nor could I help almost running into Kye as she stopped at one of the inspection tables outside of my notice.

"How's inspecting, Elena?" she asked, her eyes on a woman behind the desk as I stepped out of the way.

The woman—Elena, I remembered and burned it into my mind—chuckled. "It has been worse. How's hunting?"

I squinted, watching the woman pick up her pen. I wasn't looking at the basic ink-tipped metal utensil. I was looking at the woman herself. Because unlike the rest of the rangers, the uniform she was wearing wasn't navy blue. She wore cloth of a bluish purple tinge that culminated in a hood over her hair.

Kye smiled. An actual, genuine smile this time. "*It* has definitely been better,"—she spared a glance my way—"but I think I might have a shot this time around."

Elena playfully tilted her head back. "What makes you so confident?"

"What can I say? Killed some quality game this time around," Kye said. Then her face scrunched a bit as she looked down at the black spike in her hand. "At least, I think so."

I shuddered, rolling my neck. "Quality or not, it certainly put up a fight."

Elena tore her eyes off Kye and looked to me. Her smile wavered. "And you are?"

"Agil," I said, my name rolling off the tongue. "I was Kye's partner this hunt."

This time, it was Elena's turn to chuckle. She glanced back over at Kye. "Really? She *never* partners up. Too much of a lone wolf for that."

My former cellmate rolled her eyes. "He got me out of a difficult situation once, and he wanted to come on the hunt." Kye flicked her eyes to me. "But there's no way he was going out without a partner. So… here we are."

I scrunched my nose, tightening my grip around the hilt of my blade. "Might've been better if I'd been given any information on what I was hunting out there."

Kye raised her head at me. A gesture that barely did anything as she was half a head above me anyway. "I don't see how that would've changed much. Hunting with you was like guiding a lost puppy."

I rolled my eyes again, pushing the antagonism away. I was a knight; I deserved better. "Right. As if you *didn't* go wandering out into the trees at random."

Elena snickered, not even trying to hide her amusement. "Do you have your trophies?"

Kye nodded and placed the terrifying spike down on the table before going to untie the bag on her waist.

Elena almost took a step backward. Her expression darkened and her lips twitched before any actual words came out. "What is this?"

"My exact reaction," I muttered. Kye didn't seem to notice.

"A trophy," the huntress said. "A bit unusual, but I figured it would still count."

Elena glared at the thing for another second. Then she shook her head. "Well, I'll be the judge of that… Where are the rest?"

"Right here," Kye said as soon as she'd unfastened the bag's drawstring. Within the next few seconds, the various body parts she'd removed from all her prey were spread out over the table.

My lips curled into a sneer as I watched the woman in robes pick up each 'trophy' like it was an ornament to be stocked on a shelf. But instead of stocking them anywhere, she squinted at each for a few seconds before scribbling something down on the paper in front of her. Oddly, she was inspecting each trophy with care and finesse like it was second nature, but she hadn't even touched the black spike. Something about it, even in her eyes, was deeply unnatural.

After half a minute of standing around, I realized I had no idea what she was doing. The feeling of ignorance grated on me. I was on a new continent and living a completely new life, yet I barely knew anything. Not even the basics of the magic that was so prevalent. If I wanted to improve—if I wanted *experience*, I needed information as well.

"What are you inspecting the trophies for?" I finally asked.

The inspector stopped, blinking for a moment before looking up. Beside me, Kye nodded in recognition as though she'd been expecting my question the entire time. "For traces of magical energy," Elena said. "It's how I score them."

The idea registered somewhere in my mind, reminding me of magical lessons I'd long forgotten. "How do you do that?"

Elena narrowed her eyes. "The same way any other soul manipulates energy." I nodded as if I understood perfectly. "I've gotten used to not so much manipulating energy but detecting it. I have a high sensitivity to the presence of magic." She narrowed her eyes, rolling her own explanation through her head before letting it out. "In the same way you can feel the air… lighten whenever it's being casted through, my soul works in a similar way, except more detailed."

I nodded slowly, silently wishing I'd paid more attention to my royal courses on magic. "Interesting. I've never met anyone like that."

Elena returned my nod without meeting my gaze another time. Instead, she focused on the second-to-last trophy in her hand, squinting at it and writing something down before putting it aside.

"For example," Elena continued as she eyed the revolting black protrusion. "*That* feels… off. It reminds me of a terror, even though it's not winter yet."

I furrowed my brows. Kye had mentioned the same term back in the woods. "A terror?"

"Ghastly things," Kye said. "Mindless creatures that are practically the magical manifestation of fear." My eyes widened and I opened my mouth, but Kye cut me off with a turn. She raised a finger at Elena. "Does it still count as a trophy?"

The inspector squinted, not bothering to lift her head. "The cycle doesn't start until after winter… What did you find this on?"

One of Kye's eyebrows shot up. "On a pyre wolf."

Elena straightened, the doubt receding from her eyes. A confused sort of curiosity rushed in to replace it. "Strange." She carefully watched Kye's smile. "It should count, then."

Without another thought, Elena picked up the murky black *thing* covered in silvery scar-like lines. She shivered as soon as she started watching it. After a few seconds, she tore her gaze away and set it aside with the rest of Kye's trophies. Hesitantly, she wrote one last thing on the paper in front of her.

"It almost feels like terror flesh," Elena said after setting her pen down. "Almost, but not quite. I'm not sure exactly *what* it is... but I'll count it."

Kye grinned, the corners of her lips nearly touching her ears. "What does that put my total at?" The excitement in her voice was nearly palpable.

Elena grinned as well. "Thirty-three. A clear second, at the moment."

Kye pumped her fist, her smile somehow widening even more. She shot me a sidelong glance and, despite myself, I smiled as well. I'd assumed the hunting competition was not very important, but judging off Kye's reaction, it obviously held some weight. She was more excited now than she'd been at any point since I'd first met her.

"Who is leasing?" she asked.

Elena turned back to us with a none-too-subtle grin. "Tan and Myris. Who else would it be?"

Kye's elation dampened a hair. "I thought it was them, but I had to make sure. I had to be absolutely *certain* that I beat Jason this time."

I let out a sharp breath of amusement. Kye shot a glance back to me that showed exactly how much she wanted to shove the win in his face. And remembering the boastful swordsman, I was on-board with the reaction.

Elena looked down at the paper in front of her. "Jason only scored twenty-nine this hunt."

"*Only*," Kye scoffed. "Dammit, Elena. I've broken thirty *once* before this."

"Well, he *normally* breaks thirty," Elena said with a playful grin. Kye rolled her eyes again in a lighthearted way, the gesture doing nothing to hide how happy she truly was. "But you did beat him this time. I'll be looking forward to his reaction at..."

Elena trailed off, jerking her head backward. All at once, the background noise in the clearing faded out. Something stirred at the back of my mind. I blinked, and Elena did too. Her eyelids flitted rapidly as if she was trying to adjust to some new source of light.

An uneasy feeling settled in my gut.

And it seemed that Elena was feeling the same as she turned to look at me. No. She turned to look *past* me. Her eyes were angled upward, scanning the sky right above my head. Beside me, Kye raised an eyebrow in curiosity. I opened my mouth, a string of questions ready to pick apart the situation.

Then I heard it.

My lips snapped shut.

A powerful, earth-shattering screech ripped through the air. It silenced any sound still in the clearing. And as my eardrums rang, I figured it had silenced whatever sound was left on the *continent*. Flipping through memories, I realized I remembered that sound. It stuck out as a point of wonder—something I'd kept in mind for a reason.

That reason became clear as I turned my head.

There, perched on the branch of the tallest tree around for hundreds of paces, was a bird. A bird that I'd seen before. Flowing, elegant green feathers. Golden talons that gleamed in the afternoon sun. A regal posture that reminded me far too much of a king—it was all there.

As soon as my eyes caught on the magnificent creature, I couldn't take them off. My gaze became frozen in place, captured by the sheer power of its form. The bird captivated my attention, holding my soul hostage in its beautiful sea of natural greens. All of my mind became enraptured by its image; even the dormant force from the back of my mind lifted.

From what I could tell, the bird was holding the entire clearing in a state of pure awe. In my peripheral vision, everyone else was staring at it. It glared down at us, tilting its head and scanning the crowd for something.

Once its golden eyes got to me, they froze. They didn't bother scanning any longer; they had found what they wanted. Using my eyes as windows to the soul, the bird searched me. It searched me for something specific, something it only found when the presence deep in my mind shifted again.

"It's here," a voice called out. As if floating on the wind, it drifted to me and ripped me from my state of enchantment. At once, everyone removed their eyes from the bird and looked to the source of the sound. Even the regal creature stopped searching me for a glance at the voice.

As I turned around, I was met with another fantastical sight.

A tall woman with platinum blonde hair stared at me. Her body was decorated in robes of the same deep blue color of the rest of the rangers but lined in silver as well. A hood half-covered her head, casting her face into her shadow. Except, that was, for her piercing blue eyes, which were directed at me.

I shifted in place, instantly aware of the weight her glare brought along. But there was also something else. Unlike any of the other rangers, she had a special symbol adorned on her chest. Right above her heart, the same sigil decorated on the lodge's front door was woven into the fabric. A crescent-shaped arrow gleaming silver instead of gold.

A screech. I shuddered, already twisting. The high-pitched sound tore through the air as only a final sign of the bird's disappearance. When my eyes scanned the trees, it was nowhere to be found. But when I turned back, I realized the woman in silver-lined robes hadn't looked. She had kept her stare exactly on me.

"Why was it here?" she asked.

Nobody responded. Everyone only looked around dumbfounded, waiting to see if somebody else had an answer to her question. Even Kye, who normally always had some quip at the ready, was speechless.

The woman gritted her teeth and closed her eyes.

"You," she said as she pointed directly at me. "Come with me."

CHAPTER TWELVE

The silence was the worst of it.

I shifted, flicking my gaze across the room to keep from frying as the Ranger's leader stared at me. Looking around, all I saw was the same elegant office draped in the same dim yellow light. After Lorah had called me out, she'd escorted me through to the back of the lodge. Down hallways I'd never been in and past doors I'd never seen before. She and the two rangers flanking her had led me to what I could only assume was her office.

And what an office it was. At the head of the room, where I was still standing and waiting for her to speak, sat a large wooden door. Similarly to the door that acted as the entrance to the entire lodge, her door was lined in dark, polished wood and adorned with the Rangers' symbol. A crescent-shaped arrow. Except, like Lorah's robes, the symbol was inlaid in silver instead of gold.

After the door though, the room only became more magnificent. As far as I was concerned, it was the largest room in the entire lodge, and it acted more as a living space than specifically an office. Obviously the room's main purpose was work—the papers scattered across the desk Lorah was standing behind told me that—but it also seemed to be used for more. On the far side, a myriad of exquisitely designed pieces of furniture sat, even culminating in a bed that rested on a raised platform in the back.

All in all, the room reminded me of the chambers given to royal scholars back in Credon. Still, no matter how familiar it felt or how comfortable it was, I couldn't help my own shallow breaths. Since the moment we'd entered, Lorah hadn't said a word. All she'd done was stare. And despite the fact that it hadn't even been half a minute, the frozen *quiet* of it all was grating on me.

I shook my head. Just because she didn't want to talk didn't mean I had to stay silent. She'd called me in here, and I wanted to know *why*.

I cleared my throat, opened my mouth, and—

"What makes you special?" she asked.

I froze, my lips twitching with readied words. Now they seemed redundant.

Rendered useless by the strangeness of the question echoing in my ears.

Snapping my lips shut, I blinked in disbelief. Lorah didn't budge, imperceptibly raising an eyebrow instead. Her question still stood. And as it circled in my head, I could only get more confused. Ideas and theories spun with my thoughts, but with a dry swallow, I didn't let any of them out.

"Excuse me?" I asked, tilting my head forward and arching my eyebrows.

She smiled. Nothing more than that. "What makes you special?" she repeated.

I blinked. "I'm not sure I understand the—"

"You have to be aware of why I called you in here," she said and steamrolled past my words. I bit down, curling my lips. Dealing with bluntness and disrespect was something I was only getting used to at a painfully slow pace.

"I have an *idea*," I finally said. "But I don't understand your earlier question."

Lorah's smile wavered. After another second, she sighed. "It didn't stare at anyone else, you know." Her smile shot right back up after that and so did the burn on my skin. "I could feel it. But it didn't come for me. No, it stared at *you*." She pointed toward me with the same intensity as before.

My expression broke. In her eyes, I could see warmth; I could see care and respect. But toward me, it was masked. Covered in the layer of doubt I was getting tired of seeing, as if I was shrouded in all too much mystery for me to have earned my place.

"The bird," I said dryly. Lorah brushed the hood off her head as she nodded. "I don't *know* why it stared at me." Movement pulsed in the back of my mind. I gritted my teeth and tried to shrug the feeling off. "I've seen it once before, but I —"

Light flashed in the room, stealing words from my mouth. I squinted, taking a step back as the torches on the walls all flared. I blinked as the air around me lightened.

Lorah relaxed her fingers and tilted her head. "You've seen the Aspexus before? Where?"

"Yes. I saw it on my way to Sarin…" I trailed off, something about her previous question sticking out to me like a sore thumb. "The Aspexus?"

Lorah dropped her eyebrows before shaking her head and mumbling something under her breath that I couldn't hear. "The bird. That is its proper name." I nodded slowly at that, my eyes narrowing with each passing second. "Now what do you mean you saw it on your way here?"

I raised an eyebrow. "I mean exactly that. On my way to Sarin, I saw the"—I waved my hand as if summoning the correct term to my lips—"Aspexus during a rest."

The Ranger's leader opened her mouth but bit words off before they could come out. Instead, she just squinted at me and rubbed her chin. It looked like she was trying to work through confusion as much as I was. But as her eyes bored into me, each one inspecting my very soul, I knew she had more tools than I did. The presence in the back of my mind retracted as though trying to hide from her queries.

Again, I shook my head. "Look, I'm not sure what—"

"Describe your meeting with it before," Lorah said, cutting me off. This time I didn't even bother sparing a reaction.

"After walking all morning, I stopped to rest on a rock." I had to keep myself from growling as I exaggerated the extent of my physical labor. My body had truly only let me walk on for less than two hours before giving out. "When I did, that bird came. And actually, it did the exact same thing as this time. It stared at me for only a moment before flying off."

Lorah clicked her tongue. "Interesting. There was nothing else to the encounter? No reason why it came to you in particular?"

I shrugged. "Not that I can think of... I was the only person for hundreds of paces around." Lorah nodded at that; it was obvious that she wasn't satisfied. In truth, I *could* think of a reason that the bird came to me, but I decided to hold my tongue.

"The Aspexus needs more of a reason than that," Lorah said. "It doesn't take interest in the mundane."

I narrowed my eyes. "Do two brief encounters really count as interest?"

Lorah looked up and widened her eyes. "The world's observer *stared* at you. More than once, in fact. It does not take these actions lightly." Then, watching the doubt I was making sure to display on my face, she continued. "You must understand the Aspexus' power. It's not just a regular bird of prey."

"I know that it isn't," I said, stepping forward. Honestly, I didn't know much about the bird at all, but I did know that I wasn't too keen on getting dragged through the dirt because of something I'd never learned about. "I simply don't understand why brief glances seem to matter so much."

"For the world's sake," Lorah said, throwing her hands up. "The last time I saw the Aspexus was when I recruited Tahir." I opened my mouth, but Lorah already had her finger raised. "A former ranger and prodigious mage." My lips pressed shut in short time. "Servants visiting our lodge happens once per decade if they're generous. And yet, the Aspexus showed up today. For *you*."

I arched my brows. "Servants? What are you—" I stopped myself, stabilizing and trying not to sound like a blundering idiot. "I'm not familiar with the term."

"Servants of the Soul," Lorah said as if that cleared it all up. "Sentient extensions of the World Soul's will."

My eyes widened. I had to fight to keep them from becoming dinner plates. Lessons and stories from my youth rushed back at the mention of the World Soul. It was at the center of every creation myth; it was the progenitor of all the world and the source of all magical energy. But as Lorah's words filtered onto my conceptions, a whole swath of new questions arose.

"The Aspexus is a Servant?" I asked with the straightest face I could manage.

Lorah grinned. "Yes. And *that* is why this matters so much. The Aspexus is the eternal observer, the world's eyes and ears. It does not interest itself in human affairs unless they are important to the world itself."

I tilted my head. Slowly, my eyebrows dropped. "You think the Aspexus is interested in me?"

"That's why I called you out in the first place," Lorah muttered. Then she shook her head and raised her voice again. "There are no such things as 'brief glances' with the Aspexus. It observes all equally. Yet, it came to stare at *you*."

A brush of movement against the interior of my skull. "What does that mean for me?" I asked. Thoughts swirled in my head, mixing information with the unknown and summoning ideas from the void. Out of the nearly infinite answers to my question, though, I just hoped the correct one had nothing to do with the beast.

"I was hoping *you* would tell me that," Lorah said as she scrunched her nose.

"With Tahir, it was interested because of his magical potential." Lorah raised her hand; the light level in the room raised with it. "There was something about his soul… something *special*."

Another twitch from the back of my mind. "Do you think this makes my soul special somehow?"

After a few seconds of silence, Lorah sighed. "I don't know, which is why I was hoping you did." She turned to me and squared her gaze with mine. "I can feel some magical presence in you, but it's distant. Disconnected. Almost like some sort of phantom limb." My lips slipped apart as I took another step forward. Lorah continued before I could get a single word out. "But it's there. It has to be. The Aspexus doesn't interest itself in the mundane."

I furrowed my brows. Mundane? The image of myself rose up—my faded blonde hair being kissed by the wind as I stood on the ramparts of my king's palace. I smiled. Even if I wasn't important to the world itself, I was anything but mundane.

A brown strand of hair fell in front of my eyes.

I raised my eyebrows in surprise, staggered for a moment before the realization slapped me like a hand of time. Right, I thought sourly. Things were different now.

"Could it… be a mistake?" I asked. In my new body, frail and inexperienced as it was, there was no way the world had taken interest in me.

Lorah cocked an eyebrow. "What are you saying?"

"I'm not a mage," I said bluntly. "This body of mine"—I gestured to myself, still draped in what amounted to little more than rags—"has never done anything great." Inwardly, some part of me recoiled at the very statement, but I couldn't bring myself to explain further. Even as I thought about it now, my story sounded like one straight out of an insane mind. No. I didn't need another reason for her to distrust me. And even still, there was more truth to my words than I wanted to admit. "I came to Sarin because I had nowhere else to go. Even if I have seen the bird before, there's no way it's interested in *me*. I may have been somebody in the past, but here I'm simply… mundane." My nose scrunched. "A nobody."

My words cut through the air like a knife through butter. Lorah's eyes widened, and I sighed, trying not to let on how much my own words had cut me to the core.

"No one is nobody in my lodge," she finally said. She leaned forward on her desk and tried to meet my eyes.

I didn't particularly want to see that layer of doubt again. "Right. Like you even know my name."

"Agil," she said. I froze, flicking my eyes to her. Where I'd expected to see doubt, I didn't. Instead, the warmth, care, and respect that I'd seen before was all that shined through.

My brows knitted. "How did you—"

"*Kye*," Lorah started, "reported to me about her assignment a while ago. And seeing as you were the reason she was able to escape when she did, your name naturally came up."

I blinked, the formality in her tone not connecting to the warmth in her eyes. When she smiled again, the interrogating leader she'd been for the entirety of our exchange melted away. And as I realized myself, that meant more to me than I'd thought.

"Oh," was all I got out. It was strange feeling speechless after a life of giving formal and calculated reports.

Lorah tore her eyes away from me, inspecting the pile of work on her desk. "I don't allow people to live in my lodge without knowing who they are," she said without lifting a finger. "Additionally, your picking up of the slack, so to speak, regarding undesirable assignments has not gone unnoticed."

I nodded. I hadn't expected her to not notice me. I hadn't expected to be some sort of ghost living in the lodge without anyone knowing. I'd come to Sarin because I'd needed to get to a town. And I stayed with the Rangers because it was the best chance I was going to get if I wanted to improve. If I wanted to train —to still become the best.

"I'm still getting acquainted with Sarin," I said. "And Ruia as a whole, I suppose."

Lorah cocked an eyebrow without looking up. "The continent seems to be getting acquainted with you as well." She scowled down at her desk. "As do my rangers."

An amused breath fell from my lips. "Some of them have, yes. Taking assignments that they don't—"

"Look," Lorah said, cutting me off once more. I snapped my lips shut and tried to move past the interruption as best I could. "Are you sure you don't know why the Aspexus is interested in you? Something you're not telling me?"

A foreign feeling of anxiety washed up from the back of my mind. A shiver coiled down my spine, but I didn't let it on. Rather, my lips tweaked upward into a tiny smile. "I honestly don't think it even *is* interested."

Lorah scrunched her nose at that, still scowling at the papers in front of her. "Fine. Unfortunately, I don't have all the time in the world to question you about it. So I'll have to trust you on that." The smile on my face grew another inch. "But… if you were wondering, you don't have to vacate the room you've been living in. That was Tahir's old room, anyway. You can… you can stay in it."

My smile warmed even more. "Thank you."

Lorah nodded shallowly, the ghost of a smile breaking through before she waved me off. "You're dismissed, then."

I nodded. There was no point in pressing further. No point in testing whether or not she'd been telling the truth about my stay. Because no matter how I felt about Ruia and its unorganized chaos, I needed a bed. I needed a place where I could be of use, where I could become someone that could achieve my goals.

And so I kept my mouth shut, only sparing one last wave at the woman now hunched over her desk before slipping out into the hallway.

The polished wooden door clicked shut, pitching the world back into silence. Except this time, the silence wasn't cluttered. It wasn't filled with unanswered questions or a stubborn gaze. It didn't grate on me.

For the first time in my entire life, I felt a little bit at home.

CHAPTER THIRTEEN

"Why exactly are we out here again?" I asked.

Kye glanced back with both eyebrows raised. She weaved around a tree without even looking as a smirk grew on her face. "Do I need to keep repeating things for you?"

I glared at her, stepping around a tree myself. My movements were much less graceful than hers, despite the fact that she was carrying a bag . Biting back grumbles, I didn't give her the satisfaction of hearing my frustration. "Not if you gave adequate explanations to begin with."

A chuckle sounded behind me. I twisted, a shallow grin blooming at my lips as Myris stifled laughter. As soon as he saw me looking at him, he straightened up and regained all of the harshness he normally exuded. The older ranger then tilted his head and cocked an eyebrow at Kye, who was rolling her eyes.

I let out an amused breath, my eyes wandering down to the blue cloth uniform now covering my skin. In reality, Kye's explanation had been adequate enough. I understood the basic concept of whatever ritual I was being subjected to. I was becoming a ranger, after all.

After my conversation with Lorah, it had basically been decided—despite the distrusting objections of some of my peers. And I'd been open to it; it was as close to giving myself some sort of knightly purpose as I was going to get. But as we trudged through the dense, twisting forest that still looked like unordered nonsense to me, I still didn't entirely grasp *why* we were doing it.

"It's a rite of passage," Kye said. "You already passed as far as Lorah is concerned, but being a ranger is more than gaining her approval."

I turned back to her, my fingers curling around the hilt of my blade. "I understand that. But why this?" I gestured to the forest around us.

Kye angled her head. I could see the glint of frustration in her eyes. "We live and breathe this forest, Agil. This is where we see if you're capable." Her hand moved past the quiver on her waist and unsheathed a knife. "If you're going to be staying in the lodge, you might as well be useful."

"You *should* be," came Myris' voice as he trudged up next to us. "Being a ranger is also more than practicing swordplay in the comfort of the lodge's training room."

My grip tightened, but I let the comment roll off my shoulders and kept my attention on Kye. "Are all rangers recruited this way?"

"Not in the same way you were," Kye said. "But it isn't entirely unprecedented. Most rangers come from towns we've heard of before, for example."

In the corner of my eye, I saw a smile tugging at Myris' lips. "Do all rangers do *this*, then?" I asked.

Kye let out a dry chuckle. "They sure do. Some call this a test of personal wilderness competence, but I just think it's good fun. A great way to break in the newest recruits, if you ask me." Myris didn't hold back his smile any further.

"That it is," he said. "Although, I don't remember you being quite as excited when you were in his shoes."

Kye's chuckling stopped. She shot Myris a glare. "Well, I got into the spirit of it rather quickly. And you can't say I'm not ranger material any more, now can you?"

The older ranger raised a hand, his smile not wavering in the slightest. I narrowed my eyes. "You were a guide when Kye did this?" As far as I knew, the test of personal wilderness competence—a formal title felt natural to me—was always administered with two guides. Usually veteran rangers who were there to save the novice if anything went wrong.

"Correct," Myris said. "It seems that I was in the same situation back then as I am now. My crop of interesting assignments loves to run out just in time for me to babysit the new inductees."

"What he's *saying*," Kye translated, "is that he has nothing better to do."

The older ranger tilted his head and shrugged. "I can't argue with that. But I do blame Lorah for not *giving* me anything better to do. Making sure a ranger can do something they should already be able to do isn't particularly at the top of my list."

"Right," Kye said sarcastically. "As if you couldn't have free pickings of whatever assignments you wanted." She stopped twirling the knife in her hand and pointed it in his direction. "You'd already been with the rangers forever even when I was doing this two years ago."

I furrowed my brow, glancing over at the experienced ranger in a new light. Despite his grey hair and the crinkles around his eyes, he still looked young enough. Younger than my father had been when he'd died, at least. But on a continent full of magic, I really couldn't know how old he actually was.

"At this point, I'm sure Lorah is screwing with me," Myris said. "Back when I did this, she was still regularly going on hunts herself. It was during the time when Arathorn would still make it his duty to know as many rangers as he could by name." Myris flashed a thin smile, shrugging his shoulders. "He was such a fresh-faced lord, then. That was before he realized just how much time it takes to run an entire town."

My posture straightened at that. I knew the stages of how a ruler adapted, after all. I'd protected enough of them in my lifetime. It was usual for them to make time for everything at the start—to try and impose a good first impression on the people they were meant to rule. Eventually they receded from public eye a bit as the work piled on, but it would've been a lie to say that I didn't respect Arathorn for balancing it like he did.

"Though, back then there were far fewer rangers than there are now," Myris continued. "For me, it had been quite the challenge to find a guide. Luckily, Tahir became available one day and I went with him."

There it was again. That name that Lorah had used. The former ranger who'd stayed in the room I now called my own. "Tahir was your guide?" I asked.

Myris turned to me with a subtle nod. "My only one. Despite the fact that he'd only been a ranger for a few months at that point." Myris' eyes gradually drifted to the ground. "I hadn't even had a second of doubt about going off with a single guide, though. Tahir would've been able to watch over a dozen rangers, as far as I'm concerned."

Kye nodded, her expression blank. After a few seconds of silent walking, she smiled again. "And yet you still had trouble dealing with a single wispbear."

Myris' eyebrows dropped. "I got the short end of the stick, you know. The one I fought was their apex or something." He straightened up. "How did you even know about that?"

"Lionel told me," Kye said and caused Myris to curse under his breath.

My fingers twitched on the hilt of my blade. The words of my companions mixed around in my head, tearing up worries wherever they went. Already, from the half-hour walk we'd taken from the lodge, my feet were starting to ache. And if whatever test I was about to go through had given Myris trouble, I wasn't so sure about my chances.

"How necessary is this, anyway?" I asked. Because to me, it seemed overly casual. Something designed only to either give a ranger bragging rights or send them to a healer in quick time. Unlike the oaths of loyalty I'd taken as a knight, this seemed… stupid.

"If you want to become a ranger," Kye started, "absolutely necessary."

I narrowed my eyes, drumming fingers on the pommel of my sword. "It seems dangerous. Idiotic, even."

Beside me, Myris's glare nearly punched me in the face. In front of me, Kye only laughed as she scanned the trees again to make sure we were still heading in the right direction. "Some might consider it that, but if you can handle it, it isn't that big of a deal. If it helps, you can think of it as doing your part to return balance for the World Soul."

I slowed, my face contorting. "How does this have anything to do with the World Soul?"

"Well, think about it," Kye said. Her amusement all too quickly bled into irritation. "These are some particularly… magically dense creatures." I nodded slowly even though she wasn't looking my way. "And killing them is just one more soul for the reaper to return."

A dark hand wrapped around my spine. Only Myris' suspicious gaze kept me moving step after step to keep pace.

"Excuse me?" I asked, images of the beast flying through my head. Its tattered cloak, its ancient scythe, its bony smile—I reviled it with all of my being.

Kye turned around this time. "You'll let the reaper take one more soul back, is what I said."

My eye twitched. My fingers froze in place. My conception of Death cracked as new information trickled into my ears. Kye's words flooded the boiling pot of my mind and melded with Lorah's explanation of the World Soul. When the pot was finally done, I only had one question to ask. No matter how much I hated even thinking it up.

"Is the reaper a Servant?" I asked.

Kye slowed her pace, flicking her eyes to me. In them, I couldn't see doubt anymore, only confusion. As Myris jerked his head back, he ended up being the person to respond.

"Of course it is," he said. "How else do you think the energy in living souls is returned?"

Myris squinted at me. Kye raised her eyebrows. But as the rhetorical question shot through my mind, piercing everything I'd ever thought up until that point, I waved them off. "I'd never connected the dots, I suppose."

Instead of displaying the shock I was feeling, I just let my eyes droop and trudged on. In my past life, I'd known about the reaper. Everyone had, even if nobody was entirely sure. The beast came for all when it was their time and harvested their soul with a single swing of its scythe. As far as most were concerned, the beast was a predestined part of life. Something that couldn't be challenged.

But I'd challenged it. When it had come to end me, I'd parried it for the first time on pure speed and instinct. Yet still, it had ripped me away—taken my soul from everything that I loved. It had been impressed with me, but it had tricked me all the same, cursed me with a new life to die a second time.

Though, I had survived, I thought with a smile as I kicked my metal boot against the dirt. I'd survived enough to make sure the beast would pay. But if it worked for the world… maybe my fight with it had been useless. Maybe I would've lost no matter how powerful I'd been. If it worked for the world, perhaps it was simply a part of life. A balancing act in nature.

Some part of me screamed against that. I furrowed my brows and shook my head, disregarding the sideways look Myris gave me. The beast couldn't be a balancing act. It was cruel, disgusting, hateful. It brought chaos to the world, ripping families apart and ravaging kingdoms into shambles. The sight of my wife bleeding out into our grass flashed from a dream of weeks past. I gritted my teeth. The beast… it was the antithesis of balance, of order, of everything I'd spent my life trying to protect.

I flexed my fingers, ready to unsheathe my sword at any moment. Because not only was it horrid, disgusting, *unnatural*—it could also be fought. I'd parried it myself when it had come for me. I'd kept up with it, trading blows and fighting off advances. My life had only come into its hands because of weakness in my mind. Because I'd fallen for its trick.

Even the thought of the vile thing, the thought of it coming for me or anyone close to me—I hated it. Looking up, I watched my two companions scanning the woods to keep us safe. Even them, I realized. The thought of the beast coming for Kye, for any of them… something deep inside of me rejected it with white-hot vigor. As a knight, I couldn't accept it. If the beast came with its scythe…

I wanted to be ready with my blade.

I straightened, forcing poise into my steps and welcoming the resolution solidifying in my head. Suddenly, Kye's logic made a lot more sense. The Ranger's rite of passage didn't seem as daunting. Because I—

"We're here," Kye said. She stopped, holding up a hand that I almost ran right into.

I blinked; my thoughts screeched to a halt. Myris stopped as well, his movements becoming stricter and more careful. Before I knew it, air lightened around me and the familiar twinge of magic tickled my lungs. I breathed out, moving to the side and opening my mouth to ask what was going on.

"Don't," Kye whispered before I could even get a word out. "They have incredible hearing."

I furrowed my brows, getting ready to ask what she was even talking about. Stepping around though, I saw it too. I saw the large burrow that Kye had her eyes locked on. The small mound of mossy rock and grassy dirt that sat at the edge of the clearing in front of us. Well, if it could've even been called a clearing. In reality, it was just a section of the forest where the trees ceased being five paces apart and suddenly decided to be ten instead.

But it *was* a large space, and as I noticed after following Myris' gaze, well-traveled as well. The grass was packed down and places where the brush had been cut through were visible even now.

It was perfect for a battlefield.

Once again, I opened my mouth to ask a question, prepared to keep my tone hushed like Kye's had been. However, I was interrupted. This time by a sound.

At the very edge of my hearing—a sound soft enough that I didn't even think it should've registered—I heard scurrying. Small claws skittering across dirt. Looking forward, I had no doubt about where the sound was coming from.

I shook my head. "Okay. So what's going on?" I tried to keep my voice as soft as possible.

Myris turned to me. His eyebrows dropped. "We're here." He repeated what Kye had already said, only continuing when I shook my head at him. "This is where the test happens. It's the only place where we know wispbears congregate."

I nodded slowly, adding the information to the pile of things I didn't have the context to understand. "And what is a wispbear?"

Kye turned to me, her eyes sharp. "Exactly what it sounds like." She didn't even let out a quip like normal. "A combination of a wisp and a small bear, from what we know."

My eyes narrowed. "Helpful."

Myris bit back a grumble. "They're old creatures. Native to our forest." He curled his lip at me. "As you should already be aware of."

I had to stop myself from rolling my eyes. In the weeks that I'd been living in Sarin, nobody had ever mentioned a wispbear. It had never shown up in any of the stories from my youth. But with the mythological idea of a wisp in my mind, I came up with a rough picture of whatever we were hiding from.

"Okay," I finally said. "What *are* they, though?"

"They're magically enhanced bears, basically," Kye said. "They scurry like small bears and hunt like small bears, but they burrow like… some other animal."

"What?" I asked. The rushed, whispered briefing I was being given was nowhere near comprehensive. And if I didn't have a good idea of my enemy, hunting it became much more difficult.

Kye glared at me. "I'm informing you about the thing you're going to kill." She smiled. "So shut up." I sealed my lips. "These things have unbelievable hearing and decent noses, but they're practically blind. It's probably why they can spend so much time in the dark."

"Why do I have to hunt a wispbear though?" I hissed.

"They're mostly passive," Kye continued. "But if they do wander to Sarin, they're not easy to notice until they've burrowed under someone's house or eaten an entire week's worth of food."

I raised my head, the idea becoming clear. "So you use this to thin their population?"

Kye nodded. "Yes. But these things are also related to wisps, so it's not an easy test by any means. From experience, I can tell you these things are not simple to deal with by yourself. They're sensitive to even the slightest twinge of active magic."

My lips tweaked upward. "Oh. They are?"

"Why do you think we've been casting this whole time?" Myris asked. Despite his unimpressed tone, he smiled.

"You *want* them to detect you?" I asked

"Luring one out would be a lot more difficult without it," Kye said. She took the bow off her back and thumbed through the arrows in her quiver. "But for most rangers, that's the hard part. Hiding from these things is basically impossible."

As confusion receded, my iron grip rushed right back. "How many do I have to fight?"

Kye stifled a snicker, glancing over at me for only a second. "One. That'll be challenge enough. And these things are collective, but not collaborative. If any of them come out, it'll only be one."

"You'll be glad it's only one," Myris whispered under his breath.

Kye notched an arrow in her bow, sharing a glance with the older ranger. "We'll be watching if anything goes horribly wrong, though."

A weight I hadn't even been aware of lifted off my shoulders. I sighed, nodding and adjusting my grip. Then, only noticeable as a break in the ambience, I heard it.

On the far side of the clearing, the scurrying was getting louder. The small footsteps echoed as it neared. It seemed Kye heard them too as her smirk widened.

"I wouldn't spend much time waiting," she said. Then nodded to Myris and repositioned, circling somewhere farther away from the clearing without another word to me.

My mouth opened, but I shook the words away. There was no point it protesting further. Kye's words rang true as the approaching sound grew louder still.

I unsheathed my blade, the longsword I'd gone for this time gleaming in the afternoon sunlight. My fingers tightened around the hilt with the intent never to let go, and I stepped into the clearing to face whatever I'd gotten myself into.

I took a deep breath, fresh air circling in my lungs as I flexed my muscles. Still weak and paltry compared to the refined, reflexive ones I'd built up in my old life. But they were better than they had been, at least. Grasping onto my resolve and letting the maneuvers, stances, and applicable patterns of attack run through my head, I grinned. As the shadow of the small beast approached from the burrow, only one thought rose to the surface of my mind:

Let the fight begin.

Things were not going according to plan.

I scrambled, taking advantage of distance to surge through the brush and attempt at hiding. With the aches in my feet and the gash in my leg, it was the only course of action that made sense. The only one that would let me regroup and think of something *else* to do.

Flicking my eyes around, I spotted a rock less than a dozen paces away. Without another thought, I ran toward it. Scrambling through the clearing with all the speed my tired, uncoordinated body could muster, I tore through a bush and behind the rock.

Thorns bit into my skin.

I grimaced, locking my teeth together to keep the indignant grunt inside as pain erupted over my leg. Small, bleeding cuts felt like fire on my skin. They matted and stained the parts of my ranger's uniform where there weren't holes. Steeling myself, I skidded into the dirt as quietly as possible and scurried behind the natural piece of cover.

Still wincing, I hauled my leg forward and watched them. The new, bright-red scrapes and cuts glinted off sunlight as I tried to hold pressure on with the hilt of my sword and keep them from bleeding too much. The dirtied gash on my other leg flared up in pain as if to remind me of its existence. I stifled a scream and ignored it, not particularly fond of playing the deciding role in a competition between my legs to see which of them could retain the most annoying injury.

But I didn't get to stew in my frustration long. I heard it again. At once, focus on my own injuries stopped and I strained my ears. Paces and paces away but getting closer, the clawed skittering was back.

I slumped, pressing my back against the stone and sealing my lips.

The wispbear's footsteps neared. Quickly. Frustratingly so. I gritted my teeth, clutching my blade low and ready if it ever came around. Sure enough, I could hear it sniffing again. Which meant two things for me: it was trying to detect any magic it could, and I had to hope the smell of my blood wasn't pungent enough over the rest of the forest.

As opposed to how most rangers probably felt, I was more concerned with the latter.

Despite my comments on her explanations, everything Kye had said before the test's start had proven correct. As I'd quickly found out, the small brown animal with light blue veins showing in its fur did have unbelievable hearing. Practically any sound I made was detected by the damn thing, and I'd only combatted it by not bothering to hide my location. Though, it hadn't been as dangerous as it could've been because their little black eyes were useless. While it was nothing at all like fighting any other human, I hadn't worried about the thing tracking the subtle movements of my sword.

But—as the one thing Kye *hadn't* mentioned—the wispbear was quick. No matter what advantages I gained in close combat, the creature would simply scurry away. It would maneuver with such speed and without losing any coordination that I could barely strike it. Not with the lackluster speed my new body had, at least. Over the past two weeks, I'd trained enough that if I landed a strike, I could make it impactful. But one thing I didn't have was finesse. I didn't have the coordination or muscle memory to deal with a dextrous opponent.

Even though the worst the creature had done to me was bite my leg, I'd only sliced *it* a few times. Not even enough for it to slow down.

And as the fight went on, I was tiring. It was not.

Anger simmered in my mind. I scowled, keeping my ears perked and my eyes sharp while I lashed out at my own body. Keeping my teeth locked, I had to stop myself from cursing my own muscles out right there. In my past life, I'd been so responsive. So ready to execute whatever attack crossed my mind. Now, I couldn't. The reaper had cursed me with the inability to.

The repeated sound of sniffing ripped me from my thoughts. I widened my eyes, raising my sword again and glancing to the side. Through my battle-heightened clarity, I heard the wispbear's footsteps merely paces away. It was at the bush I'd torn my leg up at and still sniffing up a storm. Still straining itself to detect any magic present.

Oddly, that gave me confidence. The more it sniffed, the more it wasted its time. Because I wasn't a mage; I couldn't have casted magic even if I'd wanted to. And after my thoughts of the beast, the thing in the back of my mind had receded or covered itself so thoroughly that it was unnoticeable.

The most dangerous sense of a wispbear for most turned out to be a blessing for me.

I shifted, moving my legs as silently as possible and repositioning to attack if the wispbear came around the corner. I knew it was approaching. I just had to be ready when it came.

Time slowed to a crawl around me. Seconds ticked by like hours as I waited, my eyes narrow and my blade ready for the annoying creature. Ready to end the test and get it over with already. Since they'd repositioned, I hadn't seen Kye or Myris, but I knew they had to be as impatient as I was for it all to be done.

As the wispbear approached, its growling teeth coming into my peripheral vision, I froze. It snarled, sniffing again before angling its ferocious head in my direction. Blood thundered in my ears and my fingers tightened around my blade, but I couldn't strike.

Until a pained growl rang out, that was. I widened my eyes. In front of me, the wispbear struggled, its jaws snapping only half a pace away. It writhed in pain as the thorns of the bush dug into its fur and held it in place for a second.

A second that was just long enough.

I lurched forward and raised my sword. Purpose once again filled my tired muscles and before I knew it, my blade had torn through the wispbear's back. Its furious growls had tapered down to dying whimpers and the world had taken it away. I let out a thousand-pound breath before tearing my blade out and raising my arm.

"That took... far too long," I said. After not even a second, I lowered my arm and groaned. Fatigue riddled my bones and the thought of rest lured my eyelids to close. I didn't close them, though, if only out of spite. In my old life, I hadn't felt real fatigue in years. Now I felt it regularly, and I was getting tired of it.

A flurry of rustling noises sounded the entrance of my companions into the clearing. Kye came out first, an arrow still notched in her bow and wide eyes on her face. Myris stepped in after her, his face drawn and annoyed. I didn't, however, miss the amused look in his eyes.

Kye shook her head. "You're stupidly lucky."

Chuckling myself, I could only nod at that.

"Luck is definitely a word for it," Myris said. I tilted my head at him while sheathing my sword. From what I'd heard, his usual harshness had all but eroded away.

Kye crouched, eyeing the wispbear that I'd killed. Blood still stained and matted its fur, but the light blue veins had gone grey. There was no doubt it was dead. "Guess you're one of us now," she said.

A smile crept onto my face. I nodded, the simple sentiment of what I'd just accomplished nearly taking all weight off my shoulders. I was a ranger now, I reminded myself. I had a home again, a responsibility to protect, a *purpose*.

"I guess so," I said, my legs taking the moment to remind me of their wounds. The fact that I now truly owned the blue uniform they were ruining almost made it worth it. Almost. That was the keyword. "Now... which way leads back to the lodge?"

CHAPTER FOURTEEN

Shit.

I dashed to the side, an arrow splintering on the wood where my shoulder had been. My eyes bloomed as I watched the object, blood roaring in my ears.

How the fuck was I supposed to get out of this?

Another arrow flew toward me. It curved in its signature pattern, shifting course on the wind as if to fake me out. I knew the trick. I stopped in place. The arrow missed me, sailing through the air and leaving a sharp blast of wind in its wake. Taking the brief moment of respite, I scanned the area around me.

I was still dozens of paces from the nearest tree.

With arrows flying my way, the prospect of an open space had been an exciting one. Leaving the dim, cramped forest was an idea I'd welcomed. But, as I was quickly learning, my excitement had been unwarranted. Instead of fighting out in the open where my sword would reign over a bow, I was just more of a target. My adversary had stayed in the woods, scoping me out and shooting at me whenever they wanted.

It was *not* better than before. It was, in fact, much worse. Before, I'd been able to weave through the trees. Constantly worrying about running and getting my blade caught in bark, but at least protected. There was some form of cover—a confusion that came with the natural chaos of the woods. Now though, in an open space, I was a reluctant object of target practice.

The twang of a bowstring sounded to my left. Pursing my lips, I dashed, ducking low in hopes that the arrow would fly over my back. A few moments later the air slightly above my ears split while an arrow barreled through it. Heaving a breath as I ran, I didn't give into exhaustion. I flicked my eyes to the left. The arrow had come from that direction. My target was there, and I still had to catch them.

My thoughts swirled, berating me again. If my enemy continued gaining advantage on me—if I *allowed* them to continue gaining advantage, I'd get too far gone. Barely more effective than a chicken with my head cut off. Because even if I kept my evasion perfect—something I doubted I could do in my current body—I still had no chance. As soon as either of us landed a successful hit, it was settled. And having to dodge was only tiring me out. It was making me easier to hit over time.

That was something I did not want to be.

Keeping the movement in sight, I charged into the woods. The brush rustled as my enemy maneuvered in response. When they moved away, far quicker than I could have possibly caught them, I had a dilemma. If I stayed in the clearing, I was a strafing duck. But if I chased through the forest again, I'd be in the same situation as before.

My sword wasn't very useful if I couldn't figure out where my enemy was, but they knew the forest better than I did. They knew tactics, patterns, and spots of hiding I couldn't have possibly been aware of. I had to play it smart—to come up with an idea that put *me* in the advantageous spot.

Either way, it seemed like I was out of luck. With their limited supply of arrows—one that had to run out at some point, I kept telling myself—I may have been able to outlast them. But even then, they were faster than me. They knew the forest better. It would be a wild goose chase with a goose I wasn't even sure could be caught.

My lip curled in distaste, aches already starting to set into my muscles. The hilt of my blade brushed against my fingers, cool leather sliding on sweat-soaked skin. But even as the afternoon breeze ran through my hair, I couldn't focus on the small things. A realization was rising in my head, and it left a bitter taste on my tongue.

I didn't know what to do.

An arrow speared the air beside me. I flinched, twisting and stumbling to the side as I brought my sword out. The metal of my blade slashed through the air right where my instincts had screamed an enemy would be. There was nobody there, of course, but the arrow was a good reminder of my situation. A good warning for me to get my shit together.

Scanning the trees, I steeled myself. Primed my stance and adjusted my grip. I had to be ready—more so than I had been. In my new body, I couldn't help but find myself more distracted, but now was not the time for it. Movement flashed somewhere across the clearing. Close enough to have a sightline on me but far enough that I couldn't reach them without getting hit.

Instead, I whipped my head around. I flicked my eyes across the sea of brown and green until they eventually locked on a thick slab of bark. A tree wide enough to provide cover. I didn't waste time surging toward it.

Keeping my eyes sharp, I turned my head to the side. At the edge of my hearing, I could've sworn I heard a hissed curse of frustration. It moved, heading toward me. Still, as they changed position, the reverberations of a bowstring echoed off the trees.

My eyes widened, a jolt of fear catching me in the throat as I closed the final paces toward the tree. Moments bled into painful hours, but I kept with it. Clenching my fist around my blade, I dove.

For a moment, I almost expected to have miscalculated my own speed again. But the ground came up under me with a dirt-filled thud. As my mind caught up, I waited for the arrow to strike me, for the piercing pain to come into effect.

It never came.

As a full second passed, I let a smile grow at my lips.

Below me, a dirty patch of grass sprawled under my legs. The slowly registering pain from my fall was working its way through my muscles, but I hadn't been hit. I hadn't miscalculated *again*. I'd made it to the tree and bought myself some time to think.

In the distance, I heard movement. The slightest rustle of the leaves. A twig breaking. My enemy… they were good at moving in stealth—too good even, as I'd discovered. But I had an advantage. Something my new body had that put my old one to shame.

My senses.

From the very start, I'd noticed the eyesight. It had felt sharper and more acute when the howling winds had nearly torn my fresh body to shreds. From there, it had taken longer to get. It was harder to notice.

My old body didn't have *bad* senses. Not by a large margin. They were actually pretty damn good after they'd been honed over decades of experience. But they weren't everything I could've asked for, even if I hadn't known it before. Especially in my later years, they hadn't been perfect.

Not like the ones I was getting used to now, at least. As much as I despised the way my new, youthful vessel functioned, the senses seemed to be perfect. No matter what I'd tasked them with, they'd come through. My eyes could see farther and clearer. My nose could detect even faint scents on the wind. And my ears... my ears were phenomenal.

If anyone in my general area made almost *any* sound, I would hear it. Even as I kept tabs on slow, calculated movements in the forest around me, I found it strange. At first, I'd thought I was either imagining things or getting lucky, but it was more than that.

And I wasn't one to complain.

Truthfully, my old body was still better in almost every way. Each day since I'd been reborn on a new continent with everyone I loved ripped away from me, I'd gone to sleep in hope that I would wake up and it would all be over. As if the second chance at life I'd been given was some torturous dream. A nightmare the beast subjected me to for its own amusement. Having better senses wasn't compensation for having to live a completely new life.

Though, I supposed, it definitely didn't hurt.

An arrow struck through the air, tearing the ambience in half and shattering my thoughts into pieces. It curved, flying two heads above where I was pressed up against the bark of the tree and sending a stream of cold fire through my veins. It sucked me back out of my false sense of security and into the danger I still had to figure out how to get out of. I cursed under my breath.

I was better than that.

Getting up with new intent and shifting so that I was no longer an easy target, I focused outward. My brilliant eyes scanned the forest. My perked ears listened for any sign of danger. My swirling thoughts worked overtime, desperately trying to grasp at anything to work with.

As I thought, flipping through old tactics and maneuvers I'd learned in my youth, the image of my father came up. His dark hair, faded blue eyes, and warm smile stared at me. Even if it was a little clouded. There was some memory attached to the image. A memory that I could *use*. As I worked toward it, pushing through the fog, I heard the words. One of his many pieces of advice.

Everyone's always losing, you know.

The advice echoed through my head. And like a sprawling web, ideas connected into something cohesive. Something that felt so obvious once I'd realized it.

I was being stupid.

A disgruntled scoff fell from my lips, aimed at myself. The entire time, I'd been thinking that *I* was the one who was losing. That *I* was the one behind. The entire time, I'd been the one to keep up, the one who was always running away. But it didn't have to be like that. As my father had believed, there was no such thing as advantage in a fight. Everyone was always losing as long as they hadn't won yet.

Both of us desired the win as much as the other.

And as the plan came together in my head, I focused even harder on my surroundings. I tuned out all of the background noise. Searched for a specific sound.

Moments later, there it was. A bow being drawn; an arrow notching in it. Closer this time than ever before.

A grin grew across my lips. As both of us knew, getting closer to me was not the best course of action. Not for my adversary, at least. But they were getting impatient. They had to be. I heard it in the reckless footsteps, in the hastier breaths.

They thought they had me up against a wall, that they had the upper hand. But as my father's words reminded me, one should never assume they have the advantage. One should always fight like they are losing until they come out on top.

I readied myself, steadying and bringing my sword up. Keeping my body relaxed, I tried to appear as lost in thought as I had before. I tried to lower expectations and make myself vulnerable. It would only feed into their impatience. All I had to do was stay calm and wait.

Footsteps grew closer. Seconds bled together. I fought to keep myself from shallow breaths. The world seemed to stand still as the moment built. And as her last step sounded off, breaking a twig in the dirt next to my tree, my blood ran cold.

I dashed out. Crouched low and trusting the fact that the arrow would've been aiming at my chest, I ran from behind the tree. My muscles screamed, but I stuck with it, pulling my sword with me the entire way.

The air zipped shut above me, signaling the arrow before sound even reached my ears. It had missed, and I smiled as soon as it did. Flicking my eyes up, I caught the blatant surprise painted on the chestnut-haired woman's face for a fraction of a second before my blade slashed across. Flinging my arm out, steel crashed through the air. She noticed the maneuver and tore out of the way in an instant, but that was fine with me. I'd intended that. As she spent the time culling her surprise and grabbing for another arrow, I was already getting away.

She readjusted faster than I'd anticipated, but it didn't matter. It was what I'd wanted her to do; it bought me just enough time to slow her down and disappear into the trees. For the past half-hour, she'd been hunting *me*. For the next half, I wanted to be hunting *her*.

Thunderous blood filled my ears as I ran. Swerving between as many trees as I could, I didn't spare a single glance back. I didn't need to. Not really, at least. The point was to reset our arrangement so that I could take advantage of my own strengths and remove whatever ones she'd assumed.

In the dense, twisting forest, both of our weapons had benefits. With a sword I had to worry about maneuvering and getting into the appropriate range. Her bow required vigilance. It required her to know the environment, to have a line of sight, and to use it. Even though she had a greater range, she needed to know my location.

I made it as hard as possible for her to do that.

After a couple of seconds of running though, I stumbled. My foot slammed into a stick and my body staggered. Cursing myself quietly, I surged on. The strain in my chest worsened with each breath. But I kept going regardless, holding my form to the standard I wanted to reach.

I needed to be better. To be as good as possible. To be *flawless*.

The past few weeks had gone well after becoming a ranger. The assignments of hunting along with the training I'd already done had benefitted me. Building muscle mass, heightening my awareness, and finally giving context to the pile of information I had stacking up in my mind. But while I was making progress, I still had a long way to go.

That was why we were out here in the first place, after all.

Tracking a suitable tree for cover, I shot my off-hand out. Bark scraped against my skin, but I held tight and swung myself around to hide from view. The sound of my footsteps faded from the forest. I held my breath. Now was the time to wait.

I knew she'd seen me running. She'd seen the direction. She could've tracked me pretty well if she'd been attentive and patient. But she was neither of those things at this point in the fight. I just hoped that my surprise attack had disrupted her enough to have lost sight of where I'd gone.

Taking a breath, I locked onto that hope and listened. The chirping of birds. The rustling of leaves from the canopy above. A horn blaring in the far distance. An arrow being notched in a bow.

I found it.

Somewhere behind me and to the right. That was where the sound had come from. I latched onto it, focusing to its location above everything else. Listening intently, I couldn't hear any footsteps. After a few seconds, I became baffled. Where I was sure I should've heard at least the faintest sound of movement, there was nothing. It confused me a little, and it worried me far more than that.

Was my hearing failing me? It hadn't done so thus far.

Was she that good at hiding her footsteps? It seemed unlikely. Though, I didn't truly know what she was capable of when she pushed herself.

Was it a facet of her magical abilities? It could've been, but for some reason, that seemed insufficient. It wasn't satisfying, as if there was some answer I wasn't seeing. As if I was distracting myself with a bunch of useless questions. I pushed away the worry; I didn't have time for it anyway.

The light twang of a bowstring. Eerily similar to the sound before, the noise drifted to my ears. It was louder this time. Closer. But still, I heard no footsteps. No other evidence of movement as far as I was concerned. Somehow, she was getting closer. And as she did, one thing became abundantly clear.

I didn't want to be behind a tree as she did it.

The decision rushed to me in an instant. My addled mind accepted it and, sharpening my senses once more, I inched away from the tree. Out to my left so I could scope the area.

Around me, I saw nothing abnormal, only the dense woodland. I didn't catch on anything, or even pay attention to a specific area. Even with the blue outfit in my mind, I couldn't find her form in the trees.

I moved on.

Weaving between more trees and placing my feet down carefully, I got closer to where she probably was. My sword stayed ready at hand, and with each step, anticipation filled my bones. I blocked out anything and everything that I could ignore, which only made me painfully aware of one thing.

I was *loud*.

No matter how much I tried to be quiet or how lightly I placed my feet, I could always *hear* my steps. I hadn't trained in stealth, and I was in an inherently different environment than what I was used to. Even back in Credon, I hadn't snuck around much. I hadn't done much tracking. But the truth was, I hadn't needed it.

Leaves rustled ahead. I pushed away my thoughts and stared toward it. My eyes narrowed, picking apart the scene in front of me for all it was worth. Yet still... she wasn't there. I didn't see anything.

A weird sense of dread flooded me. The kind of sense that I couldn't focus on or strain. As if somebody was watching me, their gaze burning the back of my neck. But she was nowhere to be found. My mind churned through it all though, puzzle pieces fitting in one-by-one until I figured it out.

By that time, however, it was already far too late.

I turned, my eyes round. My blade shot up, slicing through the air where I expected the arrow to come, but it had already done the damage. The feathered metal slammed into my side and tore flesh with it. Gritting my teeth, I let out a muffled screech and staggered. Pain erupted like pricks of fire all over my skin underneath the blue cloth of my tunic.

"And that is that," Kye said from above. I twisted, glaring at her with bulging eyes. My left hand clutched to my side tightly as though it could physically rip the pain out of my body.

"Fucking *hell*," I muttered through my teeth. The leather handle of my blade shook with how hard I grasped it.

Kye chuckled, a smirk already on her face as she strung her bow back over her back. "Surprised you much?"

I didn't need the snark. "No," I said. Then grunted in pain. "Not really." At the last second, I *had* figured out why there had been no footsteps. I'd figured out where Kye actually was.

"I didn't expect you to come back like that," she admitted off-handedly. Her tone was dry and unimpressed, contradicting her words as to not give me *too* much confidence. "I wasn't planning on leaving the ground to beat you, you know." Without sparing much thought, she climbed down from her perch in a tree.

Rolling my eyes, I barely even had time to think of a response. "Right," I said. Then mumbled, "Fuck… Can you get over here with the leaves already?"

Kye rolled her eyes, immediately reaching into her quiver for the leaves.

I cursed, half at the pain and half at myself. For the longest time as a ranger, I'd been given basic things to do. Meeting other rangers, hunting game, doing the menial tasks I'd filled in for before. But the entire time, I hadn't been able to get the beast out of my mind. I hadn't been able to ignore all the faults in my new body.

I wanted to be as good as I possibly could. I wanted to be better than the beast. And the way to do that was training. For nearly my entire first month in Sarin, I hadn't trained with real stakes. Not with actual weapons. I'd only ever sparred. So when Kye had mentioned leaves that numbed and healed light wounds with incredible efficiency, I'd seen an opportunity.

With leaves that could act as a replacement for most medical supplies, I'd concocted an idea of training that made it feel more real. That honed my actual skills, senses, and tactical reasoning. Though now, in a body that felt more pain than I was used to, I wasn't exactly ecstatic about my idea.

Walking up to me, Kye finally produced one of the flat leaves along with a bandage. I took them readily, sheathing my sword in the process. After a shaky breath, I grabbed the arrow near its tip and tore it out.

A gravelly shriek echoed through the trees. I winced, only barely seeing Kye's grin waver when blood started matting the cloth of my uniform. Thankfully though, the arrow didn't splinter; it came out without trouble. It still left a bleeding, burning hole of pain where my flesh had been, but it could've been worse. Without waiting any longer, I placed the leaves against my wound, wrapped the bandage, and tied it off.

At first, it felt like hell. The burning became worse and I had to lock my teeth to prevent yelling. Then, after a few more seconds, the pain started to numb and I was finally able to take a full breath.

"Okay," I said, my voice lightening. I teetered. "These... really work." Deep breaths entered my lungs as I staggered some more, only stopped by Kye placing a hand on my shoulder.

Blinking away the numbing haze, I glanced at her and smiled. The concern in her eyes melted. "You okay?" she asked.

"I'll—" I stopped myself, a pulse of pain breaking through. Then it vanished and I steadied. "I'll live."

"Good," she said, a genuine hint in her voice. I raised my eyebrows but she shook me off, a smirk rising again. "If you don't live, that'll be embarrassing."

I glared at her. "Very... funny."

She stifled a laugh. "You are not hardened for wounds yet, are you?" I tried to glare again but couldn't. Instead, I only nodded. Kye let out a bemused chuckle. "I should get you to our healer, shouldn't I?"

At that, I could do nothing but agree.

CHAPTER FIFTEEN

The sight of the ranger's lodge felt like a blessing from the world itself as we approached.

Breaking through the trees, fresh air brushed across my skin. It ruffled my hair, sending brown strands wilting in front of my eyes. I smiled, not even bothering to brush them away.

From ahead, Kye glanced back at me. Her eyes narrowed as she saw my smile, but she angled her head toward my bandaged side. I waved her off, trying my best to ignore the receding numbness and the pain that was inching its way back. Instead, focused on the forest behind us. No matter how many times she proved it, I was still amazed by how easily Kye could navigate the gnarled woods. After hunting in them for weeks, I could still barely find my way around. Some parts were becoming familiar, but those were few and far between. Most of it just looked like a twisted, unattended mess to me.

Maybe I needed more time with it or maybe I wasn't observant enough. Either way, I had more important things to think about.

The leaves were wearing off.

Slowly but surely as we'd walked the final stretch through the forest, the soreness of my body had pressed in. The exhaustion and fatigue had shown its true colors after the fire of battle had retreated. And despite the wonderful numbing effects of the leaves, it hadn't stayed bearable for long.

I grimaced. "How long are these… leaves supposed to last?"

Kye turned on her heel, not missing a pace as we walked across the clearing. "Sano leaves," she corrected. My eyebrows dropped. "But it depends on what they're treating. For surface wounds or bruises, they'll last hours. But for something more serious"—she gestured to the bloodstained bandage tied across my waist—"they can wear off pretty quickly."

"Good to know," I said, straightening up and composing myself. Complaining about the pain wouldn't do any good and I knew it. Then, however, I took a sharp breath a little too quickly and my lungs rejected the air. I coughed, my side rippling as waves of pain broke through the numbing effect.

"*Fuck*," I cursed under my breath as I got the coughing under control.

"Calm down," Kye said. I sneered at her. "We're almost there." Letting it go, I forced another complete breath into my lungs.

Getting shot in the side wasn't enjoyable by any means. Though, in the grand scheme of injuries I'd sustained, it wasn't the worst thing in the world. The danger and real consequence of being shot with an arrow had made training better, at least. It had put fear into me; I'd pushed myself even harder than normal. Plus, it was the first serious flesh wound I'd sustained since joining the Rangers, and I finally got to meet the famous healer I'd been told so much about.

Whoever their healer was, they had quite the reputation. Apparently, leaving their office wasn't something that suited them very well, and that was for good reason. I'd been told that they had almost mastered the ability of manipulating energy to get a body to heal itself.

If the fanciful stories were to be believed, their healer could speed up the process of healing from days to an hour. Even quicker than that with extra effort. As a practical person, though, I was skeptical. With how annoyingly painful the gash in my side was becoming, I found it hard to believe that anyone could've let my body repair in an hour. Again, I reminded myself that things were different now.

But even that seemed hyperbolic. Back in Credon, the mages that we *did* have usually devoted themselves to a healing profession of some sort. Yet, not even the most powerful among them came close to the healing speed I'd been told.

"Arathorn?" a voice asked. Looking up, I matched it with the chestnut-haired woman currently slowing her pace in the lodge's anterior hallway. Blinking rapidly, I hobbled toward her, the image of Sarin's lord already fresh in my mind.

Somehow, the smile on his face was even more charming than what I'd imagined. Glancing over Kye's shoulder, I watched as the man in an elegant suit leaned back on his heels and nodded toward the ranger.

"Kye," he said, his voice as smooth as ever. "Coming back from a hunt?"

"Training actually," Kye muttered almost unconsciously. She shook her head. "What are you doing here?"

Arathorn bobbed his head, brushing black hair off of his forehead. "It was little sudden, but I came to discuss possible missions for rangers with Lorah. Something dreadful came to my attention just today, and I couldn't think of anyone better to handle it."

Despite her confusion, a small smirk sprouted on Kye's face. And despite the pain in my side, I found myself smiling as well.

Kye folded her arms. "What kind of something?"

Arathorn's smile dropped off, his expression souring. "The..." He clenched his jaw. "The bandit group that was rumored to abduct people from Sarin is active again. In our area, even." Straightening up, the Lord of Sarin adjusted his collar. "They may be harassing our own traders, which"—he took a deep breath —"is not something that can continue. Now is not the time for such issues in Sarin. There are dozens of matters I would rather deal with than reaffirming the safety of citizens who should already be safe."

By the time he finished, my eyes were wide. For a moment, the worry I felt for the townsfolk overpowered my pain. As if slighted by my shift in attention, though, the gash in my side sent a pulse of retribution.

"I couldn't agree more," Kye said, her voice softening. Pushing past a grimace, I nodded in agreement, leaning against one of the hallway's walls.

Arathorn's eyes flicked to me. He tilted his head and smiled, taken aback. "Agil, right?"

I blinked, my expression softening. "Yeah." The simple fact that he remembered my name bolstered me more than I would've admitted out loud. "I was Kye's..." Another wince. "Her training partner today."

The Lord of Sarin tilted his head back, glancing down at the bandage wrapped around my side. "Right. Apologies for taking up your time."

I shook my head. "No. It's... it's fine. It's good that you came to the Rangers about the bandits anyway."

The charismatic ruler exhaled sharply. "Of course. This city wouldn't be able to prosper without its rangers. I know it as much as every single citizen of this town that you all do more for us than we could ever repay."

One of Kye's eyebrows shot up. She glanced back, smugness radiating from her lips. I nodded half-heartedly, only giving part of my attention to her. The rest was draped in respect and captured by the smiling man in front of us.

"Thank you," I said, the words coming out in a heavy breath.

At once, the Lord of Sarin raised his hands. "I'll get out of your way then. After discussion, Lorah has already assigned a ranger to investigate the unsavory bandits, but I do have many more tasks on hand. Many that might be completed even more effectively if a ranger took the reigns."

I raised my eyebrows as a grin widened across my lips. Kye didn't feel the need to show quite as much appreciation. "Thank you," she repeated with one final nod to her lord. Then the started ahead and pushed into the training room, nearly pulling me in her wake.

I blinked, stepping forward on instinct. After offering an awkward half-bow to Arathorn, I followed the huntress' lead through the warm comfort of the lodge. As we barreled forward, the numbness on my side continued to recede. I bit down, focusing all of my efforts on ignoring the pain. The empty training room and back hallway flew by without my notice until Kye asked a question.

She glanced sideways at me, one eyebrow cocked while the hall passed around us. "Have you met our healer before?"

I tilted my head, turning slowly and stiffly as to not agitate the hole in my side. "I've heard about them." A wince broke through my mask for a moment. "But... no, I don't think I've ever met them myself."

Kye snickered. "Oh. Alright."

My eyebrows dropped. "What is that supposed to mean?"

"Nothing," Kye said, doing a poor job of hiding her amusement as we rounded a corner into a hallway I'd never been down. "He's a bit... much, is all. Be warned."

I rolled my eyes, but Kye only deepened her grin and shrugged. Another second of silence ticked on. "What should I be warned of?"

Kye slowed to a stop, swallowing a chuckle as we made it to the healer's office. "He's very... *passionate* about his work."

She left it at that, turning away from me and looking up at the door in front of us. As I glanced around, the sparse doors that looked like they led to storage closets were all unfamiliar. All made of the same rough wood that contrasted heavily with the polished, high-quality doors of the ranger's quarters.

Right in front of us, though, was one very different. It was wider than most, but it was shorter as well. Kye would've barely had half a head of clearance if we walked through. Besides the size though, the only difference was the symbol. Instead of gold, or the silver inlaid on the entrance to Lorah's office, this crescent shaped arrow was red.

Without even waiting another second, Kye shot a reassuring look my way and pushed into the room. Hinges creaked as wood swung in, and a high-pitched murmur sounded off from inside.

"Bullshit!" someone yelled. Before I'd even crossed the threshold, a smile was tugging at my lips.

The room we walked into was larger than I'd expected. Larger than most others in the lodge, for sure. But it was hard to get the full scale of everything because of the mess. In the far corner, a small bed was pushed against the wall. Over the floor, scattered papers and what looked to be plant parts were littered everywhere. And directly to our left as we walked in was a desk with a short, bearded man standing on top of it.

The pale-skinned man that I assumed to be the healer had bushy brown hair that culminated in a beard wholly unfitting for his stature. And from the look of it, he was more than two heads shorter than I was. Though, it was hard to tell because he was currently stomping on his desk and muttering foul curses under his breath.

"Galen!" Kye shouted. The man froze, his foot stomping one last time before he turned to us. A disk of ink swished to the side and painted the already stained wood with another splotch of black.

"Oh," he said. As I pushed back another wince, I almost started laughing right there. Instead of a low voice that I would've associated with someone of his looks, he spoke in a sort of high-pitched squeak that reminded me of a child. "Hi there."

I nodded, trying to keep myself together. The older man gestured to both of us before crouching down and hopping off his desk, making sure the red liquid in his hand didn't spill as he placed it into a square wooden holder. He wiped his hands on his version of the ranger outfit.

"Sorry about that," he continued. I barely held back a chuckle. "I was, err... venting my frustrations about a compound I'm... dealing with."

Beside me, Kye snickered. I glanced at her, my eyes going round, but Galen didn't seem to mind. I also let out a little chuckle at the fact that he looked like the mix between a child and a middle-aged man all the while sounding like it as well. His voice was gravelly, but also high-pitched. With his short stature, chiseled jaw, and bushy beard, it was quite the sight to behold.

"Agil and I," Kye started, getting back on track to why we were here. She paused, taking a short breath. Probably to make sure she didn't laugh. "We were training in the woods and I shot him in the side. The wound's been bandaged, but it should still be healed."

Galen's awkward smile dropped. "Alright then." He pointed at me. "Agil right?" Jerking my head back, I nodded. "Okay. Come lie down here and I'll see what I can do."

His voice was serious… somehow. It had shifted as soon as Kye had mentioned the fact that I'd been wounded. His request even sounded like an order with his controlled tone. As I bobbed my head, I didn't think I could've disobeyed if I'd wanted.

"Okay…" I said, giving my version of a weak smile as I walked over to his couch. Multiple raspy grunts of pain sounded off as I swung my legs up onto the cushion.

Galen smiled a bit more genuinely and turned back to Kye. "Is there anything else I should know about the injury?" Kye opened her mouth, but he continued before she could speak. "I see that you've already applied sano leaves, which is a good start—and probably how he managed to get back here without collapsing." He shared a glance with me as if expecting a rise from that. "But I want to know if there's anything you're not *telling* me."

Kye gave him a forced smile, obviously not saying what was on her mind. "No… I don't think so. It was a standard arrow. And, uh. There wasn't anything particularly abnormal about the circumstance."

Galen paused for a moment. Then he beamed. "Great! Then that'll be all. I can take care of this pretty quickly." He waved toward the door. "I think you can leave." With that, Galen turned away from Kye and started over to me.

As he walked, Kye rolled her eyes. She spared one last scowl at the back of the short man's head before smiling at me and slipping out of the room. Galen didn't seem to notice any of it, however, as he was still beaming when he got to me.

"Let's see what we can do about getting you all fixed up!" he cried. I cringed, half in pain and half at his strange enthusiasm. He almost sounded like a mother. Except, that was not something I associated—or wanted to associate—with the man standing over me.

Without asking anything else, he reached over and started to untie the rough bandaging I'd done on myself in the forest. Tension slipped from my waist. The hole in my side flared up, sending pin-pricks of fire across the surrounding skin. The sano leaves went lax, removing their residual effect almost immediately.

A chill shot up my spine. Shuddering, I felt the pain ramp up without continuous contact with the leaves. My skin felt sharp and fresh, letting warm blood flow out to stain my uniform even more. I winced the entire way while Galen removed my bandaging and tossed it to the side. He took each of the leaves, bloodstained or not, and placed them in a separate pile.

The stench of dried blood and torn muscle filled the room. I wrinkled my nose, but Galen didn't seem to mind. Tilting my head, the confusion overpowered pain for a second as I tried to figure the little man out. With his bare hands, Galen poked the skin around my wound and rubbed any blood off on the torn cloth.

"Could you—" I started, pain lancing up through my side.

He held up a finger to stop me. Surprisingly, it worked. "I know what I'm doing. I'll be done in less than a minute." He waggled his finger and I could see some of my own blood dripping down it.

Grimacing, I let him continue. With the awkward, burning, painful feelings tearing through my flesh at every touch, I didn't trust him. In fact, I wanted to punch him in the face. But my rationality kept me in check. If the stories I'd heard about him were true, I wouldn't have to endure it very long anyway. I'd get healed better than I could in most other circumstances. So begrudgingly, I put my hands down and left the short man to his work.

After prodding me for about half a minute, he finally looked satisfied. Pulling his hands off me, he wiped some of my blood on his uniform. Still, he smiled.

"Looks like a quick job." He snapped his fingers. "Shouldn't take more than… two hours maybe?" That number calmed me more than anything else. Hope sparked in my chest as I settled back a little further.

Galen walked over to his desk and took a white cloth rag from it. He used it to wipe the residual blood off his fingers, completely ambivalent as more spilled out through my wound and I let loose a string of curses into the air. My nose twitched, but it was no use. The disgusting smell would stay until I was fully healed.

Being a fighter by trade, the smell of blood wasn't unknown to me. I was familiar with it because I had to be.

That didn't mean I enjoyed it.

After finishing what I assumed he thought of as cleaning his hands, Galen threw the towel back onto his desk and walked toward me. He mumbled something, and with each step, his eyes moved to a different area of the room.

"Alright," he finally said, sitting down on the couch next to me. "You might feel lethargic during this."

I squinted, nodding wearily. The prospect of sleep sounded quite nice, actually. But as soon as he said it, I became suspicious. I took it as a challenge. If I was *supposed* to get sleepy while he healed me, I would world's damned stay awake.

My wound burned again with another jolt of pain. More blood poured out of it, the stench setting a sour taste on my tongue. This challenge wouldn't be hard to complete, I ventured. Between the pain and the horrible smell, I didn't see myself having an easy time just dozing off.

I looked back to Galen. He had his eyes closed and his arms brought close to his sides. I opened my mouth, about to ask him what he was doing. He held up a hand to silence me.

"It'd be best for you if you *didn't*"—his tone jumped in severity on the last word—"interrupt my concentration."

With exhaustion pulling my eyelids and pain searing my side, I wanted to sneer at the half-man. Instead, I snapped my lips shut and followed his command. Again, the strange control in his voice made me listen.

Galen started moving his hands, the air around them seemingly splitting to allow their passage. Something changed. Slowly at first, then more rapidly, I felt a warm feeling growing. It originated in my chest but slowly moved down to where I needed it most—the source of agony in my side. The warmth coddled my wound, wrapping around it while locking all the pain away.

It started to heal.

I could still smell the vile scent of dried blood, but I couldn't *feel* it anymore. I was happy with that. As Galen continued moving his hands, air lightening by the second, I didn't exactly know what was going on. All I knew was that I wanted it to continue.

Pulled along by the warmth, my mind focused on my side. I felt it changing. As the warmth spread and pulsed—almost like a living thing, I felt my body healing.

Like the process that normally took days, my body started putting itself back together, and it felt *great*. With each heartbeat, blood pumped around my body, and in my side, I felt it *rebuilding* my flesh. The gash stopped bleeding. The pain faded away completely. A heavy tiredness pressed down upon me.

My eyes drooped as energy moved elsewhere. I was only focused on the feeling that had replaced the pain, and before I knew it, rest was taking me. The beautiful, lovely abyss was tempting me, and I couldn't resist. My eyes flitted shut after a while, but I barely even noticed until it was already too late.

———

Blackness.

That was all I saw. If I even *was* able to see. For some reason, the concept of sight—of having eyes—was foreign. It didn't relate to my current experience as if a figment of my imagination instead of reality. I didn't have a sense of sight anymore. I was *feeling* the darkness instead. And as time marched on, that was all I was able to feel. The pure, crystal-clear blackness that somehow felt full of life. Everything I'd ever seen, felt, or heard was before me. Masked as blackness, sure, but familiar all the same.

Soon though, that familiarity came to an end.

"Why—" a voice said, abruptly cutting off. The sound mingled with my soul, feeling both intrinsic and unknown. I listened to the voice, stretching my soul to experience its words.

"How—"

"Where—"

"Gone." A note of finality surged into the voice. It echoed, finishing without being cut or warped by the darkness. Emotions rose within me. They washed over me like raging waves in a storm.

And I saw the light.

A white spark flew through the darkness. It struck like a shooting star, enchanting my soul and capturing my attention. For some reason, I felt close to the spark. I felt sympathy for it. I felt hope, even though I had no idea what it was.

The spark hit something in the black and flared. It flared into a soft white flame that burned on nothing and wavered in an absent breeze. I watched the flame, experienced its existence with my soul. It watched me back, displaying every part of itself in an idle dance.

"No—" the voice said again. White flame froze in tandem with it, warping a the broken tone.

"Don't—"

"I'm not—"

"Dead." The flame blazed once more. Its heat hollowed, coldness eating at it from the inside and corrupting the once-pure tendrils of fire. Waves of disgust swept over me. Waves of anger. Waves of hatred that somehow resonated deep in my soul. Then the flame dwindled, shying away from my presence.

"They—" the voice started. It came strong, the words piercing through darkness before being abruptly snuffed out. The meaning fell away. Broken. Fractured. Incomplete.

"I couldn't—"

"Find—"

"I want to…" It trailed off. The flame shriveled, its heat directing away from me. I wanted to reach out to it, to respond to it with my own words. But no matter how hard I looked, I couldn't find it. My voice was somewhere lost in the black. Distant. I couldn't even respond to the crashing wave of sadness that broke over my soul.

I watched the flame uselessly. If I'd had eyes, they would've teared up.

"Please." Its final word fell through blackness. The sound muffled, once again becoming lost in infinity. And as it went, the flame followed. Flickering with a passion that I felt strangely close to, it shrunk.

Then it burned out.

———

A loud slam ripped me back to the world.

I jolted, my eyelids slamming open. Squinting at the light, I held up one of my weak hands to block rays of sun from my eyes. Moving my muscles, soreness took over. It ached to my very core with such mundane lightness that served no other purpose than to annoy me. Angling my head, I pushed myself up against the cushion I was lying on. A pulse of pain washed over my head, making me wince.

Then I felt my side.

I grimaced hard as searing pain ripped through my gut. It tore into muscle like an axe, sharpening as if to make up for lost time. Though, after a second of pure agony, it stopped. While straightening, the pain receded to match the rest of the soreness and left me utterly confused.

Slowly, I remembered. Everything came back and I darted my eyes down. There, beneath a patch of stained and ripped fabric, was a pale scar. Around the scar, my flesh looked completely healed. As though there had never been an arrow stuck in it at all. After a few seconds of bewildered disbelief, I chuckled.

"Agil," someone said. I blinked, but the laughter didn't stop. I couldn't have stopped it if I'd wanted. The excellence of the healing I'd received was… unbelievable. Knowing that it had only taken a few short hours put grand ideas in my head. "Agil!"

I stiffened, a chuckle cutting off in my throat as I turned. My blurry eyes adjusted again until I finally noticed the tall, brunette woman standing in the door way. She tilted her head at me, halfway grinning as she glared.

"For the world's sake, calm down," she said. I furrowed my brows, noticing the blue cloth, black belt, and metal boots of the Ranger uniform. All at once, clarity broke through and I recognized the voice.

Sparing one last dry chuckle, I rubbed my eyes. "Hey Tan." She scrunched her face, still smiling at me. I pushed past the sarcastic annoyance. "What do you want?"

"While I'm glad you were able to take your beauty sleep, the world beckons." She crossed her arms, glancing sideways at the short man rolling his wrist as if trying to get her to speed up. Galen looked over at me as soon as he saw me staring. He did not look amused. And I ventured only half of that had to do with the glass vial in his hands.

I raised my hands. "Right. Okay. What's going on?"

"You have an important meeting," she said.

I nodded. Then shook my head. "A meeting?" I asked, my voice far more surprised than I'd intended. It was strange, though, that someone needed a meeting with me. Outside of the lodge, almost none of the townsfolk knew who I was. And I'd already met with Lorah earlier in the week.

Tan smirked at me, showing off an expression I was getting all too tired of seeing. "Yes. Somebody has requested to speak with you. About a task you might be qualified for?"

My expression darkened. I darted my eyes to the floor, the memory returning piece by piece. Something about Tan's expression helped along an idea in my head.

"Who?" I asked without even looking up at her.

In the corner of my eye, Tan's expression dropped. "Arathorn."

CHAPTER SIXTEEN

Sarin was lively as I trudged up the street.

Afternoon sunlight gathered over the town. It glinted in my eye. It warmed the cobblestone beneath my feet. It gave light to the busy square still filled to the brim with people buying and selling their wares.

But still, I wasn't feeling any of it. No matter how many cheerful voices echoed around me or how many alluring smells drifted to my nose, I didn't care. I *couldn't* care. I didn't have the energy to. All I could do was drag my sore body through the street, rolling the situation over and over again in my mind.

After Galen had fantastically healed me, I'd immediately been thrown back in. There hadn't been a single waking moment of rest. Because as soon as I'd woken, Tan had told me of a meeting I had with Arathorn. The town's fanciful lord and professional charmer. He wanted to see *me*. He had a task for *me*.

On the face of it, it wasn't that unusual. But I'd only spoken with Arathorn a few times, and I was far from a well-known figure. The fact that he had a task ready and wanted to give it to the newest ranger in town felt… off. It felt suspicious somehow.

It was completely possible that all Arathorn wanted to do was talk with me about a simple opportunity. About something small that he was giving to me just because I had nothing else on my plate. That explanation, though… it didn't satisfy. All I could think about instead were all of the *other* possibilities.

I scowled, clutching my chest and trying to steady my breaths. The film of dread in my gut stirred. I swallowed, trying to keep it away, but it wasn't very effective. Back in Credon, as a knight, I hadn't ever had much to worry about. Not after I'd established myself, anyway. Things had been simple. Straightforward. I'd been able to handle whatever had been thrown my way.

But on a new continent, I wasn't as sure. With so many things that I knew nothing about, I couldn't even say for sure what I was worried about. It was a kind of ignorant anxiety, and it grated on me. No matter what, it didn't change my duty. Arathorn wanted to talk to me, and I would talk despite whatever complaints my—

An apple flew in front of my face.

I blinked, stepping back. Only a pace ahead of me, a green apple struck into my vision and then out. For a moment, I assumed the fruit would land in the street. But right after it, a child barreled through to catch it, dashing away after she did.

"Sorry!" she called to me and continued running through the square. I chuckled. The warmth of the sun felt nicer on my face.

Flicking my eyes around, I could only smile. All in all, Sarin was a great town. Even if I hadn't spent much time in it—even with my head spinning with worries, it had a way of making me feel better. It had a way of making me feel welcome, despite the fact that I'd only just arrived.

Another blast of wind ruffled my hair. I turned, shielding my eyes with a hand before the form of the town hall came into view. Slowly, my hand dropped. It curled around the grip of the sword on my waist. I took a deep breath, letting the large, raised wooden building loom over me for a second. Then I walked in.

Pushing out of the autumn sun, the town hall's front door creaked when I entered. One type of warmth was traded for another as the crackling fire bathed the room in a soft orange light. After the doorway, the town hall opened up into a wide meeting and lounging area with chairs, tables, and a small podium at the head. Off to the right, the stone-lined fireplace burned the last of its fuel. And with the light chatter of the few townsfolk waiting in the hall, it was a nice break from the lively town square.

Then the dread acted up again. Doubts rose up and I thought about backing out, but I didn't. My brain scoffed at the ridiculous emotions.

Darting my eyes to Arathorn's office, a guard in light armor stood to its left. Squinting, the average man's face registered in my head. I'd seen him before. He'd been with Arathorn the first time I'd met my lord.

Swallowing my illogical fear and walking up to the guard, I smiled. "I'm here to meet with Arathorn."

The man raised an eyebrow at me. "Name?" He stared with suspicious resolution in his eyes, his face blank. It was as though he'd never seen me in his life. I curled my lip, frustrated by the formality. I knew he was just doing his job, but it didn't feel right for him not to even remember who I was.

"Agil Novan," I responded, keeping up the fake smile. My fingers tightened on the hilt of my sword.

"Very well," he said, cocking his head and moving out of the way. "You may walk in." He stepped in front of me again. "But do not disrespect Lord Gairen."

I nodded and bit back the quips that rose to my lips. I'd been spending too much time with Kye, I realized as my lips tweaked upward. Truly, I had no intention of disrespecting Arathorn. He was still my lord, regardless of whatever ghost I'd thought had been in his eyes.

Another second of silence was all it took before I'd crossed through the door.

As soon as I entered, I furrowed my brows. Dragging my eyes across the room, I almost thought I was in the wrong place. The office that sprawled out in front of me was not the one I'd expected. It was obviously an office, but it was quite… messy. In the dimly lit room, the ground was cluttered with objects. Boxes, books, stray papers. The scattered nature of it all contradicted everything I thought of Arathorn.

The office wasn't large by any means. Certainly not as large as I'd imagined it, at least. And it didn't have any windows except for a single one high up on the back wall. Even the only source of natural light in the room was blocked with metal bars. Below it, Arathorn worked diligently, apparently not bothered by the low light. On his large, polished, and actually organized desk, his pen streamed across a piece of paper.

Stepping forward and making sure to avoid a book on the ground, I nodded. The desk, at least, *was* what I'd expected.

The floor creaked under me, betraying my presence. Arathorn's hand froze and his brows furrowed before he glanced up. As soon as he saw me, he smiled.

"Ah. Agil, hello!" He set his pen down, his smile deepening. "I was expecting you, as you probably know." His hand motioned to the empty chair on the other side of the desk and I walked toward it. "But you're a little later than I anticipated. Did you have difficulty getting here?"

I smiled, trying to pass it off as genuine. Which was becoming easier and easier by the second because of Arathorn's infectious charm. "Not particularly. Though, I was asleep when you called for me."

Arathorn tilted his head. "Asleep? At this time? What reason did you have for being asleep?"

"Nothing special. I'd just been recovering after getting shot with an arrow in training."

The Lord of Sarin relaxed. His shoulders slumped ever so slightly and his smile rushed back. "That makes perfect sense. I'm glad you could make it." Looking down at the paper in front of him, he picked up his pen again and wrote one last thing. "Your lateness worked out well, too. It allowed me to finish up the last of my work before we got to talking." He placed the paper on a small stack to my left. "I didn't want to distract myself from this conversation. It is quite important."

I squinted, keeping my guard up. "Right. What exactly is this conversation about?"

For a moment, he just stared. Without blinking, his eyes studied my face. "This is about an opportunity I have for you."

"Oh," I said. Weight slipped off my shoulders, and I sighed, composing myself. I pushed the worries away again. It was nothing suspicious. A simple opportunity, exactly as I'd guessed. "That sounds good for me."

Arathorn chuckled. "Yes," he said, his lips splitting wide. "I think so too. It is a task as you've been told, and it is one very close to me." His gaze hardened. "It needs to be handled with care, you see?" I nodded slowly, my fingers tightening. Arathorn sniffed and smiled. "But I do think you are the correct person for it."

I raised one of my eyebrows and squared my shoulders. "What kind of opportunity is it?"

Arathorn stared me directly in the eyes. "An opportunity for you to prove yourself as well as visit a town very close to Sarin." He tilted his head, grinning. "I need someone to retrieve a package for me. It is extremely important, and I am tied down here in Sarin. So, naturally, I need somebody else to do it."

I stared back at the Lord of Sarin. Glittering blue shone back at me, perfectly covered in his mask of charisma. "Why do you want me?"

Arathorn kept our eyes locked. "Do you remember the first time we ever spoke?"

I nodded. "You came to the lodge while I was sparring."

141

"Yes!" Arathorn exclaimed. "I watched your fight then. And I remember being impressed by your skill. It has amazing potential, you know." I nodded, locking my teeth. I knew *all* about my own potential. "Then I learned of you becoming a ranger." His nose twitched. "A welcome addition, if you ask me. So with your progress since then, you are easily a viable candidate."

I nodded, recognizing the flattery. It was true that I'd progressed since becoming a ranger—the training session I'd had with Kye was proof enough of that—but there was more to this. There was more to what Arathorn wanted. There was still a question I couldn't quite understand. Straightening up, I asked it myself.

"Why *me*, though? Why not any of the other veteran rangers? I'm sure they're more experienced than I am."

Arathorn's smile wavered. He leaned back, doubt reaching into his gaze. "You think you aren't up to the task?"

My eyebrows dropped. "That isn't what I'm saying. I'm perfectly capable of taking advantage of the opportunity." My lips curled upward. The years spent in a royal court still had their uses in this life.

"Good," Arathorn said, raising his hands. "I wouldn't offer it to someone who wasn't capable. And if I am correct, you have no other pressing matters at the moment?" Reluctantly, I nodded at that. A look of assurance settled on his face. "You will have the chance to take a more experienced ranger, if you would like, but I think you are a great candidate."

Despite myself, I squared my shoulders. Held my head high. Stiffened my posture. It felt good to have my lord recognize the progress I'd made. It was true, after all. And I had no doubt that retrieving whatever package he needed wouldn't be an issue. As a knight, I'd traveled long enough distances before. "Thank you."

Arathorn waved a hand in my direction, lowering his head. "Of course."

The way he smiled, though, reminded me of my own doubt. Staring into his eyes, I focused on the sparkle. The confident glint in them that made him so friendly. I focused not only on it, but past it as well. And for a split second, I saw it again. The interest—the desire hidden beneath waves of charismatic acting. A sharp reaction shot up from the back of my mind.

Before I knew it, I'd stepped back, my eyes widening. I broke eye contact with the Lord of Sarin and flicked my gaze around the room. All of the objects this time seemed tainted. Nothing was innocent; it was all bad. Whatever I'd seen in Arathorn's eyes... something deep in my mind rejected it.

Shifting uncomfortably, my eyes roamed. Books, papers, containers, miniature statues. An array of knick-knacks that told the story of Arathorn as a successful lord to his town. In front of me, I could see him leaning forward and waving at me, but I didn't pay attention. I couldn't pay attention. Not as my eyes locked on one specific thing.

There, lying on the ground behind his desk, was a knife. I tilted my head, fighting the shiver that slithered down my spine at the sight of it. It wasn't just any knife. It was high-quality, sharpened, and the tip of it was covered in blood.

Why was it covered in blood?

I blinked, trying to wipe the anomaly from my vision. It didn't work. Thousands of theories flew through the back of my head, but I didn't move my eyes. Each idea pulled at some irrational fear stemming deep in my mind. Something based on a memory I didn't even recognize.

"Agil?" Arathorn asked. I froze, finally turning back to him while the presence within me receded from control. He watched me with furrowed brows, concern shining through his eyes. "Are you alright?"

I took a deep breath. Shook my head and cleared my thoughts of whatever overactive fear had overcome me. "Yeah," I said, trying to choose my words. "I'm fine... Just a little thrown, is all. Still... feeling my wound from earlier today, I guess." I had to stop from cringing at my own lie.

"Oh." He didn't look convinced. "Maybe springing it on you was a bit sudden."

I shook my head. "It's fine, truly. I'll do the job." I got myself back on track, trusting in the years of discipline I remembered to carry me forward. "What would I have to do?"

Arathorn looked momentarily relieved before bringing his smile back. "Well, as I said, I need someone to pick up a package for me. The knight commander of Norn, Lady Amelia, has something for me. Norn is the gateway to the mountains and an ally for Sarin. It is very important, and I don't have the time to collect it."

New names swirled in my head. I noted them both, shoving them away to ask about later. "All I need is for you to get the package and come back. Travel to Norn, tell Lady Amelia I sent you, and all should be well." The confident, friendly smile made it all seem so simple. "In fact, I'll even give you my imprint for validity." He reached into a wooden dish onto his desk and produced a small ring with elegant engravings on it. "If they ask, this should prove everything well. Just don't lose it."

Arathorn handed me the ring and I took it, slipping it on my finger without much of a second thought. Too many things were going on inside my head to think about some imprint ring. I'd dealt with royal seals before in Credon. It wasn't a difficult concept to grasp. What I *did* need to ask about was my destination.

"I'm not familiar with Norn," I said and tried to keep my tone level. Arathorn nodded slowly. "Is there a map I can use to get there?"

The Lord of Sarin scrunched his face, apparently confused by my question. He stared at me for multiple seconds in silence before regaining composure enough to respond. "No. That won't be necessary. If you don't know where it is, then take someone who does. I won't prevent you from taking a companion on this trip."

I smiled, bobbing my head. I leaned back on my heel and rolled the task over in my head. As far as I was concerned, it was simple enough. And with the allowance of bringing another ranger along, at least it wouldn't be boring. Whatever package Arathorn wanted delivered was obviously significant, but I could handle it. Yes, I could handle it. Leaving Sarin would be good anyway. Experience is what I'd wanted, after all.

"Great," I said. "Is that all?"

Arathorn raised his chin, taking a long breath in through his nose. Then he smiled. "That is all I have for you. You can set off anytime soon, but I'd like the package back here within a week."

I nodded, burning the instructions into my mind. Before I'd been noticed by the Knights of Credon for my swordsmanship, I'd done odd-jobs around the city. I knew the style of being a second-rate postal service. And it would've been a lie to say I wasn't interested in meeting other knights. The idea of such disciplined protectors on a continent of disorder was intriguing to say the least.

Extending my arm and holding out a hand, I nodded one last time. "I'll get it done."

My lord beamed, holding out his own hand to shake mine. "Good. That is all this meeting was for, so if you need to leave, you may."

A glint of something flashed in his eyes. I tore my hand away a little more abruptly than I'd intended, my lip curling in distaste. Swallowing dryly, I tried to mask the sudden disgust washing up from the back of my mind with a smile. I turned around, stepping around the mess on the floor on my way to the door.

Trying as hard as I could to push the worries from my mind, I left the room with brand new purpose in my steps.

CHAPTER SEVENTEEN

By the time I got back to the lodge, my purpose had drained into indecision.

A wave of warmth washed over me as I entered. It brushed against my skin and once again provided a welcome change from the oppressive sunlight outside. Though, this time as I heard the door open, I didn't get the same respite. As opposed to providing a calm contrast to the busy streets of Sarin, the inside of the lodge mirrored them. Since I'd gone out, it looked like most of the rangers had finished their assignments for the day. The training room was packed. At least five rangers stood around, chatting or eating. And I would've placed a bet on even more of them lounging in the kitchen.

"Agil," a voice said. The sound of my name brought a smile onto my face as I turned. Tan stared at me from the wall next to the weapon rack. She had one eyebrow raised and her arms folded as if she'd been expecting my arrival. "You're back."

I nodded, my brows pulling together. Despite the casual commotion around me, I straightened my posture at the slight edge in her voice. "Yeah. I see most everybody else is as well."

Tan nodded, a smile tugging at her lips. "What was the meeting with Arathorn about?"

I stopped, leaning back on my heel and bobbing my head. That was what she was interested in, then. I sighed, walking closer.

"It was about an opportunity," I said, trying my hand at the signature ranger smirk. She snickered, the sound barely audible above another ranger laughing.

"He did say he had a task. What did he rope you into doing?"

"He wants me to get a package for him," I said. I didn't see any point in hiding it, and despite her bemusement at my predicament, I didn't see anything wrong with it either.

She narrowed her eyes. "From where?"

"A town called Norn," I said. Rolling the new name over in my head, I was reminded of the decision I had to make. Reminded that no matter how easy retrieving a package sounded, I didn't even know where Norn *was*. "Actually, I need—"

Tan chuckled. I stopped, furrowing my brows. The sound was short and dry, but she couldn't hide the amused sympathy behind it. "That's a harsh mission."

I squinted. "Why?"

"A man like Arathorn doesn't get the usual kind of packages." Tan pushed herself off the wall. "And Norn… isn't the friendliest place, especially for a ranger."

I dropped my hand to the hilt of my blade. My fingers tightened as I remembered Arathorn mentioning knights in Norn. He'd seemed so amicable when talking about it. Jovial, even. From the look of near-disgust on Tan's face, I faltered. Perceptions of the town in the mountains differed wildly, it seemed.

"What do you mean?" I asked. "Why would—"

The loud creaking of a door cut me off. I snapped my lips shut, trying not to roll my eyes as I turned toward the sound. Kye's face walking toward where Tan and I stood, however, killed my frustration in an instant.

She looked frustrated herself, in fact. Her steps were rushed and her hand was balled as if she'd walked out of the kitchen for the sole purpose of punching someone in the face. But as she approached us, her features softened. And looking past her, I saw the source of her frustration in the first place.

Jason chortled, nearly choking on the bread in his mouth as he slapped a hand on the back of another brown-haired ranger. A ranger I'd seen before but that, to my own frustration, I couldn't name. The slim man chuckled himself, apparently unbothered by Jason's idiocy as he muttered another joke.

"Well…" Tan said, slowly dragging her eyes away from the scene.

I turned, shaking my head and focusing on the decision I still had to make. "It doesn't matter, actually. The task isn't difficult. All I need is a guide, or someone with a map that can show me where I'm going."

Tan shrugged, sparing a smile at Kye. "I've never been to Norn."

I bit back a groan, the soreness in my body only heightening my irritation. "You're the one who told me about that meeting in the first place."

Her eyebrows dropped. "I'm just the messenger. I didn't know what he'd ask you to do, or where he'd tell you to go. But—*anyway*. I have to go meet someone in town." She smiled at me, waving to Kye before just walking off.

"Oh, come on. Could you at least—"

"Good luck on your opportunity," she said while turning her back. She slipped out the door a second later, followed swiftly by a separate pair of rangers. I leaned my head back, biting off curses as the decision reasserted itself in my mind. It still nagged. I still needed to know where the hell I was going.

"What opportunity?" Kye asked. My eyes shot wide and I turned on my heel, instantly smiling at my former cellmate. She furrowed her brows, cocking her head toward the door. "What's up with you and Tan?"

I shook my head and held up a hand. "Nothing." Doubt glinted in Kye's eyes as she squinted, forcing my hand against my neck. "She just wouldn't help me with something."

Kye nodded slowly. Unconvinced. "Help with what? And what were you two talking about anyway?"

My lips tweaked upward. "We were talking about what I need help with. I just got back from a meeting with Arathorn."

Kye jerked her head back. "Why did Arathorn want to see *you*?"

I couldn't help the smile from breaking through on my face all at once. "For a good reason, actually. He had a job for me. He wants me to… retrieve a package for him." My fingers tightened around the grip of my sword. "The only *problem* is that I don't know my way to the destination. I need a guide."

Kye angled her head back, nodding in understanding. Then she chuckled as she realized my situation. Her gaze darted to the door, the laugh bubbling out of her throat only rising in intensity. I rolled my eyes half-heartedly.

"Well, I definitely feel bad you have to deal with Arathorn," she said.

I stopped, already shaking my head. "Don't. He's not difficult or anything. But I have to go to a town called Norn, and I still have no idea where it is." Even saying it made my grit my teeth. After spending more than a month in Ruia— more than a month in the new life the beast had cursed me with, I'd adjusted. I'd *learned*, and I'd gained experience. But the fact was, I still knew almost nothing about the continent I was living on.

Kye narrowed her eyes on me. She was studying me, scanning my face as though to check if I was joking or not. "Norn… Why do you need to go to

Norn?"

"That's where Arathorn's package is. It's where he—"

"In Norn?" she asked. Her voice raised enough that I almost took a step back. Then, my smile wavering, I noticed the near silence the room had settled into.

Looking back at Kye, I nodded. "Yeah. He said it was important to him, and that he trusted me to retrieve it because he couldn't leave Sarin." Kye's lip curled in distaste. "As I said though, the only problem is that I don't know where it is. Arathorn suggested I take a guide. Another ranger who *does* know."

My eyes fell on the chestnut-haired woman expectantly. After a moment, she noticed, flicking her eyes up to meet mine. "No," she said bluntly. "I'm definitely not going to Norn. Not again."

"Why not?" I asked, my fingers relaxing as Kye stiffened.

"I'm not facing their knights after…" She shook her head. "Not after what happened with Tahir."

There it was again. That name that I kept hearing. The former ranger who never got more than a passing mention yet was somehow on everyone's mind. He was special in some way, I knew. I didn't know anything more. "What do you mean?"

Kye opened her mouth and hesitated. Her breath skittered as if she'd been given bad news of some sort. "The knights don't care about rangers over there." Her tone darkened almost imperceptibly, but the way she scowled made sure I didn't miss it.

I straightened up, trying to shrug off the antagonism again. Except this time it was different. It was aimed at knights instead of me, but I couldn't help entangling myself in that. It seemed almost justified, in a way. Like there was a story behind her reluctance—a story about Tahir that I hadn't been told.

"What are you talking about?" I asked.

Kye grumbled something under her breath. "They don't care," she said. "During my first year as a ranger, Arathorn offered me an opportunity too." She tilted her head. "Well, he didn't ask *me*. He asked Tahir. And *he* needed other rangers. Lionel and I went along."

The words spilled out of her with a nearly caustic edge. I knew all too well where the story was headed. "You went to Norn, then?"

She nodded. "They needed our help because Arathorn owed them a favor. Something about a trade agreement about metal. But instead of asking for trade in return, they asked for assistance. All they said was that they were spread thin and they needed extra support." She tightened her fist. "What they *didn't* mention was that they needed support to quell cult activity." I furrowed my brow, questions rising. Kye continued before I could even get a sound out. "Next thing we know, we're fucking *galavanting* through terrain we know nothing about to help the Knights of Norn."

I held up a hand as Kye took a breath. "What does this have to do with them not caring?"

Kye shot me a glare as harsh as nails. My eyes widened and my lips snapped shut. A wry smile grew on her face. "As we went around dealing with cultists, Tahir did most of the work. At the time... I was the newest ranger there, and we held ourselves pretty well." Her expression darkened. "Well enough that we didn't even question it when they gave us a special target. Something important enough for them to warn us... but *not* important enough for them to send along additional support."

My head tilted back. "Ah." Kye pursed her lips before nodding. I cringed, painfully aware of the silence. "What... happened?"

Kye straightened her shoulders, composing herself. "The target was a dragon."

I coughed, my eyes bulging. *"What?"*

"According to Tahir it was, at least," Kye said. She rolled her shoulders. "I didn't see it. He warned us to stay back. Then he went in and came out on his last limb." A moment of silence passed like an eternity. The tension froze against my skin, and no matter how many times I opened my mouth, I couldn't bring myself to break it. Finally, I didn't have to. "They treated him when we got back but..." She averted her eyes. "They hadn't cared enough to offer support even though they knew the target. They'd said they 'couldn't afford to spare any of their guard' or something like that."

Kye stared at the ground, her metal boot tapping on the wood. I stared at her, my eyes slowly scanning her face. Even despite the casual look she was trying to force, she couldn't hide the bitterness. She couldn't stop herself from putting up her guard.

"Oh," was all I got out. She looked up at me, the stiffness in her posture melting away. Yet, something about her reaction felt... wrong. Improper. It was the kind of thing I'd had to learn to get over when first training to be a knight. "At least it was somewhat understandable."

Kye straightened. For a second, she just blinked at me. *"What?"*

I fought back a cringe. My fingers flexed on the leather grip of my sword. "They were desperate, weren't they?" Kye's eyebrows dropped, so I answered my own question. "If they requested the assistance of rangers from Sarin, they must've been."

Kye nodded slowly, distrust creeping back to her form with every syllable I uttered. "They were in the process of rebuilding at the time anyway, and the cult had been slowly gaining ground for years."

"Exactly," I said. "And probably the only reason they were able to hold out as well as they did was because of their guard. Their active fighting force. Their knights. That organization and discipline must've saved the town from a much worse fate."

Kye eyed me. The beginnings of a sneer formed across her lips. "What are you trying to say?"

I sighed. "I'm just saying that at least what they did was understandable. They had a code and they stuck to it. They followed it because it was best for the city." Memories of my past life streamed back to me, stretching from my first induction as a knight to my days studying in the royal courtyard. Learning about history and magic. Even the corrupt continent itself. "It's something I think much of Ruia could benefit from."

My voice trailed off. I raised my eyes again to look at the huntress. But where I expected to see the same slight frustration and exasperation, I saw something different. I saw something much worse. For the first time since I'd met her, she looked angry. Her eyes bulged, her nostrils flared, and she stared at me as if in some sort of furious shock that I'd done something horrible.

I widened my eyes, stepping forward. "What's—"

"You don't get it," she said. Sharp words cut me off and sliced far deeper than that.

I stopped, tilting my head at her. "What are you talking about?"

She took a deep breath with surprising control. "You don't *get it*—you don't understand." She raised her fist at me. "You can't get it through your skull, can you?"

I stepped back. "Get what through my skull? What are you—" She held a hand up. That was enough to stop me in my tracks.

"Look," she said, staring me in the face. Her voice stayed controlled. Clear. But I didn't miss the edge in it either. "I don't know what kind of abandoned, peaceful, isolated, world's damned backwater town you came from—but things don't work like that. They don't—" She stopped herself, biting back words that would've cut deeper than intended. Deeper than what she'd already said, which felt like shoving a knife through a scar that was all too fresh. "Tahir didn't make it, okay?"

Her voice softened with the last sentence. In the pure and absolute silence of the room, it rang out clearly. I blinked, trying to swallow bitterness down my dry throat. "I'm sorry. I…" Couldn't think of anything else to say.

I'd dealt with death before; I'd dealt with the effect it had on others. I was even still dealing with its effect myself. But that had been back in Credon, I reminded myself. Back in the world I'd grown up in. In the kingdom I'd lived in for decades—a place where I knew all the rules. Here… it wasn't quite the same.

Kye threw up her hands. "Don't bother. That was a long time ago." Some weight lifted from my shoulders. "Ruia just… it doesn't *work* like that. It's a wasteland out here—everyone for themselves." She shifted, her eyes falling to the floor. "Circumstances don't always work out in your favor." She scowled, adding a new edge. "They have a code in Norn, and it works. I can't *deny* that. But no matter how well it's worded, their enemies don't care. For the cult, the doctrine is the same as it has always been. Stay alive and achieve their goals. Prioritized in that order."

As soon as she stopped talking, the silence rushed back. It took advantage of the finality to steal life from the room. Even with her explanation and the now-conflicting ideas in my head, I wasn't too fond of the quiet. "Well—I didn't know any of that. Nothing about Norn, anyway. Before today, I'd never even heard of the place."

Kye folded her arms. As I looked at her, the doubt was back. That sharp, guarded look I'd seen on first meeting her in a cell. It was back, as if everything I'd done since then had just been washed away.

"Well, now you've heard of it," Kye said with a dry chuckle. Her eyes flicked back to mine. "But no. I'm not going back to Norn."

I blinked, my mouth slipping open. Kye didn't wait for my response. She spared me a half-wave before hauling out of the training room and into the back hallway. At once, I started after her. Except… something about the pure silence in the room stopped me. Something about all of the eyes directed my way.

Cringing slightly, I turned over to where Jason was standing. Even he was speechless. His eyes were wide in a sort of stunned surprise, and his lip was curled as though he'd just eaten something disgusting. I raised my eyebrows at him.

He blinked, straightening up. "That was a bit of a shitshow. I guess you wouldn't know, but Tahir is a sensitive topic around here. In general." He tilted his head at me, distaste melting away with his own arrogant amusement. Most of it, anyway.

I sighed, running a hand over my face. My mind spun with complaints about myself and feelings of regret to back them up. For a second, I almost wished that I could've gone back. That I could've started the interaction anew. But I knew it was as useless to consider as staying locked in my head while I stood in the same spot. No matter what lines I'd overstepped, I still had a task. I still didn't know where Norn was. I still had a decision to make.

And despite the past few minutes, I still knew exactly who I wanted it to be.

Without waiting, my legs spurred into action and I pushed myself across the training room as quickly as I could. The overly-attentive eyes of the other rangers only motivated me to go faster. By the time I'd made it into the back hallway, I couldn't stand my own thoughts. They kept spiraling and latching onto fresh memories. They grated on me. I shook my head and scanned around, hoping I wasn't too late.

It seemed luck was on my side.

"Kye!" I called as I rushed up to my former cellmate. As soon as she heard my voice, she stopped opening the door to her room and turned to me, unamused.

"You can't just leave like that."

She shrugged. "I've finished all of my assignments for the entire week, actually. I can do whatever I want."

I sighed, my gaze dropping. "You know that's not what I meant."

Kye shot me a glare before nodding. "I *know*, but if you couldn't get the hint, I'm trying to get you to leave me alone." She spared a sarcastic smile my way before stepping into her room.

"Hey, will you—" I started, but she was already closing the door. I caught it before it could click shut. "Just wait for a minute, will you?"

From inside, I heard an audible groan. Then she opened the door, the guarded look in her eyes as prevalent as it had been when she'd walked off. "Fine."

"Thank you," I said, relaxing. "Now… Look, I need a guide to Norn."

Kye rolled her eyes. "I'm not going back to Norn. I'm sure I made that crystal clear."

"I know," I said, holding my hands up. I met more resistance than I'd expected when my fingers slipped off the hilt of my sword. "I know. And I'm sorry that I didn't know about Tahir." Kye scoffed, so I corrected myself before she did it for me. "I'm sorry that I don't know about a lot of things." My teeth struggled not to grit together. I'd lived an entire life already—one filled with more experience and accomplishment than most would ever see. The life the beast had cursed me with though…

It was different, I told myself to cement it in my head. Things were different now.

"That's all you wanted to say?" Kye asked. Her tone ticked up a note, but I could tell she was unconvinced.

I shook my head. "I still need a guide. If I didn't even know about Norn, I sure as hell don't know where it is."

"Find another ranger," she said. "Most of the veteran ones have either been there themselves or been present at enough trade negotiations to know where it is. Bother them instead."

"Are you sure?" I asked, trying to push past her exaggerated smile. "Tan said she's never even been."

The chestnut-haired woman in front of me chuckled. Her smile grew a fraction more genuine. "Right. That's only because *she* doesn't like to leave Sarin. She says it's *cozy* here." I stifled a laugh at that. Kye didn't spend much time off track. "But there are other rangers, you know. Why not ask Myris or something?"

I couldn't even hide my utter lack of amusement. "How well do you think that will go over?"

Kye couldn't keep her deadpan up for long. She snickered. "You should ask him and see."

No, I said inwardly. Myris didn't trust me as it was, and asking him to act as a guide would only buy me a ticket to the lecture about things I should've already known. In front of me, Kye's lips curled back into the smirk that I wasn't sure anyone in the lodge could go a day without. I shook my head. "Not happening. And it's not like I'm well-known to most rangers here anyway."

Kye tilted her head, but she couldn't argue with me on that. "I guess. What about Lionel?"

"Lionel?" I asked, blinking as I considered the charismatic, raven-haired ranger. I hadn't had more than a passing conversation with him, but he was never one to turn down an opportunity when presented. Then, as if my mind was rewarding me, I remembered something surprisingly relevant.

"No. Don't do that—you and I both know Lorah made Lionel investigate the new activity of the bandit group." Kye offered a wry grin. I sighed and tried to match her with one of my own. "You know… there is a ranger that I *know* has been to Norn before."

Kye cocked an eyebrow at me. Her lips parted, about to fall into my trap. She got it before she did, though, and the realization settled over her face with a glower.

"I said I'm not—"

"If you went once, you can go again," I said. She stopped, words dying at her lips as she straightened up. "You can't let the ghosts of your past control you." I rewrapped my fingers on the hilt of my sword. "You can't let the work of the reaper affect your decisions."

Kye glared at me, her gaze harsh. Despite it, I could see her guard dropping little-by-little. "I'm not letting—I just don't want to go to Norn."

"Plus," I continued, my tone lightening. "I'm *definitely* not going with Jason, so if you don't come, you're stuck here with him." Kye's strict expression broke away with a laugh. I offered a light smile—one softer than any I'd given since my rebirth. "Please."

She sighed, rolling her eyes and making a completely unsatisfied noise in her throat. She ran a hand through her hair. Eventually, she yielded. "Fine. I'll… I'll go. But I'm going to hold you to this being a simple task. Norn isn't far—I'm not trying to be away for long."

I nodded at that as quickly as I could. Her words meant the decision was made. They meant that I could finally stop ignoring the soreness in my body and get some rest. I smiled far warmer than I'd expected of myself.

"After this, we're even," Kye said, trying to hide her own smile as she shook her head. "Now leave me alone." Without waiting another second, she stepped back and closed her door.

Solid wood slammed shut in front of my eyes. My smile didn't fade in the slightest.

CHAPTER EIGHTEEN

It all happened so fast.

After convincing Kye to come with me to Norn, the next few days passed in a blur. Despite the simplicity of the task, there had been more preparation than I'd expected. I'd prepared for trips before—as a high knight, travel had been half of my job. But here, things were different. Here, I actually had to *learn* about my destination. It wasn't a place I already had conceptions of based on stories from my youth. No rumors, no tales, nothing. It was exactly like all of the other things I'd faced since the beast had cursed my new life.

Entirely new.

And that novelty had led to multiple things. Namely, it had led to decisions. After reporting the task to Lorah, Kye had given me a run-down of Norn itself. She'd told me her experience of traveling there and made sure I was fit for travel at all. After that, the decisions had only just started. I'd had to decide who would pick up my assignments while I was gone. I'd had to decide what to bring—what weapons and equipment. And all of it had only served to remind me of one of the few things I'd actually *disliked* about being a knight.

"Are you fucking ready yet?" Kye asked from the doorway. I chuckled. At least one of my decisions hadn't been that hard to make.

I smiled, narrowing my eyes on the weapons rack again as a knife balanced in my hand. Shifting it back and forth, I feigned interest in its weight and composition. After all, I actually *was* interested in those things. I'd just made the decision already.

"I'm still choosing," I lied, my lips cracking into a wry grin. The longer I spent with the Rangers, the more devious I found myself becoming. It was enjoyable to indulge in some of the childish things I hadn't done since my previous youth.

"Just pick one already," Kye said with a groan. In the corner of my eye, I saw her slump back against the wall while she twirled an arrow between her fingers. My grin only deepened.

In reality, I was only choosing between what backup weapon to bring. As a knight, I'd never had to worry about it because my sword had been able to tear any of my foes to shreds. Now, I didn't want to take the chance. No matter how much I hated admitting it, Ruia was more dangerous. It was unknown, and I wanted to go prepared.

I tapped my foot and brought the knife up in front of my face again. Its metal tilted at the very edge, sharpening even further with an unreflective grey tinge. It was tipped with blue silver, I noted. One of Kye's favorite weapons to use. So naturally, I asked her about it. "You think this knife would be useful?"

Kye threw a glance my way. When she saw the knife in my hand, she rolled her eyes. "Yes. You *know* it is—now stop dawdling. If you don't choose, I'll put another hole in your side."

I finally broke, my face contorting as a laugh bubbled up out of my throat. I turned to Kye and tilted my head. "Wouldn't that just hold us up even more?"

She shrugged. "Maybe. But I'd get to shoot you again, and I say that's worth it. Dealing with you isn't my job, you know. It's your own grave."

Her signature expression made me chuckle. "Fine. I'll take the knife."

"Great choice," Kye said. "Now can we go? We're wasting daylight."

Finally, I yielded. I took the knife and holstered it on my waist where I'd already placed the sheath. Still grinning to myself, I turned back to Kye and rolled my wrist. "Yes. We can go."

She rolled her eyes again and walked out the door without me. I chuckled, pushing myself to a brisk pace as I caught up. The bag dragging down my shoulders reminded me of exactly what we were doing. As a ranger, we rarely carried more than our weapons and a few extra supplies. Carrying the brown bags that I'd always seen on the shelves was a strange experience.

All I had in mine were rations, my extra uniform, and my bedroll, but the additional weight reminded me that this was it. For the first time since I'd arrived, I was actually leaving Sarin.

Although, at least I didn't have to carry as much as Kye did. Along with all of her own supplies, she was also carrying the extra equipment and medical supplies that she'd insisted on bringing but hadn't let me carry for fear that I'd complain.

I scoffed as I caught up. "How far is Norn anyway?"

Kye turned to me. "Not far. It shouldn't be more than a day's travel away on foot." The signature smirk tugged at her lips. "Though, traveling with you, who knows. It could take up to a week."

I exhaled sharply. "A day's travel it is, then."

Kye laughed, tilting her head as we made it to the base of the climb to the main part of town. "I am still holding you to that. If this takes longer than it needs to, you are getting another arrow stuck in your side."

I sneered. "It won't. I made sure of it as soon as I picked you as my guide."

She jerked her head back at that, sparing a sideways glance at me. Then she grinned. "What's that supposed to mean?"

I snickered. She already knew exactly what I meant. "It's impossible enough that you already know our forest as well as you do. After going to Norn once, I'm sure you know the way by heart."

"I travel a lot," was all the response I got as we started up the hill.

I smiled. "It shows. I've never even seen anyone here use a map."

Kye slowed, and I had to slow as well just to keep pace. Looking at her, she squinted as if I'd just proposed an unsolvable problem. "A map? How the hell would any of us get a map anyway?"

I blinked, instantly cautious. In Credon, maps had been a common commodity. They had been made of entire regions, kingdoms, and some of the continent. They'd been available to anyone who had enough coin, and I'd always carried one of wherever my king had sent me off to. Here… things were different. I had to remember that.

"I don't know," I said carefully. Kye shook her head slightly and started walking normally again. The confusion didn't recede. "Do you not have a single cartographer here in Sarin?"

Kye shook her head, still blinking. "Are you kidding me? With how expensive they are and how quickly they get outdated? A map-maker would run out of business before they even started."

I scrunched my face. "How—" I stopped myself, trying to calm the presence of my past life. Back in Credon, map-making had been an easy process. A few professionals skilled in pen-work could create and copy them easily. But in Ruia, it must've been different. In some way, it made sense that a was unreliable here, but it still irked me. "How does anyone get anywhere without one?"

Kye scoffed. "They know where they're going," she said, as if it were the most obvious thing in the world. "Either they have been to their destination before or they don't go at all. It's that or getting lost."

My eyebrows dropped. It still felt... wrong to me, but I nodded anyway. I kept the rest of my questions inside and catalogued them away to come up at another time. Better not to push it further, I reasoned. After all, I had enough to worry about as it was.

I just let the silence that had settled continue as we walked on. Into Sarin's square and past the sweeping town hall. Through all of the bustling commotion that melted my confusion in an instant. As we ambled, we even got a few waves and nods from the townsfolk. Most nodded to Kye in respect for her service. But some nodded to me, offering the kind of respect that I hadn't felt in months. The kind of respect that I'd earned in spades whenever I'd returned to Credon triumphant. In Sarin, it came in the form stray glances and esteemed smiles as opposed to cheers and decorations, but it was respect all the same. It felt good.

From my experiences with the townspeople, I knew that they respected the Rangers. Revered them, even. To the town, we were seen as protectors—as providers that allowed Sarin to exist at all. I supposed that wasn't very far from the truth. Every time I'd been in town, it was always bustling. Busy and cheerful yet accepting. And I hadn't ever figured out why.

Before coming to Sarin, I'd been tricked by Death. I'd almost starved in the woods. I'd been taken prisoner by bandits. And I'd learned that the second chance of life that I thought I'd earned was on a corrupted continent instead of my own.

Yet, Sarin was different than that. It was a welcome contrast to the bitterness and the danger that felt safer and more content. It gave me a place to sleep. A place to train. A place to gain the experience my new body so badly needed. It gave me a purpose, and one that wasn't that different than the one I'd had before. I'd protected citizens as a knight, and I did the same thing as a ranger.

It only made sense that people were grateful.

The near-afternoon sun glinted in my eye as we left the square. We turned down a narrower street that led past houses on the outskirts of town. That led back out to a path all too similar to the one I'd arrived on. But as the commotion faded behind us, I couldn't help feeling bad. And it wasn't about the uneven roads or mouth-watering smells we were leaving behind. It was that we were leaving at all. We were walking right out of safety, right out of home.

"Leaving this place is harder than I thought," I said, shaking my head with a dry laugh.

Kye turned to me and nodded, casting a glance at what we were leaving behind. "It really does have that kind of effect on you, doesn't it? It sucks you in just to spit you out sometimes."

I bobbed my head, twisting around to spare one last look at the collection of wooden buildings I now called home. The town that had made me feel welcome on a foreign continent and even in foreign skin.

When I turned around, I was met with yet another unfamiliar sight.

Stretched out in front of us as the cobblestone path degraded back into marked dirt lined with stones was a huge field of grass. Unkept and unwieldy, just like it had been during my first days in Ruia. It was scattered with jutting rock formations that seemed to reach to the sky. To my left, the same forest I'd been hunting in for weeks stared back at me. And to my right, the same intimidating mountains loomed over as if taunting us with the future.

Kye stretched out her hand and pointed in the direction of a patch of trees that led up to the mountainside. "Norn is in that direction." She held a hand on her hip. "Didn't need a map to tell me that."

I laughed, my mood lightening. As she walked forward, I was tempted to take a look back, to take one *last* glance at what I supposed was my new home. But I resisted. I looked at the sprawling land in front of me instead and ran to catch up with my companion.

The only way to go was forward.

CHAPTER NINETEEN

It was dark.

After traveling for the entire day, we'd only just broken into the loose set of trees that was the last barrier before Norn. Yet, even though we were close, dusk had already descended. We were chasing the last rays of sunlight as they retreated from the world..

As Kye had said, Norn was only supposed to be about a day's travel away from Sarin. On foot, at least. But as the night crept in, stealing the last vestiges of light from the world, it looked like we were going to have to make camp. We were going to have to abandon hope of reaching Norn before it got too dark for us to continue through the trees.

That hadn't happened yet. There was still sufficient light for us to see the greens of the leaves above, and that was more than enough. Despite the aches of soreness dragging us down, we walked on.

For their part, at least the trees that led up to the mountains weren't nearly as densely packed as the ones I'd become used to. In the evening twilight, the twisting branches that blocked out moonlight weren't anything to scoff at, but they weren't a big issue either. Even though as a knight I'd never had to do much navigating through thick woods, the environment around me was paltry. I'd risked my life in much worse.

Still, with night setting in, I wasn't one for taking chances.

"Should we look for a place to set up camp?" I asked my companion in a low voice.

Kye turned to me, raising an eyebrow before shaking her head. She didn't even take the chance of talking. She only notched the arrow she was carrying in her bow and trained it on the shadows in front of us. I could feel the slight lightness in the air that betrayed her magic.

"When?" I whispered.

Kye shot me a glare, straightening up. "If I remember correctly, there's a side-clearing soon." She flicked her eyes back to scan everywhere the light didn't reach. "We'll get there and camp a ways out. But I don't want to—"

Rustling. Low and nearly inaudible, the sound of disturbed leaves drifted to my ears. I stiffened, my fingers curling around the hilt of my sword. I darted my eyes around. Tried to pin-point the source of the noise. When I did, Kye already had an arrow trained on the spot. I slowed my pace as the rustling grew, ducking lower as I waited for some horrible abomination to appear.

A small bird flew out through the leaves.

I blinked, furrowing my brow as I watched the little, red-feathered creature spiral in the air. Kye stopped as well, her bow dropping as she relaxed. After a few seconds, it turned away and darted back into the leaves it had emerged from. At once, unease settled in my gut, and Kye shot me a sidelong glance.

I'd seen that look before. There was a question in her eyes, and I could only nod when I realized what it was. She had a suspicion. And after hunting with the woman a myriad of times, I trusted she was right. There probably *was* something else hiding, and I didn't want to be caught off guard.

We crept on, step after step through the dark. Grass crunched under our boots, but among the oppressive silence, it almost didn't make a noise as if swallowed up by the night's maw. I straightened, scouring the trees ahead more cautiously than I had in too long. Because typically as hunters we didn't have to be as careful as our targets. That, however, only worked if we knew that we were the predators instead of the prey.

Memories of brief hunting lessons trickled to the forefront of my mind. Ones from both past and present—from both my father and the Rangers themselves. But no matter what point in my life they came from, they said the same thing. We had to assume whatever was out there was hostile, and we had to be ready for the worst.

My lips pressed into a thin line. I squinted, letting my thoughts spin in the background as to not overtake my attention. I needed to be as alert as possible for any—

Another rustle. I froze, perking my ears. The sound was more distant this time. It was farther away, and as I heard a shrill chirp, I tensed up. The bird. I strained my ears, trying to locate it in the increasingly dark unknown.

Remotely, I could hear movement in the brush. Movement and... something else. Something unfamiliar, and a bit odd. It sounded sharp yet muffled and erratic, like the distant gnashing of teeth as if some beast was just now finding its dinner.

My skin crawled.

I looked up, holding my sword low. Kye shot me a glance. I pointed at my ears. She got the message in short time. Then, taking a deep breath, she closed her eyes and concentrated. The brisk air lightened even further around her, swirling with energy.

After another second, the sound came back. Sheer and grinding. Kye's face went pale, a realization washing over her. My stomach churned as she turned toward me, her eyes as wide as the moon. She knew what the sound was, then. She *recognized* it. And the accompanying fear did not bode well for us.

Kye grabbed my arm. I twisted, my eyes blooming like fearful flowers. "We need to split up," she hissed.

I shivered, ripping my arm from her grasp. Split up? The idea sounded insane to me. Some creature was lurking in the woods—it was hiding from us. And if its sound had been enough to scare Kye, I didn't want to meet it on my own. I had no doubt about my own ability with the blade, but in my new body, I didn't want to take the chance.

Kye noticed my hesitation and shot me a cold glare. I met her gaze with a nod, and she nodded right back. Despite myself, I understood. I *remembered* the lesson she'd given me when I'd first become a ranger. Whenever our dynamic switched—whenever we became the hunted instead of the hunters, it was better to split up. Sometimes it didn't make sense, but it gave more safety to the group overall.

I repeated her advice in my head. The words bounced off the edges of my skull until I convinced myself to follow them. I knew the premise was that if one of us got attacked, it ensured the other wouldn't be. All one ranger had to do was be as loud as they could to alert the rest of their group to either help or leave and save themselves. So when Kye gave me another firm nod, I swallowed my worries and nodded back.

Without waiting another second, Kye bolted into the trees. She left me standing in open air like a fish out of water. I almost opened my mouth, almost tried to call out to her one last time, but I bit it back. When the wind slapped me in the face, I spurred into action.

I skulked between the trees as carefully as I could. My footsteps clattered softly against the dirt, but in the splitting quiet, they were almost all I could hear. Around me, the world seemed frozen. It was unnerving. Besides for the howling wind, nothing else moved. Nothing else made any sound. Not even the creature lurking in the dark.

Rolling my neck and pushing away the fear, I didn't give in to it. Not like I had when I'd first been chased through the woods by a pyre wolf. With Kye here, there was no way I was leaving. No way I was leaving her to deal with it alone.

I just had to stay vigilant, I told myself. That was all. I repeated the words through my head as I stalked through silent brush, and they kept my nerves in check. It seemed to ward off the distracting thoughts that had grown since the beast had applied its dreadful curse. If I kept—

A noise. I wheeled, steeling myself and straining my ears. Sharp and raspy, it sounded like something taking a breath in the trees to my right. It wasn't immediate, but it was close enough. I threw up my guard and raised my blade, ready when the noise came back.

My blood ran cold when I recognized what it was.

A sniff. Short, feral, and distinctly humanoid, something was smelling the woods. It was smelling for *me*, I realized. I took a step back, scanning the shadows for some form. I couldn't find one. I couldn't find anything in the dark—a fact that worried me most when the sniffing came back.

It came, lilting on the air as if trying to blend in with the ambience. But I latched onto it. I tracked it as it sounded again, and again, and again. Until at one point, it approached far too close, and something instinctual inside me screamed that I wouldn't hear it again.

I twisted out of the way as the creature surged from the trees. Even though I'd been expecting it, it was still fast. Too fast. Faster than it should've been. I only barely leapt back as pale flesh filled my vision and I swung my blade down into it. Contact rattled through my hand when steel tore through the thin black cloth covering its chest and ripped flesh as it went.

When I tried to pull it out though, my eyes widened in horror. In the next second, I'd expected to be dashing away. Instead, my blade was lodged in place as if the blood trickling over it had latched on and refused to let go.

My eyes widened in horror, a scream catching in my throat as I wrenched backward. Resistance pained my muscles, but eventually I tore the blade out and stumbled. As soon as I looked up at it though, it was already dashing again. The blurred mixture of tattered dark grey cloth and pale skin was on me in an instant. I tried to block with my blade. It was a useless attempt.

I went flying.

With a force far greater than I thought possible for the humanoid creature in front of me, it threw me. Thin arms pushed me back, cutting themselves on my blade, and I hit the ground *hard*. My back slid on the dirt and a dull pain draped over my skull as I grimaced in agony.

My vision blurred. I tried desperately to raise my head, to scramble away with whatever power aching muscles could provide. Only when more fire poured into my blood was I able to sit up, my thoughts spinning. I bit back the pain and gripped my sword, holding it at the ready.

Scanning the trees around me, I tried to blink away the blur. To push back the haze of painful disorientation so that I could locate whatever feral thing had treated my body like a rag doll. As soon as it had rammed into me, I'd seen it running from the corner of my eye. Somewhere back off into the trees. I needed to know *where*.

Clear hearing came back when cold air struck my face. I strained my ears, trying to grasp at any sounds that I could. For a few moments, everything was still; all I could hear was the pounding of blood in my ears. Nothing else. Only the repetitive thump and the terrifying, deafening silence that surrounded it.

Then I heard it. My blood froze, only adding to the breathless pain in my chest. From the trees to my left, the rustling returned. I whipped my head in its direction, ignoring the throbbing of my skull. My hand tightened around my sword and I stumbled to a hunched position. I scoured the trees for anything. Any speck, or rustle, or—

Movement. The thing came running. My eyes bulged, straining to track the pale beast as it rushed toward me. Despite its humanoid form, it moved at inhuman speeds.

166

It had closed the gap before I could even get a breath into my lungs. I lurched backward, preparing my blade when its face came into view. The thin, waxen, human-like face stared at me. It wore a crooked smile with cracked lips that only stood out against the color on its face. Well, that and its grey, bloodshot irises that were full of something. Full of an insatiable want, a desire, a *hunger*. As soon as I looked into its eyes, a deep fear washed up from the back of my mind and cut me to the core. The strike I'd been ready to make faded before I could do any damage.

Pallid, claw-like fingers swung. They aimed at my neck in uncoordinated movements that gave me just enough time to interrupt them with my blade. For a moment, the ice-cold fire in my blood pushed back the fear and I sliced through the creature's wrist. Blood flowed out over steel as I attempted to haul it out. As before, however, it wasn't quite that easy.

The creature wasn't fazed by the strike. It stared right into my eyes. With its other hand moving at a speed I couldn't counter, it grabbed me by my tunic and lifted me off the ground. It bored into my eyes. A shudder wracked through my body at the revolting sight, and some instinct deep inside of me rebelled, slicing forward with my sword.

The creature just grabbed the sharpened blade.

Using its long, horrifying fingers, it grasped the sword without hesitation and ripped it from my hands. The bloodied weapon clattered in the dirt, useless. It left *me* useless. Defenseless. Overcome by increasing panic as a fate that I feared more than any other reared its head.

I balled my hands. Curled them into half-fists and started striking the vile thing. I kicked my feet out at it, brushing its tattered cloth and bruising its ghastly skin. It reeled, wheezing some kind of horrible breath and inhaling sharply through its nose. But still, it didn't falter. Instead of dropping me or running away, it just stared into my eyes.

My mind fogged over despite my best attempts to stop it. All I could think about was the terror. The unnaturalness of it all. It pulled at deep, fragmented memories that I barely even remembered. Showed me sights I'd never seen. Yet somewhere in the fog, a spark of hope sprung up. It reminded me of… something else. Something I could have been doing to stay alive.

Latching onto it, all that I did was scream.

Louder than ever before, my shriek split the air. It rattled off through the trees and would've alerted anything listening in for hundreds of paces around. All it truly seemed to do, though, was anger the pallid monster holding me up. Slowly, its brows came together and its nostrils flared again.

It slammed me into the ground.

When my eyes flitted shut, I once again felt control over my body. But as soon as I hit the ground, that control was knocked from me like air being pushed from my lungs. I wheezed, blinking rapidly as an ache spread into my bones. Above me, the creature smiled and crouched, slashing again for my neck. I raised my arms and covered my face, trying to defend from its strikes. All I got were burning cuts on my skin and blood spilling out over my arms. In pure desperation, I kicked out at the thing. That only bought me momentarily relief. It kept up the barrage. It kept up the pain.

The creature growled. Its lips cracked open and it tried for my neck. I rolled out of the way, sliding over the dirt as the creature missed me by inches. But despite my singular save, I knew it was in vain. Every second, its attacks became more vicious. They became more savage and unrelenting. I couldn't keep it up forever, and deep inside, I knew I was going to die.

The visage of the reaper loomed over me like a phantom. I gritted my teeth, rebelling against its image. It had been the one to curse me to this life, after all. It had been the one to trick me—to exploit my mind and force me into a new body. On a new continent. To face new threats that I knew nothing about. But still, I lived on. Because whether it had been intended or not, my vitality was a blessing. It allowed a means for my end—a second chance against Death.

That second chance was not ending tonight.

I twisted, curling my fingers into a fist and throwing it toward the humanoid *thing*. My knuckles cracked against its jaw, sending its head twisting. It regained composure in short time, but I was already brandishing my fist. This time from below, my bloodied fingers rammed up into its chin. The creature staggered, fury entering its bloodshot eyes. Then it sniffed at me once more and resumed the assault.

I curled my knee and forced it upward, interrupting the dreadful attacks. It growled, the savage sound sending a shiver raking down my spine. But I kept at it. I kept fighting back with every last dreg of strength I could find. Some part of me still expected death. It still expected that in an instant, I'd hear the rattle of the reaper's scythe and it would be all over.

But that's not what I heard. Instead, with its claw-like fingers still dug into my arm, it wailed. A bloodcurdling screech emanated from its lips, overpowering everything else in the air. Eventually, the wail trailed off, leaving only the faint sound of sizzling beneath its skin. I squinted, perking my ears and scrambling backward at the opportunity.

The twang of a bow.

An object struck through the air and tore into the creature's shoulder. The sizzling sound grew louder, as if its blood was literally boiling. It shrieked and growled, writhing before returning its eyes to me. Once more, they filled with unbidden anger, but even that was interrupted. Another arrow followed quickly after and lodged itself in the side of the creature's head.

The soft sizzling grew louder still, burning until the feral thing hunched over.

I scuttled away, staggering up to a stand as I made sure my body still worked. Scrapes, cuts, and bruises littered my skin. Blood flowed from them and stung against the brisk air. I was alive.

It hurt. It hurt like hell. Everything did. But it was a sign of my vitality. It kept me grounded in reality and offered a better thing to focus on than the slowly-softening screams of the demonic grey-eyed monster. Stretching my legs, I confronted the soreness and the pain.

Something felt off.

I knew I was alive—the exhaustion itself was proof enough of that—but I didn't feel whole. Some aspect wasn't the same as before. My muscles twitched and my fingers flexed in anticipation of some object that wasn't there.

I only thought for a moment before I found my answer lying on the ground. There, in the dirt a few paces away, was my sword. A million-pound weight lifted from my shoulders

"You okay?" a familiar voice asked. I furrowed my brow, grasping my blade anew before turning to see who it was.

It was Kye. A breath slipped between my lips. Of course it was Kye. It couldn't have been anyone else. "I-I'll live."

She nodded at that, taking another step forward toward the nightmarish creature. "At least for the world's sake it's dying." Before her, pale flesh twitched in the dirt. Its movements dampened, and dark blood stained its tattered clothes. "I'm just grateful I don't have to see the reaper come to take its soul."

I froze, my hatred of the beast piercing the haze of exhaustion. "What?"

"I'm glad I don't know it," she said. "That my soul doesn't care enough about its soul to witness the moment of passing. And I'm glad it's passing at all." Kye's lips twitched into a smirk. "Because that was my last sunlight arrow."

"I'm glad, too," I muttered. "It can be taken away with no one to watch it for all I care. I don't even know what it *is*."

"A kanir," Kye said. She fixed me with a glare that put weight into her words.

I stiffened, the term resonating somewhere in my memories. Somewhere I couldn't access through the ceaseless waves trying to pull me under. Whatever it was, I knew that it was bad. "Oh."

I nodded a bit, words getting lost in my mind. I wanted to ask more questions —about kanir in general or about the arrows she'd used. But it all seemed like too much work. It was too complex of a task when I was barely staying balanced as it was. I needed rest. True, healthy rest. My brain allowed me the one question that mattered.

"Can we find a... a place to set up camp yet?"

My companion froze, straightening. She glanced at me, finally taking stock of my battered form. Then she nodded. "Yeah. It's too dark to make any more progress, regardless." My head bobbed lazily. "You must be glad I brought sano leaves, aren't you?"

A dry chuckle fell from my lips as she started off. I glanced back at the demonic thing that had attacked me, my eyes questioning its existence. But I didn't even get that far. Questioning was too much effort.

So I just clutched my sword close and followed my companion into the night.

CHAPTER TWENTY

We walked toward the gate in silence.

Masterful stone brick stood above us. It implored us, looked down on us by sheer force of its stature. From what I'd learned of Norn, I knew it had been built for the mountains. And I knew it had been built out of the mountains as well. It was seen as the gateway to an almost separate world composed entirely of stone. As I looked at its walls, I realized none of the stories had done it justice. Truly, the massive and intricately inlaid entrance reminded me of something greater— something I would've seen back home.

Something that demanded my respect.

I held my tongue as we approached, unconsciously softening my steps. Dirt crunched under my metal boots so quietly that the air devoured the sound. It never got far enough out as to disturb the spell of silence that the magnificent wall imposed on the valley. As I got closer, my breaths became shallower. The hairs on my back stood on end. And even the dull pounding behind my eyes dampened.

My companion made no such effort. "Are you doing alright?" Kye asked, her voice echoing off the walls and shattering the silence into pieces.

I turned, my sore fingers wrapping around the hilt of my sword. "I'm fine." And I regretted every word as we made our way up the steps. A pulse of pain radiated through my head. It forced me to wince and reminded me of the fatigue that still hadn't left. After using the sano leaves that Kye had brought and getting a night's rest, the pain was manageable, but that didn't mean it was enjoyable by any sense of the word.

I grunted, rubbing my forehead with my hand. Behind me, Kye chuckled. With the blunt soreness in my bones, my frustration rose like hot air. I glared straight at her. She didn't falter. I swallowed a curse as the pain passed, casting my eyes back down at the smooth stone steps. Truthfully, I wasn't angry at her. With how she'd saved my life the previous night, I really *couldn't* be. Still though, I wasn't in the greatest mood.

My eyelids flitted. I let them slide shut, shaking my head as memories of the previous night resurfaced. I saw the thing again—the pale Kanir lunging at me. I felt the resistance its flesh had given my blade. I smelled its blood boiling among the cold air. Only the small size of my breakfast kept me from throwing up at my feet.

"Excuse me," came a steady, powerful voice that ripped me back to the present. I opened my eyes and lifted my head, meeting the armored form of a gate guard. I stopped, my fingers twitching and my mind suddenly racing to figure out what to say.

"We're Rangers," Kye said before I could process what was happening. "We've come on business from Arathorn, the Lord of Sarin." The guard's stance didn't waver. "And we have business with Lady Amelia." *That* made him shift. His posture stiffened at the mere mention of the knight commander's name.

The guard offered a weak smile before looking over to his partner. Across the way of the gate, the other guard nodded at the silent question that had passed between their looks. A moment later, the one in front of us turned back and nodded readily. Finding no sign of a lie in Kye's words, he stepped out of the way.

The interaction happened so quickly that words were still registering in my sore, addled mind even after I followed Kye through the gate. Passing the two guards on our way in, I saw them eying both of us. But I also saw the confidence plain on Kye's face.

"What was that?" I asked as I caught up with her.

She raised an eyebrow at me. "What are you asking about? The guards, or my suave entrance?" My brows dropped and I nearly rolled my eyes on reflex. I stalled my emotions long enough to clarify.

"Both," I said. "Why did they let us through with such little hassle?"

Kye's grin danced across her lips. From the corners of my eyes, I saw the shapes of houses and shops passing by in a blur, and I only swallowed my grumbles. Wrangling Kye into a simple conversation was costing me valuable scenery.

"Because of our contacts. I'm sure the guards know about the Rangers, and Arathorn for that matter." Kye rolled her wrist. "But even if they didn't, mentioning Norn's knight commander was a simple enough way to get by. I don't think either of them were willing to risk their post by denying us entry."

"It was so… quick, though," I said. My brows came together as memories of long past streamed by. In my past life, I'd had to work for my name to hold meaning. For it to hold weight. And it had only truly been that way after the formative years of my life.

"Yeah," Kye said. The longer she went on, the more amusement bled out of her tone. "Her name holds weight." Then my companion turned away and picked up her pace, forcing me once again to follow in her wake.

The town—which I was quickly realizing was more of a city—rushed around us. A flurry of houses, shops, and buildings scattered the sides of the paved street. After the rough path we'd been walking on all day, the smooth and even stone was a welcome change of pace to my feet. The road beneath us was reminiscent of the town's walls, and so was everything else. As my eyes flicked from building to building, the same expert stonework held all of them up, too.

For a brief time, the pounding in my head receded. It got muffled by my inquisitive and wondrous thoughts. The city around me sprawled both with intense organization and clarity as well as nearly the same clamor as was in Sarin. My time to watch, however, was all too brief, and the pain came rushing back as soon as we stopped.

Kye dragged me to a halt alongside her. The buildings, stalls, and public works stopped moving in an instant. Blinking, I snapped away from a stone statue in the center of the street and looked toward Kye.

"Why did we—"

"*That*," Kye started, interrupting, "is the Knight's Barracks." My companion narrowed her eyes and raised a finger toward the large building in front of us. My scouring eyes shifted to the columned stone structure. Without thinking, I was already picking apart the implications of the name, but when I saw it, my mind screeched to a halt.

It looked absolutely impeccable.

Tucked away from the rest of the buildings and built straight into a part of the mountain that jutted out, the stone masterpiece stared at me in innocent beauty. Back in Credon, we'd had stoneworkers. Expert ones, even. We'd held them to high standards and enlisted dozens of them in works to construct monuments or palaces.

Yet... I'd never seen anything like this.

At the building's front, a set of perfect columns held up the start of the level ceiling. Each column carried simple yet elegant carvings that looked intricate even to an untrained eye. And on the front of each of them, different emblems were inlaid directly into the stone. As I scanned them, I could only figure that they were emblems of different knights. They were all lined with thin silver borders that glittered perfectly in the limited sunlight.

My hand relaxed, slipping off the grip of my sword. I gawked. The world faded around me as the columned barracks froze me in awe and reminded me of memories I'd long since forgotten. Blurry images of my youth cleared as though dust was being brushed away. And the pain that had hit me when we'd stopped retreated as if shying away from the reminiscent beauty.

More and more details of the building revealed themselves to me. I implored it with my eyes, some deep part of me wishing it would return to me the life that I'd forsaken.

It wouldn't; I knew it wouldn't. I shook my head and remembered the mission. I wasn't here to get distracted. I was here to retrieve a package, and that was it.

"That's probably where she'll be," I said as I turned to Kye. She gritted her teeth. "We should go in." My companion folded her arms and didn't move. She kept her eyes narrowed in a hard gaze as though she was trying to win a staring contest with the stone.

I furrowed my brows. I pushed away pain once again. "We have a job to do, you know," I said. The discipline and loyalty and training from my past life rushed back, brought out by the city around us. Kye's scowl only deepened. I could see gears turning in her head, even if she stayed resolute and unmoving.

A sigh slipped from my mouth. Half of it came out as a groan. I didn't want to be here. Not in Norn, anyway, no matter how much the magnificent stonework wanted me to think otherwise. My body ached, my head pounded, and I wanted to get back to a restful bed as fast as I could. But we had a job to do —one that Kye's stubborn attitude was not going to stop me from doing. I opened my mouth.

"I'm being careful," she said before I could get a word out.

I blinked. "What?"

Kye shifted her weight, tilting from foot to foot. "I'm being *careful*. I don't want to go in there unprepared, or have them dismiss us. We're here on actual business, and I won't have the fact that they don't care about us interrupt that. A simple task, that's what this is supposed to be."

My gaze dropped at that and I leaned back on my heel. That was what it was about, then. She was nervous. Hesitant to confront the knights after what had happened the previous time. Honestly, I couldn't blame her. She had a good reason for it all. But glaring at the barracks would do nothing but waste time.

"Sure. We still have to do it, though," I said.

Kye wheeled around to glare at me. She didn't hide at all how unamused she was. "I *know*. It's just… bad memories. Past experiences with a relationship that has been rocky from the start." I nodded, throwing up a hand, but she wasn't finished. "It's been more than just me. More than Tahir, too. I just… can't afford *not* to be careful."

I sighed, shaking my head slightly and ignoring the onlookers staring at us from the street. In the middle of the day, two people simply standing before the Knight's Barracks would've seemed weird, I supposed. And that didn't even take into account our clothes. I shrugged it off. "I get it, but you knew we were coming here. We both *knew*. This isn't a difficult—"

Kye shook her head. "It's nothing you need to worry about." Her words cut through mine like a hot knife through butter. I stopped, taking a step back as a familiar expression started on her face. She took a breath. "We should go in. We have a job to do, after all." Sparing me an exaggerated smile, she started off toward the building.

"Right," I muttered as my eyebrows dropped and I followed directly in her wake.

The barracks greeted us with a blast of warm air. Cozy, comfortable air that was such a stark contrast to the brisk autumn wind outside that it felt like being transported into another world. Shaking my head, I scrunched my face and tried to adjust to the orange light. When I did, the only thing that awaited me was more grandeur.

In all, the Knight's Barracks appeared to be nothing more than a repurposed cavern. It was lit sparsely enough with torches that it held a fiery glow yet also warmed the space. Stray beams of light glinted off dozens of pieces of metal in my vision, and I couldn't help but smile at the sight of knights at work. Unfortunately, my head took the influx of new information as an opportunity to start pounding again.

I cringed, tearing my eyes away from the crackling fireplace on the right side of the room. It bathed the surrounding seating area in a dim warmth, kissing each individual table and gleaming off each individual weapon. As I scanned over the rest of the room, I couldn't help but be impressed at the tall, carved pillars. They held up the ceiling like titans of stone and cut the main room into coordinated sections. Between the pillars and the walkways, though, was where my eye was really drawn.

Throughout the cave, what looked to be dozens of black mats were set up in miniature sparring areas that reminded me of the training room in the lodge. However, these training areas were more open and of a much higher quality. Quality that the knights dancing over them took full advantage of.

Even as Kye walked on, apparently disinterested with the activity of the barracks, I grinned. My fingers tightened around the grip of my sword and just the sight of other knights ignited a fire within me that I hadn't felt in years.

One of the knights, draped in half-plated armor trimmed in blue, was wielding a hammer instead of a sword. Despite his powerful build, he danced around the mat as quickly as an assassin would. He dodged and dashed around his opponent, waiting for particular moments to strike. As we walked by, he grinned and ducked low, swinging his body around and tearing the hammer with it.

A muffled clash rang out against the stone walls.

The defending knight recoiled from the blow. He staggered backward, pushing off from where he'd successfully blocked the strike with his shield. Regardless of that, though, he did not look satisfied. Seemingly out of his control, his shield-bearing arm trembled, shaking uselessly. Still, he was far from done. A bead of sweat dripped down the man's temple as he brought his sword around and sliced his opponent straight in the arm. Silver metal bore into the blue-trimmed half-plate, denting it and causing the hammer-wielding knight to reel in pain.

No sound emanated from the battle this time.

The sword-bearer stopped, shaking off the last of the tremors from his other arm. He flicked his eyes back toward his enemy and charged into him shield-first. The hammer-wielding knight staggered, nearly falling over on the mat as the silent barge forced him backward. The sword-bearer brought his sword down and—

"There," Kye said beside me. I blinked as it ripped me out of my stupor and reminded me of reality. Turning, I furrowed my brow and followed her finger across the room. In a secluded personal sitting area, another knight in plated armor watched the room.

Right, I reminded myself. Lady Amelia. We were on a job, after all. We'd come to see *her*. There was no sense in getting caught up in the training around us, no matter how interesting it was. No matter how much it let me recall my own days as a knight, training in a barracks and learning technique after technique until I could wipe the floor with them all.

I shook my head. "Lady Amelia."

Kye nodded, pushing forward again without a word. I followed in toe, forcing away the muffled sounds around me and focusing on our target instead. The knight we'd been tasked with meeting stared out at the room as if studying it intimately. She wore what looked to be reinforced plate, yet seemed unburdened by its weight. Almost carefree about it, ticking her foot back and forth while still holding a cold and calculated look like she was solving a problem and didn't want anybody to know. As soon as I met her eyes, she was staring right at me.

A shiver crept down my spine as her dark brown irises locked with mine. After a moment, I straightened up and nodded to her, offering a respectful smile. All she did was turn away.

"We have a job to do," Kye grumbled.

I snapped away from the intimidating knight and picked up my pace. "I know we do."

"I'm reminding myself," she said, relaxing her arms. "We don't need to speak with her long." I nodded while Kye squared her shoulders, as if reassuring herself with her posture. "And don't get distracted."

My lips tweaked upward. I stifled a chuckle and moved on with her, walking down the designated pathway toward our target. The muffled sounds of battle still rung out around us. The knights still dueled with as much fury and determination as they had when we'd entered. But I ignored it all. That was, until a question came up.

The distinct, shrieking clash of blades didn't echo at all. "What's with the sound in here? None of the fighting is nearly as loud as it should be."

Kye spared a glance back at me, one eyebrow raised. "The black sparring mats. They're enchanted by soundweavers to dampen the sound produced above them." Then she turned back around. "We have one at the lodge, you know."

I rolled my eyes. "I *know* that. But nobody ever mentioned it was magical. It looks like any other training mat."

Kye bobbed her head. "Truthfully, it isn't that complex of a spell. Or, not for a competent soundweaver at least. Someone who has done it enough that it's almost as simple as manipulating heat." I nodded slowly, accepting her words as truth. I'd heard the term of soundweaver before—one of my king's scholars had studied the field—but enchanting an item was new to me. As far as I'd known, that was something delegated to myths alone.

"Interesting," I said as my eyes flicked around. "These knights have almost a dozen, though. How come we only have one?"

Kye slowed her pace. She scrunched her face. "If you'd be willing to have one enchanted yourself, go ahead and get us another." Her voice trailed off into a baffled chuckle.

A crack of sound. As though the air itself were ripping.

I turned, wincing as the fleeting noise tore through the dull commotion of the barracks. It broke through its own muffled cover and echoed off the cavern walls, ringing in my ears. My lips pressed into a thin line and I dropped my hand around the handle of my sword. There, only about a dozen paces away from us on the sparring mat that was the source of the sound, a knight stumbled backward. He shook his head furiously. And his opponent was taking advantage, swinging at the man with immense force and whipping the tip of her blade up near the neck of her opponent.

The man almost whimpered as another crack split the air. He grimaced and fell to his knees.

"Offensive soundweavers," Kye grumbled under her breath. "Such little respect for our world's damned ears."

I turned to her, my eyes blooming. "I thought you said sound created on the mats was muffled."

She chuckled. "It is. And believe it or not, that *was* muffled. We were lucky our ears only felt as much of it as we did."

Lines appeared on my forehead. I raised my eyebrows and glanced back to where the agile knight was lying on the ground. His face was contorted in what looked to be a permanent grimace. Even though the soundweaver standing above him was wincing herself as if suffering from a headache beyond proportion, it was still clear that she'd won.

I didn't stare at the scene for long. My fingers relaxed and—at the repeated realization that even among knights, I was little more than a fish out of water—I walked in silence. Kye happily obliged, keeping her comments to simple grumbling under her breath as we made our way across the room. As soon as we did, her demeanor changed.

"Lady Amelia," Kye said in a calm, controlled voice. Cheerful at the edges but firm enough to command attention. I nearly took a step back as she smiled at the sitting knight, surprised by her diplomacy. "We are Rangers from Sarin, and we have business on behalf of Arathorn."

Lady Amelia chuckled. "I know." She didn't even get up. "I'm quite familiar with you Rangers. As well as Arathorn's *important* package. Do you have his imprint?"

Kye stiffened, keeping her smile carefully wide as she turned to me. Her eyes widened, restrained fury dancing within them. I nodded and held up my hand before sliding the gold ring off my finger and holding it out.

"Of course," I said. "We wouldn't come requesting on his behalf without verification. I have it here."

The stoic knight smiled. It was a thin, practiced smile, but a smile nonetheless. She leaned forward without moving from her seat and grabbed the ring out of my hand. Her eyes studied it for a moment, lazily glossing over the engraved golden surface before throwing it back.

"Good," she said. "Not that I doubted you, but I can never be too careful."

The way Kye clenched her fist made it clear that she agreed. "So, the package?" The last hints of cheerfulness she'd started with drained away.

"We'll get to it." Lady Amelia side-eyed us. "It's of sensitive material, as you may know."

Kye sneered. "I know. I just want to make sure that we know what to expect this time. I'd rather not get blindsided with a package this significant to our lord." The professional, almost reverential tone felt odd coming out of Kye's mouth.

Lady Amelia squinted. Her head tilted, and I didn't miss the way her fingers curled as if grabbing the air by its neck. "This time? I don't think I've ever dealt with you before."

Kye didn't falter. "No. Not you specifically. But your knights have, and I simply want assurance that nothing will go sideways."

The commanding knight shifted, glaring at Kye. Still, she didn't waver. Not even when Lady Amelia pushed out of her chair and onto the ground. Instinctively, I took a step back as if the ground itself had tilted away from me. "You assume something will go sideways?"

Behind us, the muffled sounds of battle slowed. They lessened as if each battle was coming to some kind of abrupt end. Kye, however, didn't even seem to notice. "I don't assume anything. But we can never be too careful."

I stumbled, my stomach lurching as the ground tremored under me. After a moment, I caught myself and staggered to a stand. Unmuffled and unbidden sounds of creaking wood drifted throughout the cavernous space.

Lady Amelia took a step forward without notice. "I will not stand here and take implied accusations." The ground tilted again, shaking slightly as she spoke and sending light tremors through my feet. I widened my eyes, grasped the sword on my waist, and tried to stabilize. As the ground shook again, I was only half successful.

Momentarily, Kye teetered. She glanced around as if to check where she was standing before taking a step forward toward the knight commander. When she did, the ground calmed. The groaning of wood stopped. For the moment, everything was fine.

"Look," Kye said through locked teeth. "I'm not trying to be rude, but this package should be handled with care. If we could just—"

She never got to finish her sentence. Wood creaked anew in the background. All sounds of fighting turned into drowned-out, inaudible discontent. The ground tilted again, nearly throwing me from my balance. I unsheathed my sword, ears twitching at the scrape of metal against its scabbard.

But when the ground truly started to shake, I glanced at my companions. Kye's eyes shot wide with shock, and even the stoic knight's lips quivered in unmistakable surprise. Behind us, creaking wood turned to breaking wood, and one thing became blatantly clear.

Everything was *not* fine.

CHAPTER TWENTY-ONE

The world itself was shaking.

I fell to a crouch as the thought occurred. My grip tightened. My breathing accelerated. Blood pounded on the insides of my ears, ice-cold fire seeping in with each passing moment. The aches and pains in my muscles receded, despite the shaking, and I scrambled to balance myself over the stone.

I looked up, trying to keep my mind in check. To push back the fog. I couldn't let confusion overpower me. Because as soon as it did, I was all but useless. I furrowed my brow and squinted, scanning the room. Clattering metal itched at my ears. It joined the splitting wood in my hearing. But what I didn't hear were voices. No large outcries. No panic. These were knights, I remembered, not common folk. They were trained better; they had no need for such things.

I repeated the thought in my head, trying to calm my addled brain. If they weren't freaking out, then neither should I. There was no *need* to, I told myself. So I didn't. I kept my lips pressed shut and my senses keen.

From the corner of my eye, Kye crept up to me. She glared, entirely serious. Her form rushed up faster than I would've imagined in her crouched position, stalking with her bow at the ready. When she reached me, an arrow was already notched. How she'd found time to ready herself when she'd been arguing only moments before was beyond me. But it didn't matter. I had to stay focused.

Turning to her as steadily as I could, I pressed my hand to the floor. Cold vibrations slid up my arm like a snake underneath my skin. "What… the hell is happening?"

"I… don't know," she said, her tone firm among the chaos. Afterward, she spared a glance backward. Over toward the knight commander who was still somehow holding her ground.

When Kye looked back at me, she cocked her eyebrows. The intent was palpable. It disturbed my gut just to think about it—she thought we were being set up. That Lady Amelia had caused whatever was taking the cavern by storm. A bead of sweat trickled down my temple as I tried to balance while I thought.

After a second, I shook my head violently. The movement sent agony rippling across my skull. I ignored it and focused on Kye. Her idea didn't make sense. I knew Kye didn't trust the knights here—and I knew she had a good reason, but the implication was more than a stretch.

A strong tremor shook me. I stumbled backward multiple paces, my hand scraping on the stone as I pushed off to stay stable. When I staggered straight, I flicked my eyes back to Kye. I watched the steady anger rising on her face. I didn't let it sway me. With as much composure as I could summon, I shook my head. Kye glowered.

I crept toward her. "It can't—" My body jolted, pushing breath from my lungs. "It doesn't make any sense." She curled her lip at my response, but I knew she understood. Her fingers relaxed on the bowstring and she released tension from her shoulders.

A relieved breath fell from my lips. I teetered, forcing my body upright and ignoring the waves of pain ripping through my exhausted bones. Instead, I focused on the room. From what I could tell, there were more than a dozen knights in the barracks. All heavily armored. All highly skilled. I clenched my jaw even harder as my mind raced with possibilities.

Spawned from both irrational fear and rational preparation, battle encounters flew through my head. One after another. Stance after stance. I didn't even know if I'd be able to beat one of the knights in my current body, but that didn't mean I wouldn't try. Then, turning my head to my companion, I noticed something. Her eyes were darting between the knights as well, and her fingers were twitching as well.

She was doing the exact same thing.

Warm pain flashed through my arms with another powerful tremor of the rock. My thoughts followed it, conjuring images of the forest. Images of the kanir and its blatant ferocity. My body moved on automatic to balance myself as the simple image of the thing set a taste of sulfur on my tongue. Fear screamed at me. I pushed back, ignoring its calls to falter and using it for another purpose instead.

Never again.

Fight scenes came back to replace terrible memories. I latched onto them, flexing my muscles and clutching my sword. I could imagine myself swinging it. Dodging and weaving. Executing maneuvers. It felt right.

An immense crack of pure noise broke the violent ambience.

I jolted, wincing at the sudden and familiar sound. Whipping my head around, I blinked away the blur in my eyes to see the woman I'd watched before. The soundweaver who'd caused her fellow knight to cower in pain. Somewhere across the room, she was casting again. Except this time, after the noise, the ground calmed. The world responded to her cries, and she forced more and more energy into it until the shaking died down enough.

After a flurry of boisterous noises reverberated energy straight into the stone, the quaking calmed to a light tremor. It settled enough that standing up became an achievable goal. A goal that, as the rest of the tumultuous noise dampened too, most of the knights were achieving. Coming up from their hunched, crouched, or lying positions, the knights rose back up on their mats and looked around. From the corner of my eye, I saw Kye do the same.

"It's over," a familiar voice said soft enough that it didn't grate on my ears yet loud enough that it echoed off the walls. I knew who it was before I'd even turned.

What I saw, though, was not what I'd been expecting. Lady Amelia stood with her head hung low as her words trailed off. That had been expected. But she was also still standing perfectly steady, her feet planted in the exact positions they'd been in when the shaking had started. Painted on her face was a fractured, pained look that felt burdened by more weight than she let on. And under her feet, I could even see small dents in the rock where her heels had dug in.

The awe of it didn't reach Kye the same way. "What in the world's name was that?"

Lady Amelia took a breath. "A quake of some kind."

Kye's eyes flared, and she took a step back. "*Obviously* that's what it was. But that's not what I'm asking."

Lady Amelia straightened, her mask of composure recovering. "This isn't the first." She darted her gaze up to watch the confirmation from the knights around the room. "They have been happening more frequently in recent times."

Kye took half a step back. The look in her eyes softened. "Why?"

The single word said everything. It dragged with it all the curiosity. All the anger. All the confusion. All the memories. I knew it as much as they did about quakes, after all. They weren't specific to this continent. As one of the most primal features of the world's wrath, they happened everywhere. Even back in my home kingdom, they'd wreaked havoc on our land.

A memory burrowed its way to the surface as my eyes fell to the floor. I remembered my home. During my childhood, before I'd ever been to a royal court, we'd dealt with a quake. Even now, despite so much of the past blurring away—fading before I even have a chance to grasp it, I remembered that morning. It was seared into my mind.

The way I'd woken up. The shaking. The chaotic vision of broken glass and splintered wood. Dirt flying through the fields. The rock that cut a gash over my knee. My mother's screams.

The quake had decimated our crops. It had forced us into debt. Stolen whatever money we'd saved up to help my father in his condition. I remembered it all so clearly. Because that was when I'd begun my odd-jobs, after all. My little quests. That was the year I'd first picked up a sword.

"—and she may be back," Lady Amelia said. I blinked, rising out of the restless waves to return to reality. I turned, surprised by the knight's low and foreboding tone. The sorrow was clear, but there was more to it as well.

Kye averted her eyes. "Who?" she asked, the question hanging in the air. To me, it looked like she already knew. But she was scared of the thought. Scared enough to hope it was something else.

Lady Amelia's eyes locked with my companion. "The mother of destruction." Kye's face flashed pale. "Rath herself… she may be returning. Her slumber may finally be over."

Kye swallowed and took a step back. My eyes widened, the unknown information somehow scaring me too as Kye's face paled. I didn't understand what the knight commander had said, but I didn't *need* to. My former cellmate's reactions were enough. With the mention of the new name, I mentally set aside the question for later and simply let the silence stand in the room.

And stand it did. As soon as Lady Amelia's words had finished echoing off the cavernous walls, the left-over quiet held us all up by the throat. It challenged us to speak in a way so deceitful that none of us dared follow its call. Everyone seemed to know what Lady Amelia had said. They all knew the context behind it. But I would've sooner been caught dead than letting my question echo in the void.

Kye lowered her bow slowly. She flicked her eyes up, holding a stare with the knight commander. Fingers twitched as she took the readied arrow and put it back in her quiver. Her shoulders slumped as she did.

Kye shook her head. Then she swung the bow over her shoulder and strung it on her back. As soon as she did, her brow furrowed. I saw determination racing back.

"Really?" she asked, the single word echoing.

Lady Amelia broke the stare. "Yes. The Scorched Earth have returned more powerfully than we expected. And their… activity in the mountains has coincided with the quakes."

Kye wanted to curse. I saw it painted between the lines on her face. But she held her tongue. And so did I, placing my sword back in its sheath.

"However," Lady Amelia said and raised her voice. "The rumors of Rath are nothing more than that. Rumors. False information proliferated by her cult to bring destructive myths back into our minds." She straightened up. "It has nothing to do with you or your organization." Color returned to Kye's face. "So, I suppose we should retrieve what you came for, then."

The ghost of pride floated at Kye's lips. She nodded. Lady Amelia nodded back, turning toward me and doing the same a second later. I bobbed my head, returning what appeared to be a friendly formality.

The knight commander then pursed her lips and furrowed her brow. She stiffened her posture—however that was still possible given the way she was already standing. The sound of her step forward all but announced her address to the room.

"Knights of Norn," she started, her voice booming. "I have the obligation to escort these two representatives from Sarin"—she gestured back toward Kye and me—"to a package for their lord. It is in the apothecary's guild, which is not far. However, given the quake, we can never be too careful. I will be taking at least two of you with me."

A soft murmur weaved through the crowd of the knights like a disgruntled snake. Though, it didn't get loud enough to disrupt their leader. They all listened. A few looked concerned, but just as many of them were poised and prideful. As Lady Amelia cleared her throat, the murmur ground to a halt.

The knight commander scanned the room. "Rik." She pointed to the large hammer-wielding knight I'd been watching when we entered. "And Vlad." Her gaze slid over the crowd toward a taller, sword-wielding knight of slimmer build. They both had the same light-blue trim on their armor. "You two are coming with us."

A smile grew on the face of the hammer-wielding knight. He nodded, sparing self-referential glances toward his peers before walking over. The other knight— Vlad, she'd called him—appeared unfazed. He collected his weapon, sheathed it, and started toward us.

Lady Amelia smiled. "The rest of you stay on high alert." Her voice dropped lower. "And start cleaning up the barracks." A murmur spread through the remaining crowd at that. It died with a simple glance from their superior. Without any further complaint, the knights got to work.

I narrowed my eyes and stepped closer to Kye. Despite the growing smile on my face, I kept the intimidating leader in my peripheral vision. Because with the quake that had just occurred, I had no reason not to be cautious. No reason to trust someone my companion was shaky on to begin with. But flicking my gaze to Kye, I had another topic in mind.

"Who's Rath?" I asked in a hushed tone.

Kye froze. Her jaw tightened. But after a second, she lent to my ignorance. "A high dragon," she said. I blinked, images conjuring in my head at the simple mention of a dragon. Kye tilted her head. "The… the first, actually. Supposedly the most powerful of the dragons to ever exist." Kye rolled her shoulders. "Her draconic soul can conduct and manipulate enough magical energy to split a mountain in half." Kye swallowed. "As well as raze the remaining rocks to ash, as far as the myths go, anyway. I only know of her from legend… old, unproven, impossible legend."

I nodded shallowly, trying to store away the information in my head. Licking my lips, I found my mouth dry and coughed. Kye shot me a sideways glance; I waved her off, taking a deep breath as memories streamed back. Stories, myths… legends just like Kye was talking about. We'd had them in Credon—about dragons, even. Though, none specific enough to mention a dragon by name. None that were *true*.

The sound of a certain knight clearing her throat brought me out of my thoughts. Looking toward Lady Amelia, I saw her staring directly at me. She raised one eyebrow and cocked her head before turning on her heel.

A heartbeat later, we were on our way out. The commanding knight commander dragged her summons along with her. Kye followed behind them. And once again, I fell in line only a step removed as she left, passively dragging me in her wake.

―――

The apothecary's guild was larger than I'd expected. At first mention, I'd assumed the guild building to be a medium-sized stone structure that mirrored a bureaucratic office. I'd thought of it as the administrative headquarters for the apothecaries, storing supplies and acting as a office where they would organize.

I was quite wrong. Instead of separating the management from its primary workplace as had been common in my home kingdom, the apothecaries in Norn combined them. They created the enigma of a building that was an oddly functional hybrid of sparse offices and large hospital main spaces. The expansive and elegantly designed structure consisted of the same masterful stonework in its foundation and supports as most other buildings of Norn. But it also used much more wood and glass in its construction, letting in natural light and only adding to the magical tinge that seemed permanent in the air.

Straight from the entrance, the building stretched into a space littered with desks, chairs, and research equipment on one side and a plethora of infirmary beds on the other. Working in tandem with the large windows, intricate sconces sat on nearly every pillar of the building's interior and gave the area a cozy, golden glow.

From the moment we'd arrived, Lady Amelia had barreled ahead without stop. And as we stormed past the various apothecaries still working or cleaning up damage from the quake, she didn't appear to be letting up. Watching the dark, strained, and exhausted expressions on the mages around me took away my urge to even look at the other side of the room. The quake would've been particularly damaging here, I guessed. In a place that actually cared for real *people.*

Still, we marched without hesitation. Nobody stopped Lady Amelia and her guard of knights all the way until we approached a polished wooden door tucked away at the back of the building. Halting in front of it for only a second, the knight commander glanced around before opening it and leading us inside.

A curious grin sprouted across my lips. The room we walked into looked like a back room—one that wasn't accessible to the common-folk of Norn. And judging by Lady Amelia's slower pace along with her increased hesitancy, I wasn't far from the truth. The space was dark—much darker than the rest of the building had been, and it was lit without a single window.

Marching straight as an arrow—despite Kye's reserved apathy about it all—we made it past the tables and chairs. We walked past the racks of glass vials and notebooks that looked completely unharmed, almost as though the room had been completely detached from the destruction of the quake outside. I shook a shiver off my spine, eying the knights ahead. Even though I trusted them more than my companion did, I couldn't help the sense of unease that scratched at my neck.

Then we stopped. I blinked, twisting forward to see the clean-cut stone brick that made up the back wall of the room. There, embedded in the rock, was a metal box. Made of what appeared to be matte, unpolished steel. It was locked shut, and it didn't have a handle or any other mechanism for which to open it.

Lady Amelia stepped toward it. The lack of such things didn't deter her in the slightest.

For a moment, I considered opening my mouth. I considered rattling off a question about the room we were in, the box she was attempting to open, or what package Arathorn had even requested. Yet I found myself pursing my lips instead. Unable or unwilling to disobey the will of silence in the room.

Lady Amelia took a deep breath. The simple sound reverberated off smooth stone walls. She extended her hand and pressed it firmly against the surface of the safe. Instinctually taking a step back, my unease thickened. My eyes flicked around, and everything felt... wrong. I'd assumed she was trying to *open* the box, but—

Movement. I widened my eyes, turning and scouring the wall. Still standing before the metal box, Lady Amelia's face contorted. It became pained. Tense. Drawn. As though she was focusing on something I wasn't aware of.

Movement. Again. I furrowed my brow and dropped a hand to my sword. As far as I could tell, the motion was coming from the wall, from out of the stone itself. But when I watched it, all I saw was grey. Stark, motionless grey. Then the movement came again as a stream of slight tremors through the rock.

The stone was moving, I realized. Not shaking. This wasn't a quake again. But it was trembling in coordinated, squared lines as if a worm was burrowing between spaces in the compact rock. The recognition of it made all of the tremors obvious and revealed the stone wall almost as something living. A sort of creature with energy pulsing through its veins, each leading in lines toward the metal safe. They worked in tandem with the subtle movements of Lady Amelia's fingers.

I stared in awe at the display of magic. The display of manipulating energy to change the world itself. It was the kind of magic foretold in myths in my home kingdom, the kind supposedly long lost to time. But things were different here, I reminded myself. Especially that which I'd thought impossible before my first encounter with the beast.

A soft click echoed through the space.

My lips parted as questions rose to my tongue, as thoughts raced through my mind and started my imagination running wild. I wanted to confirm what I thought. I wanted to know about Lady Amelia and her magical abilities. After living in Ruia for more than a month, I knew far more about magic than most scholars from my past life, but it still wasn't enough. If I wanted to make the beast pay, I needed more than that. I'd wanted experience, after all. Knowledge came directly along with that.

I straightened up. "What kind of—"

Lady Amelia turned, her eyes straining not to widen and her face flushed faintly pale. Her worried posture cut me off before she'd even said a word.

"It's gone."

Beside me, Kye shook her head. She stepped forward and glared at the knight commander, her fingers already twitching toward the bow on her back. "What do you mean it's *gone*?"

Lady Amelia turned to her. Brown eyes met Kye's with a gaze of pure ice. "I mean it's gone. My statement was as simple as that."

Kye squinted, furrowing her brow. "How can it just be *gone*? Isn't this safe well-guarded? Our lord's package was extremely important to—"

"I *know*," Lady Amelia interrupted. She cut Kye off before the huntress could ramp up. "This room is kept unknown. It is guarded by both physical and magical means." The knight commander glanced back at the now-open safe. In the middle of the metal box sat an equally empty holder for some kind of vial or sample. Lady Amelia clenched her jaw. "The package *was* here. But it isn't anymore."

I heard the force in every word—the anger bubbling just under the surface. She hadn't been expecting the package to go missing, then. She'd expected to come into this room, retrieve it, and send us on our way. I could see it all in the stunned concern painted between the lines on her face. She'd *wanted* to deliver it, I realized. And yet…

Unease scratched at my neck. I sneered, grasping for my sword as I strained myself. Perking my ears and sharpening my eyes, the unease only heightened its presence. Something was off.

And I could tell I wasn't the only one to feel it either. Beside me, Kye stopped as well. Her glare softened toward the knight commander and she leaned back. Light air drifted out from her only a moment later as energy swirled in her eyes and she started casting. As she started straining her ears and concentrating on… something.

A slam.

My blood ran cold, flooding with white-hot steel as I whipped around. My fingers tightened around the hilt of my sword, tearing it out of its scabbard as quickly as I could. Scanning the other side of the room, I took a deep breath. I was *not* getting caught off guard this time.

Flicking my eyes to the wooden door, I furrowed my brow. It was… closed.

Motionless and undisturbed, exactly as we'd left it when we'd entered. There was nobody there. Nobody who had entered. Though, possibly someone who had exited. The simple fact that I didn't *know*, though, was what irked me the most. I gritted my teeth and hunched over, battle stances already playing before my eyes.

"*You mortals never learn,*" a voice whispered. Cold, sinister, and ever-present. I shuddered, going rigid as the words both echoed off the walls and off the inside of my skull. It wormed its way into my consciousness and taunted me. I bit down harder, trying to shrug the sound away.

Steeling myself, I dragged my gaze across the room as smoothly as possible. I searched every shadow, corner, or crevice I could find. Yet... there wasn't anyone there.

"*Doing what you do... it cannot go unpunished,*" the voice whispered again. It enveloped the entire space, staying at the same volume despite pressing in from all sides. I pursed my lips, latching onto its words as best that I could. Partially so that I could understand what it was saying, but also so that I could picture its source and imagine tearing them to shreds. But no matter how much I focused on it, I couldn't find anything else. No other information or direction that it—

The corner.

I froze, darting my eyes over. There, appearing almost out of thin air to lean against the wall like he'd gotten bored of existence, was a man. Tall with tanned skin and fiery red hair, the man leered. His eyes flicked over to us, glaring and holding our collective attention in the palm of his hand.

My eyes widened. My heart thundered. My mind spun, lurching into action as I scanned over the man to take stock of his form. After all, I had no idea of how long he'd even stay in the physical world. Judging from his standard cloth pants and a tunic that were both lined in sharp orange, he almost looked ordinary. That connection stopped as soon as I saw his ash-black boots that appeared to wriggle around on their own. I swallowed, my gut tying into knots. Then, as if on cue, the man gestured out to all of us, pointing with metal gauntlets that looked to be made of permanently scorched steel.

I clenched my jaw. My breathing accelerated. No matter how long I stared at the arrogant man, the dangerous flash in his eyes didn't go away. The piercing contrast of his blue irises tore through my soul as though he already knew everything about me.

Well, everything about *him* made me sick.

"Who the hell are you?" someone said behind me. I turned, recognizing Lady Amelia as she cocked her head.

The red-haired man chuckled, the sound worming into my consciousness like a parasite. I turned, watching as he took his sweet time to respond. "I would say that is none of your concern… But I guess it really is, isn't it?"

"So who the fuck are you?" Kye asked. Her eyes flared with energy as she casted furiously, already notching an arrow in her bow.

The man didn't chuckle this time. He only stared for a moment. Mocking. Baiting. Taunting us with the simple fact that he was alive. "My name is Keris, if that is what you were requesting. But I feel like you would like more." None of us showed a response to that. We didn't offer an ounce of satisfaction.

Keris' smirk dropped as he watched us carefully. The blue in his eyes sharpened. "I am here to correct an injustice," he said, cutting straight through his own bullshit. "You took something from the mother, and I am simply allowing it to be returned." He leered, burning hatred punctuating his gaze. "And making sure it is not taken again."

I stopped, stepping back half in confusion and half under the weight of his stare. Taking a breath, I ventured it was more of the former. Because I didn't know who the hell the red-haired man was and yet he was accusing me. He was claiming that I'd stolen something from him when I'd done nothing of the sort.

I blinked and shook my head. The realization came down like a crumbling mountain.

Kye appeared to come to the same conclusion. She whipped back toward Lady Amelia and growled. "What exactly *was* that package?"

Lady Amelia hesitated, her eyes flicking back and forth between the ranger and the imposing man. Grinding her teeth, she stepped toward us. "Dragon's blood," she whispered.

The world around me slowed. It ground to a screeching halt as her words echoed in my head, bringing up too many related ideas to count. Dragon's blood? How did they get dragon's blood? I swallowed, only adding to the lump in my throat. Why did Arathorn *need* dragon's blood?

Beside me, Kye straightened up. She swallowed her curses and drew the arrow in her bow further back, still aiming at the intruding man.

"Too much of it, too," a voice said right next to me. I jumped, snapping my head back to the actual threat in the room. The man—Keris, he'd called himself—grinned. "It does not fare well for you to be getting on her bad side when *her ire is so near.*"

A brief, splitting wave of mental pain. It sliced through my brain like a million pinpricks before falling away and leaving confusion and anger in its wake. I glared at Keris, the hairs on my neck standing on end. Something about what he'd said was... wrong. Shaking my head at all of it, I let my eyes bore into the grey cloth of his tunic.

Keris chuckled, the laugh morphing into a demonic cackle in short time. "Although," he started, rolling his metal-clad wrist. "You are almost no threat to me. As I am sure you would all agree."

The corners of his lips tweaked upward. A motionless glass vial shattered across the room. I flicked my eyes to it, fighting them not to widen too far. Keris' lips tweaked downward again, and another vial broke in time.

"Then let us leave," Kye said, her voice slowly losing life as the man revealed the extent of his power. The dread I'd felt before ceased being an itch and transformed into a scar that reminded me all too well of how screwed we all are.

Instead of giving a response, Keris laughed. His laugh warped into a cackle. The color of his eyes changed, shifting out of piercing blue at the edges and turning to a color that reminded me only of an undying flame. And then his cackle picked up, booming throughout the room as my vision was filled with light.

CHAPTER TWENTY-TWO

Blood roared in my ears as the flames moved toward me.

A frozen second in time hung in the air. It was as if the world was waiting for my reaction, teetering on the edge of its seat to gauge whether or not I would get scorched alive or make it out with minimal burn. As the fire of battle flooded my veins, I studied the real fire in front of me. I watched the writhing ball of it— tinged with red and flaring with energy. Its heat licked at the surface of my skin, taunting me with pain that was sure to come. But as my mind spun uselessly in the void between thoughts, I knew it couldn't last forever. I had to decide before the world got fed up with watching at all.

My chest was pressed to the floor before I could think anything else. The ball of fire exploded against the stone behind me, flaring in a flash of light lined in red. Thoughts still spinning, my instincts carried me faster than my thoughts. Briefly I felt a searing pain on the side of my head along with the vile smell of smoke. Of burning hair, I realized. Without giving in to the pain, I swatted it out and gritted my teeth.

Flicking my eyes up, I saw Keris still laughing. His wicked, incessant cackle rang out in the room. It echoed off the walls and whispered in my ears at the same time. I shook the sound away, forcing myself to focus. Whatever Keris was, I already hated him from the depths of my gut. No matter what he'd said amid the arrogant warnings and diabolical laughter, he'd stolen something from *us*. He'd attacked *us*. He was going to pay for it.

I swallowed, staggering to a stand. Wiping dust and char off the cloth of my uniform, I felt sweat trickling down my back. In an instant, a shudder wracked my body as I realized it was becoming hotter. With Keris' continued laughter, the air itself was erupting with heat. I cursed to myself and scanned the room for anything useful.

The flick of a bowstring. I turned, catching an object flying through the air from alongside me. The same sound repeated only a moment later. Arrows. Kye was firing arrows.

I watched the blurs streak toward Keris. An unsuspecting target, as far as I was concerned. The man's eyes were still sealed shut as he laughed, after all. Then, however, I heard the sound of wood breaking and metal grinding on rock. My smile dropped.

Turning, Keris flashed me a grin. The same, fiery intent lined the outer rim of his piercing eyes, but I didn't get much time to consider his changing physicality. Without another thought, he pointed a metal-clad finger at me.

My mind stopped. The world around me spun uselessly before I could figure out what had happened. I was running, I realized at some point, with my blade gripped tight and my eyes darting over the room from form to form.

Then my brain caught up. My senses reacted at the same time, warning me of the red glow emanating from under my feet and the flames licking at my heels. With a jolt of mortal fear, I pushed on even faster. I dodged around wooden tables and chairs while my mind raced. As it started to all click back into place, I saw Kye running opposite me, on the other side of the room. Scrambling as she went to notch another arrow in her bow.

A sound behind me stopped my line of thought. Metal skidding on rock, I recognized. In an instant, I knew what it was. The knights. They were here too, I reminded myself. It wasn't just us. But as my eyes flicked back to Keris, that didn't feel like much consolation. The furious, fiery eyes were on me. A growl rose out of my throat. I swerved, ducking past another table as a large form flashed in the corner of my eye. A man draped in metal armor while holding something high over his head. I barely got time to process the image before it left my periphery.

Thunderous footsteps rang off the room's stone walls. Finally wavering, Keris' eyes moved from me and toward the hammer-wielding brute. Flicking my gaze back, I smiled as Rik raised his hammer even more. A sneer formed at Keris' lips and he stepped forward, flexing his fingers too ready for the attack.

I pushed harder, forcing my tired body forward. Keris was close now. Only a few paces away. Eyeing him, I could see his guard was up. He was ready for an attack, but I had to try anyway. I had to execute the maneuvers flooding my head —because I didn't want to know what Keris would have time to do if I didn't.

Swallowing my fear, I swung.

My sword shot out. Steel sliced through the air as I brought it down, stopping halfway and twisting my body around. The movement wrenched my wrist, sending a volley of pained signals to my brain, but it was worth it. He would've tried to block, I reminded myself. But my blade would already be somewhere else.

I strained my muscles as I forced metal up under Keris' guard. Or, what I'd *thought* to be under Keris' guard. When I felt the solid, immovable contact rippling through my arm, though, I wasn't so sure. My eyes bloomed. I wheeled backward, kicking against the stone to force myself away. But with his metal gauntlets, the pyromancer didn't have a hard time keeping his grip.

The sharp scraping of steel on steel echoed through the room. I tore my blade backward, my muscles shrieking. It wasn't enough, and Keris just threw my sword away with another cackle. I stumbled to the ground, my balance and grip slipping. The blade of my sword clattered to the floor beside me.

"You must understand that I am mightier than you," he said. I didn't look up as the words poured into my ears. "Right?"

The stone beneath me burned. It erupted into heat and I scrambled, grinding my teeth and grabbing my sword. I did *not* want to get torched again. I staggered up, my feet in protest as they found solid ground. All the while, though, the red-tined glow grew ever-brighter.

Then it went out.

I blinked, weight slipping from my shoulders. A loud clash of metal rang out and the heat was gone. I spared a sincere and grateful prayer to the world before retrieving my sword and pushing myself as far away from the crazed pyromancer as I could.

After only a second or two of running, my body slid on stone. Before I even knew what I was doing, I twisted my head back. But unlike… whatever I'd expected, I only caught an eyeful of wood. I'd slid behind a table.

The loud clang rang out again, more broken this time; my respite was gone. I cringed at the sound. My ears whined with overstimulation, complaining in the same way the rest of my body did.

I sighed. Then collected myself and lifted my head out above the table to scan the room. This time from a different angle—and, more importantly, out of mortal danger. Instantly, I saw Keris. The smug, furious expression that turned strained at the edges as he held up a hammer being forced upon him. Vibrations shot through his arms, ruffling the grey cloth. And as he fought to resist, his legs looked near buckling.

Movement flashed in the corner of my eye. I turned, my eyes narrowing on the second knight—Vlad. He was running toward the fight with his gloriously-cut longsword at the ready. Pure determination etched itself into his features and, as though bored, his fingers drummed on the sword's elegant crossguard.

A loud growl brought me back. It reminded me of the immediate threat, especially as the temperature spiked in the air around me. My burning skin pleaded, but I didn't pay it any mind. As my gaze snapped back to Keris, I *couldn't* pay it any mind. Despite Rik's best efforts, Keris pushed out. The brute of a knight went stumbling backward. Pure, unbidden shock tore the previously-giddy knight's resolve to shreds.

A new understanding of Keris grew in my head as I watched him stand there, seething. It was not an understanding I enjoyed.

Rising as a thought from desperation, I tried to reach to the back of my mind. I attempted to grasp for the white-hot power I'd felt all those weeks ago when on the brink of death. The presence in my head shifted, shying away from my probing attention. The sight of the battle in front of me didn't help, either. All that did was impose a sort of mortal fear that paralyzed it, forcing the heat to go cold.

Cursing, I shook my head with gritted teeth. I had to stay alive on my own.

In the center of the room, Vlad ran in next. He stared down the flame-haired man with blank eyes and slashed out. I winced, already expecting it when Keris shot out his hand, ready to catch the strike with metal gauntlets. But the strike never came. Surprise bloomed on my eyes as I watched Vlad duck to the side. His feet carried him with an unnatural level of finesse, twisting into Keris' peripheral vision before he leapt into the air.

For a moment, the look on Vlad's face changed. His stoic shell cracked and a grimace shined through as he flew. In an action that seemed impossible, the knight kicked his foot out and pushed off of nothing. It was as if the world behind him had crystalized into a platform just so that he could haul his blade down from above.

My mind whirred for a moment, replaying the last second. The movement flashed over and over, sticking out like a sore thumb. Though, even as awe washed over me in waves, I didn't get time to rest. Heat around me rose once more and held me up by the throat. Keris threw his scorched gloves up recklessly in an attempt to block the strike. But as the blade came down, all he could do was save himself more damage. His arrogance earned him a shiny red cut on his cheek.

"You insolent..." he started, the words sounding distant this time. They didn't trickle into my ear with all of the concentrated conceit I'd come to expect. The pyromancer's eyes flared dangerously—and Vlad seemed to notice. The stoic knight backpedaled, throwing his blade up to block, but the movement was only half-effective as Keris' hands covered with tendrils of red flame.

"It is unwise to interfere with things you do not understand."

A flash of light consumed my vision. The next thing I knew, Vlad was surging backward, grunting in pain as flames scorched his armor. A second later, the fire cleared, and Keris lunged through it already swinging. My eyes barely tracked the flame-trailed movements. Faster than human, Keris' fists came down to leave charred dents in Vlad's plate.

The defending knight retreated, quickly turning it into a run. He left Keris standing among the heat by himself, a satisfied smirk draped in pain decorated on his face. The crazed energy the pyromancer still had sent a shiver down my sweat-soaked spine. I shook my head and cleared my thoughts for the moment. Fear would get me nowhere. I had to remember that. Instead, I furrowed my brows, strained my ears, and focused on the other thing I'd noticed in the room.

Kye.

Dozens of paces away, the huntress darted backward. She narrowed her eyes and watched Keris carefully, readying an arrow in her bow. As soon as the vile man opened his mouth, she let that arrow go. It streamed through the air for only a second before a truly irritated grunt sounded in its wake.

Darting my eyes over, I saw a blackened gauntlet move to his chest. Keris tore the arrow out only a moment later, the confidence on his face not wavering in the slightest.

"Nuisances," he said, his voice low and firm. A trickle of blood poured out of the wound, but Keris didn't mind. With a fire that he created on his finger, he cauterized the bleeding hole and discarded the arrow on the ground.

"Just nuisances," he repeated without hesitation.

I swallowed, my skin sweltering and my throat drying. The longer I watched the insane fire-mage, the worse it got. The more the breadth of his power expanded before me and cemented a singular thought that I had been *trying* to ignore for the entire fight.

Spurred on, I forced myself to think. We needed a plan, obviously, and we needed one quick. Or we needed *something* at least. We couldn't sit where we were for long. All that did was make Keris angrier, and the fact that his power appeared unfaltering at that terrified me.

I *also* realized that I had to move. Even if I didn't have a plan immediately, I couldn't hide behind a table forever. Especially not one made of wood. So, taking a deep breath, I rose to my feet.

As I'd expected, Kye was in the same spot. In the middle of the room, the two knights were engaging Keris again—clashing in shrieks of metal and being pushed back by plumes of flame. I cursed under my breath, tearing my gaze away before I became too entrenched in the scene. Instead, I focused on the back of the room—on Lady Amelia. She stood completely immobile, her face carefully passive as she looked on.

I blinked, trying to refresh the world as though that would've nullified the sight. It didn't. If anything, it only made my doubt rise higher while I watched her. Distantly, my own paranoid dread whispered to me and tore up images of betrayal. Yet even as a hand fell to my blade, I didn't buy it. With the tight, terse look on her face, she didn't look in the spirit to be a traitor. She looked, in fact, more like she was preparing something. And her eyes led directly to Keris.

My anger melted away with a single breath. As I stepped forward, a loud ringing sound resonated throughout the room and came followed by a screaming grunt. Alertness poured down my spine with the realization that I had to *move*. On instinct, I surged, my intended destination forming a moment later.

Keris was distracted. I knew that he was—the mess of metal clangs and grunts told me enough—and Lady Amelia had a plan. Whatever she was doing while standing stock-still and watching all of us sweat and blister, I hoped it was worth it. In the mean time, I just had to survive. And that meant only one thing.

My metal boots beat against the stone floor as I scrambled across the room, side-eyeing the knight commander. I didn't even bother looking over at the fight. It wouldn't have been any use to me anyway. The noises were enough to tell me it was still raging, and as long as I heard them, Keris wasn't coming after *me*.

Lady Amelia didn't budge. As I looked over her for a frozen moment, I could only narrow my eyes. I could swear I saw it again—the denting of rock underneath her feet.

Kye was searching through her quiver when I arrived. She snapped her gaze up to me before twisting back toward the fight. She was keeping an eye on it, then, as her fingers thumbed past arrows. Every few moments, she would raise one up before tossing it right back down. As soon as I slowed next to her, she clenched her jaw and bit back a cruse of annoyance.

"What are you looking for?" I asked, my voice carrying more like a hiss.

She didn't bother to look at me. "I was looking for any arrows that could be useful. But so far I've found jack *shit*." She kicked her foot against the stone, wrapping fingers around her bow.

My eyebrows shot up. "Useful arrows? Are the pointed ones not enough?"

She shook her head. "I mean *imbued* arrows," she said as though the term meant anything to me. Vaguely, I remembered rangers mentioning it here and there during preparations for hunts, but I'd never bothered to learn more. I wasn't an archer, after all. "I got Lorah to work on some before we left, but *apparently* I used all of them up last night."

I shuddered, remembering the dark forest and the feral kanir. Waves of disgust and fear washed up from the back of my head. After she'd killed it, Kye had said something about sunlight arrows—a statement I hadn't questioned back then. Now I almost regretted it.

I shook my head, gesturing to Keris as he burned a split piece of wood and threw it in Rik's face. "Do you know who the hell *that* is?"

Whatever passion had been left on Kye's dropped. She scowled instead. "No. He said his name was… Keris, but I've never heard that in my life. Not even in legend." She coughed once, the lines in the corner of her eye sharpening. "Even though with that kind of magical stamina, he almost reminds me of a mythical hero."

I swallowed, trying to ignore the torrid air as I glanced back at Keris. Another flash of red-tinged flame erupted from his hand before Rik got the message and leapt backward. The previously-confident knight cursed and coughed. Keris' eyes just continued showing that same color of an undying flame.

He had to slow down at some point... didn't he?

My question was interrupted by more movement. Vlad reared away from the flames, regained his composure, and slashed again. Keris growled, the haunting sound echoing in my ears as he jumped back. The swipe of Vlad's steel missed him by inches. A wicked smile grew on the pyromancer's lips before it was quite literally blown off.

Keris stumbled, a gust of air washing over him. Red hair ruffled backward and caught the madman off guard. The slim, stoic knight twisted and sliced again, forcing as much concentration as he could into a blade of air that actually made Keris curse in pain.

"Dammit," Kye said, ripping my thoughts away. "That won't be enough. This guy has more stamina than anybody I've ever seen."

I could only nod at that, staring in horror for a second longer while Keris matched Vlad with every flick of the blade. He caught them all and rolled forward in a surge of fire. The longer I watched, the more my hope dwindled.

"I don't know what we *can* do," Kye spat, breathing heavily as air regained its weight in her vicinity. She took a step back as she stopped casting, wincing and rubbing her forehead. "And it's not like *she* is doing anything."

I knew who the huntress meant without asking. "She has a plan," I said with a nod that confirmed the statement with more belief than I had. It would have to be enough, I decided.

Kye snorted derisively. "How would you know?"

"I just know," I said, forcing weight into my words and leaving no room for argument. Kye seemed to hear it too as she straightened. I took a shallow breath and prayed to the world that I wasn't lying. Because if I was, we were in even more trouble than I already thought.

"Well," Kye started, nearly wheezing in the oppressive heat. "What the fuck do we do now?"

Turning back, I opened my mouth to respond, but nothing came out. In truth, I really didn't have an answer. I really didn't know. There was a vague idea in my head about tactics and distractions, but it fell flat. It didn't feel like it applied in a fight filled with unending flurries of magic. Not in a fight where we were so seriously outmatched.

In my old body, I was sure I could've done more. I could've danced around the pyromancer and tricked him with maneuvers executed so perfectly he would've tripped over himself. I could've gotten the upper hand if I'd focused. Now… I wasn't so sure. I was stronger than I'd been weeks ago, sure, but not strong *enough*. I didn't trust my faulty muscles with the life they protected.

I couldn't face the beast again so soon. Not like this.

"Maybe nothing," I said, still eyeing the two knights that were keeping the fire-mage occupied. They were slowing down noticeably—succumbing to the heat, their injuries, and exhaustion. But they were also fairing rather well together against Keris. They were doing some damage, at least.

"Nothing?" Kye asked. I assumed she'd meant the question to be pointed, but it fell short as she coughed. "He looks occupied, maybe even strained at this point, but I'm not convinced. They won't last for long—and from the looks of it, his flames aren't running out anytime soon."

I nodded shallowly, the sounds of their battle overwhelming even my pounding pulse as I watched. My eyes flicked across their forms and tracked every movement. Studying. Analyzing. Waiting for any kind of opening.

Shrieks of resonant metal echoed through the room. Rik growled, having already discarded his levity. He pushed forward with his hammer and forced through Keris' guard. Only for the knight to be pushed away in a flash of fire a second later.

Vlad came running in right after, continuing the dynamic the two had started on. He pushed off crystalized air behind him and flew with all the force he could muster, a trembling whirlwind of air circling his straight blade.

The pyromancer staggered, coughing air for a moment before he turned back. Vlad was ready, though, and he sliced his blade out without the need for magic. Keris was barely fast enough, ducking under the strike and hauling the knight away as cut strands of red hair fell through the air. Vlad went tumbling.

Keris smiled, teetering in place. His fierce eyes faltered for a moment, flitting as he tried to keep balance. But unfortunately for us, there was no one to take advantage. No one was close enough or ready enough to do damage to his unguarded state. Even when Kye notched another arrow in her bow, it was already too late.

The heat in the room soared higher. Sweat spilled off my skin, matting the blue cloth of my uniform with grime and soot. Keris' lips ticked carefully upward, and with each moment, the ferocity returned. It stretched even further than before as blood trickled down his nose and he stared toward the ceiling. The faint, fiery image of something incomprehensibly terrifying floated in the air behind him.

Then it was gone.

Whatever he'd done had finished. He'd become even more crazed than normal. Even more powerful than normal, I was forced to realize. As tendrils of flame wrapped around his body, culminating in bright red bursts on his fingers, I knew something horrible had changed.

"*Imbeciles,*" he said, but his lips didn't move. The word simply radiated through my mind like one of my own thoughts had gone rogue.

I shook it off, pushing away the terror and taking a step back. I darted my eyes back toward Lady Amelia. She stared at the pyromancer wide-eyed before redoubling her focus and pressing her feet into the ground.

She still had a plan. She needed to focus. We needed to *let* her focus. We needed to buy her time.

I swallowed, my mouth a desolate wasteland as I gathered courage. "Cover me!" I yelled back at Kye as my body lurched. In the corner of my eye, I saw her turn to me. But I didn't stay to see her reaction. I didn't have time to.

My legs screamed at me to stop. They screamed in tandem with the fear and dread still circling in my head to turn back. They tried to get me to falter—to fall, even, as it would've been preferable to getting my face burned off. I didn't listen to them, of course. I knew better than that. There was no place for any of us to flee, and if we didn't do something now, we would all meet each other as plumes of smoke. No. I kept my body moving with an iron grip and just prayed to the world that luck was on our side.

A moment later, an arrow shrieked past me. It sliced through air like butter and would've pierced Keris in the face had he been any normal soul. Unfortunately for us, however, he was a far cry from such a description. He dodged to the side easily with a scowl on his face. As soon as he did, another arrow came through and forced him to do the exact same thing.

Cursing, he turned toward Kye. He directed the full brunt of his rage at her and sent pillars of searing flame in her direction. My heart froze for a moment as she yelped, but I just had to hope the sounds erupting behind me belonged more against the stone wall than against my companion's charred flesh.

I tried not to think about it much. I needed to keep my focus ahead.

That was exactly what I did. Sweeping in as dexterously as I could, I swung my sword from the side. Keris turned to me a moment too late, his eyes flaring with rage and confusion before reaching his hands out. But my maneuver hadn't been that simple.

No. I stopped myself in place and spun, stepping around to angle another strike up against the side of his leg. Sweltering air streamed around me and, before I knew it, my blade had gotten stuck in something. Without bothering to figure out what it was, I pushed forward. Keris screamed in agony before the hilt of my blade started to burn my hand.

Blinking, I leapt back. I let go of the sword only for it to start glowing red-hot. Keris stared down at it and ripped the burning steel from its lodging in his leg. It erupted in flames before he slammed it into the wall behind him. Then, without even waiting for my reaction, he stepped toward me.

A flash of light. A hand against my chest. A hellish cacophony of pain.

I hit the ground *hard*. My body skidded on stone while jolts of torment tore through my spine and up to my already aching head. The world spun fleetingly around me as I slipped from control. As the exhaustion's roots took hold and dragged me deeper and deeper.

"Simply a nuisance," I heard Keris say as my eyes flitted.

I'd given them a chance, I told myself with whatever conscious thought I could retain. He'd been distracted long enough with my attack. They had to do something. *Someone* had to do something.

A clash of metal. A gust of wind. An explosion of flame.

Keris cackled, the noise still filtering into my ears even if my brain could hardly make heads or tails of it. "You—" he started.

The ground shook.

I coughed and lurched upward, ice-cold fear forcing lucidity upon me. Glancing up at Keris, though, he looked just as confused. He took multiple tentative steps while staring at the stone below him—only for it to shape in a single frozen instant and grow into shackles that kept him stiff and immobile.

That sight was enough to calm my fear. My body slumped back, resting against the heated rock as the world spiraled away.

The sound of metal footsteps. Yelling. A few sighs of relief.

"You," a voice said. Lady Amelia, I noted lazily. "How did you break in here without consequence?"

"What is this?" asked another voice. Keris, I assumed based on its erratic, raspy quality. "How does one control the world itself with their magic?"

A silent moment of satisfaction as footsteps passed my ears and toward the trapped man.

"How did you get in here without consequence?" Lady Amelia repeated.

A laugh. One that sounded far too sinister.

"You cannot disgrace her children and ask questions about the punishments," Keris said.

"How did you *steal* it," Lady Amelia asked, the iron in her voice raising me from the depths of the dark abyss for a moment.

A soft, restrained yelp.

"You should not…" Keris started, his voice shaking. "You should *not*…" His tone ramped up in both severity and volume this time. A belated look of horror dawned over my faint features before I could even see what was going on.

"Not *what*?" Lady Amelia asked. "Am I going to require further action?"

A cackle. One as recognizable as it was terrifying.

"Further action shall most certainly be necessary."

Heat. Smoke. Choking, blistering air. I couldn't breathe. I couldn't think. My body was dying—slipping far into the void. Sizzling and tearing. Cracks through rock. Something exploded in front of me. It sent me tumbling a few paces. I felt

206

pain, but a white flame came to heal me. It coddled me. I didn't understand.

"Where did he go?" a strained voice asked. I couldn't discern its source.

More smoke filled my lungs. It mixed in with all the rest, hazing together in a grey fog that blocked out thoughts. I tried to cough it out. My body wouldn't listen. I grasped tight for my sword. I realized too late that it wasn't there.

I was dying, I told myself as my consciousness drifted. Falling. Draining. Twitching in too much pain. I saw the visage of the beast—its silver scythe was there waiting for me. I couldn't stop it. I couldn't face it now. Yet I had no other choice. It was happening all the same. The abyss came to swallow me up.

I just hoped the darkness would be nice.

CHAPTER TWENTY-THREE

I awoke far too slowly.

Darkness swirled around my mind. I floated before it, waxing and waning between stray beams of light hitting my eyes. Or, I assumed they were hitting my eyes. As I felt consciousness come back at a snail's pace, I wasn't really sure about anything. All I felt was an odd emptiness—one lined with frigid cold. It enveloped me and forced my soul down as if telling me I wasn't ready to be alive.

I didn't challenge its orders at first. There was no need. Even with the cold, I didn't mind it all that much. It wasn't as though I could feel anything. It wasn't as though I even remembered the concept of *feeling*. No. I just floated there. Still. Content. Alone.

Until I wasn't.

A flicker of light was the only sign I got that something had changed. White and warm, it felt close to me. And this time, it came with sound. The soft and comforting crackle of flame. I turned toward it—as best as a soul could turn in directionless blackness. The white flame flickered, wavering as it stared at me. For some reason, it felt familiar, but remembering why took too much effort. I adjusted my attention and watched it instead because it was more interesting than the dull blackness was.

Yet the longer I watched it, the more aware I become. The more full the emptiness felt. Its waves of white-hot warmth melted away the cold and pulled me up. They washed over me like crashing waves—making me lucid enough to even realize what waves were. Its warmth spread out through my soul and equalized until it was sure I was alive.

The little flame dwindled right after. Its flaring tongues calmed until the darkness swallowed it up and I felt its presence recede. I felt it flee into the back of my head as though it had only come out to make sure that I was alright.

As soon as the last scraps of light were gone, I jolted up.

My head pounded. My body ached. And yet, I felt alright. I felt I could breathe again instead of coughing up smoke. I could lie back onto something soft and comfortable instead of a burning stone floor.

A burning stone floor that Keris had ignited, I remembered. Pulses of pain washed in with my memories, replaying them in front of my eyes one-by-one until I couldn't take it anymore. Shaking myself slightly, I creaked open my eyes.

Haze. That was all I saw for a second as the world seemingly stumbled over itself in deciding what the space around me looked like. After a while, the fog started to clear. The stone pillars and wooden tables rose out of the blur. A soft golden glow mixing in with what I could only assume to be evening twilight descended over the room. Blinking some more, I recognized the infirmary bed below me and the desks on the other side of the room.

I was still in the apothecary's guild.

That realization brought a sigh along with it. And with that sigh, I slumped back. I let my head fall onto the stiff pillow that still felt like heaven to my overworked muscles. My body settled back, letting tension out and forcing me to realize how sore I was instead.

I grimaced, nodding silently to myself as I remembered what I was feeling. The dull, hollow soreness that would persist in my muscles for however long it took them to get used to the fact that they were whole again. It was the drain of healing. A good thing, really. I'd felt the same way after Galen had healed me in the lodge. Though, this time I supposed I wouldn't have to go make a deal with Arathorn directly after waking up.

A chuckle slipped through my lips. My chest rose with it and sent me a jolt of agonizing pain originating in my ribs. I cringed, freezing in place before lowering myself down onto the cushion of the bed.

"World's dammit," I muttered to myself. In truth, I didn't know whether the exclamation was more aimed at my body or the events that had hurt it in the first place. Probably both, I ventured while relaxing my neck. I shifted myself into the most comfortable position I could find to sleep off the soreness and be ready for action the next time I woke up.

I barely got ten seconds of respite.

"Oh! Look who's awake," a new voice said. Cheerful and masculine, I recognized as I raised my head to glare at whoever dared disturb me. My bitterness fell away as I saw the beaming man in singed white robes. An apothecary.

"Yeah," I mustered, my face contorting. "How long was I out for?"

"Hours," the apothecary said. "And that was *after* the healing, which took almost two hours by itself." The man inclined his head to me as he spoke. I got the message rather quickly.

My head bobbed a firm nod. "Thank you," I said. "I guess I'm fortunate this all happened in an apothecary's guild rather than a shop or simply out in the street."

The apothecary's smile softened at that and he nodded again. Light air rolled off him as he walked up to the side of my bed. When he let a hand down on my shoulder to impose the blissful warmth of healing, I really did have to be grateful. After the abyss had taken me in its grasp, I could only assume the apothecaries had taken care of all of us. I had to give them respect for that.

"I'm Marr, by the way," the man above me said. "I'm one of the healers on duty at the moment—and I'm the one that had to drag you into this bed for treatment."

I sighed, nodding a fleeting thanks to him.

"Right," another voice said. Not Marr, this time. I turned, the warm feeling working its way down toward my chest and repairing the stiff flesh that was still damaged there. I blinked away the oncoming haze to see another apothecary glaring green eyes at me.

No. She wasn't glaring at me. She was glaring at Marr.

"Don't even start, Rina," Marr said. Glancing back at him, the cheerfulness was almost entirely gone and replaced with a tight expression that reminded me of a sibling rivalry.

As the woman apparently name Rina walked up, though, I had a hard time believing the two were related. "Start what?" she asked, her voice calm and uninterested. "I'd just like to add that you weren't the only healer who worked at this bed."

My brow furrowed. I shook my head, glancing back to Rina. She eyed me, a slight smile rising at her lips. Had she healed me too?

"I didn't claim anything of the sort," Marr shot back. Air heaved around me as he lifted his hand from my shoulder and folded his arms. A pulse of fatigue shot straight up my spine.

In the side of my vision, I saw Rina open her mouth again, but I didn't let her start. I was already shaking my head. "Why were there two healers attending to me in the first place?"

My expression darkened. Back in Credon, I'd normally only had a single healer attend to me day after day while I'd recovered from battle wounds. Depending on the severity, another healer had joined on occasion to make sure I'd been in the best shape. But the healers in Ruia were far superior to the ones I'd interacted with back home. And then, I'd been a high-knight—somebody deserving of as many healers as could be available. But here? As a ranger?

Marr was the first to make a sound after my question hung in the air. He chuckled. "You *needed* it, in all honesty. Your injuries were the worst out of the bunch, all things considered. Burned skin, blunt bruises, more cuts and scrapes than you have fingers and toes." I held up a hand to the man and nodded, hoping he'd stop. He didn't. "And I bet you didn't know you broke three ribs back there."

I froze, my fingers twitching in the air. As if on cue, a wave of soreness washed over my chest. I winced, lying back. "No... I didn't know that."

"Well you did," came Rina's far less enthusiastic tone. "You're lucky we could fix you up as soon as we did. You were top priority because of how bad it would have been for all of us if you hadn't made it."

For a moment, her statement made sense. Then though, as I was reminded of my new life, I furrowed my brow. "Why was *I* top priority?"

Rina turned, shaking her head slightly at me as though she didn't believe I'd asked the question at all. "You're a ranger aren't you?"

"Yeah," I said, nodding slowly. Still, I didn't see how a lowly ranger could have been deserving of such treatment when actual *knights* had been injured almost as severely.

Rina flicked her wrist. "You're a representative of Sarin. And even if such basic concepts evade common folk, it's simple diplomacy that you don't send back representatives crippled or dead."

Oh. Color drained from my face as I slumped back further, recognizing what she'd said. Whether it made sense to me or not, she was right. Retrieving Arathorn's package *was* a diplomatic mission—almost reminiscent of the royal work I'd done for my king's court.

"We were told to get the rangers taken care of first," Marr added as he walked around toward the foot-end of my bed. "You two are important for this city's relationship with Sarin."

"Hell yeah we are," said a very groggy voice that I would've recognized anywhere. Kye, I realized before immediately turning to my side. Sitting in a wooden chair a few paces to the left of my bed, the huntress was still rising from sleep. She blinked herself alert and ran a hand through her messy hair.

Rina shot Kye a hard glance, scrunching her face and offering a sardonic smile. "And we can't sour that relationship. Sarin is where we get all our grain." She then made her way over to another bed.

"Right," Marr chimed in. "It is quite hard to grow grain out of the stone of a mountain!" He shrugged lightly and squinted at Kye for a second. The huntress waved him off dismissively as she stifled a yawn. "Plus, the Lady gave rather resolute orders after we managed to get open that back door to investigate."

"Orders to save face," Kye muttered. I turned to her, raising an eyebrow as she straightened up in her chair. "Orders to maintain pretty political partnerships. Nothing else."

I shrugged, unable to stop the grin growing across my lips. "Maybe... But it got us healed, anyway. We have to respect that, at least."

Kye grumbled something unsavory under her breath before simply nodding. Shaking herself fully alert, she turned to me and brushed locks of chestnut hair from in front of her eyes. The smirk rose up before she'd even started talking. "I guess we do partially. But I'd give more credit to the actual apothecaries who healed us." In the corner of my eye, Marr perked up.

"That would make sense," I said, my eyes narrowing on her and the wooden chair she was sitting on. "Why didn't you get a bed, by the way?"

Kye raised an eyebrow. "I did. You think I would've let them heal me in this thing?" She gestured down to the split wood of one of the chair's four legs. "No. My injuries were child's play compared to what you brought on yourself." I didn't miss the flash of pearly whites with that. "I was back on my sore ass feet after less than an hour. But they wouldn't let me out of this place, so I came over here to check on you. Out of boredom."

I nodded slowly, not entirely convinced. "Then you fell asleep in that chair?"

Kye shrugged. "Fatigue doesn't play around." She brushed a hand over her forehead, rubbing the side of her temple as if to relieve a headache. "And neither does soul drain."

"I suppose there are some benefits to not being a mage," I said before the rational part of my addled mind could catch the comment. I knew it wasn't proper—and that there really were more advantages to the use of magic than disadvantages. The dry laugh I got out of Kye made it worth it.

"Right. Because you were in *such* good shape after Keris laid you out."

A chortle bubbled out of my throat before I could catch it. As her words registered in my head, it dropped dead through the air. Phantom pain spread out over my spine and I stretched as though shaking it away. Red-tinged flames flashed in my vision. I cringed, slamming my eyes shut and shaking my head.

Then, turning back to Kye, I opened my mouth to—

A slam echoed through the space. It cut right through my thoughts and drew my attention to the corridor that led out of the building's main space at the back. Toward the back room where a crazed pyromancer had attacked us, I reminded myself.

Solid, metal-clad footsteps followed the sound along with a murmur of voices. My eyes narrowing on the corridor's mouth, I only heard the voices getting louder and louder until the knights producing them walked in. With Lady Amelia at the head, I recognized. My head flooded with questions that I wanted to ask the knight commander. Questions about not only Arathorn's package but also about what we were supposed to return to Sarin with. As dread once again itched at the back of my neck, something told me it was *not* a good idea to return empty-handed.

I'd said it would be an easy task, after all. How hard could retrieving a package realistically have been?

I cursed myself silently before swallowing old ignorance. "Lady Amelia!" I called. "What are—"

The knight commander slowed, turning on her heel and causing the other two knights flanking her to do the same thing. For a moment, she just stared at me with a gaze harsh enough to kill the words at my lips. Then, though, she smiled.

"They're alive, then?" she asked. Marr started to nod to his superior, but Lady Amelia didn't need the confirmation. "Good. Make sure they stay that way."

Without waiting for a response or even watching for a reaction, she continued on. Her small procession of plated warriors barreled through the remaining space and out the building's front door into dusk light. I let my eyebrows drop and curled my fingers into a fist.

"World's dammit," I muttered again. I turned to Kye. "Where are they in such a rush to get to?"

My companion scowled, her hands only barely resisting fists. "Away from *us* is what it looks like." She sat back as her scowl deepened. "I told you the knights don't care."

Her words grated on me, but I had to nod. The disrespect of not even getting a single adequate word in response from the knight commander won out against petty mental complaints about my discipline. "Maybe not."

Walking back over, Rina laughed. She shot me a knowing glance before calming herself and rolling her wrist. "They're going to the Temple to the World," she said. My eyebrows raised. Such a name reminded me of the temples we'd built back in Credon. The elegant monuments we'd constructed in the world's honor and as a way to gain its favor. The more devout among the kingdom's populations had believed those temples had been the reason Credon had flourished for as long as it had. Though, I knew it'd had more to do with our unmatched skill in both military and diplomatic strength.

"Why there?" Kye asked, curiosity winning out over disgust.

"To organize," Rina said, her disinterested tone creeping back. She took a small metal utensil that I didn't recognize from the wooden table next to my bed before walking off. "They're initiating a new plan of attack against cult threats."

A shiver crept down my spine. I swallowed dryly, remembering far too well the threat only one of the cult members had posed to our group. Granted, I had trouble believing there were many other mages of Keris' power on the entire continent, but that didn't mean they weren't still dangerous. Keris had invaded

214

Norn directly in his theft of Arathorn's package. If Ruian tactics were anywhere competent, that would've been treated as an act of war.

"Cult threats…" Kye mumbled to herself. Glancing over, I saw her cross her arms and kick metal boots against the cold stone floor. Her tone was nonchalant on the surface, but I heard the way it wavered.

"If only one of them can do that, world knows they really are a threat," I said.

Kye turned to me, color draining from her cheeks a bit. "Yeah…" She shook her head. "They aren't a threat to *us*, though. The cult lives in the mountains, and they've never threatened Sarin for the entirety of its existence. It's Norn's issue, not ours." Her scowl returned. "We're just unlucky that their activities happened to interfere with our business on this occasion."

I fought back a sneer as her words processed. She was right in one way. Luck had most certainly not been on our side as Keris had nearly melted us alive. But I wasn't convinced that whatever cult they were dealing with in Norn wasn't Sarin's problem. From what I knew, the two towns were allied. In a place as lawless as Ruia, that was a valuable relationship.

Plus, as I replayed the fight over and over, I still couldn't get over Keris' repeated mention of *her ire*. Whatever it was, it only brought fear and waves of mental pain whenever I thought about it. And knowing about Rath—about the legends of a dragon powerful enough to raze mountains… I worried that the issue of the cult was something that would be felt well outside of Norn.

With a torrid swallow, I pushed the thoughts away. They were too much in my tired state. I knew they were important, but… not now.

I asked a question instead. "Kye?" The huntress turned, unknotting parts of her chestnut hair that had been matted at some point during her healing. "What… happened at the end there?"

She froze. Her posture stiffened and she pursed her lips as if the information itself was too dangerous to let out. Eventually, though, she did. "After you went down and started spluttering on the floor… Lady Amelia's plan actually worked." I nodded slowly, working her explanation through the fragmented memories I already had. "For a while, at least. Turned out that the entire time, she'd been focusing on readying the stone. On preparing the world itself to act as a weapon for her." Kye chuckled. "A stone mage, you know. As rare as they are,

I'd never expected a *knight* to have that kind of power."

I sneered, playing it off as a wince instead. "She... she trapped Keris in rock, right?"

Kye bobbed her head. "But then as she tried to get information out of him, he just kept repeating himself. He kept warning us of some ire and ramping up in intensity until his entire body was engulfed in red flame." Kye stopped, her face going pale for a moment. "He exploded out of the rock in a really furious flash and... vanished. I don't know how he did it, but nobody saw him after that. Not even any of the apothecaries who'd been trying to get into the room from the start."

Unease scratched the back of my neck again. Dread built back up in my chest. "He disappeared," I said, "in a puff of smoke."

Kye stared blankly for a second before nodding. "Yeah. And he left us empty-handed. However he took Arathorn's package doesn't really matter now that it's gone. We have to come back from this *simple task* with nothing." I cringed as she shot a glare my way. Then she settled back and sighed. "Though, I still don't know what Arathorn wanted with dragon's blood in the first place."

Kye crumpled with another yawn, letting her words hang in the quiet air for a moment. I didn't respond this time; there weren't words with which to do it. Instead, I just let the silence sit as I thought. I let in the annoying, pestering thoughts that had been eating away at me since the first moment I'd realized Keris' power.

I'd parried Death once. I didn't know if I could do it again. Not with the body I was in, anyway. The first time, I'd been nearly at my peak form. And even then the beast had tricked me. It had thrust me onto another continent to die. I'd only *survived* through my own will and determination. But my life in Ruia wasn't temporary. It wasn't something that would end and eventually lead me back to the kingdom that I loved.

No. Things were different now. I had to remember that. On the corrupted continent, I had to face even more danger than I'd faced as a high-knight. And, I supposed, I had a lot to lose by now too. A new home. An organization that I felt solidly apart of. People that I cared about.

The reaper always loomed above all of it. Its scythe always watched, just waiting for its chance to harvest a soul—to rip it from the world and everyone it loved. The beast didn't care. The beast couldn't care, as far as I was concerned. And if I wanted to keep it at bay—much less make it pay for what it had done—I needed more.

More training. More assistance. More experience and knowledge. I had things to protect now, too, and I wasn't letting the beast rip me away in the same fashion as before. It was only more fuel for my fire, the burning passion of potential that I knew I could reach.

Lying in an infirmary bed inside a body riddled with fatigue, I knew it wouldn't come now. And based on the power of the threats that seemed ever-increasing on the horizon, I knew it wouldn't come soon, either. I would do it, though. I knew that I would.

Just… not right now.

CHAPTER TWENTY-FOUR

The trek back was ruthless.

I walked, pressing my foot into the dirt and rolling my shoulders. Small movements to to keep my body moving. That was what the apothecaries had advised when I'd asked about the soreness that was still there after a full night's rest. Though, that was *all* the advice they'd given before sending us off. I did it either way. If I kept moving, I'd get used to the pain at some point. That was what I told myself, at least.

Sharp rays of sunlight pierced through the canopy above. They danced on my face, moving in warm, wavering patterns as I walked under the imperfect cover of leaves. Veering away, I shielded my eyes with a hand. But no matter how hard I tried to protect from it, the sun bit me anyway. Its golden light stung the side of my head—right where I'd been burned.

I shook myself. Blinking and relaxing my shoulders, I tried to ignore the searing pain that had since healed. Taking a large whiff of the smooth, natural smell of the forest path, I tried to forget the scent of burnt hair. It was harder than I thought. Never again, I decided as my hand crept up to my scalp to pat where brown locks of hair had been only a day prior.

A sigh fell from my lips while I wandered on, my eyes downcast and my mind whirring. In general, the treatment I'd received at the apothecary's guild had been much better than I'd expected. If their descriptions of my wounds had been correct, I'd been lucky to make it out at all. And for all that I could say about magic, having elixirs made of herbs and plants that collected the world's latent magical energy had made for some quality painkillers.

I wished I could've taken some with me.

One of my legs screamed as my boot fell crookedly in the dirt. I winced, clenching my jaw and correcting myself as quickly as I could. This time, I didn't even curse myself. After the battle with Keris, it was as if my body refused to cooperate, instead holding a passive resentment for what I'd done to it. As another pulse of pain raked across my skull, I couldn't entirely blame it.

When I'd taken the job from Arathorn, I really had assumed it to be simple. I'd assumed I would've gone to Norn, retrieved the package, and returned.

Letting out a sigh, I tried my best to relax, tried my best to take in the ambience of the forest. World knew my ears could pick up on it all. The birds chirping high above. The wind rolling through the leaves. Even the scurrying animals hiding in the brush dozens of paces away. Still… I wasn't feeling any of it. Despite my warm surroundings, I felt bitter.

And Kye felt about the same way as we trudged along the path. Although I guessed her bitterness came from a slightly different place than mine. She hated the knights more than anything, it seemed. I still couldn't have felt that way if I'd wanted—it felt like a slap in the face to the past life that I'd lived, to the citizens I'd served and protected back then.

I didn't tell her any of that, though. It wasn't as simple as that. The beast had cursed me with a new life—and there was no reason to force the past and present to collide. There was no reason to try and bring what was now a continent away into this new life. Things were different now.

Kye kicked the dirt up ahead. My eyes flicked to her, watching the way she shrugged brown hair over her shoulder. There was no finesse in the action. No extra flair or emotion. It was blank and bitter, just like how both of us felt. She hadn't talked since we'd started.

I knew she'd talk when she wanted to. It wasn't my business to go about trying to get her to open up. Not when I felt the same way, especially not when she hadn't pushed it with me on our way into Sarin all of those weeks back. I was a ranger now, and I'd convinced her to come along on a simple trip. A simple journey that was supposed to gain me information and experience.

Well, I supposed it had done both of those things. I just hadn't predicted the shaking of stone or the fire and flames.

A sharp breath escaped my lips. And we'd left so *early*, I reminded myself. Even now that we'd been traveling for over an hour, it was still before midmorning. The apothecaries had woken us up after letting us stay a single night in the infirmary and then kicked us out. Lady Amelia hadn't even come to see us off. Not that I'd expected her to, though. But a knight with as much honor as she displayed… it left a foul taste in my mouth.

With the breeze drifting over me, my mind wandered back to the fight. It replayed the action in my head just like I'd been doing it since it had ended. What I saw didn't sit well.

I remembered the knights' forms. Their little inaccuracies and over-aggression that had given Keris the upper hand. Because no matter how strong the knights had come at him, his power had made everything simple. His manipulation of fire—the least complex form of energy from what I'd been told—had been enough to outpace all of us. No matter how many times I thought about it, that fact kept bringing me back to one thought.

I was afraid.

He'd fought off all of us single-handedly. He'd kept up with multiple opponents and pushed them away. And as much as it pained me to admit it, his dexterous form actually hadn't been terrible. It had been fluid and practiced. He'd stayed arrogant the entire time, and at no point had there been doubt in his mind that he would win. That he would at the very least escape with his life.

Well, his life and the package we'd gone there to collect in the first place.

I ground my teeth and looked up, remembering the package. The *important* one that Arathorn had been so eager to receive. Dragon's blood. That was what it had been. No matter how much stray information I gathered from odd questions here and there regarding dragons, I still had a question I couldn't answer.

I lifted my head, forcing a little bit more purpose into my steps. "Why did Arathorn want dragon's blood?"

Kye twisted her head, slowing only a hair. She widened her eyes as though surprised I was even still walking behind her. "Why did…" Her face contorted. "How the hell would I know?"

I grumbled, taking a deep breath and using the nature around me to calm myself. "Well, why would *anybody* want dragon's blood? What's so special about it anyway?"

Kye just stared at me for a moment, her body on automatic as her attention directed toward making sure I knew how dumb my question was. I gritted my teeth, trying to push away the irritable frustration simmering underneath my skin. I *knew* my question was stupid—it was the blood of a dragon, after all. But there was more to it than that. Arathorn wasn't simply a collector. He'd said that package was important. He'd wanted it for a specific reason.

"I don't know," Kye finally said. She threw up a hand. "People want it for any whole lot of reasons. Depending on what legends you believe, it has any number of properties."

I raised an eyebrow, tilting forward. "Properties like what?"

Kye bit back a curse and forced a deep breath. She came back at me with the most derisive smirk I'd ever seen her give. "It's the blood of a fucking *dragon*, what do you expect? If you can think of a property for it, somebody probably believes it acts that way. People understand as little about dragon's blood as they do about dragons themselves."

I nodded, my head bobbing slowly. "What are the most widely believed properties?" I figured it was a good place to start. If Arathorn had wanted that vial, he probably believed in some aspect of it that was useful to him. Some aspect that he'd probably heard from somebody else.

"I don't…" Kye started, slumping her shoulders. "There are a lot of them. Too many to sort through. Dragon's blood has been said to do anything from increasing the soul's capacity for magic, to curing vampirism, to enhancing physical abilities, to attuning one with dragons themselves… The list goes on."

My eyes narrowed. "How are there so many rumors? Where did they come from?" I chuckled dryly. "I mean, it's not like dragon's blood is common… It can't be."

Kye shook her head. "It's not, obviously. Outside of that vial that we almost got burned alive for back there, I've only ever heard one other credible story regarding it. And that was…" She dragged her eyes on the dirt. "That was years ago in a completely different part of Ruia."

"How do the myths come about then?" I asked, trying to connect what information about Ruian myths I was being told with the ones I'd learned back home. In Credon, the blood of a dragon had been cursed. It had been used in dozens of horror stories where it transformed people into chaotic monsters of destruction. But that was all they were. Stories. Ideas made and changed by the imaginations of people who didn't know better. I assumed the same thing was true in Ruia—the only difference being that the myths here had actual ground to stand on.

"I couldn't tell you." Kye gave a half-hearted shrug before turning around again. "As I said, people understand dragon's blood as much as they understand dragons. Which is to say *not at all*. Nobody I've ever met has seen a dragon." She hesitated. "Well, nobody I've ever met has seen a dragon and lived long afterward. They're elusive and legendary. Effectively only as impactful as their myths."

That made sense, at least. In my home kingdom, there hadn't been dragons at all. It had been common knowledge that they were no more than imagination. But even still, they had influenced people. They had wormed their way into the public conscience and done anything from scaring children to having people do faulty magical rituals in hopes of joining wherever the dragons were.

In Ruia, though, they *were* real. Or, they were *apparently* real. I hadn't seen any confirmation on that yet. Though, with the world-shaking quake and the sweltering heat of Keris' magic still fresh in my mind, I didn't entirely doubt that they could exist.

Falling back into silence, my foot curled. I cursed into the air and corrected myself, stepping heavily into the dirt as if to show my body who was in charge. As frustration rushed back, my will to stay silent melted away rather quickly.

"How far until we're out of this damn forest?" I asked, trying *not* to wield my words like daggers.

Kye chuckled. "Not far… maybe up to half an hour?"

I nodded, biting back whatever twisted retort I'd built up in my mind. It wasn't worth it. I was just still frustrated. Though, I couldn't blame myself for it that much when each step hurt to take. My thoughts were still tied in knots. I was feeling my new, disappointing body a little more than I wanted to.

I huffed, the sound coming out as more of a sigh. Then, lowering my head, the sun glinted in my eye. Shying away from the spear of light, I sighed again. I wanted the journey to be over.

My fingers flexed, reaching for the hilt of my sword. All I caught was air. As the wind blew over me again, my empty scabbard wobbled slightly with negligible weight. Metal clinked in the bag strewn across my back. The knife that mocked me with its existence, belittling me with its ineptitude and uselessness. I gritted my teeth and curled my fingers into a fist instead.

A shaky sigh slipped through my teeth. I'd lost my *sword*.

After Keris had ripped the steel blade of my longsword out of his leg, he'd nearly melted it right there. In whatever enraged state he'd shifted into, the entire weapon had burst into flames. And on top of that, he'd thrown it against the wall. I'd slipped down into the abyss before I could get it back, but the apothecaries had told me the only sword they'd found had been charred, bent, and melted. Useless, in other words.

Shaking my head, I walked on. Tried to focus away from the now-stark absence of weight at my side. The pain in my legs offered to take my attention. I concentrated on it instead, feeling the soreness with each push of my foot into dirt. But no matter how intently I focused, I couldn't stop the berating from my own conscience. I couldn't stop remembering how back in Credon, I'd lost only two swords in my entire lifetime. Here... things were different. They were stupid. Chaotic. Senseless.

A soft growl built in my throat as I stared down, my fiery eyes burning holes into the dirt. Then, growing tired of even that, I flicked my gaze back up to Kye. The taller, chestnut haired ranger was still only walking a few paces ahead.

"How?" I asked, my voice soft. She slowed her pace a fraction and started to turn. I hesitated before continuing. "How is any of this even able to happen?"

Kye twisted fully, sending a wide-eyed stare my way. "What are you talking about?"

I heaved a breath. "This entire trip. The way we were treated in Norn. The *fight*. How is any of this real?" Irrationality crept into my voice, but with how frustrated I was, I didn't push it back.

She sneered at me. "You're the one who told me this would be simple. But what do you expect? Not everything can go as you want it to all the time."

"It could be better, though," I said, my eyes flashing dangerously. Kye didn't falter, only spiting me with a glare harsh as nails. I didn't falter either. "The knights there treated us so... passively. So disrespectfully."

"Of course they did," Kye said. I was already nodding my head and waving a dismissive hand, remembering her warnings before we'd come. I just hadn't pictured them as bad as they were. Lady Amelia had barely even made sure we were *alive*.

Now I knew Kye had been right, at least. They didn't care about the rangers. Not very much anyway. That didn't make up for the fact that it was a weak excuse to me. "Knights are supposed to be honorable," I said. "They aren't supposed to hold grudges. They are *supposed* to care about visitors beyond petty political appearances."

Kye laughed. "So now you're an expert on how knights are *supposed* to act?" I shrugged. "It's the knightly code."

"Knightly code?" Kye asked, waving a hand through the air. "What—"

"The code of order and integrity that all knights follow," I said, almost directly relaying the words of significance I'd learned in my youth.

Kye gave a wry chuckle. "Out of all the things you choose to know about, it's the knightly code?" I glared at her. She didn't seem to care. "And then you don't even understand that?"

I blinked, my eyes flaring. "What are you talking about?"

"I don't know what you've been told, but that is not at all what the knightly code is about." Kye stiffened her posture. "I hate the knights and even I know that. Their code is about protecting *them*. It has nothing to do with us. They have no obligation to care about us, so they don't."

I curled my lip, stewing silently for a moment. My companion's words churned in my brain slowly. Chipping and scraping against the cogs of my mind as they shattered yet another conception I'd held before. Things were different in Ruia. Who was to say knights were spared of that? My face twisted into a scowl and I killed the rest of my questions. There was no use in asking them anymore. I wouldn't magically teleport back to my old life by yelling loud enough. The beast had put me here—I had to accept that, at least.

Instead, I sighed and pushed past it. Threw it away from my attention so that the next of my worries could line itself up.

"What happens when we get back?" I asked, my voice a shell of its former self. Kye didn't slow her pace or even turn to me. I didn't need to see her to know though.

"We face Arathorn," she said, her tone firm and steady. She didn't chuckle again, only squared her shoulders almost like a wall against me and walked on.

I ran a hand over my face. We'd return empty-handed, I told myself. We'd face Arathorn *without* the package he'd asked us to get. My mind flashed to his office. I bit back another curse and bowed my head, disappointed in myself now more than ever. We would face what we had to face, I decided. It was as simple as that.

With my resolve sturdy, I followed Kye down along the path through the spearing rays of sunlight and beautiful shades of green. Past all of the tranquil sounds I could pick out without much effort. I still wasn't feeling any of it, but at least it was there. That was comforting, I guessed, if I thought about it enough.

Eventually, we broke through the tree line. The path below us narrowed and gave way back to the stone-lined one we'd walked thousands of paces on already. In front of us, the trees tapered out. They gave way to rolling plains and sparse, jutting rock formations. Ruia, I reminded myself. I lived here now.

And as we set off, I angled my gaze toward the collection of wooden buildings we could barely see raised in the distance. A thin smile grew on my face when I saw it. I lived here now, sure, but *that* was my home. The sight of it brought back my earlier question. It nagged my mind one more time.

What did we have to face?

There was only one way to find out.

CHAPTER TWENTY-FIVE

I didn't even get a break.

There was no resting after we returned to Sarin. It all happened in a blur. Walking in silence, we'd made pretty good time and arrived before the sun had descended below the horizon. But that kind of tireless travel wasn't rewarded with much relief. It wasn't rewarded with a bed or some downtime. No. After returning to the lodge and bearing through the greetings of whichever rangers happened to be in the training room, we were thrust right back to action.

Lorah called for a report of our trip immediately. Kye took that opportunity wordlessly, doing the gracious thing and letting me stay back to recuperate. I was the one who'd been injured more severely, after all.

But almost as soon as she disappeared, my respite was cut short. I had barely let my body relax for half an hour before a guard in light armor barged into the lodge requesting me. Or, more accurately he requested the package Arathorn had sent us to retrieve in the first place. But we didn't have it. So I went in its place.

Whatever Arathorn's reaction was going to be, I would have face it.

Cobblestone dragged under my feet as I walked through Sarin's square. All of the activity since arriving back passed by nearly in a haze. It all blended together in a sea of discomfort and disappointment. Before I knew it, I was on my way to town hall. Back to the office I'd been called to only days before. I doubted Arathorn would be anywhere near as cheerful this time.

A metal clang struck my ears. I twisted, shaking my head as I was ripped to reality. Looking up, I squinted in the fading twilight at the source of the sound. A young woman picked her pan up off the street a moment later. She eyed me, yawning while continuing to haul her stuffed bag back to her house. I forced myself to smile and nodded at her. She gave me a half-hearted wave before simply turning away and walking on down the hill.

Brisk air cascaded over my skin. I took a breath of it, letting it swirl in my lungs. I flicked my gaze to the side, watching the large centerpiece of town slowly become enveloped in shadow. Town hall. I would've recognized the sturdy stone base and sweeping roof anywhere.

I didn't want to go in.

But, well, I didn't have much of a choice. I pushed back on useless thoughts and shook my head, feeling the sore strain through my body. With another breath, I started up the steps. It didn't matter what I wanted, after all. I was a part of this town. I was a protector of it. Arathorn was my world's damned lord, and I would respond to his summons.

For a brief moment, memories of my past life flooded back—memories of loyalty and discipline. My honor won out, standing triumphant on the field of my mind. I furrowed my brow, held my head up, and pushed my way in the door.

The difference in temperature was stark as the door slid shut behind me. The cozy, fire-warmed air felt good against my still-bruised skin. It felt better than the brisk autumn wind I'd been walking through all day. Sparing a glance back to the door, I considered if it even *was* autumn anymore. Perhaps winter was already on its way. On this continent, I had no way to know.

I tore away from the door and curled a fist. I couldn't keep stalling, I reminded myself. Cementing my resolve, I flicked my gaze around the room. The same well-crafted planked floors greeted me. The same cozy array of tables. The same soft, wood-burning fireplace. I shifted my attention to the last of them, staring at the flames for a moment. I let their glow wash over my body while I thought. It was nice, I realized, still standing in the entryway. The welcoming feeling. The community. The *warmth*. After days of travel and too much time spent fearing for my life, it was a change of pace.

"Agil!" a voice called, grinding my pleasant thoughts to a halt.

A tall guard gestured me over from the other side of the room. He wore a fake mask of cheerfulness that disguised his obvious concern. As I walked over to him, I barely cared about his expression. He'd remembered my name.

"Yes?" I asked, keeping all edge out of my tone. Despite how bitter I felt—something my aching body wouldn't let me forget—I wanted to sound calm.

"Arathorn is in his office," the guard said, glancing backward. "He wants to see you immediately." The voice came strained, as if it hadn't been used in days. And as I approached, I noticed the bags under his eyes and the lines on his forehead.

I nodded at the man, all confidence slowly bleeding out of me as I stepped toward the door. A long second of silence passed as I stared at the handle. Dread taunted my mind. It wasn't too late to back out, it told me. It wasn't too late.

No. I shook my head, pushed away the unfamiliar fear that rose up like bile in my throat, and walked through the door.

Cold air. It hit me like a crashing wave when I stepped over the threshold. For a moment, I furrowed my brow and tried to inch out, but the door was already closed. It had already sealed me away in Arathorn's office. Glancing back, I could barely make out the wood grain in the room's dim light. I swallowed, my throat drying like a desert. Then I did my best to shrug it off, clenched my fists, and turned forward.

I squinted, scanning across the office that I had been in only days before. It was all still the same, but it was also all different. The single torch illuminating the room was almost completely burned out, and the only window at the back was boarded up as well.

A shiver crept down my spine as my eyes moved to the desk. The organized, perfect, polished desk that was burned into my memory. Even in the dim torchlight, I could see how much it had changed. The stacks of papers weren't stacks anymore, only scattered messes on the wood. The organized baskets weren't organized anymore, only thrown astray across the wood. One, even, was broken clean in half.

Something had changed since the last time I'd been here. My dread screamed it loud enough to rattle my skull. An issue in Sarin, maybe. Something Arathorn wasn't keen on dealing with. I didn't know. All I did know was that—

A glint of light. I twisted, blinking as it caught the corner of my vision. My eyes widened a fraction as I realized what it was. The memory flashed back, forcing itself upon me.

The knife was there, seared into my mind. Its ornate decoration. Its eerily sharp blade. I shuddered at the thought. Its image brought up fear—deep, dark, and unnatural. Something hailing from the back of my mind. Fear that I didn't even recognize.

I moved forward still, trying to shake the unnerving atmosphere of the space.

I poured over the desk in front of me, hoping that it would revert to its organized state, hoping that it wouldn't carry the bloodied knife. But I saw it—crystal clear in Arathorn's right hand.

Arathorn stared at me. His sparkling blue eyes bored into me with acute interest, betraying a completely different emotion than the smile across his lips.

Shaking my head again, I took a breath. "I was told you wanted to see me?"

The Lord of Sarin twirled the knife in his hand. Now-clean silvery metal gleamed in what little light there was. Whatever remnants of a smile were left on my face faded instantly.

"Yes," he said, keeping his gaze on me. "I wanted my package delivered. But"—he inclined his head while keeping a careful smile—"you don't seem to have it, do you?"

"Well," I started, "you see—"

Arathorn's sniff cut me off. His gaze stayed on me, unmoving. After a few moments, his lips curled into a grin far more wicked. "Well. What I need *you* to see is that I sent you off on a mission. And you weren't able to complete it." I swallowed hard. "I trusted *you* to do something as simple as retrieving a package from a town only a day's travel away. And *you* came up empty-handed." He twirled the knife once more through his fingers before stabbing into the desk. "*I* want to know why that is."

I gritted my teeth and forced calming breaths through my lungs. "We tried to get the package. We really did. But—"

"*But?*"

"*But*, there were complications," I continued, tightening my fists until I was sure I would've seen white in the knuckles.

Arathorn's brows snapped up. "Complications?" he asked as he pushed out of his seat. "There were *complications*? What kind of complications?"

I closed my eyes for a moment and relaxed my shoulders as memories rose up. "Firstly, we had an unexpected altercation on our way to Norn." Arathorn's fingers drummed a deafeningly quiet rhythm on the wood of his desk. I steadied. "It left me quite injured before we even arrived to collect the package."

Arathorn chuckled softly. The sound echoed through the room. "That is something you should have expected." He snapped to me. "Do you know where we live? Don't answer that. It doesn't matter anyway. That has nothing to do with my package."

Color drained from my face. "Right," I said, clearing my throat. Arathorn may have been erratic right now—he was certainly angry. But he was also my lord. "It doesn't have anything to do with your package." I swallowed my anger like a dry pill. "But we did have further issues when we arrived in Norn."

Arathorn tapped his foot, still glaring. "Like what?"

"Most immediately, we had an issue with the knights there." I cracked a dry smile. "They seemed to hold a grudge against us for some reason."

"That doesn't surprise me," Arathorn said. "Most people wouldn't immediately trust two questioning rangers who they had just met. But you had my imprint, didn't you?"

I nodded, my expression faltering. "We did."

"Did that not clear up the issues?"

I cringed. "Well. It did, but—"

"Again, not surprising," Arathorn said. He cocked an eyebrow at me, patience visibly running out in his strained eyes. "I gave you my imprint so that there would not be these issues. Yet, you have still returned to me without the package I sent off for."

My eyebrows dropped. I sighed, nodding slowly and swallowing the rest of my comments on the matter. The imprint had helped our relationship, but it had still been sour the entire way through. Even after we'd been attacked, they hadn't cared much. I knew they had no obligation to be our friends, but they were *knights*, dammit. They had an obligation to have some integrity.

"Of course," I eventually got out. My breaths slowed as I kept myself composed, a technique reminiscent of ones I'd used as a high-knight during diplomatic missions. "However, there were more troubles ahead of us after that." Arathorn furrowed his brow. I nodded. "After Norn's knight commander agreed to retrieve your package, the city was struck with a quake that—"

"A quake?" Arathorn asked, tension underlining his tone. Looking up, his smile was gone. There was no longer any charm. No careful cheer. He just showed bare frustration and concern.

"Yes," I said, my voice softening. "A quake."

Arathorn cursed something foul under his breath. "Is that what destroyed my package?"

I wheeled backward at his statement, my foot barely catching me. He wasn't concerned about the quake or the destruction it caused. He only cared about his damn package. My resolve of honor was starting to crack.

"No," I said, pushing the words through my teeth. "I'm still getting to that part."

He returned to the facade of a smile, his pale lips doing more harm than good. "Ah. Alright. Continue, then."

I did, my eyes sharpening on him. "Your package had been held in a magically secured room in their apothecary's guild. After the quake, Lady Amelia led us to it." Arathorn's eyes flashed with hope. I had to fight back a sneer. "When we arrived, it was gone."

Arathorn snapped up, sliding from behind his desk and walking toward me "What do you mean it was *gone*?"

I threw up my hands both to reassure him and to keep him from coming any closer. "I'm getting to that."

My reassurance appeared to calm the irritated lord only the slightest bit. I nodded to myself, letting out a light breath. "Okay. We didn't *know* it was going to be gone. When we got there, it had been stolen by a rogue pyromancer named Keris."

Arathorn tilted his head back in interest. The intensity of his glare didn't waver. "How did he steal it?"

I clenched my jaw just thinking of the pyromancer's smug face. "I don't know. As soon as we entered, he attacked us. Even with the extra protection we had gone with, we almost *died*." My efforts to keep frustration out of my tone were failing.

Arathorn blinked. "You had the two of you, Norn's knight commander, and extra protection as well… Yet you still couldn't recover my package?"

There it was again. *His* package. It wasn't about me. It wasn't about Kye, or the knights for that matter. To him, it didn't matter what we'd done or what we'd gone through.

"He was strong," I said, trying not to spit the words out. "A more powerful mage than I've ever seen. He kept telling us that we shouldn't have been taking such actions before *her ire*." I cringed at myself, throwing up a hand. "The possession of dragon's blood sounded really important to him."

Arathorn took a step back, his face paling further. In a speechless moment, he glanced back at the knife stuck into his desk. I bit back a grumble. He hadn't reacted when I'd told him about my injuries. Nor when I'd told him about the quake. Nor when I'd mentioned the fact that we had almost *died*. But as soon as I'd said something about his precious package, he reacted.

"What?" I asked. Arathorn jerked his head toward me, fixing me with wide eyes before his face morphed into a scowl. "There was nothing we could do. We really tried, but all that got us were burns and pain." My fingers tightened even further. "I even lost my sword for you."

Arathorn froze, his scowl deepening. The mask of charm and restraint faded from his eyes, only letting anger shine through. He stepped forward with flaring nostrils. "You lost *what*?"

I stood, stock-still for a moment. "My sword."

Arathorn took another step. The last remnants of worry fell from his expression. His crooked smile came back with a vengeance that made my nose scrunch up. "I ask a *simple* task of you out of sheer hope that you'll complete it." I cringed, already seeing where he was going. He moved closer. "You go on the journey, don't complete the task, and return empty-handed." Another step. "And you still have the nerve to complain about losing a fucking *sword*?"

I scowled. "Yes. Do you know what we had to face in Norn? Just for your package, we had to—"

"Do *you* know how important that package was?" Arathorn asked. Rage coated his tone plain and clear, but I didn't miss the underlying anxiety. Neither stopped him from stepping close enough that he was right in my face.

I felt Arathorn's breath on my neck. I stiffened, my nose twitching. Tilting my head, I averted my eyes from his glare, and I tried to take a deep breath. Tried to process the situation *rationally*. But when a faint but instantly recognizable smell caught my nose, I knew that wasn't going to happen.

Blood.

My heart nearly stopped. Ice-cold fire flooded my veins and I stared at the previously bright-faced man. The previously charming, handsome lord I'd come to somewhat respect. As I scoured over his pale skin, I disregarded the elegant suit. I disregarded the gleaming black hair peppered with flecks of silvery grey. All that I saw was an object of disgust that set a horrible taste on my tongue. Waves and waves of abhorrence washed up from the back of my mind and crashed over me until it was all I could think about.

It was like I'd eaten something vile. Except it was worse than that.

It was like I'd killed someone. Except it was worse than that too.

It was like my entire family had been slaughtered. That thought echoed in my mind.

I froze, my eyes fixed on the man who I considered my lord. The pale, sniffing, rage-filled man who I'd given my honor to. The furious, selfish man who was staring at me with perfectly piercing blue eyes that were slowly slipping from control. Him? No, I realized. He was *not* my lord.

His nose twitched, taking a long whiff of the air one more time. Movement shifted in the back of my head, only providing more disgust as it tried to hide away. It tried to conceal whatever scent Arathorn was searching for. His smile grew as he watched me, his interest completely captivated. Staring into his eyes, something shined through. Something I recognized. A part of him that I didn't stare long enough to figure out the nature of.

I scrambled backward, focusing all my energy on putting each foot on the floor. Arathorn eyed me curiously, blinking to himself. In an instant, he straightened. He regained his poise and quelled the anger to a light frustration. Then he raised his head and sniffed.

At once, control slipped from his eyes again. I saw it in the erratic twitching of his fingers. He was fighting. Fighting *something*. And losing, I realized far too slowly. He didn't have the awareness left to stop his feet from following me forward. Before I knew it, his arm had flailed out.

I dodged, scuttling back farther. Wood flew under my feet as I leapt against the door. I fought my eyes not to stay wide and pushed away panic as I reached for my sword. If I grabbed my sword, I would be able to defend myself. That was what went through my head.

A stifled curse was my entire reaction once I realized my mistake.

Arathorn lurched, his fingers swiping at me like claws. I shuffled, throwing an arm up to block as I twisted away. A slight, burning scrape raked across my skin before I got away. The previously handsome man stared at me, his eyes quivering. Words rose to my tongue. But when his body surged with newfound energy, I knew there was no talking left. There was no *him* left.

Briefly thanking the world for my body's crystal clear eyesight, I ducked. Arathorn's arm flew wide over my head, striking the air. Turning, I scoured his feral form for a weakness. It didn't take long to find. I kicked the back of his knees without another thought and pushed away before he could react.

Arathorn stumbled, knees buckling as his fingers scraped against the wooden door. After only a moment, he was back on his feet. The rage was bubbling back up. He turned slowly to stare at me. His fingers curled into fists and he stepped toward me.

Then he stepped back.

I froze, halting the motion to dodge I'd almost initiated. Arathorn stared, wide-eyed. He clenched his jaw and fought again—the charismatic sparkle shined anew in his eyes.

"I'm sorry," he eventually said. Even those words were barely more than a hiss through his teeth. Before he could stabilize himself, the hunger had returned. It wrestled away his control and consumed him with fuel from his rage. The wicked smile grew back. The creature lunged, and I knew he was gone.

I didn't even get a moment for the sympathetic part of me to mourn. It was on me again. I turned and threw myself to the side to avoid its first strike. The second, however, came quicker than I'd imagined. It charged me with inhuman speed and slammed into me hard, not wasting energy with precision.

My body reeled, blunt pain ripping through the soreness as the lazy guard of my forearms broke. Grimacing, I staggered to a stand. I stared back at the the creature wearing Arathorn's skin, and I raised my fist for a strike.

Attacks and maneuvers—simple ones this time—played through my head. They processed with the scattered books over the floor and the shelf I'd almost slammed into. Yet, even as I returned to its pale form with a smile on my face, I couldn't act. I wasn't fast enough. It was already attacking me, and all I could do was dodge.

So that was exactly what I did. Only acute fear and instinct saved me quickly enough. My body fumbled through an erratic sea of motion before I caught on something. Before I brought my brow together and forced myself upright against Arathorn's desk. More fire poured into my blood as I stared back, baring my teeth in battle-fueled rage.

Still, however, I couldn't keep up. The thing was flailing. In a flash of movement that I hardly tracked with my eyes, it came swinging at me. It flexed its fingers and grabbed for my arms. On pure, fluid instinct, I twisted away and brought my own fist up under its savage guard.

I allowed myself a smile as my strike connected.

Ara—the *thing's* arm came down and knocked mine away like a pebble. I teetered, anchoring myself on the desk to prevent from falling. Papers slid across the wood behind me, sending the room even further into disarray. I wasn't quite in a state to care.

After stepping backward, it rushed toward me unthinking. It didn't slow as it forced me against the desk and scraped into my arms with nails that felt far too sharp to be human. A muffled yelp escaped my mouth as pain streamed through my sore muscles. But I didn't put down my guard. I didn't let it break through. It wanted at my neck—I knew that much. I wasn't going to make it an easy task.

I pushed it back. It resisted, forcing its foot into the ground and leaning toward me even harder. Then its foot slipped, and it scrambled to the side in an effort to maintain balance. I twisted away, flying across the desk's polished wooden edge and glaring back at the creature before it could attack again. In a frozen instant, I turned my attention inward. I turned it to the source of the disgust crashing over my skull.

The thing in the back of my head shifted, shying away. It scurried deep enough that I couldn't even feel it while it only piled more and more fear on. More and more revulsion. I gritted my teeth and pleaded with it—tearing up images of the white flames that had engulfed my hands before. That was the last time it had helped me in a desperate situation. Well, I was in a desperate situation now.

It wouldn't listen. It was too scared. It blocked me out, and by the time I tried to get at it again, the pale creature was charging.

Another swipe. Another block. Twisting, turning, dodging. The routine was solidifying as Arathorn's body kept up with tireless rage. Each time it got close, it lunged for my neck. Each time it lunged for my neck, I twisted away. It was a game of cat and mouse, and I was growing tired of being a rodent.

I couldn't keep it up. That fact was becoming too clear. Despite the cold fire burning in my blood, I was slowing down. My body was still sore—I was stumbling more, and in the disorganized office, my movement was limited. All the while, the burning pain tearing through the cloth of my uniform was getting worse with each cut. The agony was ramping up. I was getting tired of sticky blood. I couldn't keep dodging forever. Eventually, something had to give.

As I leapt back, my foot slipping on a stray piece of paper, I knew exactly what it was. Color drained from my face as my guard became all but useless. With its inhuman speed, the vampiric creature took full advantage.

Before I knew it, I was sliding like rag doll across the wide wooden desk.

I gritted my teeth and held to a halt, keeping my head above the wood. If there was one thing I definitely didn't need, it was another head injury. In a moment of rest, I felt the cold air sting my skin where the blood was now flowing. The fatigue pulled me down and taunted me with the opportunity of closing my eyes.

I didn't listen, of course. I knew that I couldn't. My moment of relief was short-lived at best, and there was no way I would let the barbaric *thing* get at me. Though, as my thoughts ran on a fraction of a second too long, it loomed over me all the same. I stared up at it—up at the newly blood-stained suit Arathorn wore. I cringed while watching it, wishing that I would've seen it sooner. Wishing that I would've disregarded the conceptions held up by my honor and seen the truth. I wished I could've seen past Arathorn's weak facade and put more stock in the fear he sparked within me.

Now, though, my wishes didn't mean anything at all.

It clambered onto the desk and snarled. Its lips slipped open and bared the pearly whites that looked more like fangs in the dim light. They threatened me with their existence as the creature hunched over. And before my eyes could even track the movement, its claw-like fingers were grabbing again.

I pushed them away intuitively. But my movements were lazy. My body was slow, sore, and useless. The creature only redoubled its efforts to get at my neck —and my attempts to stop it were becoming weaker and weaker.

A shaky breath fell from my lips, one carrying far too much weight. My eyelids flitted, feeling heavier and heavier as blood spilled out over my arms and stained the cloth of my clothing. As darkness flickered in and out of my vision, the beast's image returned. It taunted me like it always did, spawning from the depths of my psyche to remind me of the rage I felt. Of the way the reaper had ripped me away from everything I loved only to put me *here*. It had put me on the corrupted continent, destined to die. A place where even the lord who I was supposed to honor to was deceitful. It was sickening.

And it appeared I wasn't the only one who thought so.

Movement in the back of my head. I focused on it. I tried to track it. But I couldn't. It was moving too fast. Or was I moving too slow? I couldn't tell. I didn't need to tell. My blood was draining from. The beast was coming for me. It would take me away for good this time—rip me from the world just like it had done to my parents.

My parents?

The question didn't even have time to process before a white-hot presence surged to the fore-front of my mind. I snapped my eyes open, stretching them wide and noticing the white haze at the corner. At once, control fled from my muscles. Something else took the reigns. Something different yet close, scared yet just as rage-fueled as I was.

"*Not again,*" my voice screamed even though I hadn't ordered it too. The creature above me swiped one more time, darting its fang-like teeth toward my neck. My hand snapped up, catching its neck with a fiery sort of ease before pushing the thing away.

The creature wearing Arathorn's clothes growled, wrenching out of my grip and peering down in horror. Following its expression, I saw the searing burn I'd left across its skin.

In a moment of clarity, I realized what was going on.

The white haze flared brighter at the edge of my vision. I took a deep breath, curling upward and watching the feral creature retreat from the desk. It scurried away through air. Air that I could feel, that felt untapped and powerful. It felt malleable. Changeable. Light enough to twirl on my finger. And as I focused on it, my hands grew warm. They sparked into flame that swirled around me without burning or prompting pain. They weren't working against me. The flames were part of me, through and through.

The *kanir*—as my mind forced me to think—stared on in confusion. The hunger was still there, I noticed. Even if its erratic movements had slowed. Even if its wicked smile was gone. All lifeful color had drained from its face now, and as it watched me, it licked its teeth. Only the hunger was left.

It lunged. I could feel it in the light air. I didn't even need my eyes to see it. My body dodged to the side easily, raising ready hands in an instant. I caught it before it could think twice about its action.

My burning hands tore into the quality fabric, leaving only charred shreds. I pushed it away with all the force I could muster. It stumbled back, tripping over a book for the first time in the fight, and similarly to what it had done to me before, I was on it before it could react.

The flames worked through perfect, fluid motions in tandem with my instincts. The image of my attack solidified in my mind only moments before I took it; I brought my hands down. I struck the kanir with more force than I'd thought possible. But it didn't stop there.

Blow after blow, my body worked in perfect synergy with my mind. I lorded white fire over the creature that had threatened my life and rained hell upon it. The thing that had almost cut my second chance short, I remembered. The thing that had almost forced my rematch with the beast. My hands tossed it to the floor, scorch marks covering its shoulders and chest, and it spat a dark red substance onto the floor.

Blood.

Its eyes darted to me. Its nostrils flared. It stared with only primal emotions that were all dominated by hunger before pushing up and swiping at me again.

I dodged to the side with a smile still on my face. That was all it ever did. It charged and it swung. There was no finesse to its actions. No skill or technique. There was only rage and hunger, fueling the most brutish of attacks.

My smile dropped a moment later when a hand grabbed my arm. I snapped my gaze to it, immediately moving away when I saw the pale fingers. But they didn't let go so easily. The kanir latched onto my flesh, digging its nails through the cloth and deep into my skin. I screamed in pain, bringing up my hand to do the same. In a motion faster than I thought possible, my fingers wrapped around its arm as well. A growl slipped between its lips.

My mind worked on its own. The plan only became clear to me as it was executed. I shook off its grab, holding my own grip tight enough to keep it in place. My other hand latched on to the thing, gripping it with all I had.

The air lightened even further. Every particle of it flowed past me, carrying all latent energy provided by the world. I moved that energy and changed it with my soul. My vision flooded with white. Flames licked at my skin but didn't burn. And by the time the movement was over, I saw the kanir sprawled in a half-crouch on the floor near to the door. Its pale skin was covered in burns and scrapes. Part of Arathorn's hair had burned off, and when my eyes met its gaze, I saw something it had never previously displayed.

Fear.

A new plan flashed in my head, clear and wrapped in flames. My eyes widened immediately, rebelling against the idea. I tried to bring my hands up to stop it. But no matter what I did, it was already too late.

The air became slick and I felt power surge through my bones. As I helplessly stared, a passenger in my own skin, heat erupted through the air. It jumped from particle to particle until white fire exploded within Arathorn's body. The kanir shrieked one last time before it was scorched from the inside out.

The fire fled as quickly as it had arrived, leaving only dim torchlight once more. The smoked, charred body crumpled lifelessly to the floor. White flames receded from my fingers and settled off my neck. They let me gain control of my hands, but I didn't bring them up. It was too late for that. All I could do was stare.

I'd wanted to defend myself. I hadn't wanted to die... But I hadn't wanted to *kill* it. Not while it was still in Arathorn's skin.

The thought played back in my head, echoing and echoing. Images of what had just happened flashed, skewing and tearing as my mind tore them apart. The consequences of what I'd done came crashing down on me. Each moment that passed was agony— a searing, burning pain against my empathy. I hadn't died, but all I'd done was give the reaper another soul. I'd tossed it one that I *knew*, even. My lord. Or… former lord, at least.

The distinction didn't lesson the bitter taste in my mouth.

Pressure rose against the back of my eyes. I pushed back on it, sniffling and trying to maintain composure. It wasn't as easy as I'd thought it would be, and before I knew it, tears were running down my cheek, blurring away the image of Arathorn's body frozen, soulless body.

I shook my head, wiping the tears away and forcing myself to be calm. I'd killed before. It wasn't a matter to cry over. I'd only killed because it had been necessary, and I didn't—

My vision shifted. The air around me warped, freezing to an unnatural cold before stopping. And when it settled, a horrible sight consumed my attention.

In front of me, standing over Arathorn's body with its scythe still touched against his burnt chest, was the beast. The pallid, bony form draped in a tattered cloak.

I stopped, all thoughts screeching to a halt. The white haze at the edge of my vision wavered, twisting and twitching in frozen horror. Standing stock-still, I watched the beast. It moved in slow, fluid motions as it lifted its scythe and stared at me. Barely resisting my primal fear, I stared back at it, recognizing the expression painted across its skeletal features.

Surprise.

My breathing quickened in tandem with my pulse. The beast stepped forward, nearly floating over the floor toward me. Step after step, its expression morphed back into the neutral confidence it had displayed before. And when it got close enough, it stared me right in the eyes. I fought it, trying to scramble away and tear it from my eyes. My efforts were pointless.

The darkness flared up to consume my vision. To finish the task it had set out to complete all those weeks ago.

Except this time, the darkness didn't spread. It didn't swallow my soul in a deathless maw. No. The white haze rebelled against it, blazing in bright flame. The light fought against the darkness almost out of my control, holding my soul hostage in a void to wait until it stopped.

Eventually though, it did.

The beast ceased its efforts and looked toward the ground. Confusion descended upon its face, nearly burning against the bone as though it was being scolded by something more powerful than even it.

Letting the white haze calm, the reaper echoed a low, hair-raising growl before taking another step back. It vanished in a stream of black mist, taking its lifeless presence along and leaving the room in pure silence.

For a moment, I only stood there and stared. My mind worked tirelessly to try and piece together what I'd seen. It was a futile effort. The stillness of the room caught up to me far too quickly. As I looked to the body again, a long breath slipped from my lips.

The flames faded from my eyes. The cold rushed back. The exhaustion set in, dragging my body to the floor.

And in a moment of pure humanity, I fell to my knees.

CHAPTER TWENTY-SIX

I was floating.

In a dark place somewhere between nothing and nowhere, my soul existed. Blackness filled in everything that I could perceive, but it wasn't oppressive. It didn't press in on me to murder each last ray of light. It spun in soft, elegant circles that enchanted my soul without dizzying me in the process. I felt at home as I drifted through it. Everything felt right.

At the edge of my vision, I saw a flicker of light. It pierced through the darkness around it and stopped the spinning for a moment. As my vision fixed on it, I became captivated. A warmth cascaded over me that I could only describe as comforting. The spark of white light was everything to me, and I wanted to stare at it forever.

Then it went out. The blackness swallowed it up and began swirling again. It settled over the void and distracted me with soft movements again, almost enough to detract from the uncertainty worming its way through my thoughts.

Sorrow built up in my soul. A deep longing for something I knew nothing about. Yet, the more my drifting conscious thought about it, the more I felt that I knew. The more I felt the cold, an empty stillness grown frigid at the edges. As time waxed on, I coveted warmth. I coveted the fleeting white light I'd seen for a moment before.

As if on cue, the spark flickered anew.

Soft, white flame crackled against the black. It grew slowly, as if feeding off my attentions while I stared at it. I didn't mind, though. It was as captivating as it had been before, and its warmth coddled me in the same way. It felt cozy and familiar, like I was a child out in the summer. And once the flame drifted close enough, it flared as bright as the sun. It revealed its perfect, innocent beauty and radiated out like a beacon.

Memories came after the light, almost following its lead. Waves of some feeling crashed over my mind, but I couldn't discern what it was. Images rose up, skewed, fractured, and terrifying. A man in an expensive suit. A charming smile. A dim room.

White light faded away and with it fled the warmth. The frigid tone encroached on my soul again. It wrapped me in a cocoon that felt natural yet incomplete.

I didn't get much time to stew on it before the flame flared bright again. It danced through the dark and flickered its beautiful tongues as though burning through a wind that wasn't there. More images followed the light as it waned, sending frigid tremors through my mind. An ornate knife. A scattered floor. My sense of smell rushed back along with the putrid scent of blood.

The light faded to leave me gasping in the infinite black. Feeling started to return to my body at a slow, unnatural pace. It stung against thin air and I only avoided all the discomfort by once again watching the flame.

It wavered ever so slightly. I didn't look away. I didn't *want* to look away.

Another flash of light made me regret my own thoughts as pain radiated through my limbs. The images returned, one after another. A crazed beast. A flurry of motion. A white haze. They left a bitter taste in their wake.

The light faded, giving me only momentary relief while I stared into darkness. The pain died down, my breath steadied out, and my gaze once again froze on the little light. It danced in perfect unison with my mind as if it and I were one.

Before I could relish in respite, another flash seared my eyes. It burned brighter than all the rest and brought a sharp fear along with it. The images came back, forcing themselves into my vision all at once. A black mist. A dark cloak. Cracked, bleached bone. I fell to my knees, the cold seeping into my muscles. The sound of soft crying reached my ears and it took me all too long to figure out that the sound was coming from me.

The light faded, leaving my blurred vision as the tears stung my eyes. The flame returned, dancing larger than normal. Something reached me from the edge of my hearing and I could do nothing else but listen.

"I don't—"

"Mom—"

"Dad—"

"I'm sorry—"

A strained voice echoed through the dark, feeding off the flame's light as waves of emotion washed up. First confusion, then anger, then sorrow. And finally, as the flame dwindled to barely a spark and turned its attention solely to me, I felt a sharp pang of relief.

"Thank you."

The little white flame faded into the darkness for good. But the spinning didn't begin again. The blackness didn't feel the same. It *wasn't* the same.

I didn't feel cold anymore. There was no distracting stillness or empty void. My soul had been warmed by the flame—all the way to my core. And I felt my entire body at once as a sharp noise entered my ears.

———

"Get up!"

I jerked my head forward, blinking eyes open. The dull yellow light of the sun filtered into my blurry vision through a window. It was morning, I realized through the haze. Holding my head, I felt a dull ache echoing off my bones. And when I'd collected myself, I turned to the short, bearded man who was yelling at me.

"What?" I asked, my voice strained and hollow.

Galen rolled his eyes and folded his arms. "You can't sleep in my office all day." His voice came harsh with an edge of annoyance, but its squeaky quality almost made me laugh. The dull, never-ending pain stopped my levity in its tracks.

I squinted at him while rubbing my temple. "How long have I been in here?"

The short man tapped his foot on the wood floor. "After I healed you for the second time this week"—I didn't miss that back-handed jab—"you slept here all night."

I cocked an eyebrow, my eyes widening slightly. All night? Hadn't I just been on my way to see Arathorn? On my way to deliver the news about his package? Memories bubbled under the surface of my mind, but something told me not to pry them apart.

"But you were strained pretty bad," Galen continued. I flicked my eyes back up to him. "Bruised and scraped all over. So I thought I'd let you sleep 'till morning." Galen's smile grew. "The guard that brought you here was pretty frantic too, babbling on about how he found you nearly dead." My smile dropped, the haze uncovering things I didn't want to see. "And he kept going on about something being wrong with Lord Arathorn. I could barely understand the lad by that point."

My eyes widened further, pushing past the last of the fog as I remembered. A tortured grimace took my face, dull pain stinging in each of my bones. I *remembered*.

It had killed him. *I* had killed him, with my own power. I still didn't understand it, but looking back at the crystal clear scene, I couldn't deny it. I remembered the white flames. The lifeless body. The reaper afterward.

I took a sharp breath and pressed hands to my forehead for the oncoming headache. It had all been too fast after that. I remembered the door opening. I remembered a whole lot of screaming. I remembered the shocked faces of guards that were only barely visible through my tears.

After that, it was just a blur of movement as I was carried out of the room. It tapered out eventually into black, and there was nothing after that.

"Shit," I muttered under my breath. From the corner of my eye, Galen stopped and furrowed his brow in slight concern while still staring at me. I looked up, forcing my muscles to get used to moving again. "I'm sorry."

It was all I could muster. I didn't know what else to say. The memory stung. The image of the body—of *Arathorn's* body—cut me to the core. He'd been my lord. I was a knight. And yet I'd killed him.

I shook my head and returned to the present, trying to piece back the fragments of my honor. I wasn't a knight, I remembered. Not anymore. I was a ranger. And *it* hadn't been my lord. Arathorn had been—and by the end, there hadn't been any of Arathorn left. I'd killed the kanir, not him.

As before, that distinction didn't really make it any easier.

Galen nodded softly. The warm gesture did wonders in making me feel better. "It's fine," he eventually said. "You'll be fine. And you will fully recover in pretty short time." His smile inched upward, but I could see him struggling not to scrunch his face. "You still can't stay in here for the whole day. You have…

things to face out there. And even though I like you, you're taking up too much of my world's damned time these days."

The short man glared at me again, tapping his foot louder as if trying to simulate the ticking of a clock. I nodded, noting the hyperbolic gesture with a smile. Lifting my head, I looked to the door, and then back at Galen. He only raised an expectant eyebrow before widening his grin.

I opened my mouth, ready to stammer out another question. I bit it off shortly. I knew what Galen meant, and stalling in his office pretending to be in more pain than I was wouldn't have done anything anyway. The past had happened, whether I liked it or not. I couldn't change that now. All I could do was face it. So, with a weak sigh and a bob of my head, I rose from the couch and started toward the door.

The basic motion tore at my legs as they were subjected to the smallest amount of effort. The faint, sore pain was annoying, but it wasn't bad. I'd felt worse. Far worse in the past few days, even. It just told me I was alive.

I walked past Galen without another comment and pushed through the door. The warmth and the light commotion of the rest of the lodge greeted me as I stepped out. The wooden hallway. The rough, well-cut wood. It was familiar. It was nice. A soft breath fell from my lips as I dragged my gaze over it and smiled. Then, raising my hand to spare one last wave toward Galen, I turned.

The wooden door slammed in my face.

Polished wooden inlaid with Galen's red emblem filled my vision as the exaggerated slam echoed out through the space. I laughed, the outburst escaping before I could even think to stop it. Rolling my shoulders as I turned away again, I felt the tension deep in my arms. It reminded me of what I'd done. That calmed my laughter in short time. So without wasting anymore time with my unnecessary, torturous thoughts, I walked off down the hall.

Morning light attacked my eyes as I made my way to the training room. The floor creaked under me, ramping up my anxiety with every step. When I arrived, I shook my head and took a breath before walking in. A bit of weight slipped from my shoulders as I stood before the room that had seen me flat on my ass too many times for me to count.

But it wasn't the room that gave me such relief.

"Oh look," a voice called, as smooth and snarky as always. Kye's familiar smirk shined just as bright as the light piercing in through the windows. "If it isn't the kanir-slayer himself. How's the high life?"

I watched her, my smile only growing. "Not at all what I imagined it to be," I answered as she leaned back against the wall next to the weapon rack. Chuckling softly, she took another bite of the bread in her hand.

"So how do you feel?" she asked with her mouth full.

My foot cramped up a bit as I stepped forward, causing me to grimace as if on cue. "Not too great," I admitted and shook off the pain. My brow furrowed slightly as a question rose to my lips. "How… how did you know he was a kanir?"

Kye's expression tightened as she swallowed. "Ah. Well. News travels fast in a town this size." I cringed at the statement I already knew to be true. But she wasn't finished. "A member of the town guard carrying a battered and bloodied ranger through the streets tends to get people talking." Her smugness wavered, morphing into an apologetic smile. "It didn't take people long to find out about the charred body you left or the animal corpses Arathorn kept to keep that part of him satisfied."

I paled, teetering in place as I remembered the knife, as I remembered the dry blood on it without knowing what it had been used for. Again, I berated myself for not seeing it sooner. But again, it was already too late.

"Shit," I said, making no effort to hide my shame. "What, ah. What's been the reaction so far?"

Kye straightened up, her head tilting. She shot me a caring gaze, but I didn't miss the guilt in it. "People aren't happy. Obviously. But… it could be worse. A lot of the attention isn't on you, or even the Rangers, really. I've heard too many people just scared of the consequences it could have." Her eyebrows arched upward. "They… they don't know what could happen to Sarin without a lord again. Things have been going well, you know. Better than what a lot of these people can remember in the past." Kye averted her eyes and sniffed, trying to relax her shoulders.

I nodded in shallow movements. Weight pressed down on my shoulders, and I sneered. At myself. At my ignorance, my hubris, my incompetence. I hadn't seen it—and I'd barely been able to defend myself against the kanir in my useless body. It was my fault. All of it. Even if Arathorn had been a kanir... I'd committed *murder*.

"So what happens to me now?" I asked, trying to keep my tone level.

Kye stopped, swallowing again before turning to me. She furrowed her brow and squinted at me. "Now? You just killed a *kanir*." The weight in the term felt like a punch in the gut. "Now you get some rest."

I tilted my head and blinked. Her calm, convinced words played back in my head, but I couldn't accept them. Get some rest? How could I just get some rest with everything I'd done? After only a month in the new life that the beast had forced me into, I'd already disrupted a community. I'd killed the lord of the place I now had the audacity to call my home. I couldn't *rest*.

But as I glanced back at Kye with bemused conviction, she only shrugged. She only raised one eyebrow and took another bite of the bread in her hand as though we were in the most casual situation in the world. And, even if I knew that wasn't the case, it was more true than I assumed. I wasn't in Credon anymore, I reminded myself. Things were different now. In Ruia, leadership was probably as fleeting as any other type of order. Even if that grated on me, I'd have to accept it. Maybe one day I would.

Now, though, I couldn't shake it so easily. "Just... rest?"

Kye nodded. "Rest. It's all you'll be able to do for the foreseeable future, I'd imagine. Even if most talk is on Arathorn, that doesn't mean there's not a fair share of scorn thrown our way. Thrown *your* way, specifically." She scrunched her face awkwardly. "The townsfolk know you at this point, Agil. I... I wouldn't imagine facing them would be the best idea."

My expression dropped. "Oh. Right." I rolled my shoulders, feeling the phantom weight press back down. "But, no punishment? I'm not getting imprisoned?"

Kye blinked rapidly. "What?" She shook her head, stifling a chuckle. "No. That—it doesn't work that way here. Not like it does in the stories." I scrunched my nose at the implication that justice and order were things of myth. "You're a ranger. Nothing like *that* is going to happen." Kye's smirk flashed again. "Though, I won't make any promises about how Lorah deals with you."

I nodded, a singular amused breath fleeing from my nostrils. Her words played back in my head again. They warmed me and made me feel better because of their truth. No matter how hard I tried to hold onto it, I wasn't a knight anymore. I *was* a ranger. That was something I could accept.

Then, with a genuine smile tugging at my lips, I dragged my gaze over the floor. Over the wooden planks and black mat to where Kye was leaning against the wall. She wasn't the only thing leaning, I noticed. There was another object— one that stuck out like lightning to my eyes.

A sword.

Sheathed in a beautiful but simple black scabbard, a formidable longsword sat motionless, almost like it had been waiting for me to notice it. A sliver of silvery metal poking out from the top of the scabbard glinted light into my eyes. It sparkled with a contrasting brilliance that almost made me forget all the worries that had been swirling a moment before.

Kye coughed, eyeing me from the corner of my vision. I looked up, widening my eyes. The question slipped out before I even knew it existed.

"What's with the sword?"

Kye made a curious sound, turning toward me and raising an eyebrow. I flicked my eyes down to the scabbard by her feet and she followed my gaze with a grin.

"Oh," she started, feigning surprise. "This?" She picked up the sword, holding it by the center of its scabbard. I resisted the urge to cringe. It wasn't the kind of sword to be picked up near the blade.

She balanced it in her hand and faked a sort of cursory inspection. My eyes tracked every movement. The way it swayed and steadied. It had a good weight, I thought giddily. Looking at me expectantly, she cocked an eyebrow and raised the sword in my direction. My eyes shot wide before I remembered her question.

"Yes," I said with as much composure as I could manage. "That."

She laughed. "It's for you."

I blinked, the air brushing against my empty palm suddenly much more apparent. "For me?"

"You lost your sword when we were in Norn, didn't you?" She didn't wait for my response. "Well, after having to fight a kanir, I thought you might appreciate another one."

I did. My fingers twitched in the air, desperate to get around the grip of the blade. It was a slightly bowed longsword with a simple hilt that had a curved guard at the end. I must've been nearly salivating at it because in my peripheral vision, I saw Kye roll her eyes. She scoffed once, and before I knew it, the sword was soaring straight toward me.

The ornate scabbard flew through the air with the blade and landed in my hands as awkwardly as I thought possible. It tumbled through my arms, hitting all the exact places where I'd gathered bruises. After a few seconds—and my body crouching to the floor—I caught the blade.

Staring at the beautiful black scabbard lined with silver, the awkward pain faded away. It didn't matter. What mattered was the thing now in my arms.

Moving with more grace than my body should've been able to muster, I unsheathed the sword and lifted it in my hands. The perfect silver metal gleamed brilliantly in the fleeting morning light. It was smooth, sharp, well-made.

Kye stared at me as I waved the blade through the air, getting a feel for its weight. It was heavier than the longswords stocked at the lodge. And longer, too. The crossguard was smooth and accommodating.

"Where did you get it?" I asked, keeping my gaze on the shiny silver metal.

Kye snickered, swallowing whatever laughter had been building in her throat. "It's one of Jason's blades." I stopped, my fingers twitching on the hilt. "Supposedly, it's made of a conductive metal. Something that was extra effective for him when used with magic."

I furrowed my brow. "Jason gave one of his swords to me?"

Kye raised her shoulders and was significantly less successful than before in keeping down laughter. "No," she said. "I didn't even ask him before I took it."

My eyes bloomed. "What?" The image of the arrogant swordsman yelling at me was already all too clear.

Kye rolled her eyes. "He has so many of them. It doesn't really matter." I nodded to myself, not fully reassured. "And *he* hasn't killed a kanir before." The name made me scrunch my face, bitter feelings welling up from the back of my mind. "So it's probably more useful with you anyway."

I looked back to the blade in my hand, my lips slowly curling up. As I bolstered myself and stiffened my posture, I could only agree with her. After only holding the sword for a short time, I already loved it. The longer I held it, the more I could *feel* it, as if the blade was slowly becoming part of me.

There was no way in *hell* I was giving it up.

"Thank you," I said softly as I fastened the scabbard to my belt. The weight fell by my side and I let out a breath that I hadn't even know I was holding in.

Kye smiled at me—an actual smile this time—and nodded. "No problem. Anything that both makes you more competent and annoys Jason in the process is a win in my book." She chuckled before taking the last bite of bread from her hand and devouring what was left.

My fingers wrapped around the grip of the blade. It seemed to drain my exhaustion on contact. My mind wandered for a second, caught in a fleeting feeling of bliss before a question forced my thoughts to a halt.

I blinked, the worries making themselves known again. My eyebrows dropped.. "How… How did it happen, by the way?"

Kye turned to me, raising her eyebrows. "You're going to have to be more specific than that."

I shook my head lightly. "Arathorn. The Lord of Sarin." *Former* lord, I thought bitterly. "How did he become a kanir?"

Kye's smirk drowned out whatever fragments of sincerity were left in her smile. She shrugged her shoulders. "I don't know, probably for the same reason they all turn."

The reason reared its head in my mind as memories streamed past. I didn't need to ask what she meant, I knew. Power was a constant everywhere, it seemed. I just had to be glad that in my home kingdom, greed hadn't been able to turn someone into a vampire.

"Although," Kye cut in, a tinge of something almost unnoticeable in her voice. The same way she spoke in anticipation of a joke. "Rumor has it that he corrupted himself with magical experimentation involving his own blood."

My eyes widened. That didn't sound like a joke. "What rumors?"

Kye tilted her head to the side. "The rumors that *I* just made up."

I rolled my eyes and averted my gaze. But I couldn't stop the laugh that pushed its way out of my mouth. Kye's lips tweaked up into a grin far more wicked. My laugh grew louder, overpowering the passive noise level in the lodge for a second. I shook my head to calm my addled, susceptible mind.

Kye only briefly chuckled. "No. I don't know how he turned." She pursed her lips for a moment. "Maybe one day we'll find out. But now that he's dead, it doesn't matter all that much."

That stole the rest of my amusement. The tips of my ears burned as I remembered Arathorn's corpse. Shaking my head only helped halfway. "I-I guess not."

Kye nodded shortly before grabbing the bow leaning against the wall beside her. Then she turned back, her face lighting up. "Oh. Lorah wanted to see you as soon as you woke up, by the way."

"She wants to see *me*?"

Kye stared with a straight brow. Unimpressed. I threw up a hand, already turning to the hallway that led to her office. I knew the answer to my question, after all. It didn't need clarification.

My former cellmate slumped her shoulders. "I don't know what you can hope to expect. *But*, I have a hunt, so good luck."

She flashed me a look that I just barely missed before she strung the bow onto her back and started toward the door. I had comments at my lips, other questions left to ask. But before I knew it, I was just standing in an empty room.

My gaze dropped. I clutched the hilt of my new blade with everything I had. It did wonders at making me feel better. With a breath, I turned on my heel and started off again before my thoughts could hold me up. Creaky wood flew under me as I walked down the hallways toward the office I'd only been in a handful of times.

By the time I'd reached it, it was unmistakable. Shrouded in dim light only half a dozen paces in front of me was the large wooden door emblazoned with a silver version of the Ranger's emblem.

I moved before I could even tell myself not to. I was a ranger now, I reminded myself. Things were different. I no longer answered to a king or was bound by a knightly oath. Lorah was my leader, and if she wanted to meet with me, I was going to face it head-on.

The hallway flew past in a blur, blank wooden walls only sparsely populated by equally blank doors. Step after step, the sound of my boots hitting the floor echoed in sync with the rhythmic pulsing of my blood.

I still remembered the first time I'd walked down this hall.

When I stepped up to the door, a full breath entered my lungs. It calmed me, but only slightly. My stomach still twisted in dread. My mind still raced like it always did. And even though I'd gotten more used to the anxiety my new body seemed prone to, I still struggled to bring my hand forward.

When I finally summoned the courage, the silver, crescent-shaped arrow stared down at me. It implored my soul with its form, reminding me of the matching symbol stitched into my tattered uniform. The final rays of morning sunlight that only barely reached this far into the hall glinted off its surface and shined into my eye. They melted away the rest of my doubts.

I knocked on the door.

Three simple knocks that were the standard around the lodge were all the warning she got. For a second, I waited in silence. My heartbeat slowed, the air prickling at my skin. My breathing got louder, echoing in my ears until—

"Come in."

The pleasing but muffled voice of the Rangers' leader came through the door in odd clarity. It was equal parts firm and soothing at the same time. My breathing calmed as I went to open the door.

The room was dim, just as it always was, and Lorah was standing in the center of it. She stood hunched over her desk with her eyes flicking back and forth. Her lip was curled and despite the slumped shoulders, her posture emanated poise. It emanated purpose. She didn't even look in my direction as she waved me in.

The door slid shut behind me, a soft noise drowned out by the silence of the room. I didn't dare speak. The torches on the walls, each glowing softly glowing with Lorah's characteristic yellow flame, all rose in brightness at the same rate. The Rangers' leader didn't even so much as break a sweat at the exertion.

Stiffening her posture Lorah tore her gaze off the papers on her desk and glared at me. Her eyes stayed dark for only a moment before brightening up in tandem with the rest of the room.

"Agil," she said as warmly as she could manage with the tension in her voice. "Good to see you."

I nodded, unflinching. "I was told you wanted to talk with me?"

She cocked an eyebrow, her lips curling into a smile. "Yes, of course. And I'm sure what I wanted to discuss isn't a mystery to you, either."

"It isn't?" I asked, a tiny, shriveled part of me hoping she was getting at something else.

"Arathorn." The dead man's name sent a shiver down my spine.

"Oh." I gulped. "That."

She nodded at me, the shine in her eyes brightening. It failed to comfort me like it usually did. The memories rushed back, only held back from being shown to my eyes by the importance of the scene in front of me. I pressed fingers into my palm.

"Yes," she said, her eyebrows raising slightly. "That." She crossed her arms and sighed. The yellow light of the room highlighted the shadows under her eyes. "It is quite the shame isn't it?"

I stared at her, unable to catch her gaze. Eventually, I found myself nodding along despite the vigorous hate my stomach had for the topic. "Yes." Kye's words played back to me—the rumors, the *citizens* that now didn't know what they would do. "It is."

Lorah nodded briskly. "The Lord of Sarin was a kanir, and I didn't know?" A whimsical note entered her tone, matching the light air. "Must've been quite the fight."

I froze. She knew about it. It made all the sense in the world that she would. If Kye knew, she should too. But as my hand clenched tighter by my side, my logic was doing a poor job of consoling me.

I opened my mouth, immediately snapping it shut right after. I didn't have a response. I'd fought Arathorn. I'd *killed* him. She had to think something of that. There had to be a punishment that came along with her suspicion, and I didn't have anything to dissuade her from issuing it.

"Agil," she started, her voice raising as she narrowed her eyes on me. I stared at the floor. "Do you know the most basic principle of magic?"

I blinked, my head shaking in confusion before I could stop it.

Lorah smiled. "Perhaps not." She walked over to the edge of her desk. "Well, magic is just the manipulation of the energy produced by the World Soul." I nodded, remembering all that I'd learned after living in Ruia for so long. "But not all forms of energy are the same, you know. Some are simpler than others."

I squinted, the fact registering somewhere in my mind.

She held out her palm. "See, the most simple form of magic is heat. It is often expressed with fire." A small yellow flame appeared in her hand, waving in a nonexistent wind. "The color and nature of which changes with each individual soul. However, it gets much more complex."

Her face contorted in concentration. I watched, frozen and perplexed as she killed the small flame. Her fingers twitched, the air lightening more as she manipulated the energy in it. And a beam of golden light shot across the room, illuminating everything in its path.

Lorah turned back to me with a grin. "The more complicated the energy, the harder it is to shape and control. But it all just takes finesse. It all just takes experience with using the soul as a conduit for the world's energy." Stark lines must've been evident on my forehead as I watched her curl her fingers into a fist. "Eventually even…" In clenching her hand, the wooden chair behind her desk broke into pieces with a flash of light. "You can change the objects around you."

My hand unconsciously drifted to the blade at my side, its existence reassuring me more than anything else could. The thing at the back of my mind stirred, slowly coming to attention as the display of magical power continued.

"All it takes is power, which is something that is different with every soul." She eyed me for a second, her gaze heavy enough to pin me down. "But as with all types of power, it just needs the right hand to guide it."

A shiver raced down my spine and a foreign sense of desire washed over my mind. A sense of yearning and aspiration that reminded me of training with the blade. As the sea passed me over, the feeling eventually faded. And in its wake, I noticed sharp spots of fear mixed in with the hope, spots that I couldn't grasp at fast enough before all the feeling left.

"Why are you telling me this?" I asked, trying to ignore the obvious answer to the question that was literally hiding in my mind.

Her smile dropped almost imperceptibly. She eyed me, scouring my eyes for what she knew was there before simply throwing up a hand. "No reason. It is simply something you should know."

I nodded at the transparent lie. But I didn't comment on it. I didn't invite any more questions or doubts while my thoughts were still tied in knots. So as the silence crept in, I let it hold like a permanent breath. But eventually, it was one I had to take.

"Thank you," I said, giving what few words I could muster.

Lorah nodded, her eyes tightening again. "Good. Don't forget that, if you would." She spared a light smile. "The main reason I called you in here, though, was to inform about your duties. Obviously you are not in any state for new assignments at the moment." She raised an eyebrow half an inch. "After the next few days, however, you will return to your duty." My eyes widened and I opened my mouth. Lorah didn't let me get a single word in. "Your assignments will change. Nothing strenuous, important, or in the public eye. With Arathorn gone, I will have enough work to do without the townsfolk's increasing unrest. Alright?"

I bobbed my head briskly, bowing a little with a forced smile on my face. At the mention of Arathorn, the worries came back. They continued to nag at me no matter how much I pushed them away. But Lorah was my leader, and she'd made her decision. I had to be grateful for what I'd gotten. "Thank you, Lorah."

She smiled at me, more than a little amusement shining through. "I pulled this organization up by its bootstraps you know. Rangers protect their own." Her gaze nearly burned my skin with its warm intensity. "No one is nobody in my lodge. You're a ranger now, Agil." She rolled her wrist. "Act like one."

I couldn't have stopped the wide grin on my face if I'd wanted to. Nodding once again and watching Lorah hold her head high as she walked back to the work on her desk, I felt better. The doubts still nagged, but they weren't as loud. I'd been reborn on Ruia with a vengeance. With the kind of burning hatred that stuck to the insides of my bones and cemented itself in the deepest parts of my mind. A hatred for the beast, for death itself. Before, I hadn't been able to stave it off or make it pay. If I wanted to do that now, I needed more. Which was what I'd come here for, after all. I'd come for training, for experience, for a *purpose*. And damned if I didn't have one now.

Even as Lorah shifted her attention back her desk, my grin didn't let up. It stretched far and wide with the kind of hope I hadn't felt in far too long. Things were different now, I told myself once again. But that didn't have to be a bad thing. I couldn't change the past, but I could embrace the present, and that was exactly what I was going to do. The reaper still loomed over my head—over all of our heads, in truth. But with what I'd found after its vile trick, it was almost worth it. Because not only could I embrace the present, I could work toward the future.

"Oh, and Agil?" Lorah asked. I looked up, rising from my thoughts as the resolve solidified in my mind. "Things will be changing around here, and I'm going to need everyone—including you—to rise to the occasion."

"Of course," I said as I raised my head. The answer slipped out without even a thought. After giving one last bow, I turned away. I looked back toward the door as silence spread back through the room. As my muscles screamed an aching complaint one more time, I started toward it.

Even with the grin on my face, the doubts weren't *gone*. The question that Lorah had implied still stood, and it spiraled in my head. Would I rise to the occasion?

In truth, I wasn't sure. Thinking about it brought images to the forefront of my mind. One-by-one they streamed past as though taunting me with the emotions they reminded me of. I saw Kye, notching an arrow in her bow as she smirked at me. I saw Jason, cleaning his sword as he rattled on about this or that. I saw the other rangers, hunting through the forest every day just to keep the citizens of their town safe. I saw Arathorn, lying on the floor where I'd killed him. I saw the beast, its pitch-black gaze tearing deep into my soul.

I shook my head, the doubts growing ever-larger while I thought. The images faded back into the memories they'd spawned from, and I walked forward again to try and shrug them off. It was barely effective. But as a glint of light caught my eye, I started to calm. As the silver symbol of the Rangers stared down at me from the door, I knew my answer in an instant.

Would I rise to the occasion?

Yes, I told myself. Yes I would.

ACKNOWLEDGEMENTS

Here it is. A dream come true in the form of a fantasy book. In all honesty, I can't believe I got this far, but I do have to thank everyone who made this possible. For those who don't know, this book started as a serialized piece of fiction that I wrote and posted chapter-by-chapter online. Back then, I had no idea it would turn into a trilogy, nor did I expect it would ever be a book. But… well. It's both of those things now!

For starters, I want to thank the beta readers of this book—the individuals who took the time to read the unfinished version of this novel and give me feedback on it. Seriously, I cannot overstate how much I appreciate each and every one of you.

Ford, thank you for writing up such an in-depth and constructive review of the novel. It helped me fix a lot of things. Erk, thank you for being the greatest typo-spotter I've ever had the pleasure to meet. The prose in this book is the way it is in a lot of spots because of you. Illrememberthismaybe, thank you for being my resident super-fan, for reading the unpolished version of the book and reminding me that *hey, this might not be absolute crap.*

Beyond them, it would be a disservice for me not to mention the people from which my knowledge in both writing and book-making stems. All of you have been not only excellent friends but also teachers at one time or another. Inorai, Hydrael, Elven, Static—each of you have helped me in one way or another to become the person that was able to make this book. Thank you, from the bottom of my heart.

Next, I'd just like to give thanks to the readers who read along chapter-by-chapter as this was being written. Owen, OriginalWolfpack, Cz, Rw, Magnamiouskoala, HighlandAgave—the list goes on, and I know I wouldn't be able to list everyone out with my memory being the way it is. To all of you readers, though, I appreciate you. This would not have been possible without you.

Now I suppose I'll thank the communities that were invaluable to me writing this book. Primarily, I want to thank the WritingPrompts and RedditSerials communities on Reddit. Not only for the platforms that they provide, but more importantly for the amazing people who make them up. The fantastic individuals who have given me so much support, so much motivation, so much critique, so many laughs. Luna, Potato, Zub, Yugi, Sol, Faren, Aly, Lee, Nova, Nick, Bread, Aman, Lilwa, Pyro, Quark, Tens, Glo—this list could go on forever. Without you guys, I would never have become the writer I am, nor would I have had the best single year of my life while doing it. You all are awesome. I hope you know that.

And finally, I want to express my gratitude to my patrons who have financially supported me on Patreon. Well, *patron*, since there is only one at the time of writing this. Still, thank you for believing in my work. It really does mean the world.

$5 Tier: Ramy

Interested in reading more? The next two books of the trilogy are slated for release in 2020. Keep an eye out for the titles *Rise and Fall* as well as *Life and Death*.

This series, along with others, is also updated in rough-draft form chapter-by-chapter as they are written on the author's website:

www.reddit.com/r/Palmerranian

Printed in Great Britain
by Amazon